A

Guide

to Being Just

Friends

ALSO BY SOPHIE SULLIVAN

Ten Rules for Faking It
How to Love Your Neighbor

A
Guide
to Being Just
Friends

A Novel

Sophie Sullivan

ST. MARTIN'S GRIFFIN
NEW YORK

First published in the United States by St. Martin's Griffin, an imprint of St. Martin's Publishing Group

A GUIDE TO BEING JUST FRIENDS. Copyright © 2022 by Sophie Sullivan. All rights reserved. Printed in the United States of America. For information, address St. Martin's Publishing Group, 120 Broadway, New York, NY 10271.

www.stmartins.com

Designed by Gabriel Guma

The Library of Congress Cataloging-in-Publication Data is available upon request.

ISBN 978-1-250-62420-8 (trade paperback)
ISBN 978-1-250-62421-5 (ebook)

Our books may be purchased in bulk for promotional, educational, or business use. Please contact your local bookseller or the Macmillan Corporate and Premium Sales Department at 1-800-221-7945, extension 5442, or by email at MacmillanSpecialMarkets@macmillan.com.

First Edition: 2023

10 9 8 7 6 5 4 3 2 1

To Kalie and Amy. You both inspire me every day
to be the best version of myself.

LOVE CANNOT BE FOUND WHERE IT DOES NOT EXIST,
NOR CAN IT BE HIDDEN WHERE IT TRULY DOES.

~William Shakespeare~

1

September

Salad paid the bills. At least, it was supposed to. If it wasn't going to, Hailey Sharp needed copious amounts of chocolate. In all fairness to her very quiet, newly opened salad shop, By the Cup, she would use any excuse to feed her chocolate addiction.

Which was why she hadn't gone the bakery or chocolate shop route—she'd eat herself out of profits.

Looking around, desperate for something to do—or eat—that would take her mind off the lack of customers, she debated going next door to Baked, the coffee-shop-slash-bakery that served the most delicious brownie lava cakes.

Her Kindle was in her purse, just a few steps away, but if she went back to the book she'd been reading, she wouldn't come up for air. She was right at *that* moment when everything was about to get so good, she wouldn't be able to tear herself away.

Her stomach growled, distracting her from the temptation of her latest rom-com read. *Whip up a salad.* Her end-of-summer special was a dessert salad, which she topped with dark chocolate shavings. She wasn't in the mood though. Had she made a mistake opening this store?

Why don't I have customers? This is California for God's sake. People love their greens and mine come in handy little to-go cups, perfect for the busy Californian.

A few people walked past the shop window. They didn't even glance in. Maybe she should change the special. With that in mind, she grabbed a chalk marker and a cloth, heading toward the door of her supposed-to-be-thriving store. *It's been two weeks. Give it some time.*

The heat hit her like a giant blanket when she stepped out onto the sidewalk. She'd lived in California for years now, though she'd only moved to San Verde recently, but some days the steady sunshine still surprised her. Deciding to put her San Verde Sunshine Cup—a mixture of lettuces, assorted yummy seeds, yellow tomatoes, and avocado with a homemade dressing—on sale, she added it to the board.

Then, because she was only human, she tucked the marker and cloth into the back pocket of her jeans and went into Baked.

Similar to her own store in layout, size, and the gorgeous picture window with seating, it set itself apart with the number of customers. Plus, the smell. *Salad doesn't smell. Hmm. Something to think about. Nothing lures people to buy like the scent of something freshly made or appetizing. Like coffee.*

She joined the line, thinking maybe that was the draw. Maybe she should add some specialty iced teas or something.

Almost every table was full. She scanned the room, once again wondering if she'd gone too far out of the box with her take-out, dine-in salad shop.

The line moved forward as people chatted and laughed over the sound of coffee machines and music. *I'll bring my Bluetooth speaker. At least then it won't be so quiet.*

Glancing out the window, she tapped her debit card against her thigh, wishing she could live in one of the apartments so conveniently located above this row of shops. Instead, she'd decided to save money by renting something smaller and farther away. The focus was the shop, and since she'd sunk all the proceeds from the sale of her apartment into this venture, that was the way it needed to be.

Forcing herself to inhale deeply and think about the scent of chocolate and the quiet hum of people, she felt her heart rate settle. The line moved forward again. *Everything will work out.* Hailey wanted to believe that one day soon, her own shop would be bustling with happy customers.

Don't even need a bustle. I'll take a steady trickle. Teens took up the center of the dining area, sitting at a long, scuffed wooden table. Most of them were on their phones despite laughing at the conversations around them. Two of the guys were flicking wadded-up paper balls back and forth. The bell jingled over the door, signaling more customers. Two guys who either really liked spandex or had just been cycling joined the line. *Maybe not the teens, but those guys should be next door getting a salad. Says you as you stand in line.*

Three women in yoga pants, workout tops, and high ponytails sat at the back of the store talking over each other, loudly, about dating. They looked like salad people.

"Next," the male barista called. He didn't look familiar and Hailey definitely had regular-customer status. Tara, the shop owner, must have just hired him.

Hailey pulled her loyalty card out of the pocket of her cell phone case. Chocolate would never have to doubt her commitment. "Hi. How are you today?"

His pierced brow arched like the question confused him. "Fine? You?"

"I'm great. Thanks for asking. I'll have a vanilla latte and three mini chocolate caramel scones." *They're mini. They barely count as one.*

"Name?"

One day, when she hired staff, she'd ask them to not sound bored. "Hailey," she said, watching as he wrote her name wrong on the cup.

She shuffled to the end of the high countertop, continuing her visual inventory of how her shop was different than this one. There was a free online marketing course that her cousin had sent her a link to. She needed to register for it.

A man at a corner table caught her gaze. A little zip of energy—like a shot of caffeine—whipped through her body. She tried to shake it off even as she smiled at him. His dark blond hair, square jaw, and strong shoulders were tempting. Beyond tempting if she was honest with herself, but she needed to keep herself on track.

She'd pushed aside her own dreams for a man for too long. She'd thought she was building a life with her ex, Dorian. While he took small acting gigs, she paid the bills and supported them, thinking her turn would be next.

But her turn never came. Selling the tiny apartment she'd been smart enough to buy in L.A. when she first arrived there had been her saving grace. The reason she could move to San Verde and really start fresh. It was less than two hours away but felt like a different world. One where she could breathe. Maybe even thrive. This time, nothing was holding her back. Not even his cute dimples and sexy, assessing gaze. She'd been fooled once with a pretty exterior. Now, she knew better.

The grunty barista set her scones on the counter. She opened the pack and snuck a piece, holding in the sigh as the delicious taste hit her tongue. There was very little chocolate couldn't cure. *One more bite.* Forcing herself to close the bag until she was back in her own place, she grabbed the drink she'd ordered, offering an unacknowledged "thanks."

Turning, she nearly spilled her latte all over the man she'd been watching. He stood close enough for her to notice he smelled almost as good as the scones. Which was fine. Flowers smelled good, too. Didn't mean she wouldn't accidentally kill them within three days.

"Hi," he said, a hint of those dimples appearing. Like a yummy preview of coming attractions.

Nope. Stay strong. Dimple immunity shields activate. "Hi."

"I would have bought that for you if you'd given me a chance," he said.

Hailey glanced around in case he was talking to someone else, but his dark blue eyes were locked on her. Cute or not, he needed a better opening line. "I'm perfectly capable of purchasing my own snacks and drinks, thanks."

He frowned. "Why don't we sit down? I have a table right there." His eyes traveled along her body and she noted the spark of heat when they met her gaze again.

Not even Harry Styles's dimples could excuse his resigned tone. "I'm good, thanks."

Someone else joined the waiting area, making it hard for her to sidestep him and leave.

He sighed. "I've been waiting for you."

Oh, good Lord. Even when I'm not trying, I attract the wrong ones. A high-pitched, thankfully short, laugh burst free. "That's what they all say." Actually, none of them said that. But he didn't need to know that.

He stepped back, his square jaw dropping. His blue eyes flashed with . . . hurt? She watched him gather himself, straighten his shoulders before speaking again. "Is this some sort of game to you?" His whispered words held a hint of embarrassment.

Okay, then. He's a few tomatoes short of a full salad. Time to shut it down. Hailey stepped to the side so others could collect their purchases. "I have no clue what you're talking about. We don't know each other."

He made a dismissive noise. "That's the whole point, isn't it?"

No! The point was *chocolate*! "I'm sorry. I think you've mistaken me for someone else."

"Really. So, you're *not* Hayden?"

Huh? She shook her head, realization dawning. Empathy welled up in her chest. He really was waiting for someone. But not her. She leaned in. "I'm not."

Hailey wasn't sure what she expected, but it wasn't to have him cross his arms over his wide chest and look pointedly at her beverage. "Then explain your cup."

Her emotions were giving her whiplash. His tone sent her right back to irritated. "What about my cup?" She turned the white container slowly, saying the letters as they appeared. "H-a-y . . . wait." The not-so-capable barista had printed "Hayden" on her cup. *Damn.*

She sent a side glare to the barista, who obviously took no notice, then looked back at Mr. Grumpy. "My name isn't Hayden."

He continued to stare, so she did the same despite the number of people milling about them.

"You don't have to lie. Just say you don't like what you saw and go."

Her gaze widened even as her heart pinched. She didn't even think about her next move. With her treat and cup in one hand, she put the other on his arm and guided them to the side, out of the way.

She needed to get back to the store but she didn't want him to think something like that.

"Listen, I don't know who you were meeting and I know my cup says Hayden, but I'm not her. Whoever stood you up is rude and an idiot."

He still looked like he was having trouble believing her. At that moment, she was grateful she'd given up dating. Who needed this kind of blow to the confidence? If a guy like this was getting ghosted, the dating world was a sad place.

"You're not Hayden but you're taking her cup?"

She wasn't sure if it was amusement or doubt in his tone.

"I'm *not* her but I'll be anybody for one of these lattes." She stepped back. "Good luck."

He huffed out a sardonic laugh. "Luck has nothing to do with it." He gave her one more glance then stalked away like she'd actually done something wrong.

Hurrying back to the shop, she was both relieved and disappointed no one was waiting at the door. After letting herself in, she set her cup down on the counter, then attacked the first scone. It never stood a chance.

"What a jerk." Sure, he'd been stood up, but it was like he'd been waiting for disappointment. Not her fault or her problem. But she wondered if his date would actually show.

Midway through the second scone, she reached for her cup. She picked it up, grabbed a sharpie, and scribbled out the wrong name, wrote her own. And she damn well spelled it properly.

2

The good thing about the jerk next door—*hmm, that could be a rom-com title*—was it stopped her from going back for seconds. Could she call it seconds if she'd had three?

As she texted her cousin, Piper, the only person she really knew in San Verde, her irritation dissipated.

> **Piper**
> What an asshole

Hailey winced. He'd been a bit of a jerk but clearly there were reasons.

> **Hailey**
> I guess if he really thought I was blowing him off, that I was really lying about my name, it makes sense.
> **Piper**
> You always do this. You're such a softy.

Hailey grinned.

> It's all the scones. I need to eat more of what I'm selling. ☺

Piper
Shut up! That's not what I meant and you know it. Seriously, you ok?
Hailey
I am. See you soon? "Book" club Wednesday, right?
Piper
Absolutely!

As she pocketed her phone, intending to double-check some prices for produce suppliers, the little bell over the door jingled. It was Hailey's new favorite sound.

Two women walked through the door, chatting back and forth—a blonde who was a few inches taller than the brunette, but that might have just been the heels. The brunette wore adorable pink Converse. While they were both very pretty, the blonde looked like an advertisement for the state of California with her sun-kissed skin and oversized sunglasses. She shifted them into her hair.

Hailey smiled while trying to tamp down the excitement she felt when people came in. "Hi. Welcome to By the Cup."

"Thanks. We were heading to the bakery next door but saw the sign. I forgot a new shop was opening."

Whether it was the dessert cup or the San Verde Sunshine Cup, she was grateful for that sign. Maybe she should have had a grand opening like Piper suggested. But parties made her nervous. She'd attended so many Hollywood ones at this point that anything she could pull off felt like too little.

"I've been open a couple weeks now," she said.

"It's a great area," the brunette said, her voice low. "Your shop is adorable. It's like a blend of vintage and modern."

"Thank you." Her happiness meter soared. It *was* a great area and she'd been lucky to lease the place. "That's exactly what I was going for. What can I get you ladies today?"

"Evs?" the blonde asked. Something about her voice was familiar.

"You go first. You're better at decisions," "Evs" answered.

The other woman looked up at the menu board. It didn't make sense for the butterflies to wake up in Hailey's stomach but at the moment, everything depended on word of mouth and repeat customers. Not only was it the most effective marketing tool, it was the cheapest.

"They all look so good. Are your dressings homemade?"

Hailey nodded, stuck for a minute on the distinct sound of the woman's voice. "Yes, sorry, your voice sounds so familiar."

The two women exchanged a glance then the blonde beamed at Hailey. "I'm a DJ for 96.2 Sun."

Hailey snapped her fingers. "That's totally it. You've got an excellent voice." She *loved* that station. It was fun, engaging, and played great music.

"Unless she's singing," the other woman said quietly.

The blonde—*damn, what's her name, she's on billboards . . . Stacey!*—sent a mock glare to her friend. "That worked out pretty well for you in the end."

Unsure what they were talking about, Hailey worked to keep her cool. A radio station DJ in her shop. How cool was that? Seeing as she'd run a Craft Food Truck on movie and television sets in her previous life, one would think she'd be more chill. But since moving to San Verde, Hailey had listened to the station almost every day. They played cool games, did giveaways, and generally made listening to the radio enjoyable. A forgotten media art form.

No pressure but this salad needs to be fantastic. Do what you do— make a salad to knock her gorgeous high heels off.

"I love your station. I'm thrilled you decided to check out my shop," Hailey said. Okay, so she wasn't great at being chill. She'd had to teach herself not to openly fangirl when on set. They were all there to do a job. Her ex, an actor who got enough work to feed his ego but not make him a star, had constantly told her how childish she seemed when she gushed over meeting someone she admired. Once they'd gotten together, he'd told her not to embarrass him. It made her self-conscious, but what was the harm in telling her she liked the station?

"I'm excited you're open. I need something to counteract the brownies Tara makes," the woman said. She gestured toward the wall By the Cup shared with Baked. "Tara's our friend, she owns the bakery. I'm Stacey. This is Everly, my bestie and producer for my show."

"It's really a pleasure to meet you both. I'm Hailey. Whatever you'd like, it's on the house."

"You don't have to do that," Everly said.

"I want to. Honestly, I'm a big fan. What would you like?"

They ordered a San Verde Supreme, a Citrus Chicken Cup, and a Mexi Cup to go. Hailey chatted with them about the neighborhood and what it was like to be on the radio. Everly didn't say much at all but she was one of those people who made it obvious with eye contact and body language that she was listening.

"Thanks for the salads and welcome to San Verde. You'll love it here," Stacey said.

"Thanks for coming in," Hailey said, watching them go with a mixture of hope and disappointment. It would have been great if they'd eaten in, enjoyed the shop. Maybe live-Tweeted or TikTok'd it or something. She really did need to get some music in here.

How had she thought that would go? That the tall DJ would take a bite and swear an oath to promo the hell out of Hailey's shop? A girl could dream.

She texted Piper. Regardless of anything else, it was pretty cool to have a radio personality visit the store.

Piper
That's awesome! Give it time. Wait until they try it. You'll see.

Hailey had had enough of waiting for things to come to fruition. When she'd made the decision to leave L.A. and open up a shop of her own, she'd left behind her "wait and see" attitude. If she didn't do it for herself, no one else was going to jump at the chance.

Hailey
I guess. I want more scones.
Piper
Don't mask your feelings with food, Hails.

Hailey rolled her gaze. Piper had a degree in psychology and was working on her master's degree so she could do counseling. She used Hailey, frequently, as a test subject.

Hailey
My feelings are: you're a dork but I love you.

She stared at the three bubbles.

Piper
FYI according to Urban Dictionary, what you're saying is

dork
(n) a **whale penis**
*The **blue whale** has the biggest **dork** on earth*
By **anonymous,** February 14, 2003

And burst out laughing.

Hailey
Point proven.

~~~~~~~

The following week, she saw just enough customers to make her feel like she wasn't in a sinking ship but not enough to celebrate.

She had a degree in business and marketing but there were few industries that changed as quickly. She'd taken two years of culinary school, working for food services trucks on movie sets while she'd saved for her own truck. She was good at what she did. She knew how to run a business, but the thing about *knowing* and *doing* was they were worlds apart. Especially in the age of social media.

For instance, she *knew* Facebook advertising was a good way to improve her visibility. In order to *do* something about that, however, she needed a bigger marketing budget. She fiddled around with the cheapest options, set them up, and then went to explore her website. It was lacking. From a glance, it was bright and appealing, but there was no substance.

There were ways to make it more interactive. She'd scoured other restaurant sites and loved the ease and flexibility of them. Order in, take out, preorder meals, preorder drinks for pickups. Those things were where she wanted to go but she had to be content with waiting until the money started rolling in. Or learn how to do it herself. There was always so much to learn, she felt like she'd not only slipped below the curve but given up and watched it drive away.

While she read through an online article about successful small businesses, her shop phone rang.

"By the Cup."

"Hi. Is there any chance you do deliveries?"

Hailey glanced around her empty shop. *Think fast, Hails.* "Absolutely. There's a small delivery fee depending on the distance."

"Oh, that's fine. We've got an afternoon meeting and I was wondering if I could order twenty salads."

She wasn't often thankful for an empty shop but she was now as she did a little sideways shuffle behind the counter. She didn't even care that a couple of guys walked by with huge grins on their faces that said, yeah, we saw you.

"Sure, let me grab my pen and I'll write down your orders." She tried to keep her voice calm. *Act like you've done it before.*

As Hailey wrote down *twenty* salad orders, she fell into an easy groove of answering the questions the woman asked—yes they had organic lettuce, all dressings were homemade, there were two sizes.

"I'll need about an hour," Hailey said when she'd written them all down. That was if no one showed up.

"That's perfect." She gave the address and said to come through the back entrance of the building.

"See you soon," Hailey said.

As soon as she hung up, nerves rippled through her system. Now more than ever, she wished she had some sort of ordering capabilities on her website or one of those apps that allowed customers to order ahead. It would allow her to schedule things so she wouldn't have to worry about whether customers were going to come walking through the door while she was swamped, or, worse, show up while she ran across town.

"Work now, worry later," she told herself, turning up the music a touch. It definitely added a nice vibe to the place. Twenty salads, delivery. It hadn't occurred to her before the phone call. Living in a Skip the Dishes era—where a third party would bring your meal to your door—meant even if a company didn't offer delivery, it wouldn't impact their sales. But as a new company, she needed loyal customers before that could work for By the Cup.

Despite worrying about closing the shop, deliveries, and websites, she hummed along to the music playing from 96.2 Sun. The smell of fresh vegetables and delicious dressings made her smile. She loved having her own shop. The food truck idea no longer felt like her and when she'd come to visit Piper, they'd visited the bakery and seen the FOR LEASE sign. The location was great and it meant she'd be close to a cousin she loved like a sister.

The two customers—a man and a woman—who came through the door about twenty minutes into her huge prep seemed content to sit in the corner of her shop eating their salads.

When they were still there when she finished making and

boxing up the order, Hailey wondered how best to approach them about the fact that she had to go.

The man stood, taking the tray and leaning over to kiss the woman before he cleared it and set it on the back counter. The woman checked something on her phone then joined him, turning to smile at Hailey.

"Those were delicious. We'll be back."

"Thank you so much. Have a wonderful day!"

Hailey stood frozen a minute as they left. It suddenly hit her that one of the pieces of herself she'd lost in her relationship was optimism. She'd always been a glass-half-full girl, but for too long, she'd been content with having a glass at all. Which was good but it didn't offer much hope. She *felt* her smile from her lips to her toes. No more accepting the bare minimum. She wanted the stars? She'd need to learn to reach higher.

For the first time since she'd opened her shop, she had a good feeling about where she was going.

Today is the beginning of something amazing. She not only knew it, she *believed* it.

3

Wesley Jansen's stomach growled. He placed a hand over it as he looked over the financials for Squishy Cat Industries, the corporation he owned with his brothers.

"Food will be here soon," Everly, his brother Chris's girlfriend, said with a quiet voice and a knowing smirk.

Chris, his youngest brother, joined them in the boardroom. He had a Cheshire Cat grin on his face and a small, flat box in his hand. They'd been meeting weekly at 96.2 Sun radio station—just one of the businesses under their SCI label—since Wes had joined them on the West Coast. Chris and Noah both had a head start on establishing themselves in their communities, particularly Harlow Beach, where Noah lived. The brothers volunteered at one of the local recreation centers but also attended town halls to meet residents of the neighborhood.

Effecting positive change wasn't just about money. It was about becoming part of the community and learning about real needs. Things that mattered most to the people who had to live there. Wes needed to catch up in that regard but he was trying to get them sorted in other areas first, such as finding an office space of their own.

Not that anyone minded meeting at the station. Everly worked there as a producer with her best friend, the DJ, and it was his suggestion. Noah's girlfriend, Grace, was joining them for lunch today.

Jane, the office administrator, popped her head into the room. "I ordered enough for everyone but I'll bring your salads in here when they arrive?"

Chris nodded, thanked her, then turned back to whispering something in Everly's ear. It was good to see him so happy. Wes would never let his happiness rely on another person, but he was grateful his brothers had found love.

"You ordered salad?" Noah looked up from the notepad he and Grace were studying. "You that cheap?"

Grace smacked his arm. "I could use a salad. I'm pretty sure my blood is part brownie now. Tara has got to stop trying new recipes out on us."

"Says you. You can never have enough brownies," Everly said. She pinned her gaze on Noah. "These salads are awesome. You need to try them before you complain."

"Oh, is this the place you and Stace tried last week?" Grace asked.

Everly nodded. "Delicious."

"To a girl who eats like a mouse," Noah grunted.

Everly stuck her tongue out at Noah. "Chris had one too and he loved it."

"No. He loves *you* and therefore told you he loved it then snuck out for a steak," Noah said.

Chris laughed, shook his head when Everly looked at him. "Not true. He's lying. A man can love his girlfriend *and* salad. Noah's just not that evolved."

All of them laughed. God, it was good to be all together again. When his brothers decided to build their own lives away from their tyrannical father, Wes had hesitated.

He liked his life in New York. He enjoyed routine, knowing when all his favorite restaurants were quiet, which shops catered to locals, and he loved walking through the city. Like his brothers, what he didn't like was his father's insistence that what he did for the family business was never enough.

"Have you tried the salad place yet, Wes?" Everly asked. "I know you like your routine of coffee dates at Tara's but the shop is right next door."

Looking up from his laptop, he frowned. He'd seen it, obviously, since he lived right up the road from Baked and used one of their back tables like an office. Sure, he'd met a few dates there but no more. Not for a while anyway. "Coffee and *work*."

She smiled. Everly was so shy and reserved when he first met her, he'd thought she didn't like him until Chris explained she had severe social anxiety. Over time, she'd shown more of herself and Wes was thrilled his brother had found someone so special. Someone who grounded him but also appreciated what he brought to her life.

"Dates not going well?" Grace asked. She was different than Everly but every bit as lovely. Both of his brothers were damn lucky men.

"I'm taking a break." He was in no rush. Not wanting to talk about it, he looked down at his phone.

Wes wanted a consistent, predictable dating life. He wanted to meet a woman who enjoyed an evening out, or in, shared the same interests, and wanted her own life, independent of his.

He wanted the *like* without the downfall of *love*. It looked and felt right for his brothers but Wes had worked hard to shield them from the realities of where love could lead. As the oldest, he'd seen and understood the nastiness of their parents' divorce up close. He'd always been more attuned to tension—his father condescendingly referred to Wes as the "sensitive" child—and when his parents would start, he made it his job to distract them. They'd go play outside, find hiding spots in their enormous home, play video games, or just huddle together in one of their rooms. Wes didn't want them to feel sick to their stomachs every day like he had in the end.

Looking around the room, listening to them laugh and joke, he realized he'd done it. He'd protected them. They weren't close with their father but they didn't seem to remember the fighting or the anger.

"What are you taking a break from?" Noah asked, pulling him out of his thoughts.

Wes's skin heated like it was on fire when he thought of last week's disaster. Before he could respond, his brother continued.

"Getting a life?" Noah asked.

Grace smacked his arm again. "Stop it. Be nice."

Noah grinned, unrepentant. "Honey, you keep doing that, I'm going to start liking it." He leaned in to kiss her, making her laugh.

"Knock it off, Noah. Let's get to work," Chris said.

His brother shot Wes a "you okay?" look. Wes nodded. He was fine and he had a life. A perfectly fine one.

"I have a surprise," Chris said, glancing at Everly as he opened the flat box about the size of a yearbook. He pulled a plaque out of tissue paper and turned it to face the table so they could all see.

Wes smiled, pride and happiness pushing aside his worries. The words engraved on the mahogany-colored plaque made his throat feel thick.

SQUISHY CAT INDUSTRIES
THREE BROTHERS, ONE GOAL:
CREATING A BETTER WORLD, ONE BUSINESS AT A TIME

"For when we finally get an office of our own," Chris said, looking both of his brothers in the eye.

"It's perfect," Wes said. The last line was what distinguished them from their father. It wasn't all about money. It was about leaving behind something that mattered, doing something that mattered.

"It's awesome, bro," Noah said, no hint of joking on his face.

"Speaking of offices," Wes said, pulling up his notes on his iPad. He wanted them to take a closer look at the spaces near his apartment, above shops like Baked. It was a great location and not just because he lived down the street. Before he could continue, Jane knocked on the door, letting them know lunch was there. Looking toward the door, Wes's heart did a painful shimmy all the way to his gut.

What. The. Actual. Hell? Hayden . . . no, *Hailey* was standing right next to Jane with a box in her arms. The reddish-brown hair he'd been admiring last week while she waited at the café counter was pulled up into one of those messy but sexy buns.

She was their delivery girl? Jesus. His hands went so clammy he didn't trust himself to take a drink of his water even though his mouth went desert dry. He still didn't know for sure if she'd lied. He'd had some bad matchups through the apps he tried but that one topped them all. Either she was who she said she was and he'd looked like an idiot, or he was right, she'd seen him and lied about who she was, and, well, he was an idiot.

"Sorry it took so long," she said in that pretty voice he remembered.

Unfortunately, he'd replayed the moment about two dozen times in his head. The way her hair looked, her smile, the cadence of her voice and the sympathy in her gaze when she realized he was waiting for a date.

She stepped into the room and he had the satisfaction of watching her nearly trip over her own surprise. Their gazes locked and a strange zap—like he'd stuck his finger in a socket—whipped up his arms, over his back. Damn. He'd felt a hint of this when he saw her last week, when he approached her, but it had faded quickly in the confusion. He figured he'd imagined it by overthinking things this week. Apparently not.

He had little frame of reference but thought *this* was the feeling that put hearts in his brothers' eyes. *No thank you.* He shut that down, forced himself to remember how nervous he'd felt approaching her when she seemed no closer to coming to his table last week. He wanted a steady, reliable woman he could enjoy time with. He didn't want to feel flustered and short of breath when he looked at someone.

"Oh." She huffed out a hard, noticeable breath, making him wonder if she felt the same tightness in her chest that he felt now.

What would he say? He opened his mouth to say *something* just as Everly moved back from the table, stood up.

"Hi, Hailey. How are you?"

Hay-what? Oh, shit. She really was telling the truth. Dread filled his stomach. He was more than an idiot. He was a jerk.

"Hi," Hailey said, her voice strained. She moved, nearly fumbled the box, and then set it on the table.

"I already paid her," Jane said to Chris. "But she refused a delivery fee."

"You shouldn't do that! We made you come out of your way," Everly said.

Chris got up and joined his girlfriend at her side. "Hi, Hailey. I'm Chris Jansen. Everly brought me one of your salads last week. It was fantastic, and I'm not the biggest fan of salad."

She lifted her chin, sending Wes a lightning-fast glare no one else seemed to notice. "Thank you. I'm really happy you enjoyed them. I get that comment a lot but there's so much more to salad than what we remember from growing up and being forced to eat it by our parents."

Noah went to the box. "Please tell me there's meat on some of them."

"That's one of my brothers, Noah. He's got no manners." Chris hooked his thumb toward Noah.

Wes's stomach felt like there was one of those cartoon characters in it who couldn't move even though their legs were in hyperdrive.

"I have manners. Sorry. I'm just hungry," Noah said with a wave. He picked up a clear cup with layers of vegetables, meat, and lettuce.

Wes never imagined he'd use the adjective "beautiful" on a salad but that's what it was. Almost like a piece of art.

"Spicy Steak. Nice," Noah said, gaze moving back to the woman making Wes's skin feel too tight. "I stand corrected. I can get on board with salad that contains this much meat."

She laughed and it surprised Wes to his very core that he thought the sound was pretty. Art was pretty. Not laughter.

"That there is Grace, Noah's girlfriend," Chris said. "You know Everly and that's Wes, my oldest brother."

She nodded in his direction.

He couldn't stand it. "It's nice to meet you, *Hailey*."

No one else seemed to hear the emphasis he put on her name, his way of admitting his mistake, but she clearly did. With an arrogant tilt of her chin, she met his gaze. "You, too." At least she hadn't outed him in front of everyone.

"I'm so glad you brought the salads, but why won't you take a delivery fee?" Everly asked.

Hailey's gaze softened when she looked at Everly. "When I got here, I realized it must be you and Stacey who recommended me. I appreciate the word of mouth."

"Do you have someone watching the store?" Everly asked.

Hailey shook her head. "No. I closed it for a bit. I'm still a one-woman operation."

That didn't sound good. She could be losing revenue by delivering to them. "I'll make you a deal. Instead of a delivery fee, how about Stacey mentions By the Cup on the show? Do you have any coupons or anything? We could do one of our quick-draw giveaways."

The hope he saw on Hailey's face surprised him, made his stomach shift uncomfortably.

"I don't but you can absolutely do a draw and I'll honor a giveaway for sure."

Why didn't she have coupons? That was standard business practice. Especially for start-ups. They needed to have an advantage over their competition.

"You could give us a couple business cards. Then the winner can pick them up here and use them to verify that they won when they visit the store," Wes said.

All eyes turned to him. He hadn't even realized he spoke aloud. His brain liked navigating problems and unfortunately, he had a bad habit of not keeping it to himself.

"I don't have any business cards yet," Hailey said. He wasn't sure if she looked embarrassed or worried. Maybe some combination of the two.

"That seems like something you should have," Wes said, then realized how rude he sounded. Shit.

Noah was eyeing him quizzically. Wes's hairline felt damp. He hated this feeling—being the center of attention was bad enough but being *wrong* and in the spotlight was horrible.

"Never mind me," he mumbled, looking at his laptop screen. His skin felt too tight for his body.

"My pleasure," she said sweetly.

He didn't look up until she left, which was after a bit more chatting Wes listened to painfully. He pulled up his dating app on the screen, looked for *Hayden*.

Admittedly, it was a really bad picture. A full-body shot. It was hard to see any clear details besides the reddish-brown hair. The pixelated image hadn't been enough to go on but from a distance there were similarities. Hayden was a buyer for a small clothing company, traveled for work. What she wasn't was a salad shop owner with a death glare, a great laugh, and a very, very good reason to dislike Wes.

It was getting harder to ignore his brothers and their girlfriends as they surrounded him, clearly waiting.

"What?" he snapped, shutting his laptop so they didn't see the evidence of his idiocy.

"What was that?" Noah asked, his voice ringing with laughter.

"Nothing." Wes pushed his hands through his hair, avoiding all their gazes. "Can someone open a window?"

"Had you already met Hailey?" Everly asked. Her tone was so soft and safe, it would be a dick move not to answer.

Seeing no way out of it, he stood abruptly, heading for the window. Once he did, he stayed close to it. He needed space if he was going to embarrass himself.

"Sort of." He leaned against the wall, grateful for the slight breeze, and told them the story.

"Oh my God. I cannot believe you did that. Holy fuck you're bad with women." Noah was peppering his colorful commentary with bursts of laughter.

"Noah," Grace said firmly, eyeing Wes with compassion and empathy he didn't deserve.

"I'm sorry, Wes. That must have been awful," Everly said. She sounded like she understood the many layers of how terrible it was.

"I'm not sure which sucks more, the feeling I had when I thought I was stood up or seeing her just now and realizing I'm a complete jerk."

"It's a misunderstanding," Noah said. "I'm sure she'll forgive you."

"I don't need her forgiveness." Wes's snap ended on a groan. "Sorry. I don't like being an asshole for no reason."

He'd been fully and completely in the wrong and as the son of a man who would never admit such things, accountability mattered to him. How he treated others mattered. *Those stupid dating apps. Why do I even bother?*

"You should still explain it," Grace said, sharing a glance with Everly.

"You could just pop by the shop. She seems really nice. I'm sure she'll laugh when she realizes what happened," Everly said.

"Then you can ask her out properly," Noah said.

Chris shoved Noah's shoulder. "Knock it off, man."

"What?" Noah looked around at them. "What's wrong with that?"

"I'm not going to date the woman I mistook for someone else and made hate me without even knowing my name." Or the one he'd accidentally thought of so many times this week, he'd recognized her voice even before he'd looked up to see her face. That road led somewhere he'd carefully avoided for most of his life. Their father had his faults but he'd loved their mother. The divorce had changed him irrevocably for the worse. Wes didn't want to open his heart only to have it ripped out of his chest.

"Stacey was going to talk to Rob about ordering some salads for the gym," Everly said quietly. "She really liked it there, and Tara told Stace that Hailey is new to town so I'm not sure how many people she knows."

Where was Everly going with this?

"We agreed to meet for lunch there next week with Tara," Grace said.

Wes groaned. "Awesome."

The women he *did* like were going to become friends with the woman who *didn't like* him. Perfect.

He grabbed his laptop, shoved it in the bag, gathered his keys and phone.

"Where are you going?" Chris asked.

"To figure out how to apologize to their new best friend," Wes said. He wasn't prone to dramatics but he felt severely backed into a corner. One that had a sign over it reading DO THE RIGHT THING.

"We weren't done talking business," Chris reminded him.

"We talk forty times a day and see each other several times a week. We can catch up later. I'm sorry, Everly. I'll figure something out with Hailey."

Mostly, he meant he'd figure out how to apologize and then stay as far away from her as possible.

As he was clearing the doorway, Noah called out, "Wait, don't you want a salad?"

Noah's laughter rang in his ears as he headed for home to figure

4

Hailey was focusing on the positive. Yesterday had thrown her off her game for a quick minute when she'd seen coffee-shop guy, *Wes*, at the radio station. Not just because she was fairly certain he realized how wrong he'd been but also because he looked better than she remembered.

Not important. She turned her Kindle off, stuffing it in her purse. Sometimes, reading a few pages or chapters took the edge off for her, settled her pulse like nothing else.

Hailey checked the list of must-do items she'd created. Top of the list were getting her website updated, business cards, and looking into preorder options for customers.

Having the producer of a local radio station as a return customer was huge. She'd felt like a total rookie when she didn't even have a card to offer, especially after *Wes* was so kind as to point it out. *Positive. You're focusing on the positive.* Her skin heated remembering the intensity of his gaze.

"What would Taylor say?" Hailey asked, leaving her list on the end of the counter where she'd been sitting on one of the stools. She'd left her phone by the sink and picked it up now, pressing play. "Shake It Off" came through the Bluetooth speaker and she threw her energy into chopping, dicing, and prepping for what she hoped would be a busy day.

The three brothers were a sight to behold. Everly's boyfriend was a dark-haired cutie and the other one, Noah, was straight-up adorable. Wes? Definitely good-looking no matter how immune she wanted to be to him in a suit. She really couldn't imagine someone standing him—or his brothers—up on a date. Wondering what apps he was using, she wondered if she should put herself out there again but quickly dismissed the idea.

She didn't want to be distracted right now. She wasn't bitter about love, no matter how poorly it had turned out the last time around, but she and her store came first.

"Hey, Siri," she called, going with her gut.

"What can I help you with?"

"Text Piper."

"Would you like me to text Piper?"

"Yes."

"What would you like to say to Piper?"

"We need a girls' night. I'm thinking rom-com, wine, and pretzel sticks. What time do the kids go to bed?"

"Your message to Piper says, 'We need a girls' night. I'm thinking rom-com, wine, and pencil dicks. What time do the kids go to bed?'"

The knife sliced the edge of her thumb, distracting her from anything else. "Shit." She grabbed a napkin.

"Would you like to send this message to Piper?"

"Yes." She groaned the word. She hated blood.

"Your message is sent."

"Thanks," she said, grabbing a bandage from the first aid box by the sink. "Now can you stop blood?"

"Here are some articles I found on the internet on how to stop blood."

A low, irritated growl left her throat. *Okay, Siri. Thanks for nothing.* The cut was tinier than an eyelash. She was such a wimp. After she wrapped it, she cleaned the prep area, mad at herself but letting Taylor Swift's brand of calm work its magic.

When her phone rang, she was still cleaning so she swiped accept, moved down the counter.

"Hey. You okay?" Piper's voice came through the Bluetooth speaker loudly.

The bell over the door jingled. Hailey locked eyes with Wes.

"Hailey," Piper called.

"I'm fine. I have to call you back."

"Okay. But I don't know where to buy pencil dicks. So, you get those and I'll get the wine."

Like she'd fallen into a vat of quicksand mixed with honey, everything slowed. Piper's laughter sounded like it was coming from a tunnel far, far away. Wes's brows nearly disappeared into the hair that fell over his forehead. A snort of laughter broke through her humiliation. What the hell was wrong with her cousin? She raced to the phone, picked it up, fumbled it, turned off the speaker at the same time she put the phone to her ear and turned her back on Wes.

"Are you day drinking?" she whispered into the phone.

"I'm not the one sending dirty texts," Piper said, still laughing.

Hailey pulled her phone away from her ear, looked at the text to see what the hell was so dirty about pretzel sticks. *Holy shit*. She put the phone back to her ear. "I have to go."

"Okay. See you later."

She hung up, gave herself the time to take a few deep, cleansing breaths. When she turned around, shoving her phone in her back pocket, Wes was watching her carefully.

Her heart was beating in her ears. The only other sound she heard was her own attempt to swallow the dryness in her throat.

"What . . ." she started, and the word disappeared. Hailey cleared her throat, grabbed her water bottle, took a long drink, very aware of Wes's gaze. She set it down and tried again. "What can I get for you?"

His smile was so slight that it could have been a twitch. It was his eyes though that said everything for him. They were blue the color of the California ocean. The deep blue sort that pulled you in and made you want to swim a little deeper. *Until a wave comes up out of nowhere and drowns you.*

As though he needed time, he strolled along the display counter, his gaze moving over the fresh ingredients below the plexiglass divider. When he stopped, he was closer, near to where she'd been sitting.

It was then he pinned his eyes on hers. "I don't suppose you have an apology salad? Though, then I guess I'd be making it for you." He sighed. "I should have brought you cake from Tara's. It's delicious."

Her brows scrunched, her embarrassment over the phone call slowly fading.

Wes shook his head. "I'm rambling. I'm not very good at this."

"Apologizing?"

She watched his Adam's apple move up and down. "To being out of line. Being a complete jackass. I try not to be."

She leaned against the counter, overwhelmingly grateful they were focusing on his failings and not on pencil dicks. "There's no such thing as an apology salad but you could just say the words."

He nodded, like she'd scolded him even though she'd kept her tone even. "I am sorry. Very sorry, *Hailey*. And incredibly embarrassed."

Hailey hadn't expected him to be so forthright. So genuine. "Thank you."

Shifting in his spot, he continued to stare at her. She was curious to see if he'd add anything. When he didn't, she couldn't stand the quiet.

"I take it your date didn't go well?"

The twitch of a smile turned into a real one and the impact on her system was concerning. He moved to the stool she'd sat on earlier and eased into it, glancing down at her list, then up at her. No suit today but his jeans and light, long-sleeved shirt looked every bit as good.

He seemed to be weighing his words carefully. "It didn't go at all. She never showed."

Hailey grabbed the pen, paper, and her calendar from where they lay in front of him, storing them behind the counter.

"I'm really sorry." She meant it. It had been a while since she'd dated but she'd had some less-than-stellar ones herself.

Once again, his brows darted together. "I came here to say that to *you*."

She leaned against the counter from her side so she was across from him. "You did. Apology accepted."

"That's it?"

She laughed. "Was there something else?"

Wes folded his arms on the sleek white eating area. She only had three stools on this shorter side of the counter. The rest were arranged in front of the window on the other side of the store.

"No. I just figured you might . . . you know what? I have no idea. I didn't get to try your salad yesterday. Can I have a Wild for Walnuts?"

Happy to shift the conversation away from anything awkward, she nodded, washed her hands, and pulled on some gloves.

"So, pen—"

Her arm shot out and her index finger aimed right at him as she backed up toward the service bar. "Don't say it. We will not speak of that. Stupid voice texting."

When he laughed, really laughed, his eyes crinkled. "Sure."

"Be nice or I'll put hot sauce in your salad."

"Maybe I like hot sauce," he said, his tone shifting.

She smiled, grabbing a cup and tongs. This was better than awkward. While she put the ingredients together, she asked, "Any more dates? I mean, ones that showed."

"No. After that one I decided to take a break," he said, watching her layer butter lettuce, chopped walnuts, marinated tomatoes, and cucumbers.

"Sometimes you need one." She could understand that no problem.

"You speaking from experience?"

Focusing on her task, she gave a slight nod she wasn't even sure if he saw. "My last relationship required more than a break. I'm on a semipermanent hiatus."

His laughter brought her gaze back up. "Ouch. Must have been bad."

"You have no idea." She walked back over, put the salad and a fork in front of him. "Here you go, Wes. One Wild for Walnuts."

After he paid, she thought he'd leave. Nice knowing you, sorry for the mix-up, see you. But he didn't. He opened it up and dug in.

"Damn. This is good. I can't believe it's good for you. When people order salad at a restaurant, I always think it's a waste of a meal out but wow. Maybe I'm the one who was wrong."

She grinned, came around the counter again. "Wouldn't be the first time."

His lips fell flat but she could see the laughter in his gaze. "Well played."

Giving him some space so he could eat, she cleaned the small mess she'd made.

Grabbing the take-out menus, she wiped them down, wondering if she should get some nonlaminated ones made. If she offered a delivery service even a couple days a week, she could—

"I was thinking," Wes said.

Hailey turned when he didn't finish.

"There's no apology salad but I have other skills."

"Oh my God please don't let that be your come-on line." She hadn't meant to blurt out the immediate reaction. *Damn, brain, keep some things to yourself.*

His face blanched, paler than the plastic fork in his hand. "No! I'm not . . . I'm not *coming on* to you. I was going to offer to play with your website."

"Excuse me?" Maybe she spent too much time texting with Piper but everything he said seemed to have a double meaning. She bit back her smile when she noticed his complexion getting rosier.

He set the cup and his fork down, held his hands up, palms facing her. "Please let me start again. I work with computers and software. I'm very good at my job." He gestured to the paper she'd put aside. "Can I see that?"

Slowly, she grabbed it, slid it back in front of him with the pen. He picked it up, started moving his hand, blocking her view. "You need help with your site. I can help you make a few improvements that'll have a big impact."

He continued to move his hand over the page.

"You saw the site?"

He glanced up. "I did. When I was looking up your store, while I was gathering the courage to come apologize, I noticed your website has very limited capabilities."

She crossed her arms over her chest. "Okay . . ."

"I thought upgrading it, making it more user-friendly, maybe even putting in an advance order capability"—he put the pen down, slid the paper across—"would make a nice 'I'm sorry' gesture."

Wow. He'd drawn an adorable, lifelike salad cup, complete with a smile and happy eyes. Little vegetable sketches were arced across the page as if they were eager to head into the cup.

"On the site, we could animate some graphics, make it fun."

"You're a good artist," she said, picking it up.

He ducked his gaze as he picked up his fork. "I just sketch really."

She waited for him to say more but he didn't.

"If this is your job, you probably get paid a lot to do things like this," she said, wishing guilt didn't crowd her chest whenever people offered to do things for her.

Growing up, she'd learned that unless she absolutely had no choice, it was easier not to ask her parents to do anything for her or on her behalf. When she needed them to step up and do things like come to parent-teacher meetings, her mom would tell Hailey she "owed her" or that she didn't want to but she would. She didn't need Piper's counseling courses to know this created a panic inside her whenever she had to ask for help.

"I love this stuff. Honestly, it's relaxing for me. I don't mind. It'll take no time." Wes polished off the rest of his salad.

He seemed genuine. "How about we trade salad for website work?" she suggested.

He grinned, put the lid back on his empty cup. "If that makes you feel better, sure. Got a laptop?"

Hailey laughed. "You want to do it now?"

He shrugged. "Why not? I can show you a couple things that'll make it easier to update. I like the personal touch with the blog."

She felt her cheeks heat. "Some of the stuff I write is a bit corny."

"It's honest."

She arched her brows, noticing the way his lips quirked. She wasn't writing sonnets for salads, but she did tend to babble on when she was excited about a new recipe.

"And corny?" She put her hands on her hips, waited.

Wes pursed his lips, holding her gaze. "Can it be both?"

A week ago, she thought she'd never see this man again. Now, he was making her laugh. Life was full of good surprises. She'd forgotten that for a little while.

5

Hailey bagged up the three salads—technically two with one side of chips—the surfer dude was buying, thanking him again for stopping by the shop. Slow and steady. That's all she needed. She cleaned up the counter and went back to where Wes had taken up residence with her laptop.

"That guy was really happy you had Doritos," Wes commented.

Hailey laughed, cleaning up the counter. "Yeah. It's the first time I've had someone order a Ranch Taco Supreme minus the lettuce, peppers, beef, tomatoes, salsa, and guac." The guy literally just wanted Doritos.

"You have eight thousand tabs open," he said, picking up his lemonade without looking up.

"You're supposed to be working magic on my website, not scrolling through my tabs."

Now he glanced up, lifting his gaze to hers. "They kind of go hand in hand."

"I have a busy brain," she said, shooting him a smile.

She liked to be busy in general. Whether she was chopping veggies, writing emails, or paying bills, Hailey needed to keep her head and hands occupied.

"If this is an indication of your brain, you might need a reboot," he said. His tone told her he was teasing but he wasn't entirely wrong.

It was hard not to be surprised by his wry sense of humor. "Technically, that's what moving here was."

She hadn't meant to say it out loud and was relieved he didn't respond. Maybe he hadn't even heard her. With only an hour to go until closing, Hailey puttered while Wes did whatever the technology version of puttering was. She grabbed her clipboard and went to take inventory of what she needed to top up for the following day.

"So, a break, huh?"

"Hmm?" Wes alternated tapping on the keyboard with making notes and sketches on the paper she'd left beside him. He looked up as she set her clipboard down near her veggie bins. "Sorry, what?"

"You're taking a break? One no-show scared you away?"

His brows rose on his forehead. He had a multitude of what she'd call "serious" expressions. "How do you know it was just one?"

"Has it been more?"

"No. But you sounded so certain."

"If someone is going to go to the trouble of being on a dating app, scrolling through possibilities, and making arrangements, it feels like they're somewhat invested. Did *Hayden* ever contact you?"

He ducked his gaze again, picked up the pen. "She said she got held up and asked if we could reschedule."

Hailey grinned, walking over to him. "You should say yes and then I can sit somewhere close by, get a good look at her, and see if your vision is really bad or she's my doppelgänger."

Wes gave a half laugh, half groan. "That sounds awful. There's nothing wrong with my vision. It was a bad photo and just an all-around error."

Grabbing the clipboard, she finished the quick check of veggies and put the board away. She didn't like to overprep because she wanted only the crispest, freshest veggies.

"Why San Verde?"

She grabbed the broom, moving out from behind the counter. So he had heard her. He was a dangerous sort—the kind who listened even when he didn't seem to.

Even at first glance, when he'd walked over to her at the bakery, she would have pegged him as uptight. Type A. He was. But he was also . . . more. Smart, witty, and beneath the sarcasm, maybe a little scarred, like her?

It was surprisingly nice to have him there that afternoon to chat with. Between work and work and more work, she hadn't made any new friends.

She debated how much to say, very aware he was watching her. "When I broke up with my ex, I needed to get out of L.A. I have a cousin here. We've always been close. Since I'm not close to anyone else in my family, it seemed as good a place as any."

"Was the salad shop always your plan?"

She smiled, stopped sweeping to meet his gaze. "Absolutely not. I was going to run a food truck. But Piper, my cousin, brought me to Baked and I saw this place for lease. I don't know," she said, looking down at her shoes, then back up at him. "I don't really buy into fate or anything like that but suddenly I didn't want a place on wheels. I wanted a place to call my own." She shrugged.

"I'm not really into fate either but I do believe in following your gut. I think you're going to do well here," he said after a moment.

Her laugh was louder than she intended. "You don't believe in fate but you're a fortune-teller?"

"No. But I am an investor. My brothers and I buy and sell businesses, properties. Sometimes we go in, assess a company, find ways to maximize profits and efficiency, and decide to keep it, expand it. I know business. I'm not as much of a people person as my brothers but I'd like to think I have good judgment. Our meeting excluded."

She set the broom against the counter, laughing as she slid onto the stool next to him. "Yeah, your judgment failed you there. Or, your eyesight. I still think you should get it checked."

He gave her a mock frown. Pressure built in her chest, making it ache a little. "It feels good to hear you say I have a chance. I'm worried about the lack of customers and I put my money into getting started without thinking about how much marketing cost."

He frowned for real this time. "Are you always this open?"

She leaned back, suddenly irritated. "Why? Did I overshare?"

Wes reached out like he might cover her hand with his but stopped. "Sorry. I wasn't trying to be abrupt. I just wouldn't want to see anyone take advantage of you. Professionally. You seem like you can hold your own personally."

Not entirely sure if he'd complimented her, she shook her head. "No, not always so open." In fact, now that he said it, she was surprised at herself. "I think I thought we were starting to become friends."

"Friends?" His brows pushed together.

She poked him in his surprisingly firm bicep. "Yeah. You know, people who talk, hang out, don't get offended right away when one is abrupt or mistakes them for another person?"

"I'm never living that down, am I?"

She shook her head.

"Friends." This time when he said it, it was like he was trying out the word, seeing how it fit. "I think I like that."

Now she laughed. "You are really not great for the ego."

Wes winced. "Sorry." He sighed. "Maybe I'm not cut out for dating or friendship."

Slipping off the stool, she decided, first impressions and attraction aside, she liked him. She could use some friends and she'd never have to worry about him telling her the truth. "Nah. You're just a work in progress."

Turning his laptop, he smiled at her. "Speaking of, what do you think?"

The colors popped right off the screen and the salad cup he'd drawn had somehow made it onto the web page. She started to squeal with excitement but was cut off by the phone ringing.

"Hang on one second. I love it." She hurried around the counter to the phone. "I can't believe you did that in, like, the last half hour." She picked up the house phone.

"By the Cup."

"Hi, there. I'm wondering if I can do a preorder for tomorrow. We have an office lunch and a friend of mine told me about your shop."

She must have done her happy tap because Wes looked over with an arched brow.

"Absolutely. Let me get a pen and you can tell me what you'd like."

It was a long list. "What time were you thinking?"

"Noon?"

She hesitated. She usually had at least a few people come by at lunchtime. If she wanted to exaggerate greatly, she'd say that was her daily rush. "The thing is, I'm by myself and to deliver, I have to close the shop. Which I don't mind but around one would be better."

"How about I have someone pick up?"

"Really?"

The woman laughed. "Of course."

"That's fantastic. Thank you."

"You're welcome!"

When she hung up, Hailey felt like she could float to the ceiling.

"You know, you're providing goods. People pay for goods and services. It's expected that you charge for food and delivery." Wes had gone back to working on the laptop.

"I know, but I can still appreciate it."

He regarded her with an expression she couldn't read. "I remember the first app I sold. I was very excited."

She couldn't imagine him doing a happy tap or squealing. "How did you celebrate?"

"I didn't. I told my brothers, invested the profit, and continued working." She wasn't sure what she was going to say but he continued. "My dad considered my making apps a hobby, so it wasn't something to toast like when Noah purchased the Morgan Park properties and we turned them into condos. Or when Chris turned a small camera shop into a chain store. But I was happy."

"Being successful at something you love is its own reward, I guess," she said.

He sipped the last of his lemonade while she pulled his laptop toward her. "I hadn't thought of it like that."

While she scrolled through the new features, the add-ons like signing up for her newsletter, and the format, she grew more and more curious about the man beside her. "Is this what you do for your father?" Seemed like all three of them worked for their dad.

Something strange flashed in his gaze. "It was part of what I did at one time. We don't work with him anymore. I was groomed to take over technology in all areas since I had an aptitude for it."

"Groomed?" Who was this man?

"I have degrees in computer science, engineering, and cyber-security."

Her jaw dropped. "Degrees?"

"Yes. I graduated young. I liked learning so I did as much as I could. What do you think of the site?"

Quick change. She couldn't blame him. The tension filling the air when he spoke about his dad was tangible.

"It's perfect. Truly. Thank you."

"My pleasure. It was fun."

"I should pay you."

He shook his head. "Nope. It was my apology."

"Your apology was your apology."

He chuckled. "Okay. It's a favor for a friend. How about that?"

She hated the favor part. She hated owing people. But the friend part felt too nice to wreck the moment. She didn't even realize they were staring at each other until her heart pinched. Like it was warning her of something. Whatever passed between them must have caught him off guard as well if the hitch in his breath was anything to go on.

She pointed at one of the options. "I don't know if I should advertise delivery."

She really wanted to but she definitely wasn't ready to hire employees who could cover the store.

"That page can stay hidden until you can offer it. You know, you could offer deliveries during a one-hour opening. If you only offer three spots, it would increase demand."

Checking the time, she realized they'd chatted and he'd worked most of the afternoon. She went to the door, turned the sign to CLOSED. "I'll think about it. I'd really like to increase my in-store clientele first."

"That's fair. Did you get business cards made?" He stood, stretched.

"Since yesterday?"

He stared at her like he didn't think that was asking the impossible.

She rolled her eyes. "No. Not yet."

"You should."

She stopped herself from sticking her tongue out at him and saying "duh" like one of Piper's kids. "I know."

"You've got a good logo. It's fun and easily transferrable to shirts, mugs, and other merchandise if you choose to go that route. You're in a touristy area so that's a definite option."

Did he just have all of these ideas kicking around in the back of his brain? "Again, I need to increase my customer base."

"Flyers are a simple and effective way to spread the word."

She could print them herself.

"Have you looked at Facebook ads?"

Her spine straightened. "Not yet."

He frowned. "It's important even if you have limited funds."

Pushing away from the counter, she stared at him a minute

before letting out a frustrated groan. "Okay. Thank you. That's a lot of ideas and examples of what I'm *not* doing. But I've been a little busy. I'm on my own and funds *are* limited."

He reached over and closed the laptop. He cleared his throat, stared at the counter. "It's a lot. It can be overwhelming."

A new kind of tension pushed against her rib cage. He knew what he was doing, had done it before, according to what he'd said. He was just offering advice.

"Sorry for being defensive."

He finally looked at her again. "It's your business. People say it's not personal, but it is."

She nodded, a lump forming in her throat. It was definitely personal. "Thank you for all your help. You have a week of salads on the house."

"Not necessary but thank you. Let me know if you have any trouble with the website. It's live now and as things change you can update it."

She'd need to google how to do that. "Perfect. Heading home to delete your dating profiles?"

His grin did a weird thing to her stomach, made it feel like she was on a trampoline. Fortunately, he'd just irritated her so she was able to ignore it.

"The exciting night of a bachelor. I think I'll just stay away from them for now. How about you?"

"I'm going to go home and look up business cards."

His laughter surprised her. "Good idea. I'll see you soon, Hailey."

She locked up after him, went back to her laptop, and played on her website. It looked fantastic. She had a lot to do and think about but didn't want to go home. She wanted cake. And knew someone who loved it every bit as much as she did.

It was quiet next door, just a few tables with customers.

"Hey," Tara said when she got to the counter.

"Hi." Hailey had only spoken to her a couple times. Now that she knew the connection between Stacey, Everly, and Tara, she was even more determined to make a good impression. "I've heard great things about your chocolate cake," Hailey said. The coffee shop was open much later than Hailey's. She'd gone with demand and decided, for now, eleven to six was plenty.

"It's got a reputation. Who'd you hear it from?"

"Wes."

Her smile widened. "Ahh. He's such a sweetie. You want a piece?"

Maybe Wes should try asking out someone he knew in real life. "Two actually."

As she stepped around one of her baristas, not the bored one from last week, Tara grabbed a pair of tongs. "I've been meaning to stop by your place but things have been so hectic. There's a San Verde Shop Association meeting next week. We have one a month. We also have a Facebook group and an email chain. It helps all of us keep up to date with what's happening. Sometimes we organize sales and specials. I thought you'd like to know."

Hailey took out her debit card. "That's awesome. Thank you for telling me. I will absolutely be there. Where is it?"

Tara passed her the cake in a little bag. "Upstairs. There's a meeting room we rent out from the owner."

It seemed strange they had to pay to rent something when they all paid to rent their shops. She hadn't met the landlord yet.

"Okay. Thanks for letting me know."

"My pleasure. You settling in okay?"

Hailey nodded. She wanted so badly to sit down and have coffee with this woman, to talk about business and promos and how to get more customers. But she didn't want to seem needy and she'd received enough pro bono help today.

"For sure."

After paying for the cake, she left the shop, headed to the back parking lot to get her car. She looked up at the apartments with longing. It'd be so nice to just take those stairs up and settle in for the night. She could sit on the balcony and listen to the sounds of the square. Her place was okay but it was nothing special.

The problem with pushing aside all her wants for so long, so her ex could have his, was now she was impatient. She wanted it all.

"You have everything you need," she said, getting in her car. Heading toward Piper's house, she thought about which rom-com they should watch. *When Harry Met Sally* seemed like a good choice.

She wouldn't have thought, this time yesterday, that today would be entirely different. That was life though: it turned on a dime, and the only thing she had control of was how she responded to what happened.

6

Anyone looking his way would believe Wes's undivided attention was focused on his date. Eye contact, check. Body positioning, check. Feet pointed forward, check. But a split-second flit of his gaze had let him see Hailey walk through the door. Now, as she stood in line, his thoughts and his focus stumbled. Which made him feel rude. Which irritated him.

"So, I thought, why not? The worst-case scenario, the quiz will tell me I'm only suited to do what I currently do."

Right. Cassandra is thinking of a career change because hers isn't fulfilling. See? Multitasking at its finest.

"If anything, it might provide some deeper insight," Wes said, feeling good about maintaining the conversation even when Hailey spotted him, waved enthusiastically, then covered her mouth with her hand, removed it, mouthed "sorry." He cracked a smile but the date could easily assume this was for her.

But when Hailey gestured to his date and stuck two thumbs up with a wide smile, he nearly laughed. She was . . . unique.

"Have you ever done one of those tests?" Cassandra asked, picking up her half-skim, half-whole, five pumps of vanilla, no whip, one shot decaf, one shot regular coffee. Was it even coffee at that point?

"No," he said, doing his best not to watch Hailey chat amiably with the barista. He'd noticed when he was in her shop for several hours the other day that she had an easy way with people.

Cassandra leaned forward. "Wesley?"

His gaze snapped to hers. "Yes?"

"Let's be honest. Neither of us are connecting here and as much as we look great on paper, it's got to be more than that."

While he agreed with the first half of what she said, he disagreed with the second part. Not in this instance, but in general.

"I'm sorry," he said, meaning it. "I appreciate you meeting me though."

"Same. Welcome to San Verde. I hope you find what you're looking for." She got up, took her coffee, and sashayed away as Hailey picked up her drink and what he suspected was chocolate cake from the end of the counter.

Hailey watched Cassandra go then slowly approached his table. "I thought you were done with this?" She sat down.

He shrugged. "I'd forgotten I already agreed before I decided that. It came up on my calendar. She showed up so that's a win."

Hailey's gaze wandered to the exit then back to him. "Well? Was she the one to change your mind? Keep you on the app path to finding love?"

Wes laughed, hiding his wince. He wasn't looking for love. "No. She confirmed the hiatus."

She pointed at him. "Nice. Industry lingo."

He nodded, remembering his surprise when she'd shared her employment history. With her elegant jawline, full hair, and wide eyes, she could play the Hollywood girl next door. Instead, she'd served lunch. She might look like a leading lady but was completely down-to-earth.

Hailey opened her take-out container. Chocolate cake. "My website is fantastic. Thank you again."

She was so appreciative of even the littlest thing. "No problem. Really. I could do websites with my eyes closed."

"Sometimes I feel like I could make salads that way," she said, making a face that embodied pleasure to the point his own cheeks heated.

"Good?" The word came out like sandpaper.

She nodded, gaze at half-mast, and gave a happy sigh. She was unlike anyone he'd ever met. When she'd suggested friendship the other day, the idea caught him off guard. But sitting across from her, knowing she was the kind of woman who could wreck him with anything more, which would end with him wrecking her beyond repair, it felt like a good option. Definitely preferable to walking away. He *liked* her.

"I'm coming to collect one of my salads tomorrow. My brothers and I are looking at the office space above your shop."

She swallowed, took a sip of her drink. "I'm jealous. Not of the office space but anything above the shops. I've heard the apartments are adorable."

"That wouldn't have been my adjective of choice but they're very nice places," he said. "I live down the street in one."

"Now I'm jealous again. One day."

He smiled at the way she could put so much stock in two words. Had he ever done that? Maybe when he was too young to understand what a heavy hand his father would have in his desire to design video games. How he'd see it as a frivolous hobby and give Wes more responsibility. One of his father's favorite sayings was "Life is built on getting things done, not dreaming about them."

"I'm sorry your date didn't go well. Maybe you need to try a new approach."

Wes finished his coffee. He had a meeting soon. "I am. The no-more-apps-for-a-while approach."

She put her fork down. "I like to see people happy. You should know that. Since we're friends and all."

He meant it when he said, "I'm happy. I'd be happier if you shared that cake."

She grabbed a fork from the cup of them set on the table, passed it to him, and moved her container closer. He took a bite, thinking he needed to hit the gym.

"Delicious."

She nodded. "It's my new favorite. When I can only fit into yoga pants, I'll blame you and Tara."

He shrugged. She didn't look like she needed to worry about such things but he had a sister and knew sometimes women worried about things they didn't need to. They didn't see themselves the way others did. "It's California. That's what everyone wears anyway, isn't it?"

She leaned to the side and checked out his pants, making him laugh. "Oh! We should check out yoga."

He swallowed wrong, coughed. "We? No, thank you."

"It's good for stress."

"I'm not stressed."

"So you're naturally uptight?"

Why did people think he was uptight? His brothers teased him about the same thing. He'd had responsibility thrust into his lap at a young age. He was taught to deal with what came his way. That wasn't uptight. It was being an adult. "I'm not uptight. Plus, I've done yoga. I don't like it."

"We could go to a yoga class and then watch *When Harry Met Sally.*"

Wes couldn't help his smile. "If this is going to work, you have to try to remember I'm a guy. One who doesn't want to do yoga and watch rom-coms."

She closed her container. "Sorry. We can guzzle beer and smoke cigars." She'd deepened her voice comically.

Wes stood. "How about something in between those?"

"I'll think on it."

"I have a meeting. It was nice to see you." He meant it. She made him smile even when she said ridiculous things. He'd come to California with a built-in circle. It hadn't occurred to him, other than dating, what someone outside his circle—a friend—could bring to his life. He waved and pulled out his phone as he left the shop.

As he strolled along the sidewalk, he pulled up the text thread with his brothers. He rolled his eyes, seeing one of them—most likely Noah—had, once again, renamed the thread. Wes had labeled it "Brothers" when they'd started it eons ago. It went back so long, he couldn't even remember when they started it. In that time, Chris and Noah took turns calling it something else. Today's was "Two Men & a Wesley."

> **Wes**
> Hey asshats. Don't forget we're meeting at Hailey's tomorrow.
> **Chris**
> Why would we forget?
> **Noah**
> Because we have a life and he doesn't.

Wes chuckled.

> **Wes**
> What have you done with your life today? Let Gracie make you something to eat, show you some designs, and nod along so you don't piss her off?

Wes adored both women and was thrilled his brothers had found happiness in all areas of their lives. There was a small piece of him, burrowed deep, that could acknowledge his envy. Some people might think that with them as examples, he'd believe more wholeheartedly in the love thing. But he knew better. From their mom leaving and the women his father fell for taking up residence in their home. From their sister acting out and their dad becoming more remote with every passing day. From his father never recovering when the one woman he'd loved had finally had enough.

He'd protected his younger siblings as well as he could. It hadn't helped any in terms of saving their relationships with their father but that was his old man's doing. Wes had given them the supportive words and shoulder they needed growing up because he knew their father wouldn't. Eventually, both his brothers had left him anyway. Sure, they'd left because of work, not Wes, but it didn't make him feel any less . . . alone. They were thrilled when he decided to move across the country and join them. But they wouldn't have returned to New York for him. Wouldn't have stayed for him. It sometimes made him question anyone's staying power.

Noah
Grace wants you guys to come for a BBQ next weekend.
Chris
I'll check with Everly but I'm sure we're in.
Noah
Invite Stacey and Rob

Wes thought of Hailey and how she was working to build a life here, how Everly and Grace had accepted her with ease.

Wes
Should I invite Hailey?
Chris
Absolutely! Way to go, bro. She's awesome.
Wes
As a friend. That's all we are. You know what friend means right?
Noah
Sadly, for you, it probably means exactly what the dictionary says
Wes
Don't be an ass

Chris
You're asking the impossible. For sure, invite her.
Wes
I will.
Chris
Cool.
Noah
Tell me you don't think she's hot.
Wes
Give me a second, I'm looking for a GIF of someone strangling their brother.

Wes reached his apartment with twenty minutes to get ready for his meeting. Between missing his brothers and his increasingly strained relationship with his dad, it hadn't taken much convincing for Wes to follow them to the West Coast. He loved New York but it changed when the two people he was closest to left.

Now he was here and he was happy but he was also restless, and that wasn't something he was used to. His brothers had really found their groove. Wes didn't *have* to work. He could dive into actually creating a video game if he wanted. He'd been thinking more and more about it but still felt this nagging sense of guilt that it would be a "waste" of his time and talent.

Hell, he could spend every day on the beach with someone bringing him ice-cold beers if he wanted. His father would probably respect that more. *Why the hell do you still care what he thinks?* Glancing at his sketchbook, it was like he could hear his father's words. They were like a tattoo he wanted removed. That took time.

Grabbing an iced tea from his fridge, he sat down at his small kitchen table, next to the window, listening to the sound of low, soft music drifting out of someone's apartment.

Chris and Noah seemed so centered, sure of what they were doing. Opening his tablet, Wes reviewed his emails. He took care of all the paperwork, the tech support for each company, vetted possible acquisitions, dug into companies, and managed the investment portfolio. Professionally, he was doing everything he wanted and now, he was doing it with his favorite people.

They were going to create an empire that matched their father's. His focus was best served doing exactly what he was already doing.

He thought of how happy Hailey seemed every single time she made a sale or took an order. He hadn't felt like that about a deal or acquisition in so long it felt like a ghost of a memory.

Pushing his tablet aside, he opened his laptop, told himself to stop searching for problems. He was as privileged as it could get. He had no right to feel this little tick of disquiet. If he wasn't careful, he'd be just like his father, never content with what he had. Always needing more and not caring who he had to step on to get it.

He sighed, clicked on the Zoom link for his meeting. Maybe Hailey was right—he needed to do some yoga.

7

People were weird. But Hailey was so grateful to have a steady stream of customers today, she didn't care. Today she'd had three elderly women argue over who was paying and they nearly left without any of them doing so. There'd been a father-son duo who asked if she had anything on plates. They were followed by a group of teens who ordered individual cups of vegetables: one cup of carrots, one cup of cucumbers, one cup of tomatoes, and one cup of snap peas. They didn't want lettuce or forks. Who was she to judge? This week had been much better than last and regardless of how strange some requests were, she loved interacting with people.

"Do you use organic lettuce?" the dark-haired, dark-skinned woman asked. She'd been studying the menu for about five minutes. Her workout clothes reminded Hailey that she really did want to look into yoga. She could go alone. Maybe she'd meet new friends. *If you had your business cards ready, you could take them.* She'd only made one new pal—which still made her laugh because she and Wes were very different—but it felt like she was on a roll.

"I have that option, yes." Hailey smiled at the woman, who clearly took salads seriously. A trait she both admired and appreciated.

"Okay. I'm ready." The woman nodded in confirmation, clapping her hands together.

Hailey bit the inside of her cheek to keep from laughing at the way she announced the words. *This salad better be one of your best or she'll be disappointed.*

"I'll have seven Chicken Landslides and three Pesto Pastas."

"Did you want organic lettuce for the Landslides?" Hailey pulled on gloves, grabbed ten cups, the happy dance in her wanting to escape. She had to stop acting like having customers was a miracle. *Act like you've been there.* Ha. She hadn't though!

"No, thanks. How long have you been open?" The woman scanned the empty store before turning her warm brown eyes back to Hailey.

"I'll be celebrating a month soon. I'm really loving the area."

"Welcome to the neighborhood. I work at a gym not too far from here. I have a feeling my co-workers are going to be thrilled there's something like this close by."

Hailey had practiced making each salad so many times, it was easy to carry on a conversation while she whipped them up. "I was hoping salads would be a hit. This is California, after all."

The woman gave a happy laugh, making her ponytail bounce when she nodded. "We do like our veggies and smoothies. I'm Jaycee, by the way. I think you'll probably see me again. Do you have a loyalty reward card or anything?"

Wes's slightly know-it-all voice rang in her head. Yeah, yeah, she needed to do that. "I'm Hailey, and not yet but I'm working on it. How about today I just knock off the price of a salad?"

"Awesome." Jaycee's phone beeped and drew her attention even as the bell rang over the door.

She recognized Noah and his laughing eyes. He was followed by Chris, who had slightly lighter hair and a more serious smile. Wes was behind him and her heart did a happy little skip. She told herself it was the same one as when she saw Piper. Having friends stop by felt good.

She smiled and waved as he came through the door. "Hey, guys!"

They waved. Wes had a shy, slightly awkward smile that she

found appealing. Platonically speaking. Because there was no other category for her right now. Even if there was, she didn't want a checklist, ideas man. She'd had enough of that with Dorian. *You should wear the blue dress, it goes with what I'm wearing. You shouldn't wear those sunglasses; they're too big for your face. You should separate my laundry from yours. My clothes are more expensive.*

The guys said something to Wes that made his gaze narrow as they made their way to a table.

"I think a couple of them work out at my gym," Jaycee said.

It was hard to see Wes as a gym rat but she'd proven she didn't always get the best read on people. If he did go, it probably wasn't for yoga.

"I've become addicted to the cake next door, so maybe I should work out at your gym," Hailey said, finishing up the Landslides.

Jaycee dug around in her purse, then slid a card over the counter. "Here's a free pass if you want to try it."

As Hailey accepted it, an idea whirled in her brain. She thought about what Tara had said about joining forces with other shops, but what if she could branch out farther than the square? She should talk to Piper and see what she thought.

"Thanks. I just might do that."

Jaycee left with a bag full of salads and Hailey got a satisfying thrill out of ringing up her order. She'd planned to go to the table and ask the guys what they wanted but they approached the counter.

"Hey," she said, meeting Wes's gaze.

"Hey. That was a lot of salad." He gestured with his thumb toward the door.

"It was. Every day gets better."

"You remember Noah and Chris. Guys, you remember Hailey . . ." he trailed off.

"Sharp," she said. "I guess we didn't exchange last names. Though, I know yours."

Noah—his eyes crinkling—started to say something but Wes elbowed him in the ribs. Hailey laughed.

Wes pointed to Noah. "Try to ignore most of what he says."

Noah bounced his eyebrows. "It's nice to see you again, Hailey. Sorry my brothers don't know how to behave."

"I'm regretting bringing you both here," Wes said, shaking his head. He rubbed a hand over his smooth jaw—did he ever let just a hint of stubble grow? She bet it'd look good on him.

"Well, I'm thrilled he brought you, and I had a customer order a BLT cup with no lettuce or tomato today so you won't ring any bells for strangest order."

"They wanted just a cup of bacon?" Noah's smile was charming and bright.

She nodded. "Yup. And dressing of course. Wanna guess what kind?"

Wes's smile increased in tiny degrees. "Ketchup?"

Scrunching her face, she pointed at him. "Yes! How did you know that?"

Chris clapped Wes on the back. "Big fan of ketchup and bacon sandwiches right here."

She couldn't stop herself from making an "ew" face. "I'm sorry. To each their own. Totally legit. I dip fries in ice cream."

"That's actually pretty good. Gracie, my girlfriend, introduced me to that," Noah said, scanning the menu.

"Everly loves peanut butter and bananas together," Chris said. His smile was warm and when he said her name, his tone softened.

"Peanut butter and banana isn't a weird combination," Wes said, looking at his brother.

"It's gross, like ketchup and bacon." Chris looked up at the menu. "Let's order so Hailey doesn't unfriend you."

She laughed the whole time she made their salads—a Mexi Cup, which was turning out to be one of her most popular—an SV Supreme, a combination of lettuces, julienned vegetables, chicken, turkey, and tuna, and, for Wes, a Fruit Fetish, which the guys teased him for ordering. She informed them that the mixture of berries, mango, Greek yogurt, slivered cinnamon-glazed almonds, chia seeds, and a drizzle of honey would make them jealous.

"I'll bring it out," she said as she accepted the payment from Chris. Apparently, it was his turn.

She'd always wondered what it would be like to have siblings. Close ones, like these three. She'd had her books and loved falling into any young adult or adult romance she could but it wasn't the same. Growing up, Piper was the closest thing she had to a sibling and she usually only got to see her during school breaks. Her parents hadn't wanted children and though they loved her, they loved their marriage and alone time more. She spent most summers with Piper's family. At the time, she'd felt lucky. But looking back, she wondered why they hadn't missed her. Why hadn't they wanted to make memories with her? It made her heart twitch uncomfortably so she tried not to spend a lot of time thinking about it. Or them.

Their laughter drew her attention more than once as she made their lunches. When she brought them over, they asked her to sit. Since she had a moment, she did.

"How are you liking San Verde?" Chris asked, popping the lid off his salad.

"It's great. I haven't seen much of it since I spend a lot of hours here. My cousin lives here so it seemed like a good place to settle. How about you guys? Are you California natives?"

Both guys glanced at Wes, who answered, "We're all from New York, actually. Chris came out for work, Noah followed, and I joined them almost two months ago."

"I didn't realize you were new to town like me. We can figure out the city together," she said.

Noah finished his mouthful, a playful grin lighting up his face. "He's all set. There are multiple food options here in the square, a tech store, and every shop offers Wi-Fi."

She laughed even though Wes didn't. "I know you work at the station, Chris, and Wes does something with computers, but do you all work together on everything?"

A couple walked through the door, hand in hand. Hailey nearly bounced out of her seat. "Hi. Welcome to By the Cup."

As she made custom salads for them, three more people came in. By the time she'd served everyone, the guys were done with their lunch and Hailey felt like she could lift a car with the happy adrenaline coursing through her.

"Nice little rush," Wes said, standing at the counter, his brothers at his side.

"It was. It's getting better every day. I'm so glad you guys came in and I hope you'll come back."

"Your food is delicious. I didn't think I'd be excited about coming for salad, but the last one was so good and this one was great. I'm not sure which one was better," Noah said.

"Thank you. That makes me happy. You guys are heading up to check out the space upstairs?"

"We are. Have you seen any of it?" Chris asked.

She shook her head, glanced at Wes. "No, but I heard it's great. I have a meeting up there next week with some other shop owners."

"Wes's place is great. Everly and I live about twenty minutes from here in an apartment but Noah's looking for a house for us."

"Your voice gets soft when you say her name," Hailey said, a hint of longing fluttering in her chest. She'd thought Dorian felt that way about her at one time. Maybe he had. Their relationship felt like one of the movie sets she'd worked on—not entirely real. With a sad ending.

"Probably because I'm crazy about her," Chris said without one hint of embarrassment. Dorian had always held off on any sort of affection in public, verbally or otherwise, until he could gauge the audience of whatever event they attended. He'd told her it wasn't personal. He needed to maintain a certain image to grow his career and being tied down to one woman, at least publicly, could cost him opportunities.

She pulled out an eggplant to chop for her own salad. See? She ate more than chocolate. "I guess not believing in love doesn't run in the family then."

Both of the brothers laughed as Wes gave her a wry grin, shifting his feet.

"Nope. Definitely not. Wes is a tech geek—if he could create his perfect woman via technology, he would."

When he looked down at his feet, Hailey's heart pinched. "There's nothing wrong with knowing what you want and holding out for it. Love—the word or the feeling—doesn't make something a guarantee."

He lifted his head and his gaze was so intense it felt physical. A shiver traveled over her skin as his appreciation shone from eyes darker than either of his brothers'.

"Exactly," he said.

"You'll both see when you get hit with the real thing," Noah said, glancing at his phone. "We should head upstairs. We're having a BBQ at our place on Sunday, Hailey. You should join us. You've already met Stacey, Everly, and Grace. We live on the beach so we usually end up playing volleyball."

She wanted to jump at the chance but she didn't want to get in the way. Wes said he wanted to be friends but he had this shell, making him hard to read. "That's a really nice offer."

"You could bring a friend if it makes you more comfortable. Someone other than Wes, I mean. Noah lives by the motto 'the more the merrier,'" Chris said.

"Hey. I've gotten a lot better and I'm always careful to give you a heads-up for Everly." Noah gestured to Wes. "Plus, this guy doesn't love a big crowd either so we tend to keep it small."

She didn't know a lot about these guys but she still had a little piece of her gut she trusted. Just because her judgment had been skewed before didn't mean these weren't good people. The only way to get to know them was to take the chance. Even then, truly knowing someone wasn't a guarantee any more than love. The truth was, she'd known Dorian for six months before their first kiss. They'd dated for three years, and in the end, she hadn't known him at all.

"Noah can be annoying when it comes to the volleyball because he's a poor sport, but otherwise it's really fun. You're closed on Sundays, right?" Wes looked at the sign on the door as a couple of girls walked in.

"I am. Okay. Sure. Why not?" She moved the eggplant aside. "I'll be right with you." She pulled her phone from her pocket and passed it to Wes. "Put your number in there so I can text you."

Long after they'd left, after she'd served a bunch of customers, she was still thinking about Wes and his brothers. Her only focus when she'd packed up her place in L.A. was to get on her feet professionally. She hadn't been worried about friends or dating. She had Piper and her family.

She'd needed the recovery time with just herself to reset and remind herself that she wasn't the sum of her mistakes. Believing in Dorian for longer than he deserved didn't make her an idiot.

Piper accused her of shutting herself off, running away from her problems, burying her head in the sand like she used to do in books. Hailey had told her where to put her counseling advice before realizing she wasn't wrong. She'd had to deal with the impact of her relationship and get to a healthy place. She was in it. She *felt* it. But letting new people in still scared her. At least with Wes, she knew he was safe. He didn't want anything other than friendship. She could be herself and if he didn't like what he saw, it wouldn't wreck her self-esteem. She'd also get a chance to be friends with some seemingly lovely women and his brothers.

Dorian's words during their last argument, the final one, still rang in her ears now and again but they were quieter now.

You're no one's leading lady, least of all mine. You're a boring book nerd who serves food out of a truck, for God's sake. You aren't even the best friend in a second-rate movie. You're an extra. A nobody. You were a placeholder, Hailey.

Yeah, she'd retreated into herself a bit with those words. Then she'd kicked him out of *her* house and told him what she really thought of his acting skills.

"You say you've moved on, you're okay. Prove it. Stop second-guessing the chance to really build a life here." Now she sounded like Piper. A small laugh escaped as she swept up, turned the OPEN sign to CLOSED. At least she could tell her cousin the therapy practice was working.

8

"Let me get this straight," Piper said, taking the tray of salads out of Hailey's hands. "First he's a jerk, then he apologizes and you actually let him help you—total growth there, cous—and now you're hanging with his family at a beach house?"

"Good recap. Why do you sound so suspicious?"

Piper set the tray down and turned to face Hailey, who dug through her purse, which she'd dumped on the counter, for some ChapStick. Finding it, she glossed her lips, then put it back, looked around the room with serious envy. Piper's kitchen was a dream—one of the things they'd always had in common was their love of cooking.

"Hails. Come on. Hot guy says sorry, whips up your website, and now you're headed to a beach house in the middle of nowhere?"

Hailey's jaw dropped and she tilted her head. "Whoa. *That's* what you got out of me telling you? I didn't say Wes was hot. When I was here last, your friends offered to help me with some design and marketing. Why is it sinister when Wes does something similar?" Two of the women, sisters Megan and Rachel, ran an Etsy-style shop that specialized in all things stationery.

"Yeah but other than Rachel—who is in a committed relationship—none of my friends would want to get in your pants."

She couldn't help but laugh. "Neither does Wes. Trust me. It's a day at the beach, new friends. I need to meet people somehow. I'm not into clubbing and that's not how you meet friends anyway. How do people in their thirties start over?"

Piper came to her side and gave her a hug. "Like this, I guess. I just worry about someone taking advantage of you. Or murdering you and burying your body in the sand."

She pushed out of Piper's embrace, aware that her cousin's words echoed Wes's. "You're a jerk."

"But only because I love you. What's his last name?"

The door opened and female voices danced into the room as Piper said, "Let's look them up on the internet."

Rachel set down two bottles of wine, one red, one white. "Who are we googling?"

Fiona and Megan followed, joining them in the kitchen. Piper took over telling the women, as she got out wineglasses, about Wes and how Hailey had met him.

"That's so cute," Fiona said.

Hailey was regretting her decision to share with her cousin and didn't really think there was anything cute or worrisome about what she'd said.

Were people really so skeptical about organic friendships? Sure, she hadn't met him because he slid into her DMs but there *was* life before whatever was the newest social media app.

She followed the women, salad in one hand and wine in the other. The house was nothing short of sprawling. Two steps led from the kitchen to a living room—one of two. This one had a wall of windows and glass doors that led to the backyard. The pool sparkled in the evening sun. Outdoor furniture was arranged around the gas firepit, inviting guests to curl up and chat.

Piper's husband had taken their kids to his mother's. As she walked past family photos on the way out to the deck, she felt that pang of longing again. *Just because you don't have what she does now doesn't mean you never will.* The truth was, she wasn't ready yet. Though, she knew life wasn't perfect—below every glittery surface, there was a scratched underbelly. Piper's husband worked long hours as an investment banker. Piper ran herself ragged many days, caring for their three kids, studying at night. Everything had a downside.

With no books in sight, the women who made up Piper's "book club" gossiped about everything from who'd just moved into Piper's neighborhood to the latest entertainment news. When she'd shown up the first time, she'd been stupidly excited to talk about Jasmine Guillory's latest and greatest but the women hadn't even brought their books. Hailey had a great night but she'd had a moment of disappointment that it wasn't an actual book club as well as all the rest. But maybe she needed this more.

Rachel polished off a mango chicken salad in record time, then set down the cup. "That was delicious. I love when salads have fruit in them. Do you make all your own dressing?"

She finished off her salad. "I do. I have a similar base for several of them and then I add different combinations to make them unique."

"You're very good at it. One of the magazines I write for does an in-house working lunch every month. Most of us are remote but it's a good chance for us to bounce ideas off of each other." Fiona set her empty cup down. "If you have a card, I'll suggest you for next month."

Happiness and disappointment ricocheted in her chest. Dammit. Where was her follow-through? Her intentions were good; she'd even looked through several samples, but had been unable to decide on the overall design. "I would love that. Thank you but I don't have cards yet." *You will get this done. No more putting it off.* She'd been busier than expected the last week or two, which was a good thing, but it wreaked havoc on her to-do list.

"Actually," Megan said, lifting a small box Hailey hadn't even noticed. She set it in front of her. "It's our welcome gift. Both to the city and our very serious book group."

Tears pricked her eyes when she lifted the lid and saw the cutest business cards. She could use that word because it described them perfectly without making them less professional. BY THE CUP was written in a cursive font with her name underneath. The top right corner had a little salad cup filled with colorful veggies, surprisingly similar to the little sketch Wes had done. There was a delicate line with a swirl in the middle on the bottom of the card. The lettering was bright blue, like at her store.

"These are incredible." She sniffled. Piper put her arm around her shoulder.

"We also brought you this," Rachel said, handing her a flash drive. "It's so you can print more anytime you like, but there are also coupons and gift cards on there. The file is editable but if you have any trouble, give me a call."

"Isn't your new buddy, Wes, a tech guru?" Piper asked.

"Oh!" Fiona sat up straight, grabbed her phone. "We didn't google him."

Hailey's throat felt thick but she waved her hand in front of her. "Please don't. I don't think I'm imagining things. I'd like to believe, despite recent events in my life, that I still have some sort of gauge on people. I don't want to stalk his social media or find him on his dating apps. Other than this, you guys and Piper, I haven't met anyone I clicked with friendship wise. It seems weird that Wes and I would click in that way at all but he's got this dry humor and interesting take on life. I just want to enjoy building my new life. I wouldn't want him to look into any of you. Please." She needed to restore faith in her own judgment.

Fiona set her phone down. "That's fair. They said you could bring a friend. I'll go with you."

Setting the box of cards down, she stared at her cousin's friend. "Really? You'd do that?"

Megan said something under her breath and pretended to cough. Piper laughed. Rachel rolled her eyes and picked up her wine.

"Oh, she'll do that and a whole lot more for you," Rachel said. Her hair was swept back from her face in a loose ponytail that swung from side to side when she shook her head.

"What am I missing?" Hailey looked at Piper.

"Nothing," Fiona answered. "I'm a nice person, I like you, so I offered to do something nice."

Hailey grinned, waiting for the other shoe to drop. "And?"

Fiona picked up her wine, not a hint of regret in her steady gaze. "And I sometimes need a sidekick to research my articles."

Piper squeezed Hailey's arm. "Usually what she gets us into is harmless."

"Usually?" Hailey laughed. She wanted new adventures but she had her limits. "What are you working on right now?"

"I'm doing an article on whether or not you can find love in five minutes."

Hailey's jaw dropped. "Can that be done?" The others laughed. Instant lust, sure. Attraction? Obviously. But love? *Come on. I couldn't find it in a three-year committed relationship.*

Fiona's gaze was skeptical. "Doubt it, but I'm looking into speed dating results. People who claim they've found their forever in those few minutes."

"I find it hard to imagine. I don't even want to. I'm happy not to be dating," Hailey said. She meant it; not focusing on that kind of relationship was giving her herself back.

Piper leaned back. "I should ask Nick to set you up with someone."

Hailey huffed out a deep sigh. "I'm not ready to date again but when I am, I'm going to have to go through one of these methods, Pipes. Seriously, I'm not going back to college to meet a guy."

"Oh my God. That would be the *best* rom-com," Megan said, clapping her hands together.

A fellow rom-com lover. Piper often teased her, good-naturedly, for that as well. Hailey looked at Piper. "Listen, I know you're used to looking out for me but I've got this. You don't need to set me up. I have no intention of meeting anyone right now."

"Not wanting a relationship doesn't mean you can't have some safe fun—"

Megan shoved Rachel's shoulder. "Stop. You're going to scare her away from book club."

Fiona snorted, folding her feet up under her, nestling into the chair. "If she wasn't concerned that we haven't cracked a book either time, I think we're good. So, want a copilot? At least this way you'll be safe. It's way harder for him to bury two bodies than one."

Hailey felt like her head was underwater. Had she really thought her new life would be dull compared to some of the Hollywood glitz and glamour of her old days?

"I guess it would be good for you to see that there are other non-Dorian guys out there even if you're not ready yet." Piper picked up a bottle of wine and poured the last dribble into her glass.

The women took turns asking her questions about dating an actor and who she'd met at parties. They'd clearly held back when first meeting Hailey. This time, there were no boundaries. The conversation veered back and forth, off on one tangent, rerouted to another. It was wonderful. Hailey wasn't sure when she'd last had this: a sense of belonging. These were Piper's friends but they were accepting her, making her one of their own because of her cousin.

Her life in L.A. had consisted of working, planning for her future, and spending many nights alone in hopes that Dorian would wrap early. She'd stopped herself from really living, and worse, she hadn't even realized she was missing out.

No more. She toasted herself in her mind: to new adventures, to new friends, and to new beginnings.

9

His brother's comment about creating the perfect woman stuck in his brain. Was it so wrong that he wanted someone he was compatible with? He had no doubt his brothers would both marry the women they were with. He could *feel* their love, their attraction. But the truth was, that physical chemistry didn't equal permanence. As Hailey said, it wasn't a guarantee—though she had said it with a hint of longing in her tone. To be honest, he didn't *trust* those emotional feelings.

He waved to the woman across the way from where he stood at the patio door. She wore a red dressing gown today. He should find out who she was, send her some cake. There was something about her, even though they'd never spoken, that reminded him of his grandmother, whom he adored and missed. She waved back after he'd already settled into thoughts about what he was doing with his life, then laughed out loud.

"Now you're *thinking* like Dad." How many times had his father asked him why he was messing around with "those goddamn games" when he had the brain capacity to do something extraordinary? Of course, by that, his father meant anything that profited his own companies.

Wes was honest enough with himself to know he was similar to his father in many ways. Not the coldhearted, detached way, but certainly a left-brain, analytical thinker. His mother, on the other hand, was as far to the right side of the brain as one could be. Their union had been a disaster. They'd based decision after decision, including their elopement and four children, on a roller-coaster ride of feelings—until the ride crashed. Splintered apart.

He didn't want that. There'd been no common ground and both of them ended up lost. That was the part Wes feared most: losing himself in another person to the point that without them, he'd end up traipsing around the world like his mother or crushing everything in his path like his father.

Instead, he wanted a smoothly paved road with someone he could care about with limits. Mutual admiration and affection didn't seem like too much to ask for. Maybe it was foolish but if he could perfectly program a multilevel video game, why couldn't he plan his love life?

The dating apps weren't working. He needed the perfect balance of spark and sensibility. There had to be *some* chemistry but not so much he'd give up his soul. Or his heart. Why was he torturing himself with this? He'd been through enough change in the last couple of months. Adding dating into the equation was doing nothing more than exhausting him. Besides, his life didn't feel as . . . aimless at the moment. He smiled, thinking of Hailey. Perhaps he'd just needed a friend.

His phone buzzed with his grocery alarm. Saturday evenings were for shopping at the larger box store. It was quiet and well stocked. Leaving his balcony door open a touch, he added a reminder in his phone to schedule someone to install AC, then double-checked his grocery list against his fridge and cupboards.

If he needed a last-minute item, he could easily walk to one of the smaller convenience shops in the square. Walking was in his blood, being a New Yorker. But it was easier, on these larger, weekly shops, to take the car.

As usual, there were few customers, so he backed his SUV into a spot close to the door. Setting his reusable bags in the front of the cart, he grabbed his sanitizing spray and gave the handles a little spritz before tucking it back in the bag.

With his phone sitting on the bags, list open, he navigated his way to the left, preferring to start on one side and work his way to the other. He loved mundane, simple tasks that needed doing but required no brain power. It was typically when he brainstormed ideas for the gaming worlds or apps he created.

Six each of apples, oranges, and pears, and one bag of green grapes. As a kid, he'd play Mario Kart and then draw his own version of the worlds. He'd kept those tucked away in a sketchbook labeled BIG IDEAS. He smiled to himself now as he set back the bag of grapes he'd chosen and went with red instead. He was so naïve when he was young. He'd actually asked his father if he could help him get his game ideas to Nintendo. He had all sorts of additions they could have made to make the games even cooler than they were.

His father had squashed that idea like a fire ant. With malice and purpose.

"Wes?"

He turned at the sound of his name and his smile escaped without warning. "Hey, Hailey."

She was dressed in a pale blue hoodie and a pair of black pants that came just below her knees. Her flip flops revealed brightly painted toenails, which, for some reason, made him smile wider.

"Making fruit salad?" She gestured to his cart.

"Not exactly." He eyed her basket.

She moved it behind her back, making him laugh too loud.

"That's a lot of chocolate. I'm beginning to worry you might have a problem." He arched his brows, waited her out.

"Buying for a friend."

He laughed again. "Sure."

"Whatever, Mr. Healthy. I hadn't gotten to this section yet. I hit the important stuff first." She picked up an orange and put it in her basket. He stared at her, amused, as she held his gaze, reached for an apple, and put that in her basket, too.

"To dip in my chocolate," she said.

The wires in his brain crisscrossed for a nanosecond, heating his skin.

"Smart," he said, his voice unexpectedly gruff.

She fell into step beside him, leaned in to check out his list. She smelled like fruit and soap, which, in his opinion, was nicer than expensive perfumes.

"A man on a mission. You're very organized. Shoot. I actually need to grab some organic lettuce. I only order a small amount because most people order regular. My shipment doesn't come until end of next week. Give me a sec." She thrust her basket at him.

He watched as she hurried to the organic cooler. By the time she came back, several packs of lettuce in her arms, he'd sprayed down the handles of her basket and set it inside the lower part of his cart.

She leaned forward over her basket and let the lettuce fall. "Awesome. Thank you."

He had no idea what she was thanking him for. "You're welcome. Is that all you need?"

She shrugged. "I don't know. You have lots on your list. Mind if I keep you company?"

He stopped and stared at her. "You don't know what you need?"

She grinned and pointed at her basket. "I got what I needed under the lettuce. How come you're at the grocery store on a Saturday night?" She put her hands on her hips. "Is *this* what all the cool kids are doing?"

Pushing the cart forward, he bit back his smile. "You have no idea who the cool kids *are* if you're looking my way."

She was quiet as they turned down the pasta aisle. He chose spaghetti.

"So, still no dates?"

He glanced at her as they headed toward the sauces. "Definitely not. We talked about this. We're lone wolves. Together."

He'd been aiming to make her smile but her gaze lit up and she beamed at him. Like freaking sunshine. She lifted her arm, held out her fist. For a second, he just stared at it, then realized she was offering him a fist bump.

Wes gently connected his fist to hers, all the while shaking his head. "You are a strange woman, Hailey Sharp."

"I have been called so much worse."

She said it so casually, like it was a joke but one that was true. It bothered him. He was thinking of a way to bring it up, to ask who would call her anything negative at all, as he looked at jarred sauce.

"You're not buying a premade sauce, are you?"

He looked down, startled by the brightness of her gaze. She had very pretty eyes. "I grew out of butter and parmesan at twelve, so yes."

She smiled, patted his arm. "You never grow out of that but it's so easy to make your own marinara. I'll show you. It'll be a thank-you for the invite tomorrow. Come on. You don't need much at all. It'll be healthier and taste so much better."

Bubbles of happiness fizzed in his chest, confusing him. He did not want to date anyone. Particularly this woman as he hadn't figured her out. But he'd really hoped she'd join them tomorrow. As a friend. Was he going to find it difficult to keep that straight in his head? Or worse, his heart? *No.*

"You're coming?"

She placed two large cans of diced tomatoes in his cart. "If that's still okay. I'm bringing a friend because my cousin is worried you might murder me and bury me in the sand."

He might never figure her out. "We try not to get that aggressive during the volleyball. Noah can be a pretty bad sport but I don't think he'd go that far."

Her laughter surprised him. It rang out over the quiet music humming through the store. "I'm not very good at volleyball so it looks like I'll be safe from finding out."

"I'm glad you're joining us. You've made another friend? That was fast." He watched as she put olive oil and balsamic vinegar in his cart.

"I did. Through my cousin. Her name is Fiona. We made a trade."

His curiosity prickled but she didn't say anything else. They strolled through the aisles, him adding items from his list, her grabbing whatever caught her gaze.

"I should ask Fiona if she'll come to yoga. I found a studio right in the square."

"That doesn't surprise me," he said after a speaker announcement finished. "There's probably one every few blocks. I'm glad you have a yoga friend."

Hailey chuckled, one hand on his cart, close to his own. "A yoga friend. We still need to figure out what kinds of things we can do together that fits between yoga and drinking beer. Though, I'm not opposed to beer."

"Well, we could grocery shop. This is platonic." He grabbed a three-pack of toothpaste.

"Definitely. Cooking—I'll show you how to make the sauce. What could you show me?" She looked up at him with such a sweet expression, his breath hitched.

Noah's voice and inappropriate thoughts jumped into his head but he just smiled. "Know how to play Red Dead Redemption?"

"No."

"I'll show you. It's fun."

At the baking aisle, she stopped his cart with a gentle tug. "Do you have brown sugar?"

"No."

She pulled the cart down the aisle. "It's the secret ingredient."

"To life?"

She looked back over her shoulder. "Ha. You're funny. But no. To the marinara."

His skepticism must have shown because she set a bag in the cart then put her hands on her hips. "If we're going to be friends, you need to trust me. At least on this."

"Is that a rule?"

She nodded. "A hard-and-fast one. Agreed?" She held out her hand.

"You know," he said, an idea forming in his mind on how to keep his brain and heart on the straight and narrow. "We're creating a how-to guide of sorts."

She laughed, still holding her hand out. "A what?"

"Activities, hard-and-fast rules." He shook her hand, held it for a moment, ignoring the pins and needles feeling as their skin brushed together. Yes. A guide was a great idea. He dropped her hand. "A guide. To staying just friends."

Now she grinned a wide toothy grin. "Uh-oh, are you so impressed with my Saturday-night outfit that we need a guide to keep you from falling in love with me? Is it the color of my sweatsuit or the fact that it says 'Brat' on my butt?"

His gaze widened. "I wasn't looking at your butt." He was very curious now though. Shit. He was making things worse.

Hailey put her hand on his bicep. "You make me laugh, Wes. I'm joking, there's nothing written on my butt. A guide could be fun, especially if you illustrate it."

God. He really *liked* her, how it felt to be around her. She was happy and hopeful. It made him feel the same without any of the pressure to try and be *more.*

"When are we making this marinara?"

They continued through the aisle and he wasn't surprised when she grabbed a box of cookies. This time he stopped. "Do you need an intervention?"

Hailey's gaze narrowed. "There's lettuce in my basket."

"To sell to customers."

"I'm surrounded by salad all day. Trust me, I get my fruit and veggie quota. Life without cookies is just dumb."

"I might have to see about getting that put on a plaque," he said, surprised that he fell into teasing her so easily.

Maybe it was because he missed his sister. Everyone got on Ari's case about not knowing what she wanted out of life. She spent her days trying everything to figure it out. Even when they didn't see each other much, they always got along. This easy back-and-forth with Hailey reminded him of how easy it was to be around Ari. Because she never expected anything from anyone. She just accepted them as they were. She sure as hell hadn't learned that from their father. She was the only one who knew about his dream of designing and selling games.

Hailey was digging around in the purse she had slung across her chest. "Speaking of such things, check this out." She lifted a card close to his face.

"You got business cards. That's fantastic. They're great. Very on brand."

"That's a very marketing thing to say. On brand. Yes. They suit me and By the Cup. My cousin introduced me to her book club, which is actually just a gossip, wine-drinking club. Two of them, sisters, made these for me as a welcome-to-California gift."

"They're fantastic. That was a nice gesture on their part."

She'd started to walk but stopped and looked up at him with an earnest expression that made him want to pull her into a hug. "People have been so nice to me since I got here. You included. Thank you."

"You're pretty easy to be nice to. Besides, you need someone to monitor your sugar intake."

Slapping his arm, she laughed and walked forward. "Maybe we just need to up yours."

"I did introduce you to the chocolate cake. Oh, Tara will probably be there tomorrow. I was thinking you could chat with her about cross-marketing."

The store announced they were closing in fifteen minutes. Wes looked at his phone. He never took this long to shop. By now, he was usually home with everything put away.

Hailey lifted her basket out of his cart. She looked down at the items in it. "I derailed your shopping, didn't I?"

She had. But he wasn't sorry. "It's okay. I have most of what I needed." Several things he didn't. "Do you want me to bring up the cross-promo idea with Tara tomorrow?"

He saw, in the way her jaw set and her eyes darted back and forth, that she was about to refuse. She had a healthy amount of pride. He could absolutely respect that but wondered why. What made her need to prove herself on her own? To not ask much of another person who could clearly help her? "As a thank-you for teaching me to make marinara next week."

Her smile was reason enough. She had a great smile. It was interesting, this being friends thing. He liked talking to her, being with her, but he didn't have to be "on." Didn't have to make small talk or say he liked things he didn't. All this time, he'd thought he needed a girlfriend, but what he really needed was a girl *friend*. The best of both worlds.

10

"What's the weirdest article you've ever written?" Hailey was enjoying the ride to the beach far more than she'd expected. Like her, Fiona, who'd offered to drive, liked chatting about everything and nothing.

Fiona's lips twisted in a thoughtful pout. "Oh, I wrote one that matched your toenail polish with your favorite sex position."

Hailey nearly spit out the sip of water she'd just taken. "That's not a real thing." What did teal blue say? "Abstinence by necessity?" She wiggled her toes in her flip-flops.

"Of course not. That's why I love it. In a world full of bad news and sadness, I can't even tell you how much joy I get from writing these kinds of things."

The ocean came into view and Hailey's breath caught in her lungs. It was gorgeous. Just this wide expanse of blue that settled something inside of her.

"It's so important to do what you love," Hailey murmured.

"Try telling that to any of the guys I've dated, my parents, or even some of my colleagues."

She turned to look at Fiona's profile. Even from the side, she was lovely, with a delicate jawbone and perfect lips. She could easily be a model for one of the magazines she wrote for, but she was so down-to-earth, Hailey felt perfectly at ease. At one point, she'd felt that way in her food services truck at whatever set she happened to be on. She knew people were just people and she'd chatted with the stars as she would have anyone else.

Until Dorian. He'd explained to her the necessity of not interrupting their day, their thoughts or musings. Who even said that kind of thing? But in truth, it was one of the many things he'd said that poked holes in her self-confidence.

He'd deflated it one prickly, under-his-breath comment at a time. He'd told her that a movie star, a famous actor or actress, didn't want to get chummy with the person who knew what they really liked to eat when the cameras weren't rolling.

Of course, maybe the truth was he'd been getting a little too friendly with many of those women he didn't want her chatting with. The sad part was, she hadn't been overly surprised when she found out he was cheating. Instead, she'd been disappointed with herself for not realizing sooner.

"They aren't supportive?" Her own parents hadn't exactly thrown a party when she said she was opening a salad shop. They'd wished her luck, though, and said they'd pop in. Eventually.

"They're not *not* supportive. It's like when people are dating and everyone says, 'When are you getting married?'"

Hailey smiled. Boy had Dorian not liked that question. "Or people who are married getting asked when they're having kids."

Fiona slapped the steering wheel. "Yes! If a couple has one baby, when's the next one coming. That's how it is. They can't believe I'm enjoying exactly this place in my life. People assume I'm just working my way up to hard-hitting journalism, maybe a piece in *Time* magazine. But this is what I wanted. To be honest, if I could write full-time for an entertainment outlet, I would."

"I love that. We need that in the world. You're absolutely right, and when did it stop being okay to chase what you really want instead of what everyone thinks you should?"

Fiona tapped the signal and took the exit labeled Harlow Beach. Like most people, Hailey hadn't really explored too far in her own state. She should take a road trip. That would be fun. *Maybe after I get some more revenue.*

"I think when social media exploded and the world decided they could share or weigh in on everyone's decisions."

Lush palm trees dotted the stretch of road, the ocean in the background. Now that they were off the highway, she could see the actual beach. People sunbathed and sat, played in the water. Today was fun already. She needed this. She'd hold on to the light feeling for the next several weeks as things hopefully got busier at the shop.

"I try to avoid social media. I need to get more active for the shop but on a personal level, I've always tried to avoid it." Dating an actor and social media was a very bad mix.

"It's probably healthier. I'm on it way too much. Have you googled Wes yet?"

Hailey shook her head even though Fiona was looking out the window. "No. I don't want to blemish an otherwise beautiful friendship."

Fiona burst out laughing the same moment Hailey did. "Then don't look me up either."

~~~~~~~~

Hailey had no idea why she'd pictured a quaint seaside shanty, but that wasn't what they saw.

"Holy shit," Fiona said, arching so she could look through the windshield at the gorgeous . . . could you call a house like that a house, or was it automatically a mansion?

"Wow." Hailey's chest tightened. This was not at all what she'd expected. Wes's brother must be well off. She'd gotten the impression they all were, but there was I-can-eat-out-every-day-of-the-week wealthy and then there was I-live-in-a-mansion money.

Directly beside the beach, it had a spacious lawn, expertly manicured. There was a one-story bungalow, more like what she'd pictured, to the right. The other houses in the neighborhood seemed to range in between the two drastically different ends of the spectrum.

"Why does this seem familiar?" Fiona asked after they'd grabbed their things from the back of her Smart car.

The only thing that felt familiar to Hailey was the sinking feeling in her stomach. It was the same one she'd get right before walking into a party with Dorian. He always stopped her, like a willful child, to tell her how important this event was to his career. It was one of the many things she'd pushed down, let go, and not made a fuss about. One of the many things that made her lose herself.

"Not sure. I hear people out back." Wes's text had said to go through the gate but she hoped they'd get a tour of the house later.

They took the cutely paved path down the right side and found a yard full of people spread out. There were conversation sets on the deck and in the yard. Part of the green space, closest to the fence separating it from the neighbors, was cordoned off with posts and yellow tape.

"Hey," Noah called out from the porch. Chris was sitting on a love seat next to Everly while Stacey and what had to be her boyfriend, if her position on his lap was any clue, shared an Adirondack chair.

A very pretty woman came to Noah's side. He turned when she approached, looked down at her, and pressed a kiss on her lips.

"They're familiar, too," Fiona muttered.

"Not to me."

Wes came out of the house as Noah and presumably Grace came down to the yard.

"Glad you could make it, Hailey. This is my girlfriend, Grace," he said, offering a happy-go-lucky smile. He shared many physical traits with Wes but she'd seen hints of that smile last night at the grocery store. Wes's was much harder to draw out than Noah's. But totally worth the effort.

Grace leaned forward, her hand out. "Hi. We're so happy you came."

"I'm Fiona." They shook hands as well but before they let go, Fiona's other hand came up and she pointed back and forth between them. "The magazine! You guys were in *Home and Heart*."

Hailey had no idea what Fiona was talking about but she felt her lungs relax when Wes came to their side, a beer in his hand.

"Hey," he said.

Fiona dropped Grace's hand and offered her own to Wes but her gaze stayed on the couple. "One sec." She looked at Wes. "You must be Wes. I'm Fiona. I could spell it if that helps?"

Hailey wasn't sure if her cheeks went as red as Wes's but they *felt* like they were on fire. She bumped Fiona with her hip.

The group laughter suggested that the others already knew this story so she felt better about it. Had he told them?

Noah looked at Wes. "You do like to leave an impression."

Grace rubbed her hand over Wes's arm. "Leave him alone."

Wes gave Noah a smug grin.

Grace smiled up at Noah. "Let's introduce everyone and then we can tease him some more."

Wes stepped to the side, gestured to the porch. "Nice to meet you, Fiona. I see my reputation precedes me."

"Like Taylor Swift," Fiona said with a teasing smile. Hailey could only laugh. When Wes looked back at her, she mouthed "sorry."

The porch was wide and inviting, with a gorgeous view of the water. Chris and Everly said hello and Stacey gave her a big hug before introducing her to her boyfriend, Rob.

As Hailey took a seat next to Fiona on one of the love seats, an older man shuffled out of the house. His stark white hair looked like he'd stuck a knife in a socket. He was mumbling to himself before he reached the porch.

"Damn kids can't buy any regular beer. What the hell happened to Budweiser?" He looked at Noah with a deep frown marring his weathered face.

Noah smiled. "Live a little, man. It tastes good."

"Tastes like piss," he said, dropping into a chair. He did a slight double take when he saw Fiona and Hailey. "Where'd these two come from? None of you are good-looking enough to be surrounded by all these beautiful women."

Grace walked over to the man, put a hand on his shoulder. "This is Morty. He's like a great-great-grandfather to me." Her lips twitched.

"Brat. I'm barely old enough to be a father figure to you. You're getting up there yourself."

Laughing, Grace winked at them. "Please excuse him, he's using getting old as a chance to be miserable. He can be quite charming when he wants."

"Damn right I can be." He worked up a smile, aimed it at Hailey and Fiona and to her relief, everyone else laughed. If they hadn't, she would have had to muffle her own out of politeness.

Grace leaned over to say something in Morty's ear but they all heard it. "Behave or I'm telling Tilly."

They didn't hear his response but Hailey could guess.

She couldn't stem her curiosity. "What's *Home and Heart*?"

Grace and Noah shared a look that expressed a combination of love and affection. She might not have had those with her exes but she still believed they were out there, somewhere, waiting for her.

Grace clasped Noah's hand. "It's a magazine. Noah is a real estate developer. He bought this place intending to remodel it. He tried to buy mine as well," she said with a teasing smirk. "So he could put in a pool."

Hailey glanced toward the poles in the yard and pointed. "That's going to be a pool? Wait, is that your place?"

Grace nodded. "Yes. We're using it as my office. I'm an interior designer. Noah's supposedly a big deal in some circles so he was able to wrangle a fancy magazine to cover the remodel."

Noah put his arm around Grace, pulled her close. "Best thing to come out of it was Gracie fell head over heels in love with me."

Chris picked up his beer with the hand that wasn't holding Everly's. "None of us can figure out why."

Everyone but Noah laughed. Morty took a drink of his not-Budweiser, making a face. "Definitely not because of his taste in beer."

"Shut it, old man, or I'll feed you Tara's veggie burgers."

"Wait. I read some other articles after the ones on this remodel," Fiona said. Her gaze grew wide, then she looked at Hailey, whose heart started knocking around her rib cage. "Do you know you're in the presence of New York royalty?"

All three of the men scoffed and balked, loudly, at this proclamation. Grace rolled her eyes and Morty mumbled under his breath.

Stacey set her bottle on the table beside her, looking at Chris. "Maybe royal pains in the ass."

"Still your boss, Stace," Chris said blandly. The connections between them were harder to keep track of than who dated who in Hollywood. Wes needed to make her a guidebook for *this*.

"Somebody tell me what I'm missing." She looked at Wes. *Should* she have googled him?

Noah set his beer down on the edge of the fire table that sat between the seats. "My brothers and I used to work for our father. Pretty much doing a lot of what we do now but under his thumb. And judgment. We buy into companies, sell companies, or improve them. We each have our own skill sets and we got tired of our dad taking them for granted. Chris came here to jump through one of our dad's hoops, met Everly, fell in love. I followed."

"And fell in love," Grace said, squeezing his hand.

Fiona raised her hands. "I'm sorry. I didn't mean to bring anything bad up. I just made the connection and remember being super impressed with all of you. I was caught off guard but I shouldn't have blurted it all out like that."

"No harm. Don't worry about it. You certainly don't have to apologize," Chris said.

"No, I do. That was a total lack of social grace. Also, while we're sharing, I'm a freelance writer."

Both brothers looked at Wes, whose gaze widened. "Oh."

"I am one hundred percent here in a personal capacity and I don't write about guys like you. I write about what kind of alcohol you should pair with your chocolate. I just didn't want it to come up later."

This means Wes and his brothers are mega rich. Hailey didn't look him up because she wanted to draw conclusions based on what she learned about him. She wanted to prove she was a good judge of people. Of friends. That Dorian hadn't broken her in every single way. Last night, she'd learned Wes was a serious shopper, a list maker, and a bit of a health nut. But now, she was struggling to stop herself from immediately casting her own insecurities and past onto him.

He didn't care about how much money she had. He'd helped her for *free*. But did she want to be friends with a rich-boy trust fund baby? *He works a lot for someone who has the opportunity to live up to that label.* Still. She'd thought they were two newbies to the city both in need of a friend, someone they could bounce ideas off of or shop with on a Saturday night when the urge for chocolate hit hard.

"She really does write low-key, fun articles," Hailey heard herself say. There was a gentle buzz in her ears and she felt Wes's gaze.

"Is your last name Hale?" Chris asked.

Fiona nodded. "It is. Have you taken my quizzes? Oh my God. Are you a closet women's magazine reader?"

"It's not closet if he's willing to just put it out there," Noah said, laughing. "What'd you learn about yourself, baby brother? Are you a One Direction kind of guy or BTS?"

Noah flashed a grin at Fiona. "That is in no way diminishing what you write. They sound fun but it's my duty to make fun of my brother if he's reading *Cosmo*."

Amusement glittered in Noah's gaze and all eyes turned to Chris. Everly squeezed his hand, her other one rubbing up and down her thigh. "My mother continues to drop off a bag of groceries we don't need and several women's, and now men's, magazines once a month."

"Everly's mom is very pro sex," Stacey said.

Even though her cheeks went pink, Everly laughed with the others.

"Nothing wrong with that," Fiona said.

"Unless you're her daughter," Hailey said, meeting Everly's gaze.

Appreciation filled her warm brown eyes. "Exactly."

Fiona picked up her drink. "That's fair. My mom takes all of my quizzes but I told her she's never allowed to tell me the answers. Even if it's just which nail polish you should pair with your summer drink."

"Your articles and quizzes sound so fun," Grace said.

"I love making them. I love writing happy-making articles. The reason I recognized you guys and the house is because I was researching the magazine to write a fun article on which house matches your personality. I like to know the outlet I'm working for so I always do some prereading. You guys did a beautiful job renovating."

Both Noah and Grace beamed. "Would you like to see it?" Grace asked.

Fiona hopped up. "Yes, please." She looked down at Hailey.

Feeling atypically flustered, like she had too many facts to digest, Hailey nodded. "Of course."

Wes met her gaze. "We're going to start the burgers. We'll play volleyball after dinner. Either of you vegetarians?"

She shook her head.

He stood. "You want cheese or chocolate on yours?"

The laugh burst from her lips. "Very funny."

He was who she thought he was. Just because she had some hang-ups about rich guys who took advantage didn't mean Wes was a pompous ass who would do the same. Besides, this time, her heart was in absolutely no danger. It wasn't even involved. Just to be sure, they were definitely coming up with that guide he'd mentioned.

11

The last few hours squashed many of Hailey's worries. Rich or not, these people were friendly, funny, and incredibly welcoming. Noah and Grace made delicious burgers, Chris and Everly worked the BBQ, while Wes conveniently dropped it into the conversation with Rob that she was the maker of the salads he'd been talking about. Turns out Jaycee—the multisalad lady—worked at the gym Rob owned.

Hailey knew even cities of thousands and thousands had overlapping circles. Hollywood was like one of those steel circle puzzle games, nearly impossible to get the pieces to disconnect. This felt similar but in a good way for once.

"I'd love to stock some of your salads in my cooler. They're awesome. I've been toying with the idea of adding a café to the San Verde location but I'm still on the fence. I get some power bars and a few select baked goods from Tara. Would you be into a weekly preorder?" Rob said.

Would she be into a steady income regardless of the amount? Hard yes. "Absolutely. I can come by this week or you can drop by the shop and we can look at the menu. I can show you some of the more popular ones or I can customize them if you're looking for something specific." She sounded breezy, right?

Stacey came out from the house. Her sun-kissed skin and bright eyes made Hailey think of Kate Hudson, whom she'd met once. Like Stacey, the actress was every bit as lovely and completely down-to-earth. She joked about being a big radio star when she wanted Rob to grab her another drink but it was clear she didn't take herself too seriously.

"Tara isn't joining us. She has a council meeting for the San Verde Shop Association."

Hailey's brows scrunched. She'd said next week.

"Are you part of that?" The ocean breeze fluttered through Wes's hair, tousling it across his forehead.

"Tara mentioned it but she said it was next week." Had she misheard her?

"I'm sure Tara can give you the details," Stacey said. She clapped her hands together, looked around the group. "Time for some volleyball. Who's in?"

The gleam in her gaze made her look like a warrior. She set it on Wes. "You and your brothers are not on the same team this time."

His brow furrowed as Noah said, "Hey. Just because you lost."

Grace lifted her brows, crossed her arms over her chest. "Which you brought up *how* many times?"

Noah sidled up to Grace, wrapped his arms around her stiff frame. "Aw, Gracie. You know I love you even if you can't play volleyball."

When he nuzzled her neck, Hailey saw her lips fighting laughter. She pushed at her boyfriend. "It's the stupid sand."

"Sure. Of course it is," Chris said, leaning down to press a kiss to Everly's forehead. "You playing, babe?"

She shook her head. "No thanks. I'll do some cleanup."

"You don't have to do that, Evs." Grace now had her arms wrapped around Noah's waist.

"Trust me when I say I'd rather do dishes than play volleyball with any of you." Everly looked at Fiona and Hailey. "No offense. But you'll see."

"This feels ominous," Hailey said, standing. Gym wasn't her best class in high school. No surprise, she'd aced Foods. Loved Drama.

"I think we should be scared," Fiona said, setting her empty drink bottle on the tabletop.

"We're perfectly nice people to play with," Rob said. He tossed a volleyball he'd procured like magic in the air, catching it with one hand repeatedly. "Well, most of us."

What she remembered from gym class did *not* help her. The best she could say was she'd avoided getting a ball straight to the face. However, when she dove for the ball Noah spiked, she'd eaten a bit of sand. Sweat dripped down her back. Maybe she should hit Rob's gym.

"It touched the net," Wes said, his eyes on his brother when he reached out a hand to haul Hailey off her butt. She'd have worried about looking awkward or yanking him down but he wasn't paying much attention.

"Did not," Noah said, hands on his hips.

Hailey dusted herself off. "It definitely touched the sand."

Wes and Noah both turned to her, gazes similarly unimpressed. She pulled her cheek between her teeth so she didn't laugh.

Fiona waved her hands. "Hello. Someone want to throw me the ball? It's our serve."

Noah hooked a thumb over his shoulder. "She's right."

Hailey, closest to the ball though not close enough to have made contact, grabbed it and threw it to the other side.

"What are you doing?" Wes asked, his tone clipped.

"Passing them the ball. What's the big deal?"

"It's our serve."

She grinned, her toes twitching in the sand. Before she could reply, Chris called out, "Don't engage, Hailey. Not worth it. Noah and Wes are both poor sports."

"But only one of us can actually play," Noah called.

"Yeah. Me," Wes said, walking back to his spot.

They'd split into teams of four with Fiona, Noah, Rob, and Grace on one side, Chris, Hailey, Wes, and Stacey on the other.

Hailey glanced at him, meeting his gaze. "You're a tad competitive."

He shrugged and she could see him try to loosen the stiffness in his stance. "Noah brings it out in me."

"Wes is the oldest so he's always blamed his issues on his poor younger brothers," Noah called.

Chris snorted out a laugh. "Noah's the middle child. That comes with a whole host of its own issues."

"Thank God I'm an only child," Hailey said, getting into position.

"Me too," Grace said.

"I have four sisters," Fiona said. "I love them but you should be thankful."

Even in the later evening, the sun baked their shoulders and the sand toasted their toes. By the time they'd played two rounds, thankfully each team winning one, Hailey was exhausted.

"Moving in the sand is so much harder than on a gym floor," she said as they walked back down the path that led to Noah's house.

"There's a women's league at the rec center near you guys," Noah said. Hailey searched for a polite way to say "pass." Instead, she just smiled.

"Speaking of," Noah said, turning to Wes. "Your coding class is full. Twelve teens. It's a good sign."

An expression of happiness—different than the others she'd witnessed—crossed over Wes's face. "That's great."

When he saw Hailey looking at him, he gave one of those little almost smiles. "Noah works closely with a community center. They try to offer a variety of classes for preteens through adults."

"We're looking for all sorts of people to offer their specialties," Noah said. "Magazine writing, salad making? Gracie does a course on interior design."

Grace swung Noah's hand between them. "That sounds lofty. I do a Saturday morning session with ten- to twelve-year-olds. We use Legos to create cool spaces."

"That's fabulous. I'd love to get involved, though I'm not sure how popular salad making would be."

Noah shrugged. "You never know. Any other talents you're hiding?"

"Noah." Wes's word was an almost growl, making Noah laugh.

"Legit question, man."

Hailey thought about what her other talents could be. "No real talents but I love reading. Do you have a book club?" She narrowed her gaze at Fiona in a teasing way. "My cousin talked me into one that doesn't read books."

Fiona leaned back. "We regret nothing."

Hailey laughed. "Fair enough."

"A book club could be a great idea," Wes said. "You could involve local bookstores, libraries."

"A lot of authors have started offering online workshops and visits," Everly said, her voice so quiet Hailey almost missed it.

Hailey nodded excitedly. "I went to an online event that featured three of my favorite rom-com writers. It was so fun. They answered all these questions and played games. I was so surprised they just gave up their time like that."

Everly smiled. "For some authors, not doing in-person events lessens their anxiety while making them feel more accessible to their audience."

"We had one of Evs's favorite nonfiction authors on our podcast. It was very enlightening," Stacey said.

"You do a book club and I could do a writing workshop," Fiona said.

Hailey glanced at Wes then met Noah's waiting gaze. "Absolutely. That sounds fun. Sign us up."

The afternoon and evening had yielded so many wonderful things. Hailey felt the fidgety pieces of her soul begging to settle in and claim, "We've found our place." But it was never that easy and things weren't always as they seemed. The blind optimism of her early twenties had turned into cautious hope. That was what filled her now.

When they sat around the fire table, Hailey stifled a yawn.

"You okay?" Wes asked.

She nodded. "Great actually. Thanks for inviting us today. It's been awesome."

"We're happy Wes has made a couple friends," Chris said. "If nothing else, it'll get him out of his carefully scheduled programming."

"There's nothing wrong with a schedule," Wes said, leaning back in his chair, at ease with his brothers' teasing.

"Nothing wrong with taking it as it comes either," Noah said.

"To each their own," Rob added, lifting his beer.

"What are you working on now, Fiona, other than the house article?" Everly nestled into the crook of Chris's arm.

"I have a list of ideas so there's always a lot going on in my head. The next one is 'How Not to Date Your Ex.' It's about not making the same choices in the next partner."

"I'm glad I took the dating apps off my phone," Wes said.

"Oh, I should do a 'which dating app should you use' article. That'd be fun. Did you use a lot of them?" Fiona asked him.

Even in only the dancing light of the fire and twinkle lights, Hailey saw his cheeks darken. It was oddly charming.

"Not a lot. But that was before. I'm not using them anymore."

"I'm doing an article on the benefits of speed dating. You ever tried that?"

Wes shook his head. "The only thing that sounds worse than dating right now is doing it with multiple women on Mach speed."

Noah started to speak but Wes shut him down with a look.

"If you change your mind, let me know. I'd love some real intel, especially from the male perspective," Fiona said.

Wes shook his head, his gaze holding Hailey's, his brows arched. "This is the trade, isn't it?"

Hailey bit her lip, nodded.

"Something tells me Fiona's getting the better side of your trade. Be careful."

Hailey leaned forward, rubbing her hands near the flickering flame. "I'll have to delay judgment. That volleyball game was pretty intense."

The others laughed.

Grace lifted her glass of wine. "To family, new friends, and detours that take you exactly where you're meant to be."

They all lifted their drinks, though Hailey's was an empty cup, and said cheers.

She hoped this was actually the start of something real and solid and not just another detour. A person could only handle so many before giving up on the trip.

12

October

Wes pressed the button on the steering wheel to release his call. The CEOs of CoreTech, the newest firm he was trying to acquire, needed to be wined and dined and it pissed him off. He wasn't into courtships when he'd proven himself time and again. Ana Pergo and her brother, Aidan, owned the security company that provided digital and physical security to their elite clients. They were looking for someone who could head the cyber piece of it and all but guarantee those clients there wouldn't be breaches. That was never a guarantee but Wes was as close as it came.

He cut the engine in his truck and grabbed his messenger bag, heading toward the rec center. Ana wanted to do a dinner to finalize some terms. Wes did not. But he wanted that contract in their portfolio. Of all the tech stuff he did, cybersecurity, digging for minuscule holes and fixing them, was his favorite.

Rolling his shoulders to shrug off his mood, he walked along the cracked cement path toward the entrance. This neighborhood was right in the middle of the socioeconomic scale. Though Noah was the real estate buff in the family, it always interested Wes the way a street or two either way could show a completely different picture.

Their grandfather was big on looking at the whole picture and how, as a privileged man, he could give back but also get involved.

He'd taught them as boys that it wasn't enough to give or raise money. They needed to connect with people, build relationships that mattered. Their father's vision was entirely different.

When Noah moved to Harlow Beach and got involved with the once thriving recreation center, he'd set goals: improve it, add onto it, be part of it. Chris and Wes were excited to jump on board. That plaque Chris had made said it all. They wanted to do the same jobs but differently than their father had.

Rob, who'd introduced them to the center, said they needed to focus on sustainable programming for now, so all of them had signed up to volunteer. He was excited that Hailey and Fiona wanted to get involved. But for long-term impact, he wondered how else they could get involved. Be more than suits with money. They lived here too. Chris and Everly's kids could one day play at this very center. He smiled, thinking of his brother with kids. Of being an uncle.

The lobby was quiet, one teenager standing at the counter, playing on his phone. He looked up when Wes came in. "Hey. How's it going?"

The kid looked familiar. "Leo, right?"

For some reason, Wes knowing his name must have put his guard up. The kid pocketed his phone, stood straighter. "Yeah. Who are you?"

Holding out his hand, he waited for Leo to take it. "Wes Jansen. My brothers and our friend Rob volunteer here."

An oversized toothy grin burst from the teen's face. "You're Noah's brother? Did he tell you how I always beat him in basketball?"

"In your dreams, kid," Noah said, coming out from an open doorway behind the counter.

"You were sweating so much I almost slipped in it," Leo said, crossing his arms over his body and using one hand to pretend to hide his laughter.

Noah hooked a thumb toward the kid, clearly enjoying the back-and-forth. "Remember when we used to be this cocky?"

Wes looked at Leo, gestured to Noah with a tilt of his head. "Some of us still are."

Leo let out a bark of laughter.

Wes laughed. "Which room am I in?"

"We rented a laptop cart from the library. I put it in a room down the hall. Wi-Fi is spotty so I hope the class goes well." Noah came around the counter, gestured to the left.

"Pickup game Saturday," Leo called as they started down the hall. "Two for one if you want—kick both your asses in one game."

Noah shot the kid a look. "There's little kids here, man. Butts. You'll kick our butts."

Wes laughed. "He seems like he's a good kid."

Noah's expression darkened. "He is. Chip on his shoulder the size of this center. It's taken him a while to relax around me and Chris. He's closer to Rob. Doesn't trust easily."

"You know anything about his background?"

Noah stopped, ran a hand through his hair. "Thought I did. Because that's what we do: we look at a situation and make assessments and judgments without knowing anything. Then we step in and pretend we know how to fix it."

Wes glanced around, smiled at a couple of people walking down the hall, then looked at his brother, an uneasiness settling in his chest. "What's this about?"

Noah looked over his shoulder, a strange expression on his face. "Grandpa always said it was about becoming part of the community but that's not always the easiest thing to do. I live here. I care what happens but I feel like we're standing still. People in this neighborhood have more to worry about than just this center. Even the ones with a steady income and access to good schools."

His gaze wandered to Leo again.

Wes sighed. "We can only go one step at a time. You *are* building relationships. That matters. When people see we're not just here for a ribbon cutting or tax break, they'll realize we're part of this community, too. Give it some time. We have it." He had a quick flash of the future, of meeting Noah and Chris and their growing families for a pickup game or something fun. The sharp pang in his chest surprised him.

Noah nodded, not looking entirely sure as they walked down the hall.

"What's Leo's story?"

"Parents are both doctors. One works locally but the other travels a lot. He got picked on in school. He struggles with reading but he's smart and quick with numbers."

Wes looked at his brother. "You *do* know him. Or you're starting to. We're here, showing up just like he is, like others are."

Noah smiled, the tension in his shoulders fading. "We're getting there." His brother wasn't known for his patience.

Wes had arrived forty minutes early and was glad they could have time to chat. The gym must have been close by because he could hear the sounds of a team playing something and shouting.

"So, if we're getting there, why do you seem frustrated?"

Noah leaned against the open door. "The more we take on, the more excited I am, but it means we're spreading ourselves thin. It isn't just our work life I want to be different. I want to marry Grace. Relationships, even good ones like ours, take work. I don't know. I guess I'm just tired."

"Do they have a board of directors? That's how a lot of these places work. It's a team effort."

Noah shook his head. "The manager said the community was having trouble reassembling a board. People have jobs and lives like us. How do we get them to be part of a board if everyone is spread thin? Running this place is a full-time job. The manager is partially funded by the city but I'm betting she does more volunteer work than paid."

He nearly smiled and said what he was thinking. *You're growing up, little brother. Think first, act second.* Instead, he said, "Let me see what I can dig up about the previous board and other community organizations, see if there's any overlap. I'll find someone we can reach out to. The best way to be part of a solution is to ask the people who know what the problem is. If we can get more people involved, the work lessens for everyone."

Noah nodded. "That's a great idea."

Wes walked into the classroom, set his bag down, and went straight for the hardware. "These look decent enough. I'll get them all turned on and make sure they're all connected."

"Better you than me," Noah said, shoving his hands in the pockets of his jeans.

"That's what I was thinking about the working-with-kids part," Wes said, glancing over his shoulder as he pulled the laptops out of the cart.

Noah came over to help him, setting the laptops on the tables, opening them to speed things up. "You know what you're talking about. The kids need that. You'll warm up after a few minutes. Don't bullshit them. Be yourself. The self you are around us, not the stick-up-his-ass event guy."

Wes set the laptop down harder than he meant to. "Nice."

"It's true, man. You're fine around people you know or a no-nonsense business meeting. These kids are neither of those scenarios. They see through you, call you out on your garbage. Hell, it's almost refreshing." He laughed. "For real, relax. They just need to know you're a real person invested in what you're teaching them."

His chest tightened. He *was* a real person. He just liked to do things *right*. He wasn't great on the fly and kids were the very definition. Weren't they? He didn't spend a lot of time around them.

"Dude. Breathe," Noah said, laughing. He didn't get it. Noah didn't have the ability to feel embarrassment. Chris and Wes had seen to that growing up. He grinned, his chest loosening with the memories of how they'd ganged up on their middle brother.

"I got it. I'll remove the stick."

Noah laughed, clapped him on the back. "Who are you and what have you done with my brother? Maybe this is Hailey's influence. You're sure you're not into her?"

He was into her—just not in the way Noah was suggesting. He was excited to see her tonight, to hear her funny stories about customers. He wanted to know more about her book club idea and since he suspected she was a closet reading fanatic, he wanted to ask her about some of his favorites, see if they had any in common.

Though he wouldn't admit it to his brother—ever—he'd sketched a few funny drawings for their "guide." He knew she'd get a kick out of it. He knew he'd notice if her hair smelled like strawberries and the way her eyes crinkled in the corners when she laughed, but having pre-set the boundaries made this easier. Didn't matter if he was *into* her. They were friends. He could look forward to being with her, being himself, and not messing it up.

"Earth to Wes." Noah nudged his shoulder.

"She's fantastic. But honestly, it's nice to have a friend of my own, one that didn't come to me through you and Chris. Despite being the oldest, I never realized how infrequently I formed my own circles. I always had you guys, and Ari. I never actively looked for friends because we never needed to. Sometimes I felt like we were always surrounded by people. Hailey's different. I like her a lot. I don't want to wreck that with even the possibility of a relationship or even sex. I'd hate to lose what we're building."

Noah leaned against the table. "What if it was more than sex?"

Wes thought about that, seriously considered it as he had many times already, and realized there was another perk to this friendship. "It can't be. Hailey is rebuilding her life and her business. She's chasing and fulfilling her own dreams. She doesn't need a lover." His throat went dry at the thought of her with another man. He cleared his throat. "What I mean is, I think we both need this friendship. We like each other but we're not long-term compatible, even if either of us was looking for that. The best part is, we already know it." His brother would mock the guide for sure. "We want the same thing."

"Sometimes we don't know who we are until we find the right

person. The one that helps us see ourselves in a way we never did before."

Wes stopped what he was doing, walked closer to his brother. This was important. "You have no idea, given the frame of reference we have for happy relationships, how much it matters to me that you've found Grace. That Chris has Everly. But that's not what I want. I like Hailey. She's my *friend*. Do me a favor and tone down the joking and shit when she's around. I feel like she could be in our lives for a long time." Something he couldn't remember thinking about any other woman he'd known.

Noah studied him for a minute. Wes nearly broke eye contact but finally his brother spoke. "As opposed to whatever woman you happen to date next? You're so sure that'll have an expiry date?"

"As sure as you are of Grace."

The look of disappointment and sadness in Noah's expression was too much for Wes. His brother didn't get it. He should be rejoicing for Wes.

~~~~~~~~~

Wes expected to find teaching the concepts easy. He knew he'd be able to break down the components of coding for the novice learner. He was prepared to ask questions and engage in conversation.

What he didn't expect was how the enthusiasm of the students would transfer. For sixty minutes, he was immersed in language he loved: app development, pair programming, source codes. These kids knew a lot more than he'd assumed. A couple of them were complete novices but the more advanced learners were able to show what they knew by helping them out.

"Can we make an actual video game?" Dimitri asked.

Wes felt like he'd downed a Red Bull. "Absolutely. I think each of you should decide on a goal, whether you want to create an app, get better at the language, map out a game, whatever you want, and then we can do some whole-group learning at the beginning of each class and break off into smaller groups after."

"Have you ever made any apps?" one of the older teens, Joelle, asked.

"Several, actually." The income from those and some other software he'd developed had given him the financial padding to take a step away from his father.

"Can we look them up?"

He wrote some of them on the whiteboard, thinking about the one he'd created for Chris's girlfriend. A misunderstanding had landed Everly in a radio-station-hosted, *Bachelorette*-style dating pool. Wes had created *EverLove*, an app to help her narrow down prospective suitors. In the end, it'd been a moot point since she and his brother had fallen for each other during that time.

The kids were great about shutting down and storing the computers. When they left, he wheeled the cart out to the front cart to leave it with Leo. The older teen was on the phone when he approached.

He saw Wes and held up a finger before turning to face the wall. "I need that shift. Yeah, I get it. Okay. If anyone else calls in sick, you can put me on the list."

He hung up, shoulders slumped. When he turned back around, Wes saw him try to shake it off. "Everything go okay?"

"Absolutely. The kids were great. I'm looking forward to next week."

"Cool. Here, I'll grab those." Coming around the counter, he grabbed the cart, wheeled it into the office Noah had come out of earlier.

"You work here a lot?" Wes asked, pulling his keys from his pocket.

"This isn't my job. I volunteer one night a week here. Sometimes more if there are special events. It's part of a program called Give Back. I get to drop in whenever I want without paying."

Wes nodded, not sure how to broach the topic. "You go to school?"

The kid swiped a dark lock of hair out of his eyes, his gaze shifting. "Graduated last year. I'm working right now. I'm taking a year before I go to college." Whatever he was thinking about made him frown deeper.

"What's your other job?"

"What's yours? Other than questioning me?"

Damn. He needed to learn. Biting back his smile, Wes held up his hands, the keys jingling. "Sorry. I overstepped. I do that. I try to step in and solve problems."

The kid's lips twitched. "Knowing you have an issue is said to be the first step."

Wes nodded. "I've heard that too." He turned to leave.

"Hey," Leo called out.

Wes turned back.

"How would you solve my problem if, say, I wasn't getting enough shifts at my current job?"

Wes shrugged, hoping he wasn't about to risk the new friendship he was so happy with. Couldn't hurt to ask, right? "I have a friend who's looking for someone to do some deliveries. Maybe. She's just starting her business and the hours aren't static."

The way he leaned forward a little, how his eyes came back to Wes suggested interest. "I have a car. It breaks down more than it runs but I've been fixing it up."

He almost asked why his parents didn't help him with that—two doctors? If Noah was right about that, why was this kid struggling with small things like a reliable vehicle? Noah's words about prejudging, thinking he knew, came back to Wes. He didn't know anyone else's true story.

"Would it be okay if I mentioned you to her? I'm not sure what she'd be able to pay or what the hours would be like but it could be mutually beneficial."

He hoped like hell Hailey wasn't mad at him but how could he not act when he was right? It would be mutually beneficial. Wes couldn't help himself. He'd done thousand-piece puzzles on his own at age five. He was a born and bred problem solver.

He'd tell her why he suggested it—she might have too if she met Leo—and leave it in her court. She was getting busier every day and if she didn't get mad at his overstepping, she'd see this could really push her to the next level. Wes had run the numbers on her website and she was getting frequent visitors. It would increase if she could offer delivery, even part-time.

"Sure. That'd be okay. I'll talk to you next week?" The tiny touch of hope, the faint glimmer in his tone, was enough to have Wes smiling.

"You bet." And because he was practical and hated disappointing people, he added, "No guarantees but I think it would be a great fit."

When he left the center, drove toward home, he felt better than he had in a while. More grounded. Less . . . scattered. Lately, he'd felt like his brain was Hailey's laptop—eight hundred open tabs all vying for attention. He didn't like feeling pulled in different directions when none of them seemed particularly interesting.

When he pulled into his parking spot at home, he checked his phone. Ana had asked about a dinner meeting next week, saying she'd bring the paperwork to sign there. It was too good an offer to be put off by having to socialize for one dinner. The money from this deal could give them the cushion they wanted for other investments.

With a smile, he got out of his vehicle and thought about what he could trade Hailey to get her to come with him. This might not be what was meant by friends with benefits, but he had a feeling she'd be willing to make a deal.

13

Wes's apartment was awesome. She'd been 100 percent accurate when she assumed the space would be enviable. "I love it. It's a great size. Oh look! You have a little patio," Hailey said, sliding the door open and stepping onto it.

"There sure is a difference between the word 'studio' in New York and here in California," he said behind her, a smile in his voice. She liked that she could recognize that even without looking at him.

Other people were out on their patios as well. Vehicles moved along the street, and music came from multiple places. She leaned over the railing, hanging on tight but trying to fold her body just . . . a . . . little . . . more.

Wes's hands gripped her waist, shocking her in a duality of different ways.

"Please don't," he said, tension woven into each word.

He'd stepped back to the doorway, his gaze down, when she turned around. With a grin, she put her hand over her heart. "You scared me. I was just trying to see if I could see my shop." And she hadn't expected the zing of pleasure at the feel of his fingers digging into her hips.

He looked up, meeting her gaze. "You scared *me*. I can see it if I lean over but you're about a foot too short."

The worry she saw in his eyes, the tension that still riddled his shoulders surprised her. He was serious. She'd actually *scared* him. Like he thought something would happen to her.

Going on instinct, Hailey stepped closer. "I'm okay. I didn't mean to scare you."

He shook it off, gave her an almost-smile. "It's fine."

This close, she'd caught the scent of his cologne and of pure Wes and she had to remind herself that neither of them wanted more than just friendship. Hailey had been lonely enough in the past few years that she knew there was no "just" about it: friendship was a gift. One she'd sorely been missing. They went back inside.

The patio was off a living room that led to a sweet little kitchen. The other end of the apartment had a bedroom, den, and gorgeous bathroom. She went toward the kitchen, started unloading some of the supplies she'd brought.

"I thought I had everything," Wes said, folding his arms across his chest as he leaned on the opening between the kitchen and living area.

"I know, but I wasn't sure if you ate what you bought." She reached for a drawer then looked at him. "Okay if I make myself at home?"

He gestured to go ahead with his hand. "You thought I ate two cans of diced tomatoes and a pound of brown sugar?"

It was easy to tease him. "Hey, I don't know what your secrets are."

His laughter made her happy. "Now I want to know yours. What do you want me to do?"

"Wash your hands."

While he did that, she found a cutting board, pans, the olive oil, tomatoes, garlic, onions, brown sugar, and balsamic.

She pulled on an apron with By the Cup on the right top corner. "Okay. Grab a can opener—you can drain those tomatoes, then dice the garlic. Do you have a press?"

Wes shook his head. "Nope. But I've got knives. You want a glass of wine? I have red or white."

"Red, please."

There was a lot going on in her brain. She hadn't cooked dinner for a man in a long time. She'd never taught one how to make her grandmother's marinara. She felt that jittery buzz of excitement she'd normally attribute to attraction, but it was more. Or something else entirely. Hailey didn't have a lot of experience with the whole guy-girl friend thing but she was curious if this undercurrent of . . . what? Energy? Electricity? If it was normal.

"How was the rec center?" She turned the dial on the stove, poured some olive oil into a sauté pan as he chopped the garlic. She grabbed the onion and chopped it on the other cutting board.

"I was surprised by how excited the kids were. I think I expected some of them to need a solid push but I guess it's different when they all *want* to be there. Not like a regular school class where they have no choice."

"What did you teach?" The oil spattered in the pan so she grabbed the cutting board from him, swept the garlic in, loving the sound of the sizzle.

"Mmm. Love the smell of garlic," he said.

"Me, too. You can slide the onions in. I keep the heat high at first but you need to be careful it doesn't burn."

The onions added bonus sizzle. Hailey stirred them with a wooden spoon, picking up the can of tomatoes while he told her about coding, creating apps, and developing software. One of those areas that was fascinating but beyond her understanding.

"You don't want the juice?" he asked when she poured in the second can.

"Personal preference. If you want a juicier sauce or are adding meat, then yes. I tend to do this because I like a hearty marinara. Your voice sounds happy when you tech talk."

Wes stopped rinsing the tomato can. "'Tech talk.' I should coin that phrase. Like a TED Talk but different."

"It's literally a different language for me."

"As is this for me." He gestured to the pan.

She wondered if he'd had people cook for him. Not here but in New York. "I don't want to learn coding," she said. She knew her limits and had no problem staying within them.

"That's fair, but you're going to play at least one video game before you're allowed to leave tonight."

She continued to stir, adjusted the heat. "Are you trying to turn me into a gamer?"

"It'd be nice to go on a winning streak. I'm used to playing with my brothers. Going up against a rookie will be good for my ego."

"Until I kick your ass. I'm a quick learner."

"We'll see." He passed her a glass of wine. She knew dinnerware. She had an affinity for it the way some women loved jewelry. Turning the glass, she tipped it slightly, looked for the suspected *W* stamp on the bottom.

"Something on your glass?"

Waterford. "Nope. Just admiring your good taste." Taking a long swallow, she tried to push down the unease that came along with thinking about his wealth. She'd broken down, broken her own rule, and googled the hell out of him. He wasn't just well off. He was old-family-empire-like-the-Hiltons rich.

"My grandmother's taste. She gave each of us a set of two. They were her mother's."

Hailey set the glass down then pushed it farther from the edge. "You might want to give me a plastic cup next time. I can be clumsy."

"I haven't seen much evidence of that."

All it takes is a high-value family heirloom to bring it out in me. She remembered meeting Dorian's parents. A nervous swing of her jacket had nicked one of his mother's sculptures in the entry hall. She'd never lived it down.

"Why don't you get the water going for the pasta." Changing the topic felt easier than addressing it. "I start with a drizzle of balsamic, a tablespoon of brown sugar. I add all the regular spices you do to any other Italian dish and then adjust to taste."

She held up a spoonful for him, her hand underneath it. When he bent his knees to accept, she got caught in his gaze for a second again. It was like looking at the sky on a perfectly clear day.

"Holy shit that's good." He licked his lips.

Hailey grinned. "It takes less than twenty minutes to whip it up. Next time one of your dates works out, you could make this."

He gave her a one-sided smile. "Or, since we're becoming good friends, you can make it for me in exchange for me helping you master the art of video games."

She turned the burner down to simmer, laughing. "You're a full-on gaming nerd, aren't you? You love all this tech stuff; have you designed your own?"

When he didn't answer her, she turned to look at him. He was giving her such a funny look that she asked, "What?"

Had she missed something? Was he a renowned gaming designer and she was clueless for not knowing? Was he the Nora Roberts of tech? The Nora Ephron of action-packed games?

"I'm a businessman, not a college kid. I was a corporate executive." He turned away, busied himself with the pasta.

She didn't mean to but she laughed. "What the hell does that even mean? Isn't gaming, like, a billion-dollar industry?"

"It is. I haven't designed my own. Well, I haven't designed a fully functioning game."

Hailey felt like he'd shared something special, something private, but didn't know why. He was great at what he did. What was stopping him from making this another part of his empire?

Friends or not, she didn't feel ready to ask. Or, more accurately, she didn't feel he was ready to answer.

They let the conversation drift while she made the pasta, drained it, and covered it with marinara. She'd brought a loaf of French bread and gently toasted it. They took their plates to the living room with their wine. He had the movie ready to stream.

Setting his plate down, he gestured with his wine. "We'll watch this first, I'll show you the pleasure of video games after?"

"Just saying . . . this wouldn't be the first time a guy has promised pleasure and I've left disappointed."

Wes's mouth did a fishlike thing but he smiled when she laughed. "Jesus. I'm glad you're on a hiatus if that's true."

She grinned. "Let's watch one of the best movies ever."

He rolled his eyes. "Fine." He pressed play while they dug into their food. Two bites in, he paused the screen.

Hailey turned to meet his gaze.

"First, this is delicious. Seriously good. Thank you. Second, I have a favor."

Her heart fluttered like it had taped on a set of wings. "Okay."

"You can say no, I will completely understand. But I know you like trades so you could also say yes and have this in your back pocket for a future favor."

"Lay it on me." She actually felt herself brace for impact. Was even friendship with a guy too good to be true?

"I have a business dinner late next week. I don't like these sorts of things at this point in the negotiation. Some people use them as a friendly-handshake sort of thing—'okay, the deal is done.' But others use them as a last-minute squeeze. I never know which it's going to be. I'd like to not go alone and I definitely don't want to bring a date. Would you come with me? I mean, that's another benefit of friends, right? You could join me, there'd be no pressure personally but professionally it would loosen the noose, so to speak." His words tumbled out like he was afraid this was his last chance to speak. He actually sounded out of breath when he finished.

That didn't sound so bad. "That's it? A dinner?" She'd been to more than a few networking dinners. She knew how to play the quiet, nonintrusive plus-one.

His posture deflated. "Yes. But no. Not *just* a dinner. I'd really like to close this account. I want to focus on that but it'll set a different tone, I think, if I bring a date. Or a friend as my date."

Wes was really sewing that label on tightly. Which was fine with her. Still, she felt a weird stitch in her side. "What tone?"

"More of a 'this deal is done' tone. A 'we're all here to celebrate.' More casual." He hesitated and she could see his posture stiffen again. "Sorry. I was nervous to ask."

She smiled at him. Of all the favors, this was an easy one. For a man she assumed was used to getting what he wanted, she was surprised by his reluctance to ask. "It's just a dinner. I don't mind. Honestly. I'd be happy to."

"Really?"

"Maybe you haven't had the best of friends if asking so little made you nervous."

His smile notched up by degrees. "I guess I haven't. Thank you. Do you want to ask a favor in return or hang on to it?"

Hailey widened her grin, hoping it would ease his obvious anxiety. "When you least expect it, my friend." Then she bumped his shoulder with hers. "I feel weird about taking advantage of people when I need something but honestly, I'll do anything for people I care about. We're good. Relax."

He gave her another strange look. "I am relaxed."

She scooped up a bite of pasta. "Tell that to your shoulders and maybe even your lungs."

He huffed out a breath, like he hadn't realized he'd been limiting his air intake. "Thank you."

"You're welcome."

They sat eating for a few minutes, enjoying the quiet and the meal. She could sense he was still stuck in his own head, thinking about what, she didn't know. But she was happy to be able to do something for him. Especially when he seemed so reluctant to ask. Hailey didn't think Wes was the type to take advantage. Or the type she'd lose her way over enough to let him do just that. Maybe the friendship path just made things more clear-cut and straightforward. *Or maybe Wes is unlike the other men you've known.*

"Oh," she said, finishing up her last bite. "I wanted to ask what you thought of me doing a book club for teens at the rec center?"

Wes smiled, used a napkin to wipe his lips. "I've noticed you're a bit of a bookworm."

"You know what they say, you're never really lonely if you have a book."

"I *didn't* know they said that. But I think it's a great idea. I think the more that can be offered in the way of programming, the wider the reach will be in the community. If you write up a short proposal, Noah will take care of setting things in motion with the center's director of programs."

"Great. I've got a couple books in mind. I think this will be fun. And I know Fiona was pumped, too."

"You don't mind giving your time, helping out a friend, comping salads, but you worry about people doing things for you."

She looked over at him and she knew she could leave the comment, talk about something else. But she also knew that if she didn't learn to open herself up again, trust in someone, she wasn't going to be truly happy.

"My parents are desperately in love. Like, obsessively. I was a hurdle. An unexpected surprise and they love me. They do. But they were, and still are, all about each other. I always felt a little bit invisible, which is fine. I'm not telling you a 'woe is me' story. But I learned early to lean on myself. When *others* started to lean on me, friends, boyfriends, I felt happy. It was like the little kid in me felt seen because these people needed me. Does that sound dumb?"

He shook his head, his lips parted, his gaze locked on her.

Her skin felt too tight. Uncomfortable. Piper would be so proud of her, she thought. "When I started to need them back, feel safer in some of the relationships I chose, I ended up disappointed. It's a self-preservation mechanism, I guess."

He was quiet a moment. "We all have those."

She nodded. He wasn't wrong.

"Thank you for telling me."

"You're welcome. You're less obnoxious about psychoanalyzing me than Piper is."

He laughed. "I need to meet your cousin."

"Oh, you shall. She'll see to it."

"Should I be scared?"

Taking his plate from him, she stood. "Piper says a little fear goes a long way. Toward what, I'm not sure. Best to be cautious but I'll have your back."

The softness in his gaze was doing something weird to her insides. Not friend-like things, but she was okay with setting it aside because what was happening between them felt special. All the friends she'd thought were the real deal disappeared with her relationship. Connections she thought mattered were severed like the tie between them was the thinnest of strings. This tether she was weaving with Wes felt strong, sturdy. Like something she could count on even if it was stretched.

"I'm glad we met," he said finally.

"Me too," she said. "Let's watch the movie. No looking at me during the diner scene."

Wes's laughter was worth pushing down any feelings that weren't about friendship. She wouldn't risk losing that.

14

November

Their Saturday-night shopping trips were a highlight for Hailey.
Wes's love of routine must have rubbed off on her because it felt
strange to be doing something different after weeks of the same.
She felt like she was living in this perfect little bubble of happiness. She didn't believe in good or bad luck, per se, but she had this
hovering feeling that too much good could only be offset by some
bad. Her business and her personal life were thriving. Giving up
on romantic relationships while building new friendships—Noah
and Chris ate at her shop once a week, Fiona texted regularly—
had given her a freedom to explore new parts of herself.

The lack of pressure to be anything other than herself was ex-
hilarating. Maybe a little enlightening as well. She'd considered
herself organized but found there were some definite kinks in her
scheduling capabilities. She wanted to do it all so she sometimes
overbooked. She'd started making lists, like Wes, because she
learned she was a horrible shopper. She wasted time and money
not having a plan. One step at a time. Small steps toward the big
picture she wanted.

Fiona's name buzzed on her phone as Hailey stood in her bra
and undies. She swiped her finger over the screen, stepping away
so the only view Fiona got was the ceiling.

"Um . . . nice fan?" Fiona's voice came through.

Hailey laughed, pulled the black dress off the hanger. "I'm not decent. Give me a sec and you can tell me if this dress works for a business dinner."

"I thought this dinner was supposed to be a couple weeks ago," Fiona said.

Hailey worked hard not to make any unpleasant sounds as she worked the dress up over her hips, got her boobs situated, and did a couple gymnast moves with her arms to get the zipper up.

"It kept getting moved. Seriously, getting this dress on should count as cardio. It's comfortable but not one of those ones you could slip into easily."

"It's about time for you to start slipping *out* of your clothes. I think you should start dating again," Fiona said.

Hailey grabbed her phone, looked at the screen. Fiona had the camera up close to her forehead. "What are you doing?"

"I think I'm going gray. My grandmother went gray at twenty-one." Fiona moved the phone back. "Your makeup looks hot. Let's see the dress."

Hailey pressed the button on her phone to turn the camera and stood in front of her full-length mirror.

Fiona whistled. "You look so pretty. I don't think I've seen you in a dress."

The quiz-writing journalist had become as much a part of her routine as Wes. They went for brunch most Sunday mornings at a little bistro a couple miles from the square. Every now and again, Wes joined them. Piper frequently joined. Megan and Rachel had shown up once. It was nice to feel like she was really making a life for herself.

"Thank you. I wouldn't exactly wear this to work."

"No. But you *could* wear it on a date. Or say, a bunch of them?"

Hailey turned the camera. "Spill it. What are you getting at?" The night the girls had warned Hailey that Fiona sometimes had some strange requests came back to her. "Should I be scared?"

"No. Absolutely not. Remember the article I wanted to do on finding love in five minutes?"

"Yeah."

"My editor thinks the article would be stronger if I was speaking from experience rather than research. She found an event at a restaurant close by."

Hailey groaned, closed her eyes, then opened them again. "I was just thinking how great it is *not* to have the pressure of dating. How wonderful it is to have made a small group of friends I could count on and hang out with. It's a shame I have to eliminate you from the list."

Fiona's laughter suggested she knew Hailey well enough to know she was joking. Mostly.

"You don't have to go out with anyone. I swear. I'm not going to. I don't want to go alone. Please."

"Fine. When?"

She hid her sigh because as much as she didn't want to go, she didn't want to make her friend feel bad either.

"Next Saturday."

That's grocery night. Ugh. Not good, Hails. Routine is fine but don't get in a rut. "Sure. That sounds good." Wes would absolutely understand. He might even be happy since she often distracted him from his own list or added fun things to it. Just because she was showing growth personally didn't mean she couldn't have some fun with him.

"You're the best. Text me when you get home, okay?"

"Yeah. Shouldn't be late."

Hanging up, she went in search of a pair of low heels that wouldn't kill her feet. Dressing up wasn't something she did often. It was nice sometimes. She liked doing her hair. She'd pulled it into a low bun at the base of her neck and left tendrils framing her face.

It was her first San Verde fancy dinner experience and she didn't even have to pay. *Maybe I should wear a dress that lets me eat more.* She rubbed her hand over her stomach. The dress actually felt really good despite the awkwardness of getting it on.

When her phone buzzed again, she knew it was Wes.

She smiled when she saw his name.

> **Wes**
> I'll be leaving to pick you up in twenty minutes. Are you ready?
> **Hailey**
> Yes.
> **Wes**
> Hailey ready or Wes ready?

She stuck her tongue out at the screen. One time he'd showed up and she was still in pajamas. Brushing her teeth. But he was ten minutes early!

> **Hailey**
> Not telling. I like to keep you on the edge of your seat
> **Wes**
> If you're Wes ready, I'll spring for extra dessert AND you can choose the movie.

He'd enjoyed *When Harry Met Sally.* She had *not* enjoyed *Inception.* Now, after grabbing groceries on Saturdays, they compromised on a movie at his house. Usually a drama since she didn't want to overwhelm him with her love of rom-coms. She was, however, getting pretty damn good at those video games he loved.

> **Hailey**
> Go ahead and show up ten minutes early
> **Wes**
> You'll do anything for chocolate

Le Tiens was fancier than she expected. Worth wrangling herself into the dress. More unexpected was the equally elegant and gorgeous Ana Pergo. Hailey hadn't asked about *who* the meeting was with. It didn't matter to her; she was just there to support Wes. The flash of disappointment she was sure she caught in Ana's gaze suggested that Wes was smart in bringing her if he wanted to keep things all business.

She told herself it wasn't a whisper of jealousy when Ana looked at Wes like she wished it were just the two of them. Just friendly . . . protectiveness.

Ana's brother, Aidan, was tall, broad shouldered, and had a smile that reminded Hailey of the ones she used to see on sets. During breaks, she'd wander around and watch the filming. It always amazed her how fast a person could transform their features into different emotions. She didn't trust it.

"It's a pleasure to meet you, Hailey," Aidan said, holding her hand a touch longer than she was comfortable with.

"I'm so sorry we had to reschedule," Ana said to Wes.

Wes moved to Hailey's side, put a hand on her lower back. It was one of those moments where she hadn't realized she was missing something. She didn't miss being a couple—not really. She sure as hell didn't miss Dorian. But she missed those little things: a hand on her back or slipping hers into someone's back pocket.

"No worries. I'm glad we found a time that works. I'm eager to sign the contract."

Ana patted her satchel. "I have it right here."

"Your table is ready, Ms. Pergo," the host said.

They followed the man to a table in the corner with pretty candle centerpieces. Silver cloth napkins sat atop crisp white tablecloths. The arched ceiling was made even prettier by dark wood beams and long candelabras adding a warm glow.

Once they were settled and the wine ordered, the small talk

started. This was the first time Hailey had been with Wes in this sort of setting. While he was attentive to the conversation, he didn't contribute much more than direct answers. When Aidan told a funny story about one of their clients, he laughed politely, but it was as clear as the real crystal glasses on the table that he was rusty at the socializing game. *Or it shows just how much he's dropped his guard with you.*

"Tell me about your restaurant, Hailey," Aidan said.

The waiter brought bread. Hailey picked up a piece and buttered it generously, passed it to Wes, who took it with a quiet nod of thanks, then buttered her own.

"I don't think it's in the restaurant category. Maybe an eatery? It's small and all about salads. Every kind you can imagine in a take-out cup. Not that you can't eat in but I definitely get more take-and-go customers."

"Her salads are creative and delicious," Wes said.

Hailey eyed him, curious that when the topic shifted to something business related, he participated more actively. Was he uncomfortable? Nervous?

"Do you have a card?" Ana met her gaze. There was something in it that pulled Hailey's nerves tight. Probably her own insecurities. She'd left the world of glitz, glamour, and power gazes behind with Dorian.

"I do!" She didn't mean to say it so loud and hunched her shoulders, laughing. "Sorry. So many people asked me that in the first month when I didn't have any." She passed one over.

"We do company and client lunches all the time. This is wonderful. I'll definitely be calling you," Ana said.

Hailey was excited by the thought of new customers. She hadn't come to help her own business. She didn't want to step on Wes's toes and suggest her website so she picked up her water, took a sip.

"I'd really like to get the contracts signed and out of the way so we can enjoy dinner," Wes said.

Ana shot him a dazzling smile. "You're all work, Wes. You need to add a little play into your life."

Wes seemed oblivious to the fact that Ana was interested in more than his cyberskills. Should she, as his friend, clue him in? When they pulled out the paperwork, Hailey excused herself to use the restroom.

After touching up her lipstick—it had been so long since she'd remembered she loved wearing it—she checked her phone.

Tara
Hey. Wanted to let you know the meeting was moved to tomorrow at 4. The landlord is attending.
Hailey
Thank you. Hope you're having a fun Saturday night.
Tara
Don't want to make you jealous but I'm doing inventory.

Hailey laughed.

Hailey
Totally jealous. Fiona is dragging me to a speed dating thing next week. You should come.
Tara
Intriguing. I'll think about it.

The two business district meetings Hailey had attended so far were mostly housekeeping. Parking issues, a San Verde Square monthly newsletter was brought up, and a review of upcoming events. It was nice to meet some of her fellow shop owners but she and Tara were two of the only ones close to their thirties. Hailey was surprised by how many of the shops had been around for years. Management passed down through families.

When she returned to the table, she was happy to see the

paperwork was done. Wes and Aidan both stood when she approached the table and it gave her stomach one of those whoosh feelings she hadn't experienced in a while. It felt nice to be noticed. Maybe she should put some effort into the speed dating thing.

"All good?" Wes asked.

She nodded. "Tara texted that my shop owners' meeting got moved to four tomorrow. The landlord is attending." She shrugged, not knowing if that was normal.

"Interesting. Noah has been trying to get ahold of him for a while."

"Your brother looking for more real estate?" Aidan asked.

"Always. Right now he's shopping for my other brother but he's never really not looking at commercial properties."

"You have your hands in many pies," Ana said.

Wes smiled. It was his polite one, not the one that made his blue eyes dance with laughter. "We like to be busy."

Their dinners arrived shortly after and they were able to shift the conversation to casual topics. Aidan and Hailey got wrapped up in some Hollywood gossip. She couldn't help it. She'd left that life behind but she still loved knowing who was dating who, not that Aidan could say much since his business was protecting his clients.

When the meal came to an end, Ana lifted her wineglass. "A toast. To friendship, to business, and to long, profitable relationships."

It seemed like an odd toast to Hailey but she was on her third glass of wine so she clinked happily, warmth spreading through her belly.

As they waited for the valet to bring Wes's car, she leaned her head against his shoulder.

"Have fun?" His voice was low.

She closed her eyes, soaking in his solid presence, the breeze that danced over her skin.

"So much fun," she whispered.

"I think Aidan likes you," Wes said.

Hailey tipped her head back. In her heels, she was close enough to see his gaze darken. "Funny. I think Ana likes *you*. Maybe we can double date them." A giggle escaped at the idea of them showing up at the same restaurant but with opposite dates.

"You're drunk."

"Tipsy. There's a difference."

"Still want a movie and dessert?"

She straightened, looked around like he was hiding it. "Do you have the dessert?"

His chuckle was low and familiar. It warmed her stomach like the wine. "Right here." He lifted the brown paper take-out bag.

"Phew."

"You make me laugh."

She smiled at him under the darkening night, the stars dancing over them. "That's what friends are for."

15

Wes was so relieved to have the contract signed, he'd texted his brothers while waiting for the valet to fetch his car. Hailey had leaned against him the entire time, making it hard not to notice the scent of her perfume, her contented sighs, and the way she smiled with her eyes closed.

She was still doing it as Wes set a glass of water in front of her where she lay, cheeks flush, on his couch. He didn't like the way Ana and Aidan had pushed the final meeting more than once. *You have it now. That's all that matters.* The contract. Not the way Aidan looked at and flirted with Hailey. He did his best to push that from his brain, unsure why it bothered him when he was so happy with their friend status.

"You okay, there?"

She opened her eyes, smiled up at him. "You're upside down."

Or he was standing at the end of the couch. "I promise I'm not."

"Don't worry, you look good either way. Right-side down or upside . . . wait."

Wes laughed, moved down to her feet, picking them up so he could sit. He'd never felt quite this much ease with someone. Even with girlfriends, he'd never been a naturally affectionate man. But Hailey didn't have the same boundaries he did. It had taken him a few hangouts to get used to the way she hugged or gave casual touches so easily.

It was the way Hailey worked. She burrowed. Dug a hole into someone's heart and stayed there. There were moments he felt the absolute opposite of ease—more like a spark snapping tension. But then one of her twenty-two alarms—alarms she'd set in an effort to be more organized after teasing him about his multiple scheduling apps—would ring, reminding her of the thing she'd definitely forgotten even though she swore she wouldn't, and he'd remember how different they were. How nice it was to have this to count on. He could tell her things he didn't tell his brothers and he sure as hell wouldn't tell a woman he was dating.

"I'm glad you came tonight. This is a big contract for our company. I didn't want to let Chris and Noah down." He kept one hand on her ankle absentmindedly.

Hailey sat up, reached for the chocolate cake instead of the water or the Tylenol he'd set beside it.

"As if you could." She pulled herself into a seated position next to him, close enough their thighs touched.

"The only thing about dining with fancy people is you never want to eat more than they do. Though, I was impressed that Ana ate. I can't tell you how many dinner parties I've been to where I was the only woman taking advantage of the delicious food."

He'd been to his share of those parties, too. Hated them. "It's a waste. Do you ever miss catering on set?"

She pulled the fork out of her mouth slowly, her eyes closed. She hummed with pleasure. *Snap.* Like a lightning-quick shock to his system that reminded him she was a desirable woman. One who was talking to him because he'd asked a question and zoned out for the answer.

"I'm happy where I am. It doesn't have the same job security but it's working out great. Speaking of. I think I'm ready to talk to your friend, Leo. You mentioned he was looking for work a while ago but I've only just gotten to a point I think I can take him on. Especially with my new plan."

Wes sat up. He was too full from dinner to eat his cake. "That's great. What's the new plan?"

She'd changed into a pair of loose sweatpants and a baggy sweater when they returned to his place. He'd suggested she bring them when he picked her up. That had been another one of those spark moments. She looked exquisite in that dress, but he liked it better when she wore what she did now. It put him at ease. Made it easier to think.

"I've been turning down some catering jobs because I'm always at the shop but with the Christmas season coming, it would be a great way to get some extra cash. I'm in a catch twenty-two. I can't say yes to more work without help and I can't hire help without securing more work. I'm going to interview Leo and say yes to some bigger jobs."

His heart muscles tightened, squeezing him like one of Hailey's all-in hugs. She was doing it. One salad at a time, she was building her business into what she'd imagined. "That's fantastic. I can update your website so the delivery option is live. Have you considered a preorder app? Most restaurants have that now, especially with outside delivery services. It's not a bad idea to hook up with one of those either. It would save you—"

Hailey held up a hand, set her half-finished cake down, the fork beside it. She took the pills with a long swallow of water. "Slow down. Geez. Were you just waiting to get all that out of your brain?"

He laughed, ran a hand through his hair. "Not really but they're all excellent ideas. Business is about seizing opportunities and acting at the right moment."

Her brows furrowed. "It's also about not overextending myself so I don't go under."

"There are loans you can get. Actually, there are probably grants you're eligible for, especially if you're hiring local youth." Hell, he could float her a loan.

She huffed out a breath. "I don't want a loan."

Excitement welled. She could push this to the next level easily. With a little help. "My brothers and I invest in businesses—"

"Wes. Stop." Hailey shook her head and he realized her tone was clipped.

Sitting up straighter, he pressed his lips together tightly.

"I appreciate that you're happy for me. I know you and your brothers could buy my store a million times over."

"A million might be overstating it," he said, dryly.

"I'm doing this."

Her quiet smile and determination made his heart clench. His grandfather would have loved her. "I love that you and your brothers use your wealth for good. That you want to lift small businesses up. But I want to do this on my own or not at all. Plus, it's not a good idea in this case."

"Why?"

"Friendship and business don't go hand in hand. You must know that. I'll take the catering jobs. I might actually need two employees. I figure it'll give me more flexibility with my own schedule if I hire two part-timers."

"There's no harm in taking a small loan to cover you. Especially when what you're using it for will yield results and income." Sure, business and friendship didn't mix but Squishy Cat was created for this very thing. It was the essence of Chris's plaque.

It startled him when she stood abruptly. She grabbed the plates. "I don't need saving."

Wes sucked in a breath, watching as she walked to the kitchen, set her plate in the sink. She was comfortable in his space. And he was comfortable with her *in* it. Another first. Maybe she was right. Some lines shouldn't be crossed.

"I know that, Hailey."

She sank back onto the couch and Wes shifted, unsure how to smooth things over. He'd meant to help. He felt intrinsically tied to her success or failure the way he would with . . . someone he cared a great deal about. *Like Grace or Everly. She's your friend.*

His *friend* still looked irritated.

"Piper asked if you wanted to come for Thanksgiving dinner. They're doing it early so they can go to Nick's parents'. I said I'd ask."

"That sounds nice. Does that mean you're free on the actual day?"

She nodded. "Yup." Still short.

"Good. You can join us at Noah's."

Hailey twisted her lips into a smirk. "Presumptuous."

He laughed, picked up the remote. "I know Grace already invited you."

She flopped back on the couch. "Argh. You know too many of my secrets."

Wes didn't comment. He scrolled through Netflix, not really registering anything. The tension between them was making his skin itch. He started to say what was on his mind, stopped.

"Are you mad?"

She turned her head, gave him half a smile. "No. I just don't want you to think you can fix everything because you're rich."

"Ouch."

"You're my friend. You're supposed to believe in me."

He sat up, irritation of his own rising. "I *do* believe in you. Do you think I would put my money into something I thought would fail?"

"Your money has nothing to do with me. I don't want it. I want your words of encouragement and support. I care about your opinion. I don't care about your money."

He didn't know what to say about that. Wealth was part of who he was and yeah, it smoothed a lot of damn roads. Was it wrong that he wanted to make things easier for her?

"You don't want your dad's name or money, right?"

Clasping his fingers together, he said through gritted teeth, "Right. Speaking of knowing too many secrets."

"There's a hell of a lot to be said for doing it on our own."

She had him there. He sighed. "I get it. I'm sorry."

"You don't need to be. I don't need anything other than friendship from you, Wes. I'm not a project or an investment."

He cursed low under his breath. "I never meant to make you feel like you were."

Show her. He pulled open one of the four drawers in his coffee table, his heart rate picking up. Little beads of sweat formed near his temples. *Damn. Get a grip.* Wes passed her the black sketchbook, held it a moment when she put her hand on it.

"What is this?"

"I believe in you. Your friendship matters to me. I don't want to screw that up."

"You didn't. You just think you know everything," she said with a teasing wink.

Wes laughed, released the sketchbook, ignoring the uncomfortable tightness in his chest.

Hailey opened the book, gasped. "Holy shit. I knew you doodled but Wes, this is gorgeous."

The first page of the book was an old drawing of a character he'd created and re-created a dozen times since his teens. He said nothing as she flipped the pages, making appreciative comments, running her fingers over the drawings like they were delicate, something special. He hadn't shared his art with anyone in more years than he could count.

"Wes, these are breathtaking. You can *feel* the characters' personalities coming off the page. And these worlds! They're so detailed."

Her words filled him with something he couldn't name. Pressure built in his chest. "Thank you."

She looked up from the pages, held his gaze. The oddest thing happened: the pressure in his body released and he was left with only happiness. She meant what she said; he could see it in her eyes.

"Thank *you* for sharing this with me."

He twisted his lips, didn't let himself hesitate too long. She'd given him a gift with her words. "It's a video game idea. It really is just sketches but the story, it's a game I sometimes design in my head."

Hailey's hand flattened on the page before what he'd actually intended to show her. "What's stopping you from designing it outside your head? Or at least on a virtual design program?"

He shook off the longing her words brought, unable to separate the reality that he was a grown man from the fact that his father's opinion still hovered over him like a damn rain cloud.

"My brothers and I are trying to build something together. This is just a hobby. A way to settle my brain, really. Getting into the gaming industry would require a lot of time and I've committed it elsewhere."

She was quiet so long, he wondered if she was going to say anything. "I'm sad you think that. You're very talented. You have the know-how. It seems like a waste to keep your gift in a drawer in your coffee table. And, as your friend, I don't mind saying, you're selling your siblings short by not sharing this with them."

Wes's mouth dropped open. "Guess this friendship thing comes with no-holds-barred honesty."

She grinned. "That's the way it should be. But honesty, not cruelty. There's a difference between being able to say what's on your mind and thinking you can say whatever you want."

He didn't get a chance to respond before she turned the page. And squealed. She actually bounced in her seat, her laughter filling the room.

"You made our guide! That's me! That's you!" She pointed at the character sketches he'd done of them, as if he didn't know who they were. Her delight fueled his own.

"This is adorable. I can't believe you did this."

He watched as she looked over the little sketches he'd made of their "just friends" guide. He'd done it in the form of an infographic with Hailey explaining how things worked—stacks of chocolate bars sat under a sign that said MUST HAVE, they both wore shirts that said TRUST ME, YOU MUST, and there was even a sketch of brown sugar with a tag on it that said SECRET INGREDIENT. Over the last several weeks, he'd added more doodles and sketches. It would be a fun thing to transfer to his computer, add pops of color. But for now, watching her happiness as she explored it, he didn't need more.

"This might be the coolest thing I've ever seen," she said, her voice reverent.

"Your friendship matters to me, Hailey. I might cross the line sometimes with my need to fix things but I have the best of intentions." Had he ever been that honest with anyone?

Going up on her knees, she held the book in one hand and wrapped her other arm around his neck, squeezing him tight. "You are the best friend a girl could have."

He hugged her back, unsure why her kind words sat uneasily in his stomach.

16

The San Verde Shop Association was an eclectic mix of people. The majority of them were in their late sixties or beyond. Other than Tara, the only person her age was Becky, who ran the bookstore. *I need to ask her about some books for teens.* Some of them seemed merely cordial, like Esther, who ran the Old Time Five & Dime, while others were gregarious, like Ricardo, who ran Yesterday's Treasures, a little vintage shop. Hailey needed to give each of the shops a closer look. If she hired Leo and maybe one other, she could spend a couple hours being a tourist in her own town.

"How are you?" Tara asked Hailey, coming up beside her and passing her a bottle of water.

"Thanks. I'm good. How's it going, Becky?"

The petite brunette shrugged. "I'm nervous. I don't like surprises. Oh, Tara, our books arrived."

"Excellent. We're starting a book club," Tara told Hailey.

"My cousin has one too, only they drink wine instead of reading books."

Becky laughed, her nerves seeming to fade. "That happens a lot but this one will be at my store. You're welcome to join."

"I'd love that. I'd also love to chat with you about some recommendations for a teen book club I'm hoping to start at the community center."

More people entered the room from the stairwell. The loft area over Baked was open, with a modern, industrial feel that Hailey wasn't sure was intentional. Brick walls and exposed beams could have been aesthetics or just an unfinished space.

Hailey glanced around, loving the feel of the space. "Some of these upper spaces are apartments, right?" Like Wes's, though his was farther down the square. Probably out of her price range, especially with her plans to hire, but a girl could dream.

"Yes. The ones on this side are stupidly expensive but they're gorgeous, like penthouses." Becky looked around too. "I'd love to live closer to work but I don't want to live in an apartment."

"I basically live *at* my store," Hailey joked.

"I heard you're doing interviews. That's great. Business is picking up?" Tara asked.

"Yes. I'm hoping it'll work out. I'm taking on some outside catering jobs so I need the help."

Esther, who'd so far only nodded in greeting when they arrived, joined them. "My grandson is looking for volunteer hours in the food industry. It's for workplace credits for school."

Hailey's gaze widened. "Seriously? Like, he works for free?" Free was right in her price range.

"Yes, dear." She stared expectantly at Hailey.

Tara gave a nearly imperceptible nod with an encouraging smile.

"Would he be able to come in for an interview?" *There's your professional voice.*

"Certainly. If you have a pen and paper, I'll give you his contact information."

Hailey held up her phone. "Right here."

She was typing the information into her notes when a large man ambled into the room. He was basketball player tall. *Oh. I should see if Wes wants to go to a basketball game.* Hardly the season but still something to think about. She'd heard sports were more fun in person.

"Afternoon, everyone. Thank you for coming. Let's get seated and started."

As if their strict teacher had joined them, they all moved to take a seat. The atmosphere of the room changed from easy to tense in a few breaths.

"For those of you I haven't met in person, I'm Logan Vanderben. I've owned this strip of stores for fifteen years. The market has changed a lot over that time and continues to change." He passed out packets of paper he pulled from a briefcase, and whatever happiness Hailey was feeling got sucked from her lungs as she stared down at the words.

"Times change, rent changes. I think you'll see, the increases are reasonable given the amount of time you've been here."

The rest of the words came at her in a hazy sort of blur. Even with free help, the rent increase would seriously cut into her revenue.

Tapping her fingers soundlessly on the table while others argued and asked questions of this seemingly unflappable man, Hailey felt the heavy thump of the other shoe dropping squarely on her shoulders.

"Thank you for helping me," Hailey said. She assembled the salads while Fiona chopped. Apparently her new friend was a jane-of-all-trades with a long list of random qualifications such as food prep and kitchen safety. Fiona had done all manner of things in the name of writing articles.

"It's the least I can do. Are you okay?" She set the knife down and turned to Hailey, who had fifty cups lined up along the counter.

"The increase threw me for a loop but it'll be okay. I've got this catering job and I can get others. With Esther's grandson and Leo, I'll be able to leave the store a bit more so I can handle the work. I can advertise the delivery option."

"You could consider getting an extra loan. I know Piper and Nick would totally help you. They're definitely in a position to do so. It's not uncommon for restaurants to hit some hurdles."

Tears pushed against her eyelids. Only the thought of having to restart the salads held them back. Yes. Her cousin could help, Wes could help, his brothers could help. But she'd used the sale of her apartment in L.A. to finance this venture and she was *doing* it. Her store was succeeding.

"That's the thing, it isn't a hurdle based on my business. It's the rent. It's a ridiculous increase. The association is talking about how to fight against it."

"Have you talked to Wes?"

She scooped cucumbers into each of the cups. "No. Why would I? I mean, about this." She knew why she didn't. He'd be all over trying to fix it and she was feeling just helpless enough to let him. Money and friends—hell, money and family—didn't mix.

"I know you like to pretend that he's just an everyday buddy, but Hailey, he's loaded. He probably has a half-dozen lawyers on retainer and speed dial."

Her shoulders fell. Did no one believe in her? What would Fiona, or Wes, say if Hailey didn't have a rich friend in her back pocket? She didn't like to think about Wes's money. "I'm not asking anyone to swoop in and fix my problems. This is part of running a company and I can do this. I will do this. It's a setback, not an ending."

"You know there's such a thing as having too much pride, right? I'm not saying you do. Just don't rule out all of your options because you think it says something negative to ask for help. When I decided to write full-time, I was terrified I couldn't swing it and at first, I didn't. I moved back in with my parents for six months. I felt like a total failure. Like I should have realized quitting my job to chase a dream was idiotic. Those six months damaged my pride but I recouped it when I landed on my feet."

Hailey smiled at her, doing her best to turn her own mood

around. "I appreciate you sharing that. I won't rule anything out. I just don't want to wave a 'help me' flag at the first sign of trouble."

They were finishing up the salads that Hailey would deliver first thing in the morning, dressings on the side—shoot, she needed to remember to order more mini to-go containers. A knock on the front door brought her chin up, making her realize how long she'd been hunched over. Wes stood on the other side of the door, a tall, dark-haired teenager at his side. She remembered those years well—those ages where she'd felt so grown-up, ready to take on the world, but young enough to believe the world wouldn't fight back. *Ha. Those years. You felt like that before the rent increase.*

Brushing her hands off on her apron, she went to let them in. She smiled at Wes, then greeted the teen. "You must be Leo."

"Yes, ma'am."

She locked the door after them. "Call me Hailey. This is my friend Fiona."

Wes and Fiona said hello after Leo shook her hand.

"That's a lot of salad," Wes said.

"Catering gig," Fiona said, setting the prepared cups in a flat so they could be transferred to the walk-in fridge.

"You're letting Fiona help." Wes's gaze twinkled.

"She has her food safety certificate. Trust me, it's an uneven trade at best," Hailey said, shooting Fiona a look.

Her friend laughed. "She's right. I might still owe her even after this."

"Have a seat, Leo," Hailey said.

"I'll go help Fiona," Wes said, giving Leo an encouraging shoulder squeeze.

Leo brushed a hand through his short, curly hair. He waited for Hailey to sit before taking the chair across from her.

"This is fairly informal, Leo. I need help desperately with the Christmas season coming and Wes has already vouched for you. Tell me why you want to work here." She'd never interviewed anyone before but he didn't have to know that. It was kind of thrilling but she was nervous too. She might need this kid more than he needed her.

"I like working. I'm saving for college." Simple. He reminded her of Wes when they'd had dinner with Aidan and Ana. She smiled, wondering if Wes had coached him: "say only what needs to be said."

She felt Fiona and Wes's presence and momentarily wondered if she should have googled what to ask in job interviews. She cleared her throat, reminded herself she was in charge. "You'll have a variety of duties, including helping customers, prep work, and deliveries. I don't mind training you for each of those things and others as they come up."

He leaned in, his gaze more mature than his years. "Whatever you throw my way, I'll catch it. I'll do my best. You have my word."

Straight shooter. She liked that. More than that, her instincts told her Leo would be a good fit. She was tired of second-guessing herself. She'd gotten here without any savings and would get over the next hurdle the same way. "Can you start tomorrow?"

She'd deal with the rent increase. Everything would be okay. She kept wondering if others believed in her but if she didn't hire Leo, when she knew she needed someone, it would be like she didn't even believe in herself.

"Yes, ma'am."

She shook his hand. "Hailey. Would you like a salad?"

He laughed. "Sure."

"Good. You can make your own. It'll be good practice."

She watched him walk behind the counter, wash up. Her gaze met Wes's and she saw a myriad of emotions. They mirrored what she felt. Most of which was happiness.

17

"I would have helped you make salads. This is a ridiculous trade," Wes said. They'd decided to shop right after she closed her store that Saturday because the speed dating started at eight.

"You don't have any food prep training. Plus, it's not really a trade. She asked me to go so she didn't have to go alone. I would have done it even if she didn't make salads." Hailey put two boxes of the same cereal into the cart. Wes pulled one out, set it back on the shelf.

The store was fairly quiet even at this time. Most people probably didn't spice up their Saturdays with a supermarket visit but Hailey had come to love this part of her week.

"I thought you didn't want to date." His voice was clipped.

Hailey stopped, a hand on the cart. "I don't. I'm going for a friend. But maybe it wouldn't be so bad to test the waters, you know?"

"You could try an app," he said, lips twitching.

"Would you invent one just for me the way you did for Everly?"

He laughed, pushed the cart forward. "No. Chris was so mad about that app. It was his idea but he kept complaining about the guys on it. They were all screened but he didn't like the fact that she was dating. I'm not getting involved in anyone's dating life again."

"Come with us tonight."

"What?" Now he stopped the cart.

"It would be good for both of us. Come on. It'll be fun. We'll go, see what the Love Gods have in store for us, and then go to dinner after. You like Fiona. It's for her."

Wes frowned. "For her article. I don't want to be part of an article. It's one of the reasons I was happy to leave New York."

Hmm. So he hadn't seen it. "Speaking of," Hailey said, grabbing her phone from her basket inside the cart. She pulled up the web page she'd pinned. The business section of *The L.A. Times* had released a statement from Ana and Aidan's company. Turning the phone, she showed Wes. "You might have wanted to mention your desire to stay out of the news to your new business partner."

Wes took the phone from her, looked closer. She'd committed it to memory. *New York's finest brothers join forces with former sibling models making this the sexiest collaboration since Beyoncé and Jay-Z teamed up with Tiffany's.* To be fair, it was the newspaper's headline, not Ana's. The article was her commentary on a very lucrative and hopefully successful merger.

A growly sigh left his lips as he passed the phone back to her. "She mentioned she was going to announce it. No reason for the headline though. It diminishes the whole thing. It's a great merger. An excellent acquisition on our part and instead of saying that, they talked about Ana and Aidan's red-carpet days. Just what my father needs to stick his pins in a little further." The red-carpet stuff had only been mentioned in the end, yet Wes's whole body seemed to vibrate with tension.

"What do you mean?"

He shook his head. "My father has lawyers all over everything we do, trying to find some sort of basis for suing us. It's his way of continuing to assert power."

"I don't understand how your father can be so toxic and you and your brothers are so great."

Wes gave her a weak attempt at a smile. "I think when you grow up like that, you either shut your eyes and follow suit or you open them wide and head in the other direction." They started walking, turning down the next aisle. "What about your parents? With the holidays coming up, will you see them?"

She avoided his gaze because he had enough parent issues of his own. "They booked a two-week vacation to Mexico over Christmas. They're flying out of LAX and offered to meet me there for a drink before they leave."

"How nice of them to set aside a little time. How do you seem so okay with it?"

The indignation on her behalf was oddly sweet.

She put her hand on his arm. "What choice do I have? I could keep trying to get them to include me like I did while I was growing up or I can move on and make my own life. My own family. They did their job. They raised me, supported me. They've never denied me anything. Some people only know how to love one way. I just remind myself that I don't want to be that way. It took me a bit to realize I also don't want to be *loved* that way by anyone else." Dorian had taught her many things.

The look he gave her sent an unpleasant shiver up her spine. "Some people don't know how to love at all."

Taking a new approach, Hailey looped her arm through his. "That's it. Enough of this. You're coming to speed dating tonight."

"Nope."

"Yes."

"Or no." He pulled two cans of tomatoes off the shelf, making her smile.

"Please?"

Looking up from where he was rearranging the items in his share of the cart, he groaned. "Don't look at me like that."

"Pretty please?" She clasped her hands together.

"Science fiction movies for the next three Saturdays in a row."

Laughing, she nodded. "Done. Let's grab this stuff and just order the rest online."

He sighed like she was hopeless. "We're right here. Let's finish the job. Tell me about Leo's first couple of days."

They fell back into the routine but Hailey was distracted by the idea that even though it wasn't their intention, they could both have dates before the end of the evening.

"I cannot see Wes doing this," Fiona said for the third time as they waited by the bar. They'd put on their adhesive name tags. Hailey had been tempted to put a fake name for fun but it seemed to negate the purpose. She wasn't sure anymore of her real reason for being here. To help Fiona? Wes? Herself? To see if anyone found her remotely attractive or intriguing? God. What if no one did? That'd be a kick to the head.

It's just for fun. Just for fun. It didn't feel like fun. Men and women were separated like they were at an eighth-grade formal. The guys clustered in a group but didn't really talk to each other. The women told each other how good they looked and checked each other's lipstick. Hailey felt like she was back in high school on the wrong side of the cafeteria. Fiona started chatting with a woman she knew to the right of her while Hailey's insides turned into a spin cycle.

Heat pooled at the base of her neck, making her rethink the whole leave-it-down idea. *Up. I should have put my hair up. Down looks like I didn't try. Up is sexy.* She mumbled something—at least she thought she did out loud—to Fiona and pushed through the crowd of women. She needed some air. Head down, the murmur of voices a nauseating buzz, she hurried for the front door. She saw black dress shoes before it registered she was on the straight path to a—

"Oof." Collision.

Hands gripped her shoulders, gentle but firm. Inhaling

sharply, the apology ready to tumble out, her senses immediately calmed. *Wes.*

Hailey tilted her head back, willing her lungs to resume function. She'd know his scent anywhere. It was like her favorite sweater. Nothing else felt quite the same.

"Hey. That's one way to make an impression, but I think you're going the wrong way."

She shook her head, mini hammers pounding in her temples. "I can't. This was stupid. I thought I could do it but I can't."

"Okay."

Her breath whooshed out of her lungs. No judgment or censure. Just, okay. She didn't know what to do with that. So, of course, she babbled.

"I don't know if I'm ever going to be ready to date again, to put myself out there in a way that tells someone, here's my heart, it's available for you to stomp, mess with, and screw up."

Wes wrapped an arm around her shoulder, led her to the front door. She loved that the air was warm, with just a hint of November chill. Moving them to the side of the art deco building, he braced her against the wall and stepped back, meeting her gaze. His was patient, steady, and caring.

"I wouldn't make that your opening line," he said.

Hailey laughed, smacked his chest, then noticed he was dressed very nicely in a crisp blue-and-white-striped polo, a pair of dark gray dress pants, and those shiny black shoes. "You look good."

"That's better," he said. "Start with a genuine ego boost. What else you got?"

She laughed again, the buzzing and pounding in her head receding. "I can't. Seriously. You look good. Fiona's in there like it's a day at the spa. You guys do this. I'll wait. We'll eat after."

"I think you need this more than either of us."

"Ouch."

He shook his head, took a step closer so the tips of their shoes were touching. People walked past them, going into the restaurant.

"People don't think California is ever dark. They're so used to the sun, it's all they expect. All they see."

Her brows pushed together. It was sunny here most of the time. Wes's hand reached out, rested gently on her shoulder, and a different sort of buzz hummed along Hailey's skin. All the way down to her fingertips.

"It reminds me of you. You're so positive, so upbeat. I forget you've been hurt. That you've seen the other side of happiness. You need this, Hailey. Not so you can get a date right away but so you can open the door again. Someday."

"You didn't want me to do this. You thought it was dumb. You didn't want to do it."

His smile was quiet. She loved that one. "But I'm here. Because you thought it would be good for me. We don't have to sign over our feelings tonight. We just have to be open to them."

She poked him in the shoulder. "Suddenly, you're smart?"

He laughed, dropped his hand. "Actually, I've always been smart. Above average across the board."

She rolled her eyes. "Let's go."

When she stepped forward, his fingers circled her wrist. "You're okay?"

Taking a deep breath, she let it out. "Yes. No matter what happens, at the end of the night, I don't have to leave alone."

18

So much for bowing out gracefully. He'd dressed, second-guessed his agreement the whole way here, and then decided Hailey deserved to have him tell her in person he was out. Except now, he didn't want to go. Not because he wanted to find a date—he'd rather go back on the apps than this, and that was saying something— but because he wouldn't ditch his friend.

Even though he'd felt the vibrating hum of tension when he'd seen her, which he recognized as more than just friendly feelings, she was his *friend*. Outside his siblings, probably his best friend. He truly enjoyed being with her, and seeing her upset like that unnerved him, made him want to fix it. Which, ironically, she'd hate.

He couldn't fix her past or what hurt her but he could stay and be her wingman. That's what friends did. Did anyone actually believe this shit? Five minutes for love? Fine. He could admit a spark took less than five minutes but really, what were the statistics on relationships formed in this setting long-term?

As a tall, broad-shouldered man tapped on the microphone, Wes looked over at Hailey. She seemed to be breathing a bit easier now. He'd recognized the panic because he'd been there himself more than once. She smiled, looking so lovely with her hair down, her cheeks adorably flushed. She wore a pair of dark jeans that fit her well, emphasizing her enticing curves. Her floral top had two little strings dangling right between her . . . *what the fuck are you doing? Checking out your friend?* He felt mad at himself. *The only thing you could offer her unconditionally is what you have between you now.*

"You're frowning," she whispered as the man at the front explained the rules.

"I'm not."

"Why would I lie?"

He winked at her, trying to forget that seconds ago he'd been on a visual tour of her body. "To throw me off my game."

She laughed loud enough to make the host stop, then buried her face against his arm. "You have no game." It was whispered from somewhere in the vicinity of his armpit.

"They don't know that." He loved making her laugh.

The announcer continued after someone asked a question. "If you make a connection, put a star beside that person's name and we'll explain how to make contact at the end of the night. We ask that you move promptly when the buzzer goes so everyone gets their chance to visit. The most important thing is to have fun. Very worst-case scenario, you're going to meet some new people tonight." The guy's jovial tone suited a carnival setting more than a romantic restaurant, but people clapped excitedly.

"Do we need a signal?" Fiona asked, nodding to Wes in greeting.

"Like a safe word?" Hailey whispered.

"I think we're good. If we don't like it, we can leave," Wes said.

Fiona folded her hands together, tapping her fingers with a wicked gleam in her eyes. "That's what they want you to believe."

"I get to pick the next ten activities after this," Wes said on a groan.

"Sounds like a lot of nights grocery shopping," Fiona countered.

Wes gave Hailey a mock glare. "We do more than grocery shop."

Fiona pretended to smack her head. "Right. Don't forget the

video games. Geesh. If I had your money, I'd be bathing in champagne and throwing parties every night."

Hailey bit her lip but Wes could see the hint of her smile. He looked at Fiona, saying deadpan, "Pretty sure Noah said the champagne baths aren't as comfortable as you'd think."

A buzzer sounded. "Ladies at the tables, please."

"Good luck," Wes said. He wasn't sure which of them would need it most.

His phone vibrated in his pocket but Wes did what he always did: put his focus into a decided-upon task, giving it his full attention.

The first woman he sat with, Julie, had oversized, red-framed glasses. He sat down, promising himself an ice-cold beer after this.

"Hi, Wes."

"Hi, Julie."

It was like interviews in date form.

"I'm a Gemini. How about you?"

"Excuse me?"

"Your sun sign. Scorpio, Taurus, and Pisces are not great matches for me. When's your birthday?"

"January twenty-eighth." Apparently he was the interviewee.

She clapped her hands together. "Aquarius. We're a great match."

Based on that? "Off to a good start," he muttered.

"What do you do?" She leaned forward on the table, her arms purposely accentuating the low-cut V of her blouse.

Wes looked up at the ceiling. "Cybersecurity." It was the simplest answer.

"Fascinating," she said, enthusiasm dripping in every syllable.

He wasn't trying to be a jerk but this was going to be painful. He lowered his gaze carefully, stopping at her eyes. "It can be. How about you?"

"Dog grooming. Do you have a furry friend?"

He almost laughed. "Other than my brothers? No."

She pointed at him. "Oh, you're a funny and sexy one. That's a double thread."

Wes winced. "Threat."

She stiffened. "Excuse me?"

"The term is 'double threat.'"

The buzzer went.

Only instead of being saved by the bell, it just meant he had to endure more.

~~~~~~~~~

"Drink it," Fiona said.

The three of them had left without starring anyone's names. They found a little pub around the corner, slipped into a booth, and Fiona had promptly ordered a round of tequila. The good stuff.

Hailey wrinkled her nose. "I don't like tequila."

"I'm good with whatever washes the taste of speed dating out of my mouth," Wes said, taking the shot.

Fiona laughed, lifted hers, but waited for Hailey. "Come on. You can order what you want next."

They both downed it but Hailey made a horrified face after hers, making Wes and Fiona laugh.

"It wasn't all bad," Fiona said.

"Really?" Hailey asked. "One of them asked my waist, shoe, and bra size."

Fiona grimaced. "Maybe he was into fashion."

Hailey sipped at her vodka 7. "Somehow, I don't think so. I know everyone is on edge at those things. The one guy . . . Carl. He was nice. Science teacher at the high school, three sisters, three nieces. Wants to start a family."

"Carl wants your clothes on his floor." Wes gulped half his beer.

Hailey's jaw dropped. Wes was rarely so blunt. "He does not." Hailey chewed on her bottom lip. Her continuous glances toward

Wes throughout the evening left her with the same thoughts about many of the women he'd sat with. Their admiration was easy to see in their expressions. "Peter. He was forty-one, divorced, and looking to find someone who wasn't afraid of new adventures."

"Like your clothes on his floor," Fiona said with a giggle.

Wes tapped his glass to Fiona's. "Those things are just a more civilized version of grinding up on strangers in bars."

Fiona snorted. "Jesus. Did Daddy Warbucks just say 'grinding up on'? I need to pour tequila in my ears so I never hear that again."

"You guys are cynics. Cynics without a cause." She set her glass down with a smack. "I have reason to doubt being in a relationship. Good reasons. You two are just pessimists."

"Hey. I have my reasons," Fiona said. "Guy number eight asking me if I liked sensual oils is a great reason."

Wes laughed. "One woman asked if I was into Kama Sutra."

"That's not so bad," Hailey said, her expression suggesting otherwise.

He pinned her with his gaze. "She asked how flexible I was."

Both women laughed.

The waitress came around so they ordered a plate of nachos to share and another round of drinks.

"How flexible are you?" Fiona asked when she left.

"He won't do yoga with me," Hailey said.

Wes pointed at Fiona. "You have her for that. I'm your grocery, video game, movie night friend. She can be the rest."

"Hey," Fiona said. "I bet I could beat you at Mario Kart. I'll have you know, I play with my nephew every weekend."

"Challenge accepted," Wes said.

"Can we agree, for now, speed dating was a bust?" Hailey asked.

"No way," Fiona said. "I've got wicked ideas brewing for an article. Oh, I should try out my newest quiz on you two."

"Since I'm not a twelve-year-old girl or Chris, I'm going to pass on the quiz."

Hailey nudged him with her hand. "Be nice." She turned to Fiona. "What's the quiz?"

Fiona snickered. "What kind of friend are you?"

Wes groaned, lifted his hand. "Check, please."

19

Wes didn't love crowds of strangers but when so many of the people he cared for were in one large group, it was a different story. Noah's house rang with activity. Music pumped, people laughed and talked, delicious food scents teased them along with the ocean breeze. He tried to imagine what it would be like even five years down the road. Would he have nieces and nephews running around? He smiled, pretty sure the answer was yes.

"What the hell are you smiling about?" Noah set a beer in front of Wes, passed one to Chris.

They were out on the back porch discussing their father's lawsuit. Wes was pissed off about it too, but it was hard to hang on to a bad mood with the women laughing from the grass where they played bocci.

"I'm happy. Is that okay?" Wes took a long drink of his beer, enjoying the crisp, cold flavor.

"You're happy our dad is a dickhead?" Noah glared at him.

"I think he might be referring to the scene on the lawn. Makes me pretty damn happy, too." Chris's grin went all dopey when Everly looked his way.

Grace, Hailey, and Fiona were on one team with Tara, Everly, and Tilly on the other. Morty was napping in the house. Or, as he called it, preparing himself for the Thanksgiving feast.

Noah moved to the railing and set his beer down, looking out, past the grass, toward the beach. It was usually Wes tied in knots.

"You get that even though he isn't going to win, he can drag this out, tie up our portfolio with red tape."

He didn't want to feel guilty for living in the moment. "We do. I do. I'm sorry. I had a moment of being grateful. What a weird thing on a day like today, huh?"

"Stop. Both of you. We all know what's at stake. We have lawyers to deal with this shit and deflect it. Dad wants to get in our heads, under our skin. I say we don't let him."

Wes opened his laptop, pulled up his files on Squishy Cat. "To that end, I've instructed our lawyer to go ahead and file a no-contact order. He won't be able to stop himself from doing that so we can slap back at him. Every time he violates the court order, it'll weaken his case."

Chris and Noah looked at him. Wes felt the heat of their stares. He looked up. "What?"

"You don't have to make those decisions on your own," Chris said. Sometimes Wes wished Chris was the oldest but then remembered what it had been like growing up and didn't want that for his brother. "It's an excellent step. I have a meeting next week to interview some candidates for a board of directors for the community center."

"Stop working," Grace hollered at them. "You're wrecking our game."

Noah's smile was instantaneous. "Sure, Gracie. It's our fault."

She stuck her tongue out at him, making him smile wider. Grabbing his beer, he took a seat next to Chris, across from Wes.

"God, I love her. Sometimes it messes with my head how much," Noah said, staring at the beer bottle in his hands.

Wes's attention got stuck on his brother's tone. He truly didn't mind the changes or challenges that came along with being in love. Wes was surprised by his need to squash the small seed of jealousy in his gut.

Chris tipped his head back against the pillows, let his eyes drift shut. "I get that. It feels overwhelming to have so much of your happiness tied to another person and their feelings."

It was a perfect segue for something he'd put off bringing up. Wes cleared his throat. He didn't want to piss his brothers off but reality intruded. It was his job to look out for them. "It would be worthwhile, since you're both living with women you love, to consider how tightly you want them tied to your finances in the future."

Chris's eyes popped open. He sat up straight. "Are you talking about prenups?"

Wes looked out at the yard where Hailey was bent over laughing at something Grace was saying. A warm buzzing feeling filled his chest. "Yes. As happy as you are, protecting yourselves and your assets, *our* assets, is just good business."

Noah set his beer down with a slam, making it fizz over the top. "Screw that. Grace is it for me. I'm not asking her to sign anything."

Wes rolled his eyes. "Could have called that one."

Noah made a dismissive noise. "Whatever, man. If I mess things up and she leaves me, she can take what I have. Nothing matters without her. Least of all money. She wouldn't want it but, as you said, we're *living* together, so she'd deserve her share of it."

Wes's chest tightened. This right here is what love did to a person's brain. It was this sort of thing that terrified him to his core. Would he gladly step aside from everything just to feel a chemical explosion of feelings? "Her share, absolutely. But not of our business. Would you really give up everything you've achieved, what you've worked for, what *we've* worked for, if your relationship ended?"

His father had made his mother fight for her share as a way to get back at her and, oddly enough, get her back. Of course, it didn't work and things only became more toxic. His brothers would never do that to the women they loved.

Chris held up a hand. "Don't get into this right now. You don't get it, Wes. I understand what you're saying. Noah, you know he's looking out for us. His brain only operates on one setting and that's smart business practice. But Wes, man. There's nothing remotely businesslike about falling in love."

His skin heated and he hoped his cheeks didn't darken, giving away his frustration. Snapping his computer closed, he nodded, his jaw tight. "While I haven't been in love, I do understand wanting to protect someone, which is what both of you want for your future spouses. That's all I'm doing here. Watching out for people I love." They didn't see the parallel but just as they'd do anything for Everly and Grace, so would he, for them.

"Let it go. Grace was right. It's Thanksgiving. Let's put work away. How many holidays did Dad fuck up with work?" Noah shook his head like he was remembering something unpleasant.

"Too many. Either of you talk to Mom?" Chris asked.

"I spoke with Ari this morning. She was flying out to meet up with her from now through Christmas." Wes hadn't realized until he saw her face on the screen this morning how much he missed her. He'd enjoyed talking to her so much and wished she could meet Hailey. Wished she were here now.

"I'll call her later tonight," Noah said.

The women were heading to the porch. Grace went straight to Noah's lap. Everly sank down beside Chris, nestled into the crook of his arm. Wes was happy for his brothers but he worried about their inability to separate the emotional from the practical.

"Hey," Hailey said, sitting on the ottoman. Her happy gaze landed right on him and his heart muscles pinched. *Not the same.*

Fiona and Tilly went into the house while Tara took a seat in the rocking chair.

"It's a bad sign when I'm tired from throwing a little ball around," Tara said, leaning her head against the cushions.

"Getting your ass kicked is hard work," Grace said. She took a drink of Noah's beer.

"Why is it so serious up here?" Tara looked around at all of them.

Hailey met Wes's gaze and his heart did that twinge thing again. It was uncomfortable and getting harder to dismiss but if anything, his brothers' stubbornness strengthened his resolve.

"You okay?"

"We're fine. Conversation got a bit heavy. Our dad's being a pain in the ass." Chris kissed Everly's cheek and took her hand. She gave him a shy smile but even from where he sat, Wes could see her gaze was full of love and trust. *Of course Chris would want her taken care of. Grace as well.* Maybe his brothers weren't all wrong.

"I hate lawyers. I hope we don't need one," Tara said.

Grace murmured something to Noah, who looked at Tara. "How'd it go with the landlord? That guy has an army of suits around him. It's impossible to have a face-to-face conversation with him."

Tara nearly snarled. It was strange given her typically even temperament. "I was face-to-face with him and didn't enjoy it."

Wes looked at Hailey, who was playing with the stitching on the hem of her shirt. "What am I missing here? Is this about the merchants' meeting?"

Tara gave Wes a strange look. "Yes. Our rent went up twenty-five percent."

"What?" Wes sat up straight. "That's outrageous."

"Isn't that illegal?" Everly asked.

Noah shook his head, his forehead creasing with his deep frown. "No. Not for commercial real estate. He's up to something."

"What do you mean?" Tara leaned in but Hailey still hadn't said a word.

"We want to purchase some property in the square so I've been researching it. Your bank of shops is owned by the same person. It's the most profitable strip on the square. If he's raising your rent that much, he's making a power play. He either wants the renters out so he can do something different or he's in trouble and needs an influx of cash."

Wes opened his computer again. "Who is this guy?" He didn't want to be stuck on the fact that Hailey hadn't said a word to him.

Fiona joined them, iced tea in hand. "What guy?"

"The rent-raising bastard," Tara said.

Looking at Hailey, she smiled. "Good. You told him."

Wes stopped typing, looked at Hailey. "No. She didn't. Tara did."

Hailey gave him a sassy look. "What? I don't report to you, mister."

"Now isn't the time to be funny. You just took on Leo. Are you even okay with the increase?"

Her amusement fled, her lips flattening even as heat lit her gaze. "I'm perfectly okay handling my own business. I'm working with the merchants just like Tara. We talked about this, Mr. Fix It."

She stood up to move past him, brushing her legs against his knees.

Fiona sat down next to Tara. "She's a bit touchy about her independence."

"'Stubborn' is a better word," Wes said, hurt that Hailey hadn't told him.

Fiona sighed. "You guys should know better than anyone what it's like to step away from all the support beams and stand on your own."

She wasn't wrong but that didn't douse the fire inside of him, the need to do what he could. Maybe he understood his brothers' earlier stance better than he thought. What would he give to protect Hailey? And she was only his friend. He looked at Tara. "What's his name?"

"Logan Vanderben. Owns that row of shops and three high-rises downtown," Noah said.

Wes typed in the name. He could be inside the guy's hard drive if he wanted to be but stuck to a regular Google search. Vanderben looked like a pompous ass. He reminded Wes of a younger version of their father.

"We are planning to contest it, Wes. I think Hailey is trying not to worry." Tara gave him a tight smile.

"Most food businesses go bust in the first year," Wes said.

"Thank you for your optimistic outlook, Mary Poppins," Hailey said from over his shoulder. He looked to where she was leaning on the doorjamb.

"Hailey. That's not what I meant," he said. He hated the look of hurt that crossed her expression.

"Yes it is. And you're right. But that doesn't mean mine will be one of them."

"Of course it won't," he said, feeling both in the spotlight and like they were in their own bubble.

"Because I'll work my ass off to make it thrive." Her tone was strong but her gaze was vulnerable. Soft. Sad. He really hated that.

Closing his computer, he set it aside. "I know you will. You have an incredible work ethic. But there are things we can look into to prevent—"

She held up a hand. "If you want to do something that is in *your* best interests because you and your brothers were already looking into property there, do that. Do whatever it is you all do. But don't do it for me. I do not need to be saved by anyone. I'm not in this alone."

She took a deep breath, let it out. "Tilly said dinner is ready." She turned on her heel and walked in. Wes waited until the others had gone inside, giving himself an extra minute.

She said she wasn't in this alone, but in no way did she mean she'd lean on him. Why the hell did that bother him so much?

20

No one seemed to mind that she chose a walk on the beach after dinner rather than the football game. It was lovely to have a big group of people who were comfortable with each other. A family of their own choosing for some of them. She was worried about how much she enjoyed being part of it.

Hailey had craved finding her own place so badly that relationship after relationship ended with her feeling more lost. With Dorian, he'd let her into a world that fascinated her, let her believe he felt all of the things she did, that they were building a future together, and then he snatched it away. Told her it meant nothing.

Not to her. It meant a hell of a lot to her, and even though she could feel the difference between Dorian and these people, her heart was still hesitant. And healing.

When she returned to the house, most of the group was eating pie by the firepit in the yard. Wes was on the porch chatting with Morty, who was telling a tall tale of the Thanksgiving he'd caught his own turkey.

Wes's smile settled some of the unrest inside of her, sending her thoughts in a different direction. She was definitely attached on that front. If they hadn't agreed to friendship, she'd be worried about her heart. Without the boundaries, he was a man she could fall far and fast for. It was equal parts irritating and sweet that he wanted to fix things for her. The others, too, were ready to rally and come to her defense. She'd learned the hard way, more than once, that standing on her own was essential. So was falling on her own. She wanted to be her own landing.

"The bastard nips me right here," Morty said, spreading his index and middle fingers apart to show a rough patch of skin. It definitely looked like a scar but whether or not it was really from a turkey, she couldn't say.

She sat on the couch with Wes but left a bit of space between them. Every now and again, she'd sit too close or inhale too deeply. Something would shift inside of her. Like she'd moved from perfectly fine to longing without warning. It was disturbing because most of the time, she didn't look at him like that.

Wes glanced at her, clearly biting back a smile or laughter or both. "I don't know if I could eat a turkey, or any animal, I had to catch."

Morty stood up, shook his head. "That's because kids these days are too soft." He looked at Hailey. "Not you, darlin'. You could probably wrangle a turkey with one hand and a smile."

She wasn't sure if that was a compliment. "I can honestly say I've never tried."

When he walked past them, going into the house, both Wes and Hailey laughed.

"You okay? How was your walk?"

The ocean air wafted around them with a hint of the fire. It smelled like happiness and warmth.

"It was good. I can't believe you guys played football after that meal."

"It's more fun that way," Wes said, his smile morphing into a more serious expression. "I'm sorry about earlier."

"I know. Me too. I shouldn't be so defensive."

"I shouldn't be so pushy." He looked like he wanted to say more.

"No, you shouldn't," she said, keeping her lips flat.

Wes laughed, knowing she was joking.

"I didn't think you'd forgive me so easily. I had a whole thing planned," Wes said.

"Oh yeah? Maybe I'm still mad." She grinned at him.

His laugh was sort of like the breeze and the warmth. It cocooned her, made her grateful for one more thing.

"We can do it in the car."

"Excuse me?"

He laughed. "Keep it clean, Sharp. You'll see."

They said their goodbyes with hugs and promises of seeing each other soon. Grace and Everly were coming into the shop next week after some shopping. They'd invited her along on a shopping trip but Hailey needed to check her calendar. Her catering events plus the increase of traffic at the store and training her two employees—that's right, she had two staff members—were time-consuming.

In the truck, she did her best to wait him out. She leaned her head against the seat, all breezy and nonchalant. He adjusted the stereo, checked all his mirrors, double-checked the heat settings before finally backing out of the drive. Once they were on their way, he chatted about the traffic, the meal, and the games.

"You're killing me," she finally said, looking at his profile. The moon was shining through the window, illuminating his sharp jaw and just slightly crooked nose. He had a good face. A good heart. He called her on her stubbornness but he had a healthy amount, too.

"It's been five minutes," he said.

"Since we left, yeah. But like, twenty since you said anything."

"You're such a kid sometimes."

"Says the person who plays video games every Saturday morning, in pajamas, after eating a massive bowl of cereal."

"Fair point. Open my phone. Fiona texted me her quiz."

She nearly squealed but stopped herself. "For real?" She grabbed his phone from the console between them, punching in his ridiculously long password. There was security and then there was Wes.

"I thought you were really mad at me."

She couldn't help her laugh. "If being mad at you would have got you to do one of her quizzes before, I would have lied."

"No lying. It's in the guide."

"I don't remember seeing that specifically." She pulled up the text.

"Trust me, it'll be there the next time you look."

She laughed. "Shush. Here it is. *What kind of friend are you?* Looks like we'll end up being margaritas, highballs, craft beer, or wine."

"I'm on the edge of my seat."

His blend of teasing and sarcasm didn't faze her. She read each of the questions, trying to downplay how much fun she was having. Fiona was not only adorable but brilliant to come up with this. Hailey loved it! She should get her friend to do one of these things with what type of salad a person would be.

"Your friend is late. Do you order their favorite drink, text them to hurry up, or bring it up the next time you're mad?"

Flipping the blinker switch, he sent her a quick glance. "Bring it up the next time you're mad?"

"Careful."

He switched lanes. "Fine. Order their drink. FYI, you're late all the time."

She grinned. "And not once have you had my drink waiting for me."

"I feel so much shame."

Giddy laughter escaped, made better when Wes joined in. "Okay. Your friend is wearing a color they shouldn't. You tell them, suggest a top you love as an alternative, or say nothing."

"I can't picture saying either of the first two so I guess, say nothing."

"I'm putting suggest a top I love."

He sent her another glance, this time with one eyebrow perfectly arched. "I won't wear anything you suggest."

The traffic seemed to come to a stop. Hailey angled herself against the door and the seat so she could face Wes a bit better.

"That loosens your seat belt. You shouldn't sit like that."

"Noted. Okay, you see something your friend would love. Do you buy it, text them a picture of it, or do nothing."

"Buy it."

"That was quick."

He shrugged. "You?"

"Text a picture. Not all of us have vaults of money."

With the traffic at a standstill, he had time to look over. He looked a bit tired, making Hailey's heart pinch. She knew he was stressed about his father and his brothers. "How do you know about my vault?"

With a smile, she scrolled to the next question. "It's your friend's birthday. They don't want fanfare. Do you ignore them and plan a big party, celebrate quietly with the two of you, or do you drop off a gift?"

He started to answer but Hailey sat up straight. "When's your birthday?"

His cheeks flushed. Even in the moonlit cab, she could see hints of pink on his skin. Adorable. "This feels like the speed dating thing all over again. January twenty-eighth. Yours?"

"May sixteenth. Phew. We haven't missed each other's."

"We've missed a few."

She laughed again. "You're funny tonight."

He bobbed his brows in a very uncharacteristically Wes gesture. "Just tonight?"

Hailey couldn't help look at him an extra moment before she responded. He'd deny it but she could tell by the way his dimple flashed, the creases in the corners of his eyes, that he was having fun. She loved seeing him happy. "More so than usual. Okay. Answer the question."

"I'd respect their wishes but hope to at least celebrate with the two of us."

"Okay. I just have to tally." The traffic started moving again.

"Which would you choose?"

"Same as you."

"Which would you want?"

She looked up from her phone. "I don't know. I've never had the whole fanfare thing. My last birthday I spent at a party I didn't want to be at, poured into a tummy tightener that was so tight it left bruises around my ribs."

The truck jolted. Hailey realized Wes had slammed his brakes. Horns honked behind him. "Sorry. Sorry. What the hell are you talking about? Why would you be in a tummy tightener? Why would you go to a party you didn't want to attend for your own birthday?"

Fortunately, he moved with the traffic again but his fingers were clenched white around the wheel.

There goes happy Wes. He was so protective of people he cared about. She wondered if he realized it. She reached over, ran her hand over his arm. "It's okay. Relax."

"No. That's bullshit. First, you don't need to tighten anything. Second, you should do what you want on your birthday."

"Sometimes I forget that you're the oldest in your family. You have this protective streak."

"That's not because I'm the oldest, it's because I care about the people around me. I hope I never meet that asshole you were with."

"Now you sound like Fiona and Piper."

"Excellent. Just what I hoped for."

She laughed, read through their descriptions. Her heart hummed with happiness that she was on his list of people he cared about. It gave her hope that her next birthday would be far better than her last. She'd found her *own* people. Maybe it was time to give herself permission to get attached.

"Come on," he said, his tone more relaxed. "The suspense is killing me."

With a smile, she read the results. "You are a highball. You're honest, loyal, and straight to the point. You have your friends' back even if you don't agree with them."

Something twisted in Hailey's ribs. For a fun quiz, it certainly had Wes pegged.

"Interesting. What are you?"

"I'm craft beer. Laid back, a little too much sometimes but loyal and true. No matter how much time passes, I'm the kind of friend you can always come back to."

He was quiet as he pulled out of the traffic, took their exit off the freeway.

"All these years, I've been trying to figure myself out. Turns out I should have just taken a *Cosmo* quiz."

Hailey laughed. "I'll add it to my grocery list."

"You don't make a list."

"Then I'll add it to yours." He was definitely honest and loyal but in her mind, Wes was more complicated than a simple high-ball. She never would have guessed, months ago, he'd be such a huge, important part of her life. That he'd make her think, push her to be better, support her, or make her laugh as often as he did.

He'd given her all the things she'd craved growing up. He made her feel like she belonged. As she continued to watch him as he drove, she realized it was too late for permission. She was already attached. The best she could do was hang on and hope the feelings were mutual.

21

December

In the kitchen, Hailey went through the calendar, transferring the events from her phone to the physical page and vice versa. She would *not* screw up because of lack of triple-checking.

Leo and Bryce—Esther's grandson—were both on the schedule today. Leo was currently serving a small group of teen girls and Bryce was out handling the lunchtime deliveries. Hailey thought about pinching herself just to be sure it was real. She had *employees*. After finishing inventory, making a list of needed items, she went to help Leo out front.

A couple sat by the window. The three girls he'd helped giggled on their way to a corner table. Hailey's heart was full.

"Hey," Leo said.

"Hey yourself. What are you making?" She watched him chop a variety of vegetables, taking longer than she should have to realize they all had something in common. They were either red or green.

He grinned at her, grabbing a large cup. "The Santa Salad. What do you think?"

Hailey walked closer. He'd chosen a bed of butter lettuce, followed by diced red pepper, green pepper, tomatoes, snap peas, radish, cucumber, red onion and a sprinkling of feta cheese.

"This is beautiful. I love it," she said, holding it up to turn it when he finished layering. Some of the veggies were more expensive this time of year, like the snap peas, but she didn't want to diminish his creativity or enthusiasm. It was another of those tricky situations: they cost more to make, but customers loved specialty items so they sometimes sold better than other menu items.

"For real?" The guarded expression on his face tugged at her heartstrings.

She poured a light vinaigrette with a hint of spice over it, took a few bites. "Absolutely for real. We'll put it on the menu as a December special. I'm really glad you're here, Leo."

"Thanks, Ms. Sh— Hailey. I love it here."

The couple by the window stood, waving as they left. They held the door open for Wes as he walked through.

"Hey, Wes. Want a Santa Salad?" Leo called.

The girls in the corner looked Wes's way then went back to their animated conversation, showing each other their phones.

Hailey smiled as Wes approached the counter. "Good afternoon." He looked so good in a suit, like they were specially cut to fit his body. *They probably are.* He didn't wear them as often anymore. His usual attire included polo shirts and jeans or buttonups and jeans. He looked just as good in jeans.

One side of his mouth quirked up. "Is it formal day?"

She laughed. "You're the one in the suit, you tell me."

"Just a regular day. How's it going, Leo? What's a Santa Salad?"

Leo shot her a look to which she gave a subtle nod. "It's a salad I just made up. It's red and green veggies with feta cheese."

She saw the pride in Wes's gaze when he looked at Leo.

"Nice job. I will definitely try one."

"On it." Leo got busy making another salad.

"What's with the suit?" He looked damn good with his hair tousled a bit differently, making her wonder if he'd actually styled it today instead of just running his fingers through it.

"Meeting in about an hour. Thought I'd stop in here for lunch first."

"What's the meeting for?"

"The community center."

Leo looked up. "When are we doing the fundraiser?"

"That's part of what I'll be discussing today. We're trying to hire a board of directors."

"Why? Don't you, your brothers, Rob, and Ms. Lee run everything?"

Hailey listened, curious about the answer. Wes unbuttoned the front of his suit. "Ms. Lee is the director. The rest of us are volunteers. We'll have more of a pull and impact with the community if we have a board. We'll be able to ask for different funding, get more resources. They'll research options and make decisions that benefit the greatest number of people so we can continue focusing on working with the kids and people who show up."

Leo mumbled something, shrugging his shoulders. "Just don't let them get rid of the three-on-three tournament."

Wes laughed, looked at Hailey. "How's your day so far?"

"Pretty good. I was going through my very large calendar— thanks for that, it takes up half my wall back there."

"So you don't miss anything."

"I won't miss the fact that I now have nine regular weekly orders for lunches at various businesses. Between you, your family, Fiona, and Piper, I'm getting referrals everywhere. People love the convenience of having something healthy brought in. Rob placed an order for double what he's been getting for January because he says it's his busiest month."

"Right. Resolutions."

Leo put Wes's salad on top of the plexiglass. "Here you go."

Wes's gaze widened. "Looks delicious." She hoped Leo recognized his tone as genuine.

"On the house," Hailey said when he reached for his wallet.

He frowned at her but she held up her hand to ward off his words. "Stop. Consider it a thank-you for suggesting Leo."

"Can you sit for a few minutes?" he asked.

She came around the counter, smiling at the girls who were packing up their things to leave. She was about to sit across from Wes when the bell jingled. Her greeting got stuck in her throat when Ana Pergo walked through the door. Her blonde hair was pulled back in a striking knot that accentuated her elegant features. She looked like a modern Grace Kelly. Her smile when she saw Hailey blossomed into a full-wattage grin when she looked at Wes. An uncomfortable prickle of jealousy weaved its way between each of Hailey's ribs.

"Wes! What a happy surprise. Hello again, Hailey."

Wes stood as she walked over. "Hi, Ana."

Hailey smoothed down her apron. "Hi. This is a surprise."

Ana didn't look like she frequented a lot of tiny shops in the square. Her black skirt emphasized her slim hips, the pale pink blouse adding a soft pulse of color. The purse hanging over her forearm cost more than Hailey's grocery bill for the month. She breathed through her nose, irritated at her own observations. She was past comparing herself to others. Wasn't she? She really wanted to be past that stage in life.

"I came to order salads, of course. But Wes, I actually needed to talk to you as well." She looked to where he'd been sitting. "Do you mind if I join you after I speak with Hailey?"

Wes's mouth moved but no sound came out. So much for Hailey's visit with him. His gaze locked on hers and she tried to convey a casual "sure, whatever" vibe.

He looked back at Ana, found his voice. "Of course."

Ana turned to Hailey. "Do you have a few minutes?"

The bell jingled again. A couple of guys Leo clearly knew came through the door.

Business first. Always. "Sure." Why did she feel so awkward?

Ana walked toward the counter. "I'd like to place an order for a staff luncheon we're having in the third week of December."

With another glance at Wes, who was looking at her with an unreadable expression, Hailey kicked herself into gear. "That's great. Is it a holiday event?"

Ana smiled over her shoulder, then turned back to the menu board. "Yes. Just an appreciation lunch. We'll be ordering from next door and a sandwich shop as well but I thought of you and your delightful little salads."

Hailey's fingers clenched. It was a compliment. What was wrong with her?

Ana looked at Hailey again. "I think it would be easiest to just let you choose."

Hailey pulled her phone out of her pocket, pulled up her calendar. "Okay. How many and what date?"

She took the particulars, including a credit card number, promising they'd be delivered. When Ana gave her a fancy business card, Hailey held it in her hand for a moment, wanting to scrunch it into a little ball. Or maybe *she* wanted to scrunch into a little ball until the possessiveness she suddenly felt for Wes passed.

This very nice woman is offering you business that'll probably end up being repeated. What more could you want? Maybe she was tired. Overwhelmed.

She forced a smile. "Are you sure I can't get you anything to eat?"

The boys had settled on the far side of the counter so Leo could chat with them as he cleaned up.

"No thank you. I'll be sure to share your cards with people at our company. I'm just going to chat with Wes. It was really nice to see you again."

"You too. Thank you for thinking of me."

"My pleasure." She turned and walked over to Wes's table, her high-heeled shoes tapping across the linoleum.

Hailey went behind the counter, focused on her phone, making sure she had the details she would then transfer to the physical calendar. That way, Leo and Bryce always knew what was going on as well. Her stomach grumbled, reminding her she hadn't finished her Santa Salad.

She was doing her best not to watch Ana and Wes talk, trying even harder not to wonder what they were talking about, when Leo sidled up next to her.

"You okay?" His voice was low.

She crinkled her brow. "Of course. We just got more business. We're going to have a great month."

"She's got nothin' on you, Hailey."

Hailey turned her head looked at Leo, her heart squeezing. "What? I don't know what you're talking about."

"Oh yeah?"

Her throat went dry and tight at the same time. "Wes and I are friends. That's it. I'm not interested in Wes that way. Ana is lovely. They look great together." She wanted her friends to be happy. *They're talking. That's it. It's probably business.* It was none of *her* business.

Leo patted her shoulder and went back to his friends, leaving Hailey to wonder what Wes thought about Ana. It was more than a little obvious what the woman thought of him as she reached over, placed her hand on his. Wes slipped his hand out from under hers, shaking his head.

When she rose from the table a few minutes later, she shot Hailey a happy smile. "Take care, Hailey. See you soon."

Hailey lifted her hand, saying nothing. Leo stopped talking to his friends when an older woman came through the door after Ana left.

"I got it," he said, turning that happy smile on their customer.

"Bryce should be back shortly," Hailey said, feeling inexplicably off.

She made herself busy, avoiding Wes's gaze while trying to get out of her own head. She didn't want Wes like that. He didn't want her like that. They were friends. Good friends. She needed him in her life. What she did not need was a love interest. Everything was finally going so well; she felt like she was surfacing after being stuck underwater for too long. She could *breathe*.

When she turned around from getting herself a fountain soda, Wes was standing at the counter.

"I have to go. Sorry we never got to chat." He was looking at her strangely.

Hailey shrugged, oversmiled. "We chat all the time. Not every day you get a Grace Kelly look-alike hanging out at the salad shop keeping you company."

"We live in California, Hailey. There are many Grace Kelly look-alikes."

She swallowed. Right. Might as well ask. "So, what did she want?"

A little V appeared between his brows. "She asked if I'd accompany her to an event. A party."

"Oh." She blew out a breath. Wes hated parties. He hated big crowds of people and pretending he was having a good time.

"It's on Saturday so I'll . . . I guess I'll grab groceries earlier in the day but you probably have to be here."

Her gaze widened. "You're going?" She hadn't meant it to sound so accusatory.

Wes ran a hand through his hair, mussing it up. "She put me on the spot. Some of the clients she'd like me to meet will be there."

She could feel Leo's gaze as he helped the woman so she forced herself to loosen her shoulders.

"That's great. Saturdays were meant for dates, not groceries. That's awesome." *Dial it back a bit, Hailey.*

"It's not a date." Wes's voice was tight. Quiet.

A sardonic laugh left her lips without warning. "That woman looks at you the way I stare at a chocolate brownie. It's a date. Which is fantastic. You could use one you didn't find on an app."

Wes's frown deepened, his gaze darkening. She'd hurt his feelings. Shit. What was wrong with her? She came around the counter, pulled his arm so they were away from anyone else.

"I'm sorry. I just don't want you to have blinders on. She likes you."

Again, he tunneled his fingers through his hair. "I'm not looking to date Ana. For a number of reasons, the biggest of which is I work with her."

Had the biggest been because he wasn't attracted to Ana, maybe she would have done something different. But that wasn't what held him back. Hailey needed to push this because if she didn't, it said something about her own feelings.

It said that she'd been reading them all wrong again. She couldn't do that. She couldn't have another one-sided relationship where she fell hard, then fell away. Wes had made it clear he didn't see her like that. There was one night a few weeks ago that he said she reminded him of his *sister*.

"You look good together. Even if it's not an actual date, going out with her, socializing and meeting people will be good for you."

He was watching her far too closely, his jaw tight. "I think I socialize more than enough." His voice lacked emotion. It was the tone he used when he was uncertain about something. A default tone.

"Your brothers don't count." She tried so hard to drown out the little voice in her head but it snuck through: *neither do I*. The thought physically hurt, like a needle poking into her skin.

"I'm going because it'll be a networking opportunity. Can we shop on Sunday?"

Hailey's throat went tight. He wasn't blowing her off. She *did* matter. She was just making too much of things.

A small "Wes" smile appeared. The one he used to convince her to play one more game. "Of course. I need to start Christmas shopping." With the excitement of being busy, Ana popping in, her out-of-the-blue whisper of jealousy, Hailey felt like she'd powered through a snowstorm without proper equipment. Tears threatened but she wasn't entirely sure why. *Just a tad overwhelmed. Everything is good.*

He nodded, looking at her like he wanted to say something. He reached out and squeezed her shoulder, the weight of his hand steadying her from the inside out. "That's perfect. You can help me pick something out for Ari and my mom. I need to get them in the mail."

Yup. She could do that. That's what good buddies who reminded a guy of his sister did. *What is up with you today?*

She pulled in a painful breath. "Good luck with your meeting."

"Thanks. I'll text you later."

She nodded, watching him leave.

"Made you something," Leo said, handing her a fruit cup with copious amounts of whipped cream and chocolate shavings.

She laughed. "If I could afford it, I'd give you a raise."

He smiled, soft and sweet. "Remember that when you can. It'll happen."

It would. She couldn't be sure about a lot of things because they changed in an instant. People fell in and out of love every minute. Tastes changed, friendships shifted. But Hailey could count on her shop, on things continuing to go well because *that's* where her focus—her heart—belonged.

22

"I think you need to go on your own date. Stop worrying about him being on one." Piper pulled a tray of cookies from the oven.

Hailey snuck a cooled one from the rack, breaking it in half and shoving the other half in her mouth just as her cousin turned around.

"Hey! Now you have one less to decorate."

She shrugged, popped the rest in her mouth. When she finished, she took a drink of the soda Piper passed from the fridge. "I'm not *worrying* about him being on a date. I just thought it was weird that she showed up at the store." She could have called in her order.

"Who showed up at the store?" Nick, Piper's husband, came into the kitchen wearing a Lakers hoodie and a pair of checkered pajama bottom pants. He gave Hailey a kiss on the cheek. "How's it going? Who came into the store? Someone famous?"

"Do you know someone famous, Auntie Hailey?" Cassie, one of Piper's eight-year-old twins, asked. She'd followed on her dad's heels. Her bright-red hair was up in two ponytails and she wore an apron.

"Not anymore. I used to," Hailey said, tapping Cassie on the nose, then sneaking another cookie to share with her.

"No more, or we won't have any to decorate," Piper said, her stern mama voice wavering.

"I don't want to decorate cookies," Alyssa, the other twin, said, coming in from the other side of the kitchen. She wore an outfit nearly identical to Nick's. Her red hair had been cropped to her shoulders. It was equally adorable.

Jason, their six-year-old son, who actually had Nick's dark brown hair, followed behind. "I do. I want to make mine look like Iron Man."

Nick scooped him up. "You want to make gingerbread look like Iron Man?"

Jason squeezed his father's cheeks together, nodding seriously.

Nick smiled at Piper in a way that made Hailey's heart muscles stretch too tight. "We've done everything right."

Piper laughed. "Alyssa, if you don't want to decorate, you don't have to."

"I'll decorate yours," Cassie said.

Alyssa shrugged, happy to let her twin do the work. "Can I play Animal Crossing?"

"Nope," both of her parents said in tandem.

Hailey hid her smile. She loved being around their family whether it was low-key and sweet like this or high-energy and chaotic like one of the kids' school events.

"Who came into the store?" Nick asked again, setting Jason on his feet.

"No one. Just a woman who wanted to order some lunches for her company." Hailey hoped that would be the end of it.

She'd mentioned Wes's date tonight in passing, but of course Piper wanted to dig deeper, pull out her *feelings* on the issue. She didn't have any. *Lies. You have too many.* It was fine. What did she care? It had felt weird at the time but everything was normal. As it had been before Ana showed up. Except that he was on a date with her tonight instead of reminding Hailey what she needed for groceries.

Nick looked back and forth between Hailey and his wife. "Guys, go wash up in the bathroom if you want to decorate. Alyssa, you too. Even if you aren't doing cookies."

The kids groaned but took off down the hall. Nick put an arm around Piper, kissing her neck. Hailey's heart spasmed again. Sharply. Just because she missed that particular feeling didn't mean she was upset about Wes being on a date.

"Did you ask her?"

Hailey groaned. "No. She did not. What?"

Piper frowned. "Hey. Why did you say it like that? It's a good thing. There's someone Nick wants you to meet."

"Let me think about it," Hailey said, tapping her index finger on her chin. "I think I'll pass."

Nick laughed. "That's not how I would have phrased it but, told you."

"You can't just pass." Piper put her hands on her hips.

"I think I just did." Hailey grabbed some food coloring, mixed it into one of the little bowls Piper had set out for icing. "I don't want a date."

"No. But you *do* need to meet Nick's friend because he asked us to come to Finnegan's with him. He works with Nick and is friends with the head chef. He jokingly asked Nick if he knew any women as pretty as me. Nick immediately thought of you." Piper leaned into him, wrapping her arms around his waist.

His came around her automatically. Like a needle into a groove, they fit. That's all Hailey had wanted back in the days when she'd thought there was someone for her, out there in the universe. It wasn't that she didn't think that anymore. She just didn't *need* it the way she was once so sure she did. The world didn't stop spinning when she split with Dorian. She got up every day, survived until she could *live*. Before Dorian, she'd been equally sure every guy was the one. It took her time—and none of Piper's analysis— to realize the loneliness of her childhood made her a needier adult than she wanted to be.

Now, she was happy. Really happy. Just because Wes switched plans on what she considered *their* night didn't mean there was a scratch on her own record.

Finnegan's was a new restaurant that had a waiting list as long as Hailey's torso. It was supposed to be incredible, the new "it" place outside of L.A.

"Did you tell him it would be a date?" She grabbed the green food coloring.

"No. But I did tell him you were great and would love the restaurant. There's no pressure. If you and Seth hit it off, great. If not, no big deal." Nick's version sounded better.

Hailey arched her brows. "I can get my own dates, you know."

"I do. I also know you and your cousin, who I love dearly, are absolute sweethearts most of the time but have tempers I'd rather not toy with. I like my balls where they are."

As Piper and Hailey laughed, Jason pulled on his dad's wrist. "Where did you put your balls, dad?"

The adults laughed but Jason looked expectantly at his father. "Right where I left them, buddy."

The girls joined them and they spread out around the island countertop, each of them sharing the colored icings, passing the sprinkles and other toppings. Alyssa seemed to have forgotten she didn't want to participate.

"I'm making my gingerbread BTS members," she said.

"Ambitious," Hailey commented.

"Can I come work at your salad shop?" Cassie asked Hailey.

Hailey grinned. "I'd love that but I already have two employees. But, you guys could come down next Sunday and make your own salads."

The kids looked at their mom. "Can we?"

Piper shrugged. "I don't see why not."

"You could leave the kids with me so you two could get some shopping done," Hailey said, licking icing off her finger.

Nick and Piper exchanged a glance, then both looked at Hailey like she'd offered them her first child.

"What?"

"Are you serious?" Nick asked.

Hailey smiled. "Yes." She drew the word out, wondering if there was something she didn't know.

"Baby, when was the last time we did anything together, just the two of us, outside this house?"

Piper sighed. Deeply. Like her body sagged with the effort of trying to remember. "Well, we're going to go to Finnegan's."

"Are you serious?" Hailey looked back and forth between them. "Why don't you hire a babysitter?"

"We have and we do but not so we can go out. With Nick's schedule, me finishing up my master's, the kids in activities, it just hasn't worked out."

She made a split-second decision. "Next Sunday, I'll come here. You two can go out for a few hours."

The kids cheered. Piper looked like she might cry.

Nick shook his head, patted her on the shoulder. "God bless us everyone."

Hailey laughed. "You guys are a nutty family."

"You're our family, too," Alyssa pointed out.

She wasn't wrong.

~~~~~~~~

By the time Wes picked her up for shopping the next afternoon, she'd mostly worked through the weird jealousy—if that was even the right word—she'd felt about Ana.

"What did you do last night?" Wes asked as they walked into the mall. "I texted you when I got home."

Yup. She'd ignored it. Her maturity—telling herself she'd overreacted—hadn't kicked in until after coffee this morning.

"I went to my cousin's. We decorated cookies, hung out. They have an artificial tree so they set it up, took out all the ornaments so they could decorate today."

"That sounds nice. You're not missing out on that, are you?"

"No. That's a family thing. Will you put up a tree?"

He stopped, looked at her, a serious expression on his face. "I don't know. I hadn't thought about it. Will you?"

"It's Christmas. Of course."

He smiled. "I don't know why I asked. Why don't I just help you with your tree? Then I can keep my place clean. Do you get a real one or fake?"

"Real."

"I'm allergic," he said, wincing.

She laughed. "Fake it is. Where's your list?"

His smile made her feel like they were back on easy footing. Even though she wanted to ask about his date, she didn't want to change the tone.

Wes pulled his phone from his back pocket. "Right here. I need to get something for Ari, my mom, Grace, and Everly." He put his phone away, looked at her. "And you. But not while you're here."

Her stomach plummeted. She couldn't shop in his price bracket. "We don't have to exchange gifts."

Plus, what if by Christmas, he was *with* Ana? She didn't seem like the type of woman who wanted her boyfriend buying his female friend a gift.

"What will you put under your tree?" He tugged a lock of her hair gently, smiling at her with an affection that put her both at ease and on edge.

"Presents for Piper's family."

"We can do a limit if that's what you're worried about. It can be free. We can make our own."

She narrowed her gaze at him, then started walking. "Unless you want a meal for Christmas, I don't know about that. But I like the price cap thing."

They agreed on an amount, making her feel better. She loved giving gifts. Apparently, Wes did, too. He held up two Kate Spade bags, one in pink, one canary yellow.

"Should I get Ari both of these?" He didn't even look at the price.

"Does she love bold colors?" Hailey picked up a soft blue shoulder bag.

"Absolutely. The bolder the better. She's . . . vibrant. Like our mother."

"Your voice changes when you talk about them. It gets softer, more affectionate. Why don't you invite them for the holidays?"

"Can I take those to the cash register for you, sir?" An attendant appeared at Wes's side.

He passed the purses. "Yes, thank you."

The woman looked at Hailey. "Excellent choices, ma'am."

Wes smiled at Hailey when the woman walked away. "Do you want one?"

Her eyes widened. "What? No."

"Wow." He leaned in, his breath tickling her skin. "You really don't like Kate Spade."

She poked him in the arm. "Shh. I do so but I don't want you to buy me a purse."

He nodded, still smiling. "Noted. No purses."

Not what she meant but good enough.

Hailey did her best to swallow down the question that kept trying to pop out of her mouth. As she looked at gorgeous trinkets without seeing them, she finally asked, "How was last night?"

He picked up a blue wallet, similar to the color of the purse she'd put down. "It was fine. What I thought it would be. I met clients, made small talk. I did get a chance to talk to someone who's worked with my father recently. That was an interesting conversation."

Hailey swallowed around the thickness in her throat. He didn't sound overly enamored. *It's none of your business. But it is. You'd ask if it were Fiona. Friends ask questions. Friends are all about the details.* "Will you go out with her again?"

Wes was staring at her, that little V forming between his brows. "No. Not like I think you mean. Do you not like Ana?"

Hailey put her hand on her chest, like she could push back the guilt. "Me? Of course. Why wouldn't I?" *Way to sound chill.*

Wes's brows arched. "I'm not sure."

Hailey tried to laugh it off as they walked to the register. "Ana is great. You guys look fantastic together."

He gave her another strange look. "Just what I'm looking for in a partner, someone who looks good at my side." His tone was dry but he was still looking at her like he didn't understand something.

Join the club. I don't understand me right now either. "Speaking of dates," she said too loudly. "I have one Friday night." *Why? Why did you say that?*

His gaze darted past her head, his jaw giving a subtle twitch. "That's great," Wes said. For one millisecond, she thought maybe he was questioning their status as well but then he looked at her and smiled. His *real* smile.

There you go. He's happy for you. Because friendship is all there is between you two. Which was perfect because it was all she wanted.

"Thanks. We're going to Finnegan's."

"I've heard great things. Who is he?"

They moved forward in the line. "He works with my cousin's husband."

Wes paid for his purchases, took his bags. They walked out, heading toward the food fair because Hailey wanted a drink. She turned her head, watching his profile as they walked. His jaw was tight. Was he holding back? Was she? Why was she so confused right now? She'd gotten so good at reading him but right now, he was a closed book.

"I think it's good you're dating," Wes said as she sipped the soda he'd insisted on buying.

He sounded like he meant it but the usual spark in his eyes, the one that made them look like shimmering ocean water, was missing. "It's just a dinner."

Wes shrugged. The Wes she knew was *not* a shrugger. He was a perfect-posture kind of man. "That's how it starts, isn't it?"

She shrugged, mimicking him. "I'm not sure I know anymore." *If that's true, he had dinner with Ana last night. Maybe he's just trying to be discreet or maybe it's really none of your business.*

He pressed his soda to hers but didn't smile when he said, "To new beginnings."

Hailey blinked too many times in a row. She didn't want to begin again. She wanted to keep going exactly the way they were. She'd been so worried about falling in love again, about being left, she hadn't considered that not all friendships lasted either. *That won't be true for us. We'll add it to the guide. Our friendship stays strong even when we find our people.*

She huffed out a breath, pasted on a smile. "Who's next on your list?"

"My mom. I'm going to get her an iPad."

Hailey shook her head. "I'm so glad we set a limit."

23

Wes looked around the space. Vaulted ceilings, gorgeous windows that looked out at hillsides of other homes.

"This place is fantastic," Wes said.

"What do you think?" Noah asked Chris.

"It's beautiful. I love it."

"You could buy it, give it to Everly for Christmas," Noah said, slapping a folded flyer against his hand.

Chris laughed. "Are you out of your mind?"

Noah looked over at Wes for backup. "It'd be totally romantic, right? A house? That's an epic fucking gift."

"No, Noah. It's something two people buy together. I can't buy a home without letting Everly see it."

Noah folded his arms across his chest. "Ahh. So you just don't know what she likes, huh?"

Wes chuckled, wandering the hardwood floors, loving the open concept between the kitchen and living areas.

"You're an idiot. How did you get Grace to fall in love with you?" Chris wandered the kitchen, running his hand over the granite countertop.

"Looks, charm. I'm basically the whole package."

Chris stopped, looked at Wes. "What do you think? Buy a

woman a house as a gift?" His lips quirked like he was trying not to laugh.

"Hailey wouldn't even let me buy her a purse." His chest tightened with how naturally he'd made the comparison. What he had with Hailey was obviously very different than what his brothers had. Especially since she'd all but told him he and Ana were picture-perfect. The words made his jaw ache. "I think Everly would kill you. For that matter, Grace would do the same."

Noah looked defeated. "Fine. I thought it'd be cool. You get her a tiny little box, put just the key in it. She unwraps it and is all, what's this?" Chris and Wes watched in amusement as Noah mimed the scene. "She looks at you and you're all, our future, baby." He gestured dramatically.

"For the love of relationships everywhere on earth, please stop. Also, maybe you should run Grace's gifts by us," Chris said.

Noah laughed. "I know you can't buy it without Everly seeing it, wanting it too, but seriously, what do you think?"

Chris gave a smile Wes had only seen a handful of times. Absolute contentment. "She's going to love it. Let's set up another walk through."

When they climbed into Chris's SUV, Noah took the front seat because, as usual, he'd called it first. Wes scrolled through his phone, checking his emails.

"How'd your thing go the other night?" Chris asked, meeting his gaze briefly in the rearview.

"With Ana? Fine. I sure as hell don't miss those types of events." Wes leaned back in the leather seat but he didn't miss the look that passed between his brothers. It made his neck itch.

"You know, we didn't have to take on CoreTech. If the Pergo siblings are high-maintenance, we can cut them loose." Noah turned in his seat as he spoke.

"I worked my ass off to get them. Why would we do that?"

Chris, ever the mediator, glanced back again. "We just don't want you taking on jobs you aren't passionate about. We broke out on our own because we wanted to follow our own paths. It's not about amassing the biggest companies for our portfolio. We aren't trying to prove ourselves to anyone this time."

"I know that. But CoreTech looks great in there. They're opening up a New York office. They offer both physical and digital security. It's a good match and once I finish analyzing their current system, I'll have a better idea how to strengthen and expand it. I do think we're at the point we could stand to hire a couple of assistants though. I'm tired of fielding emails."

"We could talk to Penny Lee at the community center. They're doing some résumé-building workshops. People are always looking for work. She said you guys were pleased with the candidates for the board?" Noah turned back around, staring out the windshield while Chris drove.

"Three women, two men. Two of the women were former athletes. They're all a great fit."

They chatted about other investments, their current holdings. They circled around their father, silently agreeing to put a pin in that issue. They pulled up to the radio station a short while later, where Wes and Noah had left their vehicles.

In the parking lot, they finished up their conversation about business.

"Do you want to meet at the gym later?" Chris asked Wes.

"Not particularly but I will," Wes said. He liked running, preferably on a treadmill, which he had in his bedroom. Chris and Noah were a bit more into the gym scene than he was.

"Ask him if he wants to play Wii sports. You'll get more enthusiasm," Noah said, shoving his shoulder.

"I don't see him asking you to go to the gym." Wes smirked. He knew it was just because Noah lived farther away.

"We should run a game of pickup ball at the rec center. If you guys see Rob tonight, ask him about it. I feel like we should do something for the holidays there."

"Everly asked about that. The station sponsors so many community food and clothing drives but maybe we should talk to Penny and see if there's specific needs at the rec center. A way for us to get personally involved."

"Grace would want in on that. How about Hailey?" Noah asked, looking at Wes.

His heart hiccupped. Noah asked like Wes and Hailey were a . . . unit. A couple. They might not be the latter but he sure as hell felt like they were the former.

I think it's good you're dating. Why the hell had he said that? Especially since the words felt like rocks in his mouth. The night of the speed dating, he'd kept her in his sights, wondering if she'd say yes to anyone. He'd had this odd sense of relief when she hadn't found anyone she connected with. At the time, he told himself it was because no one there had been good enough for her.

But then she'd said he and Ana looked good together. Kept acting like they were a foregone conclusion. Was that what she wanted? The idea of Hailey with someone who made her happy shouldn't have left him winded. Maybe he should put that in the guide: we will be happy for each other when the other finds a partner. This didn't feel like happiness. More like he'd been struck from behind.

"I can ask her. We're just friends." His voice must have come out sharper than he intended. Both of his brothers were looking at him with matching curious expressions.

Noah held up his hands. "I wasn't implying anything different. You guys hang out a lot. She hired Leo. I thought she might want to be part of whatever we do."

Wes nodded, rubbed his hand over his mouth. "Yeah. I'm sure she would. I should get going. I want to put together a pitch for the CoreTech programmers."

Again, his brothers exchanged a glance. It was starting to piss him off. "What?"

"Why don't you design the software?"

"What?" He stared back and forth between them.

Chris stepped forward. "You've backed off on designing the apps but you're really good at them. You like it. We were just thinking, you used to love the design piece. You could customize for Core-Tech."

"That would take a significantly longer time," Wes said. He was not only good at it, he loved it, but that made him feel like he wasn't really *working* or doing his part.

Noah lifted both arms, looked up at the bright-blue California sky. "What the hell else are we doing?" He lowered his chin, pinned Wes with a curious gaze.

"I'm not really designing anything at the moment." Though he'd had several story ideas and played around with some gaming development programs. Which was just to keep his brain busy. It was a hobby at best. Except for Hailey's Christmas present. That was more than a hobby to him. It was almost finished.

"We're just saying that we all get to do what we love. What we want. Chris and I feel pretty settled but we're not sure you do. Don't feel like you have to keep expanding our assets, adding on companies. That's not what we're about anymore."

That was part of the problem. They both knew what they were about personally and professionally. Wes had always been secure in his professional path but right now, everything felt up in the air. He didn't know where anything would land. Worse, he didn't even know where he wanted anything to land.

"Thanks for the permission to live my life." He was being an ass but he felt like his skin was too tight. Why did the idea of being able to do what he enjoyed full-time feel like he'd be letting them down?

"Whatever, man. Do what you want," Noah said, waving a hand dismissively at him.

Wes sighed. "I'm sorry. I don't know what I want to do. Sometimes it feels weird for both of you to be so settled. I felt like I was in New York but here, I haven't found my footing yet."

"Well, we have an appointment to walk through the San Verde Square property. Once we have an actual office space we can all agree on, we'll sit down, hammer things out, and decide where we all want to go."

Chris clapped him on the shoulder. "It's okay to be happy, man. We earned it. Figure out what's going to do that for you and grab on." That advice could have applied to his personal or professional life, but he was confused. The things bringing him true happiness could easily slip away. Then what?

With a smile, he said goodbye to his brothers. He really did need to figure out what his piece in their puzzle was. Noah had shifted from corporate, large-scale real estate purchases and development to a much smaller scale. He and Grace had bought a bungalow near Laguna Beach with the intention of remodeling it together. He was more than content. He was happy. So was Chris. He was technically an advisor for their holdings. He took care of the companies directly connected to the radio station but he didn't seem concerned about branching out beyond that.

What did Wes want? Where did he fit? It was the first time in his life that he didn't know.

24

Piper and Fiona did an excellent job convincing Hailey that she should buy a new dress for her not-a-date that she'd told Wes *was* a date. She still didn't know why she'd said it but the fact that he'd been okay with it was reason enough. Her brain was more settled today. Clearly defined boxes had been reconstructed. Wes, friend. Seth, date.

The mall was more crowded that Wednesday night than it had been the Sunday before. Or maybe she was just more tired because *her* store had been busy today. For-real busy. The kind she'd hoped for in those early days. If she could get through the next six months successfully, she really had a chance of things working out long-term.

Though she'd seen a gorgeous dress at the Kate Spade store when they were in there, Hailey had a budget. With Christmas coming, she wanted to be extra careful about sticking to it. Even with the catering jobs, which weren't her favorite, she was hovering on the "just making it" line. When she'd first gotten a job on set, she'd taken on the catering gigs because they seemed fun. Fancy parties with stars everywhere? Yes, please. But it was a lot of work, before, during, and after. Not everyone was nice to behind-the-scenes workers and there wasn't as much glamour as she'd hoped. The money was good, but once she and Dorian got together, he found her side jobs embarrassing. *What if you cater a party I'm at as a guest? That would make me look ridiculous.*

Focus on the good. Like what's in your hand. In a cute little shop that Tara had told her about, she held an adorable dress in her price range. It was pale blue with a fitted bodice and A-line skirt. She held it close as she followed the store clerk toward the dressing room. From the corner of her eye, she saw a black-and-white dress that took her breath away. It was stunning. A retro, Audrey Hepburn–esque style. The sleeves would rest just off her shoulders; the waist was narrow but the skirt flowed out. She'd bet anything it would make a swishing sound if she twirled in it.

"Gorgeous, isn't it?" the young lady asked, following Hailey's gaze.

It was so charmingly graceful. "It really is." She didn't want to ask.

"Would you like to try it on?"

She pulled in a breath between her teeth. She'd want it. Bad. She could tell just from looking at it.

"It doesn't cost anything to try it," the clerk added.

What if it was the same price? "Sure."

The woman grabbed one in Hailey's size and even though she caught sight of the price tag—so not in her budget—she decided to try it anyway. What harm could it do?

It fit like she'd had it specially made just for her body. She forced herself to take it off, try on the other one, which was *just* as pretty. Almost. Sort of. She texted a picture to Fiona and Piper. Why weren't they answering? Telling herself she shouldn't have come alone, she put the other dress back on and took a picture in that one, too. She waited, hoping one of them would respond. When her phone rang, she was still in the black-and-white dress.

It was Wes. She swiped her thumb across the screen.

"Hey."

"Hey back. What are you doing?" He sounded like he was typing while he talked.

"I'm trying to decide between two dresses. I texted Piper and Fiona to get their opinions even though I know which one I should get. Neither of them are replying."

"What are your options? Send me a picture."

"Uh, no."

He laughed. "Why?"

"Because you're not Piper or Fiona."

"Why are you buying a dress anyway? Is it made out of yoga pant material?"

She laughed. God, he knew her well. "Jerk. Can you imagine how cozy *that* dress would be?"

"Come on. Send me a picture." His cajoling tone made her stomach muscles tighten. He didn't use it often.

"This isn't why you called." Though a guy's perspective was one of the perks of Wes.

"No. I called to ask you a big favor. One I should have asked sooner."

"Shoot."

"Nope."

"What?" She moved side to side, watching the dress dance in the mirror. Every woman should have a dress that made her feel this way.

"If you can't ask me my opinion on a dress, I shouldn't ask you for a favor."

"Oh my God. You're annoying. Hang on."

She sent him both pictures then put the phone back to her ear. "I'm getting the blue. It's a better price and more practical."

"Hasn't come through yet. I need a dozen salads tomorrow for a meeting at the community center. I can pick them up but is this enough notice?"

"Of course. That's not much of a favor."

She heard a sharp intake of breath. "Jesus. Neither is looking at you in a dress. You look fantastic in both."

Her heart felt like it was vibrating. When Wes liked something, *really liked* something, he couldn't hide it. Not well. His eyes and tone gave him away. And his tone made her heart do jumping jacks. *Too much caffeine, that's all.* "See? Guy response."

"You should get the black one."

She grinned. "Rich guy response. I'm getting the blue. It's half the price."

"You can't go wrong either way. What is this for, anyway?"

She didn't want to say "date" again. She knew what they were. Hailey felt more certain with Wes than anyone else in her life at the moment. She didn't want to play games just to see his response to the word "date." That was a dangerous game. "My dinner on Friday with Piper, Nick, and their friend."

"Right." He cleared his throat. There was a beat of silence where she couldn't even hear his breathing.

"Wes?"

"I'll pick up the salads at noon tomorrow?"

"Okay."

He hung up and Hailey felt oddly disappointed. She put the black one back, telling herself it was silly to buy something that expensive that she wouldn't wear more than a handful of times. The blue was practical and perfectly lovely.

When she got home later that night, she made a list of salads, sent them to Wes to get his approval.

Wes

Perfect. Thank you again. I owe you.

Hailey

You never owe me. I'm happy to do it and you're paying.

Wes

Which dress did you get?

Hailey

The blue

Wes

You looked beautiful in both. Blue is a great color on you.

Hailey

Thank you

Wes

I know your schedule is tight right now but Chris is having a holiday party for the radio station staff. We were both invited.

Hailey

Yet neither of us work there

Wes

Laugh out loud. We're still invited.

Hailey

Sounds good. Also, did you seriously just type out LOL?

Wes

I don't like acronyms

Hailey

YASAD

Wes

????

Hailey

You. Are. Such. A. Dork.

Wes

If you're not familiar with acronyms, they can be bothersome to decipher.

Hailey

TWSS

Wes

Okay, even I know that one.

Hailey

Do you?

Wes

That's what she said?

Hailey

Yup. Acronyms can also be a shorthand with people you're close to. Like secret coded messages!

Wes

How do you make everything fun?

Hailey

IAG

Wes

I have no clue

Hailey

It's a gift

Wes

You have many.

Hailey

I should go.

Wes

GNH

Hailey

???

Wes

Goodnight Hailey

Hailey

Did you just make up an acronym for me even though you hate them?

Wes

I didn't say hate and yes. Some people are worth adjusting for. Your turn. You make one for me.

Hailey

IAU

Wes

Hmmm . . . It's not I owe you

Hailey

Which should actually be IOY not IOU

Wes

Agreed. I give up

Hailey

I adore you.

Wes

Damn. You win. GNH. IAYT.

25

"Why are we doing this on a Friday night?" Noah asked.

Because for some inexplicable reason, Wes needed to take his mind off the fact that Hailey was on a date. They let themselves into the space above Tara's bakery with a key she'd given them.

"We won't be long and you didn't have to come." Wes turned on the lights.

"Shit. I knew it would be perfect. We need to push him on this," Noah said, hands on his hips as he turned in a slow circle.

"It's this space, three apartments that he overcharges for, and the shops below," Wes said, remembering what he'd dug up on the Vanderben property.

"We'd own the lease on Tara's and Hailey's shops."

Which meant they could lower the rent. "That's fine. It's a great investment if we can get him to sell."

"I have some news on that," Noah said. He pulled up his phone, scrolled through something, then passed his phone to Wes. "It's an email from a friend of a friend."

The email talked about an investment opportunity that had come up. One of the names on the list was the landlord of this particular building.

Wes looked at his brother. "So he used this place as collateral to invest in a deal that didn't work out as well as he hoped."

"Now he's stuck. He's invested in the other property, which has been put on hold. He's paying a high mortgage on that one but not getting any income from it. He's using these shops to cover the cost of the deal that went south."

Shit. That complicated things.

"What does Chris say?"

"That we can push it forward but we'll lose money."

Wes swore, passed the phone back, and walked through the space. Right now, it was fairly bare except for a couple of long meeting tables, some chairs, and an empty watercooler.

Was he being too emotional about this? He couldn't push and he'd never made a decision that impacted him personally as well as professionally.

"We'll make up the loss if we buy him out, even if we overpay as incentive for him to do the deal. I'm positive. Tara's and the vintage shop are pulling in nice little profits, they've been here awhile. Those are stable. We lower the rent on those apartments, get people in them, use this space as our office."

Noah was saying all the things he was thinking. Wes turned to meet his brother's gaze. "You don't think it's risky to put him on the spot?"

Noah shrugged. "He'll tell us to go to hell or he'll be happy someone is throwing him a rope. He saves face, we get what we want. Is this about Hailey?"

"Not entirely," Wes said. His brother knew him too well. "I just want to make sure I'm not making a financial decision based on personal reasons. I'd really like for the rent to drop for her sake and Tara's. Hell, and the other shop owners. It's hard enough to keep things going in an ever-changing economy. They don't need some so-called businessman raking them through the coals because he wants a piece of a bigger pie."

"Doesn't sound like you're being too touchy-feely about it. It's okay for some of our investments to have a personal connection."

Wes strolled to the window. He really liked the openness, the high ceilings, the windows that looked out onto the street. "That goes against one of dad's cardinal rules."

"And he's sitting in an ivory fucking tower, three weeks to Christmas with not one person who loves him at his side. What's going on with you?"

"Let's go get a drink," Wes said.

Noah shrugged. "Sure. I know a place."

Wes forced himself to think about nothing as he watched the palm trees whip by from the passenger's seat of Noah's SUV.

The space above Tara's felt *right*. It was exactly the kind of space they were looking for. What they were proposing, giving Vanderben above his asking price, wasn't unethical. Financially, the cost would work out in their favor. He had zero doubt about that. *You wanted the space before you met Hailey. Before you knew she existed.* Did he want it more because he knew it would benefit her, and if so, how was that different than what his brothers wanted for their one-day wives? If he was all about protecting them and their investments, was this the most sound route for all of them? He'd been able to tell himself these confusing feelings when they texted, talked, or hung out were innocent. Simple. For the first time in his business history, Wes was questioning his own motives.

When Noah pulled up to a valet, Wes didn't even register where they were until they got out of the vehicle. Noah threw his keys to a kid in a black T-shirt. The emblem on the shirt was barely visible but Wes read it just as the kid said, "Welcome to Finnegan's."

Noah had come around the hood of his SUV to walk beside Wes but Wes wasn't moving. "Let's go, man."

"I thought this place was hard to get into," Wes said, looking around.

Noah laughed as a couple moved around them, went through the massive, open, double glass doors. "Maybe for dinner. But not for a couple drinks. The little bungalow Grace and I bought in

Laguna was sold by the owner. He said I could drop in anytime. What the hell is with you? You look like you swallowed something gross."

Wes swallowed, walked through the doors with Noah. It was a big place. It would be fine. "Nothing."

Noah gave him a brotherly shove on the arm. "When was the last time we had a hard time getting in anywhere?"

Wes glared at him. "We aren't in New York. No one knows us here."

"Why the hell are you whispering?" Noah's gaze was dancing with brotherly I'm-going-to-make-whatever's-bugging-you-worse humor.

"Hailey's here."

Noah looked around, his head whipping side to side almost comically. A tall brunette in skyscraper heels, a black turtleneck, and a black knee-length skirt approached them.

"Gentlemen. Do you have a reservation?"

Noah pulled his wallet out, flashed a card that Wes figured was from the owner. "Just here for drinks if there's room at the bar."

The woman leaned closer to the card. "Mr. Finnegan's guests are welcome in the VIP area of the lounge. Let me show you the way."

"Where do you see Hailey?" Noah whispered.

"I don't. She's on a date."

Noah's eyes widened. "Oh. Shit. Is that awkward for you? We can go."

He nearly tripped over his own feet. He'd told his brothers time and again they were *just friends*. "Why would it be awkward?"

The woman turned when she realized they weren't following. "Gentlemen?"

Noah's jaw tightened and he gestured, not very subtly, for Wes to get moving. "I don't know. You're the one acting weird. I just want a drink."

Wes lowered his chin, hoping that Hailey was tucked away somewhere in a far corner booth with a view of anything other than Wes arguing with his brother.

"Let's go," Noah said.

They followed the hostess past tables, up a small ramp to a lounge area. Everything was sleek, black and chrome. Soft lighting and folk music added nice touches. In one corner of the lounge, slightly removed from the rest of the tables, was a circular bench seat. The hostess led them there and said someone would be right with them.

Before she walked three steps, her look-alike took her place and asked for their orders.

"I'll have a martini. Dry please," Noah said, his charming smile locked in place.

"Vodka tonic, please," Wes said, scanning the groups and couples sharing meals on the floor in front of them. Their seat was like balcony seating at a play. They had a view of everything.

The drink order reminded him of the quiz. She'd loved it. When she enjoyed something, it was impossible not to enjoy it as well. She vibrated with energy. The waitress smiled and walked away, and Noah leaned both forearms on the huge round table, looked straight at Wes. "What's going on?"

"Nothing. I just don't want Hailey thinking I'm tailing her on a date or something weird. I mean, it's weird that I'm here on the first date she's had in who knows how long, right? If she sees me, that'll be hard to explain."

Noah's brows rose. "What's weirder is how many words just came out of your mouth all at once and that they were about a woman, not a computer."

"Fuck you."

Noah laughed, which made Wes grin.

"Seriously, man. I thought you were friends."

"Friends." The word had once seemed like the easiest term in the world. Now, it filled him with knots of uncertainty, a mixed-up tangle of emotions he didn't want to dive into. "We are. She's fantastic."

"Then it's just a coincidence. Even if you had the hots for her, you didn't know I was coming here."

Wes glared. "I do *not* have the hots for her."

Noah held up his hands. "I said 'even if.' Why are you so touchy about this? Maybe someone's gone a little too long without some . . . uh, touching?"

Wes shook his head, closed his eyes to take a deep breath. When he opened them, he was facing Noah's unrepentant grin. "You're an ass."

"That's fair. So, who's her date? Is he good enough for our girl?" Noah looked around like he'd spot her in the dining area. He looked back at Wes. "Who is this guy?"

The waitress returned, dropping off their drinks. They waited until she walked away to continue.

"I don't know. A colleague of her cousin's husband. An investment banker."

"Suit."

Wes laughed. "Yeah. Can't trust a suit."

Noah raised his glass. Wes clinked his against it, took a long swallow.

"I'm just saying," Noah said, even though he hadn't been saying anything. "If Hailey is going to get all dressed up in a killer blue dress, is the guy worth it? I mean, don't you want to know?"

Wes's mouth dropped open before he looked to where Noah was staring. Hailey was weaving through the crowd dressed in a beautiful pale blue dress that looked so much better on her in real life than the picture had shown. Her hair was up off her neck with little tendrils falling free. She was gorgeous.

"Close your mouth, bro," Noah said.

Her head started to swivel their way as she walked and Wes panicked. Like a freaking grade school kid. His heart jackhammered in his chest. He ducked his head, lowered his body in the booth in case she looked in their direction. Which she likely would since Noah was laughing his ass off way too loud.

"What are you doing?" he said, not lowering his voice.

Wes spoke from beneath the table. "Shut up."

His brother shifted. What was he doing? Shit. Shit. Shit. *Just sit up. What the hell is wrong with you?*

"Hi, Hailey. How nice to see you," Noah said.

Wes winced. *Fuck.*

"Hi, Noah. What are you doing—oh."

Yup. She saw him. He could almost feel the heat of her chocolatey gaze. He started to raise his body up, going slow so maybe he could convince himself this was a bad dream. *You dropped something. That's your story.*

"Hi, Wes," she said when their gazes finally met.

She had on more makeup than he'd seen her wear. Her eyes had this smoky thing going on that made them seem darker, sexier. Her lips were painted a luscious shade of red and Wes's mouth went dry.

"Hi." His voice sounded like he'd taken a trip back to prepubescence.

"What are you doing?" Her lips were twitching as she looked back and forth between him and Noah.

"Just, uh. Dropped something. Noah and I stopped in to get a drink. Unplanned. I didn't know we were coming here."

He wasn't sure if his voice or her brows rose higher. "Oh."

"How's your dinner, Hailey?" Noah asked far too smoothly.

"Excellent. The meal, I mean," she said, her gaze zipping to Wes. "The company is good, too. Oh. I'd love for you to meet Piper and Nick." She reached out and put a hand on Wes's shoulder. She'd wanted to introduce him sooner but all three of her cousin's kids had gotten sick during Thanksgiving so they'd had to postpone.

"We'd love to do that," Noah said.

The bastard picked up his drink, stood, and told Hailey to lead the way. Wes tried to get his attention but Noah ignored him.

Then they were standing next to a table with three people laughing. The beautiful redhead had enough features in common with Hailey to identify as part of her family. A dark-haired man in a suit much like the ones Wes favored had his arm around the woman. *Piper and Nick.* Across from them was one empty seat and a blond guy who looked like a surfer dressed for Wall Street.

"Oh. Hailey. Honey, you aren't supposed to leave your date and just pick up two new ones. Though, nice job, if I may say so," Piper said.

Nick arched his brows, pulling Piper closer. "You may not," he said with an easy laugh.

The other guy, the blond who had to be Hailey's date, looked at her questioningly.

"Ha ha, Pipes. Funny woman you married, Nick," Hailey said, turning to the side.

"You introduced me to her," Nick said.

"I ran into friends. Nick, Piper, this is Wesley and his brother Noah. Seth, Wes and Noah."

There were handshakes all around. Wes felt like the back of his shirt was damp with sweat. Why did he suggest a drink tonight?

"It's nice to finally meet you, Wes. Hailey's told us lots about you," Piper said.

"Same," Wes said, his throat suddenly scratchy.

"You two are investors, right?" Nick asked.

Wes did not want to talk business.

"We do a number of things," he said, cutting Noah off with a look. Noah was always happy to make new connections. Now wasn't the time. Wes wanted to leave. Needed to. He didn't want to see the way Hailey's date was looking at her, the way he leaned in when she sat down and asked if everything was all right. The way his hand hovered close to her arm. Her bare arm because the pretty dress she wore was short sleeved.

"Wes?" Noah looked at him.

"Hmm? What?"

"Nick was just saying he'd love to sit down sometime and go over our investments with us."

Wes nodded. "We should leave them to their dinner."

He looked at Hailey, saw she was watching him carefully. She mouthed "you okay?" He nodded. Tried to smile but he probably looked like he'd come from the dentist—he wasn't even sure his lips moved.

"Nice to meet you," Seth said almost dismissively.

When they left, Noah didn't say a word until they were in his SUV driving away.

"Dude. Why didn't you say you were into her?"

Wes felt like his head spun all the way around. He stared at Noah's profile. "What? I'm not."

Noah chuckled. "Oh. Okay. That's your story? Got it. Let me know when you stop lying to yourself."

Wes didn't know what to say. He had absolutely no idea what his story was. Hailey was supposed to be just his friend. Until recently, that's all she'd been. A friend who'd been hurt horribly but somehow still believed in love. Someone who made him laugh and think and look forward to things. Would she fall for this guy and get all of the things she deserved and dreamed about? The thought made his stomach feel like he'd chowed down on concrete.

He wasn't *into* her. She was Hailey. Just his Hailey. Shit. His *friend* Hailey. That's all. Yeah. That was his story.

26

Sometimes, a person worked their ass off, put in the blood, sweat, and tears, and slowly reaped the rewards. Other times, a fun and flirty quiz maker with thousands of followers on Twitter and Instagram mentioned a certain local business and the world went freaking crazy for salad.

FionaHale
@flirtyfunwriter
If you have not tried the salads from @BytheCup your life is not complete. Once you've corrected this, @ me with your favorite. #gonow #notyourusualsalad #santasalad-ismyfavorite

Hailey was lying on her bed in her apartment, feeling like she'd run a marathon after climbing a mountain. She stared up at her phone not sure what was harder to believe—that Fiona's tweet had given her a record-breaking day or that she was this damn tired from making salads. She'd had to call in Bryce and Leo. There was a line out the door. She'd stayed open an hour past closing.

Dropping her phone, she stared up at her popcorn ceiling and summoned the energy to bicycle kick her legs while simultaneously air punching and let out some of the giddy, overwhelmed laughter she'd been holding back.

Then she lay flat, closed her eyes, and focused on breathing. Re-cord. Breaking. Day. She'd done more in sales today than she had the whole month so far. Her phone rang. Moving as little of her body as possible, she pressed accept.

"Hello."

"Hi, dear." Her mom's voice came through the phone.

Surprise slowed her response. She sat up. "Hey, Mom. How are you?" Where are you was a better question. Her parents liked to be on the move, whether it was in their convertible, in a rented RV, or on a plane.

"We're good. Just packing for our trip. Are you spending Christmas with Piper and her family?"

"I'll go over for dinner. I've made some good friends and they've invited me to be part of their day." Okay, they hadn't actually but she didn't like to make her mom feel bad.

"Good. Then I won't have to feel bad about you being alone. I know we agreed to meet at the airport but we've actually found a cheaper flight out of a different airport. I've sent your gifts." She could picture her mom marking the item off on a checklist.

Of course they weren't meeting at the airport. The logical part of Hailey never thought they were. The part of her who still wanted to believe in them curled into a ball, put her head on her knees. "Same. No worries about the airport. I hope you guys have fun in Mexico."

"We're looking forward to it. How's California?"

"Good." She rolled to her side. "You should come visit."

"Maybe in the new year. How's your little salad shop?"

Maybe not so little. "Today was an amazing day. A friend of mine mentioned me on social media—"

"Sorry, dear. I have to go. That's fantastic about your friend. We love you."

Just like that, the conversation was over. Hailey was too used to the status quo to let it dim the happiness bursting inside of her. Unfortunately, the weight of her limbs, the fatigue of the day, was stronger than her excitement. She fell asleep curled around her phone, dreaming of salads.

A buzz woke her up. She looked at her phone but realized it was her apartment buzzer. Quickly, she scrambled off her bed, disoriented as she shuffled to the speaker.

"Hello." She sounded like a sick frog.

"Delivery for Hailey Sharp."

"Oh. Uh, I'll come down." Because even half-asleep, she wasn't stupid.

She had no idea what was in the gift-wrapped box she signed for. She shook it gently as she walked back up to her nondescript apartment. It was really more a room and a half than an actual apartment. Like a studio with a half wall that separated the bedroom area.

Her phone was ringing when she got back. Setting the box on the bed, she smiled when she saw Wes's face but frowned when she realized the time.

"Hey," she said, panic settling into her bones. She'd fallen asleep for an hour and a half. He was going to be here to pick her up for the Christmas party at the radio station in twenty minutes.

"You ready?"

"Nearly. Working on the finishing touches. I need to go do that," she said, already stripping off her clothes. She hurried toward the only separate room in her place: the bathroom. Swearing when she stubbed her toe, she leaned over, started the shower.

"Hailey."

"Wes. I gotta go. I have a hot date," she said with a laugh.

"Wait. You're still coming with me tonight, right?"

She froze. What the heck? "Of course I am. You're the hot date."

"Oh. I thought you meant Seth."

She stared at her phone even though he couldn't see her. He hadn't brought up running into her at the restaurant or how weird he'd been. Seth had stopped by the shop earlier this week, asking if she wanted to maybe catch a movie. They'd left it up in the air as to when but she'd said yes.

"I would never bail on you." Definitely not for Seth. He was nice and all but Wes was . . . Wes.

"Right. Of course. Is that the shower I hear?"

"Wes," she said more urgently. "I need to go."

She heard his groan as she disconnected. She showered as fast as she could without leaving soap in her hair. Fortunately, she'd been playing around with her hair last Sunday when she watched the kids so she wound her partially dry hair into a cute bun she'd seen on Pinterest. It was harder to do on her hair than it had been with Cassie's but it wasn't horrible. She applied her makeup and was proud of the time she was making until the buzzer sounded.

She looked down at her towel tucked between her breasts and swore. There was no way around this. Her dress was in her closet. If she waited until she put it on to answer Wes, he'd know she wasn't ready anyway. So she buzzed him in, left the door unlocked, and hurried to her closet.

He came in as she was pulling her blue dress out. She turned and nearly choked on her breath. Holy shit, he cleaned up well. His charcoal suit made those blue eyes shine like the ocean. His hair was styled to look messy but just looked sexy as hell. Here she was, not even dressed and he looked like he'd stepped out of *GQ*.

Her words got tangled. She might have lost a few brain cells staring at him wondering what it was about a man who wore a suit.

He gestured to her. "You're, uh, you're . . ."

She looked down and laughed. "Don't worry. I'm not wearing a towel. Wow. You look great."

"Thank you. So do you."

Her face scrunched. "Right. I'm sure I look amazing. I just have to slip this on and I'm ready."

"Oh. That's what you're wearing?"

Her heart cramped. Right. She'd worn it before. He probably had his suit custom-made by Gucci or something. He was used to women like Ana Pergo who probably never wore the same thing twice.

Doing her best to hide her hurt, she looked at her bare feet. "Is that okay?"

Wes's feet showed up in her line of sight. She looked up then followed his gaze to her bed. For one split second, heat infused her body like someone had lit a kerosene lamp under her skin.

Wes swallowed audibly. She became all too aware of her towel.

"Hailey," he said, his gaze coming back to her, running over her face like a soft touch. "Why don't you open that."

She stared at him a moment. There was something different in his gaze. Something that made her lungs feel tight. Setting her dress on the bed, she slowly unwrapped the shiny pink box.

The logo for the dress store where she'd bought the blue one stared up at her from the box. She looked at Wes. He shrugged but that new look was still heavy in his gaze. Her heartbeat short-circuited, going wonky as she slipped the lid off. Like a pogo stick gone rogue in her chest, her heart bounced around as she touched her fingers reverently to the glossy silk of the black dress she'd loved. Tears filled her gaze and she looked up at Wes, emotions tangling. Lines blurring.

"What did you do?"

"I don't know what you're talking about. What is that?" One side of his mouth quirked up.

She glared at him, opening her eyes wide in an attempt not to cry. She stood, set the box down, and lifted the dress, held it against her towel-clad body.

"Wes." Her voice came out rough.

His gaze met hers and she lost her breath.

"That's pretty. Looks familiar. You should wear that tonight."

She swallowed past the lump in her throat. "I can't accept this."

He lifted his hands, came over to the bed, rooted around in the box. "Hmm. I don't see a tag or a card. I guess you could just return it to the store." He checked his watch. "Probably closes soon. We don't really have time to do that before the party."

"Wes," she said, her tone sharper.

He looked at her, his expression one of complete innocence.

"Why did you do this?" She stepped toward him, the dress between them.

"I don't know what you're talking about," he said again, his voice wavering just a touch.

She reached up, touched her hand to his clean-shaven jaw. It was smooth, soft. Strong. He wasn't going to admit it.

"You should get dressed," he whispered. He closed his eyes for just a second, leaned into her hand. She wanted to step closer, run her hand around the back of his neck.

She started to say something—she didn't know what—but when he opened his eyes, he stepped back.

"We can figure out the dress mystery later."

She gave a watery laugh, lowered her hand. "Sure."

Leaving him there, she went to the bathroom and put on the dress. Smoothing it over her hips, she looked in the full-length mirror that hung on the back of the bathroom door. She felt . . . regal. Clothes didn't make a person. But damn, it was pretty. She snapped a picture, sent it to Piper and Fiona.

When she joined Wes, he was looking at a *Cosmo* magazine, leaning against the back of her couch.

She cleared her throat and he tossed the magazine from his hand. It went flitting across the coffee table, nearly slipping off the edge.

Hailey laughed loudly. "You look like you just got caught with porn by your mother." She couldn't stop laughing.

Wes's cheeks turned pink. He went to run a hand through his hair but seemed to remember it was styled and lowered it. "Just about. There's no way moon phases impact physical pleasure."

She bit her lip a second to stop herself from laughing. "I wouldn't know." She grabbed her small black clutch, slipped her feet into her heels, then turned to see he was staring at her.

"You look stunning."

She stepped as close to him as she could without touching his body. Heat emanated between them as she took her time, making sure his gaze locked on her own so he could *feel* her words. Understand them to their full extent. When he breathed in, slow and deep, she spoke. "Thank you."

Wes's smile told her he understood the depth of her words. He nodded, held out his arm for her to take.

"I don't even know any moon phases," he said as she locked up.

"We could look them up."

"I'll pass, thanks."

Laughing as they took the elevator down, she patted his arm. "You can borrow the magazine when you drop me off if you want."

Wes looked down at her in the dim lighting. The musty smell of old elevator broke through the scent of his cologne and there was a smudge on the mirror she didn't want to get near. Despite all of that, with him looking at her, wearing this dress, she felt like Cinderella on her way to the ball.

Dangerous territory. Life didn't end like the fairy tales. But maybe for tonight, just one night, she could pretend it did.

27

Something shifted inside of Wes as he walked through the doors with Hailey. It felt like his insides were virtual Tetris pieces, falling slowly, giving him enough time to put them in the right place. Hailey in that dress. He couldn't breathe. He tried. He really did. He pulled in a half breath, it got lodged in his rib cage.

"Are you okay?" Hailey turned to him. In the soft glow of twinkle lights and large paper lanterns that decorated the room, he could see concern etched into her features.

"Fine. My breath caught. That's all." He couldn't look at her while he was feeling this much. "I'll get us a drink." He pulled his arm from her hand and walked toward the bar.

Chris had rented a loft that people used for a variety of events from weddings to parties like this one. He'd hired a bartender, a couple of waitstaff, a caterer, and a DJ. There'd been serious arguments over the DJ among his staff.

"You okay, man?" Chris asked, coming to meet him at the bar.

"Yeah." He couldn't get more words out than just the one.

Chris clapped him on the back. "Hailey looks gorgeous."

Wes grunted, asked the woman tending bar for a shot of whiskey.

"Whiskey? What's wrong with you? Make it two, please, Stella," Chris said.

"Nothing. Just need a drink. Let it go." If he couldn't sort it out in his head, he couldn't talk about it with one of his brothers.

"Okay," Chris said, drawing the word out like he used to do when they were younger.

The shot burned, making his eyes water. It was a moment. That's all. He got caught up in . . . what? Hailey? He'd been caught up in Hailey for months now, but tonight felt different. If he was being honest with himself, which he usually was, things had been feeling different for a while now.

"Anything else?" the bartender asked, watching him carefully.

"Red wine and a beer, please."

"I'm glad you guys came even if you're being weird. The girls really like Hailey."

Wes's head whipped toward his brother. "Of course I like Hailey."

Chris just stared, his jaw working but no sound coming out.

"That's not what you said, is it?"

Chris shook his head slowly, his eyes wide.

The bartender put up his drinks. Wes set some money down, gave Chris a warning look, and walked away. All he had to do was get through tonight by reminding himself what they were building as friends was a hell of a lot sturdier than any romantic relationship could ever be. But her body in that dress, her gaze locked on his, her smile. He should have ordered two shots.

Stacey and Everly were asking about her dress when he brought her wine.

"There was no card?" Everly asked, smiling at Wes.

Hailey held his gaze even after he passed her the wine. "Nope. No card."

Stacey looked at him, whistled through her teeth. "You Jansen boys clean up good. How's it going, cutie?"

Wes was glad to be in a room that was mostly lit by strands of white lights. Warmth swamped his skin, particularly his face. "I'm good. You ladies look beautiful."

Everly wore a pale pink dress that was pretty yet understated. The real statement came from the pink Converse she wore on her feet. Stacey's dress also reflected her personality. It was vibrant and bold.

"Thank you," Stacey said. "I love getting all dressed up. What do you think of Hailey's dress?"

Wes swallowed but couldn't erase the feeling that he had something lodged in his throat. "It looks amazing on her." He'd seen the look in her eyes when he zoomed in on the pictures she'd sent him from the changing room.

She'd clearly wanted *that* dress and it was easy to see why. She wasn't the type of woman to splurge on herself even if she had the money. He knew because her gift to herself for her rise in sales had been buying ad space.

It brought him great joy to buy the dress for Hailey, have it delivered, and know she'd be coming with him tonight wearing something she loved.

"I love that there was no tag. It means the gift giver just wanted you to enjoy it. It's not about them. It's very thoughtful," Everly said, her voice barely audible over the instrumental Christmas music. She smiled at Wes like she could see through him.

Wes shook his head, took a long drink of his beer.

"Hey, how was your date?" Stacey asked as Rob joined them.

Wes choked on his drink, coughing loud and rough.

"You okay, bud?" Rob put an arm around Stacey, pulling her close to his side.

He nodded because he couldn't speak just yet. Hailey's eyes were filled with concern before she pinned Stacey with a much clearer one. "It wasn't a date. It was dinner with him and my cousin and her husband."

Stacey nodded, leaned her head on Rob's shoulder. "But he asked you out again."

Everly sent her friend a warning glance. Wes could feel Stacey pushing his buttons as surely as if her manicured red nails were poking through his skin. *Or maybe she believes what you've been selling. You keep saying you're friends. Why wouldn't they ask her about her date?*

"He did?" Wes sounded like he'd swallowed gravel.

Hailey nodded. "He did. He came into the shop but honestly, I was so swamped thanks to Fiona's tweet, I was barely able to acknowledge him. I had my best day of sales ever."

The others cheered, raised their glasses. Everly smiled, darting glances between him and Hailey. Chris joined them. Noah and Grace would be a bit late but were joining as well.

"Why are we all huddled in the corner? Mari and Mason want to get the Secret Santa going right after some food," Chris said, taking Everly's hand, bringing it to his mouth, pressing his lips to it.

"We're watching your brother learn how to drink beer," Rob said, his smile wide.

Wes glared at him. "I'm hungry." He turned, walked toward the buffet table of finger sandwiches and appetizers.

Hailey joined him a moment later. "Are you really okay?"

Her shoulder brushed his; he nearly winced with the current that zipped through his bloodstream. It was the perfect storm. That's all this was. Beautiful woman who made him laugh, had a little piece of his heart *as a friend,* and Christmas—the sappiest time of the year. Those things were working against him, making him feel things he didn't. *Then how do you explain that this isn't the first time?*

"I'm fine. Sorry. I just felt a bit off. That dress does look beautiful on you," he said, loading his plate with little bacon-wrapped pastries.

When she put her hand on his arm, he stopped, turned toward her.

"They were teasing, you know."

He swallowed past the rawness in his throat. "I know. I think you should believe what Everly said. Someone just wanted you to enjoy something you deserved."

"I'm not sure what they think I might have done to deserve it. But I'll stop wondering about the gift and just enjoy it." Her gaze told him they both knew the truth and somehow it made him feel closer to her. Like her secret coded messages. *IAU.*

He smiled, his chest loosening. "Exactly."

There. Tonight would be fine. She understood him. This wasn't one of her movies—he'd sat through *The Holiday* and *Love Actually* the week before. He wouldn't admit it to her but he'd enjoyed them both. He could enjoy them with *her* because she knew he wasn't built for a ring on his finger and a white picket fence.

"Thanks for bringing me tonight," she said, before picking up a small plate.

At least, with this, he could be honest. "There's no one I'd rather be here with."

~~~~~~~~~

Wes pulled up to Hailey's building. She insisted he didn't have to walk her to the door but he ignored her protests. He'd stopped after his shot and beer. Hailey and the other girls had carried on.

"You are a very good dancer," she said as he came around to help her out of the passenger side.

"Thank you. My mother insisted we have lessons," he said.

He held out a hand to her but she sort of slipped off the seat instead of stepping down. She misjudged the curb, her foot dropping between the sidewalk and the car, making her lurch forward. She gripped his shirt. He'd removed his jacket earlier during the aforementioned dancing.

She looked up at him, her fingers twisting in his shirt and pinching some of his skin. "Oops. The sidewalk moved."

He laughed. "No. It didn't." He helped her right herself, ridiculously charmed.

As he shut the door, she murmured something he didn't catch.

He turned, bent his head to hear her but almost lost his ability to listen when her breath whispered over his ear. "Did you see the way Rob and Stacey hurried out of there? Where do you think they went?"

He smiled, put a hand on the small of her back. He'd definitely seen the way Rob was eyeing Stacey as the night went on. "I'm not sure I want to know where they went or why." They'd been dating for months now and the attraction between them was palpable. "Are you okay? You should have water when you get in."

He held her arm as they walked up the cobblestone path to her small complex. There were twenty-five units. It was a decent neighborhood but he knew she wasn't particularly attached to her place. If the deal they were hoping to make in the new year went through, he could offer her first shot at one of the apartments over her shop. She loved his place.

"I'm fine. Don't go all mommy-hen. I'm tipsy at best. I could probably drink you under the table."

He laughed at the bravado in her voice. "Maybe if you were sitting under the table with your drinks."

"Ha. Challenge accepted."

He took her hand as she walked up the stairs. She dug through her purse, her hand nudging him because they were standing so close. When she looked up, keys in hand, her gaze drifted farther. She kept tipping her neck back.

"Oh."

Brows arched, concern brewing, he followed her gaze.

The wrought-iron lighting cast only a small glow but other than being old, he saw nothing wrong with it.

He looked down at Hailey, ignoring the way his breath hitched from the look in her eyes.

"What's wrong?" Why was he whispering?

Her body pressed closer. There might have been a chill in the air but Wes felt like he was insulated with wool blankets. Hot. Uncomfortable. In need of shedding the rest of his clothing.

Hailey gave a wistful sigh. "It seemed like a perfect moment for mistletoe."

He closed his eyes, tried to breathe past the moment that had been building for longer than he'd admit.

Her hand settled on his chest. He'd finally put all those damn pieces back into the right place and now she was touching him, looking up at him with those eyes, standing in that dress.

He'd never felt this aching need with any other woman. He'd truly believed it was because he had control of his emotions. Now, he knew the truth. No other woman had *inspired* this type of need. His control had been an illusion. He swallowed. Fine. He couldn't control his feelings but he still held the reins on his actions. Small peck. Friendly. That's all. Somewhere between maiden aunt and don't-hurt-her-feelings.

That was the last thought he had before Hailey went up on tiptoes, the fingers of one hand tightening in his shirt, tugging gently to pull his mouth down to her own.

At first it was just the press of her very soft lips, which tasted vaguely of chocolate. But then it was her mouth opening under his, moving, making it impossible for him to be still, for him to be sensible. He slanted his head, his hand moving to her jaw, his thumb caressing the smooth skin of her cheek. When she made a low, humming sound in the back of her throat, his other hand went to her hip, squeezed, and she pressed her body tight to his with enthusiastic agreement.

When her tongue touched his, his skin all but vibrated, like electricity was rushing through his veins and Hailey was the source. He couldn't get close enough and from the way she tangled her fingers in his hair, she felt the same. His hand slid around, down, pulling her up tight against his body.

It wasn't until she whispered his name so sweet and soft on her lips that he came out of the trance. He pulled back gently, listening to her labored breathing as his heart tried to jump over to her chest and take up residence there.

"Hailey." His tone was jagged.

She inhaled a shaky breath, dropping down from her tiptoes.

"Don't say it," she whispered.

He had to. One of them had to. They couldn't do this. It could ruin everything. "I'm sorry."

She closed her eyes, laughed humorlessly. "You said it."

He did. But worse, he'd felt it. Felt the magnetic pull of everything about her tugging on his common sense. She could make him forget that over 50 percent of marriages ended with not just broken hearts, but unfulfilled promises, resentment, and court-ordered spousal support.

She opened her eyes, looked at him with a sadness he hated. One he knew would pale in comparison to the heartache she'd feel when it ended. Because it would. When whatever they tried to build out of one passionate kiss fizzled, it would destroy a very special friendship.

"When I reimagine this, I'm going to pretend you didn't."

He reached out to stroke her jaw but stopped, shoved his hand in his pocket. He didn't trust himself to touch her again. "Please don't. I don't want to lose you."

Her smile was a watered-down, dim version of its real glow. "Why would you lose me? I'm right here."

Leaning forward, he pressed a kiss to her forehead, lingered for a second longer than he should have before pulling back.

"Our friendship means so much to me."

She stared at him long enough to make him want to look away. Then she nodded. "I'm not going anywhere," she said, her voice crisp and clear, like the tipsy fog had cleared.

His shoulders relaxed a small fraction. "Then we're okay?"

"We're okay. What happens at Christmas stays at Christmas."

He laughed. "Goodnight, Hailey."

"Goodnight." He thought he saw a sheen in her gaze but she turned to unlock the door.

He stepped down one step, waiting for her to go in. Once she'd stepped inside, she held the door and looked at him again.

"Wes?"

"Hmm?"

"Thank you for the dress."

He smiled, unsure why he felt like such an ass for doing the right thing.

28

Hailey was worn out by noon on Christmas day. How on earth did kids get up *that* early and still have *that* much energy? It was like Piper and Nick had let them down chocolate-covered caffeine tablets.

"So?" Piper asked, coming up beside Hailey. She was dressed in reindeer pajamas that matched everyone else's. Including Hailey's. Her first gift from them today had been a pair that made her feel more included than they could ever know. "Want kids?"

Hailey laughed, leaning her head on Piper's shoulder. They watched as Alyssa and Cassie circled around the tower Jason was building with their oversized stuffed animals. Nick was "reading" on the end of the couch. With his eyes closed, the book open on his chest.

"One day. I thought watching them while you guys shopped gave me a good sample but Christmas is a whole other beast."

Piper nodded. "Instead of just sex ed in school, teens should spend Halloween, a birthday, and Christmas with a pack of kids."

Hailey laughed again, lifted her head. "That would be highly effective. But honestly, I love your kids and I appreciate you guys letting me crash your day."

Piper turned, fixed Hailey with one of her "mom" looks. "You didn't crash. You're family. This is where you should be." She poked her in the shoulder, the mom brows lowering. "Understood?"

"Yes, Mom." Hailey bit back her grin.

"Come help me dress the turkey," Piper said, turning toward the kitchen.

"Surprisingly not the weirdest thing you've said to me."

They worked in tandem, chopping spices, potatoes, and other items for a stuffing that made Hailey's mouth water. She'd forgotten how much she loved cooking with her cousin.

"Remember when we used to bake cookies and sell them to your neighbors?" Hailey cleaned up the cutting board, dusting the scraps into the sink.

"I can't believe people paid us for them. Though, they were pretty good, if I remember."

"You've only gotten better at them." Hailey snagged a gingerbread from the pretty plate on the counter.

"You used to make those coconut ones I loved. Are you ever sorry you went with salads instead of baked goods?"

Hailey leaned against the counter. "No. I think what I have going is unique. Plus, I would not want to be in competition with Tara. She's a genius."

"Speaking of geniuses." Piper gave her another pointed look, making Hailey wish she had *not* confided about the kiss.

"We weren't."

"Have you seen him?"

"Of course. It's like nothing happened. Except it did. But I just need to put it out of my head. Onward. I'm not pining after a guy and honestly, I was a bit tipsy, he was all dressed up, it was romantic. It's Wes. He drives me nuts and makes me laugh in equal parts but it wasn't like that between us before and it's my own fault I made things messy."

"Are they messy?"

Hailey shrugged. Not really. But every now and again, she caught him looking at her in a way that made things feel . . . messy.

"No. They're good. I'm seeing him tomorrow with his family. I'm excited. I can't wait to give him his gift."

She'd worked hard to choose just the right image from his drawings to have inked and framed. In addition to that, she'd bought him a gorgeous leather-bound art book with high-quality pencils. She hoped he'd love it. He didn't put nearly enough stock in his own talent.

"I'm sure he'll love it. I'm glad to hear you're not pining away for him."

Hailey smiled. "He's my friend. There's no room for pining." *Keep saying it. Maybe it'll feel true.*

Piper made herself busy, putting the turkey in the oven and not meeting Hailey's gaze. Like a sixth sense, Hailey's skin prickled.

"You know what would make tonight perfect?" Piper met her gaze finally.

"What did you do?"

"It wasn't me. Not really. I mean, people shouldn't be alone on Christmas."

"Piper." She gripped the countertop.

"It's just us and I didn't think there was any harm and you're not pining for anyone. I thought—"

"Piper."

She winced. "Seth is joining us for dessert on the way home from Christmas with his family."

Hailey shook her head. "I'm borrowing one of your shirts."

"You're not mad?" Piper came around the counter, put an arm around Hailey's shoulders.

This might be just what she needed to *keep* her from pining. "Mad that you invited a good-looking, successful, nice man to dinner at a time when I need a distraction? No."

Piper's forehead creased with worry. "Do you need a distraction from how you feel about Wes?"

Did she? "Maybe just a distraction from trying to figure out *how* I feel." That was as much as she could admit right now.

"Then I'm not sorry. Why don't you go up and use the Jacuzzi tub? Borrow my clothes. Go pamper yourself. You've been working so much."

"You're the one with kids. Shouldn't you do that?"

Piper pulled her arm, putting a finger to her lips. They walked to the doorway that separated the kitchen from the family room. The girls were asleep with their heads on their stuffed animals. Jason had crawled up and curled into his father's side. They were all snoring softly.

"Merry Christmas to all," Piper whispered.

Hailey smiled, nudged her cousin forward. "Go rest with your family. I'll watch the food."

Her cousin went to the couch, nuzzled up to Jason, kissing his forehead, before laying her head on Nick's arm. When her eyes closed, Hailey took her phone out of her reindeer-patterned pocket and snapped a picture.

A distraction would be good.

29

Wes listened to Morty's sister, Dolly, tell them how he used to use her Barbie dolls as an audience for reading his favorite books.

Beside him, Hailey put her hand over her mouth and he knew she was hiding her grin.

Morty was doing nothing to hide his scowl. "If we're telling tales, I have some memories of you having some pretty elaborate tea parties with members of the Beatles who looked a lot like stuffed bears."

Dolly, an energetic woman with a strip of bright green in her snow-white hair, shrugged. "I regret nothing."

It felt good, Wes realized, to be sitting with this eclectic group of people. It felt more like a family Christmas than any of the ones he could remember as a kid, even before his parents divorced.

They'd decided to use Boxing Day as their family Christmas to allow for the couples to have their own Christmases. Wes had spent a quiet day finishing up Hailey's gift and texting her. He'd nearly suggested they get together but didn't want to intrude on her day with her cousin.

Chris and Everly were curled into an oversized chair in Noah and Grace's living area. The fire danced, giving off a low-level heat that worked against the breeze coming in through the open, screened windows. It was interesting, the scent of the ocean blending with the crackle of the fireplace.

The tree in the corner of their living room near the window seat was easily ten feet tall. It was decorated beautifully with ornaments Grace had handpicked. Neither Grace nor Noah had ornaments from their childhood. But they'd started a tradition this Christmas where each of the brothers gave the others one.

"One day, you'll have a tree decorated with memories," Grace had said.

Wes loved the idea and hoped his brothers both liked what he'd chosen with Hailey's help.

"I don't know how Tilly puts up with you," Dolly said, a happy grin on her face.

"Oh, he's not like this when we're alone," Tilly said, patting Morty's leg.

"I've lived with him. He's worse," Grace said. She was tucked between Noah's legs on the floor near the tree. They all had that after-dinner, post-turkey haze about them.

"Stayed pretty long for someone who didn't like the company," Morty said, taking a drink of his tea, which Wes was pretty sure was laced with bourbon.

Grace had worked for Morty after he'd broken his hip and once he was back on his feet, they'd become close enough that Grace stayed. This hodgepodge family they made up was unlike anything Wes ever expected to be part of. He glanced at Hailey again while the others went back and forth telling stories and quasi arguing.

Would she be here next year? Would she be with someone? Would he? There were moments when he forgot to push the memory out of his head that he could *feel* the pressure of her lips.

"Do I have something on my face?" she asked, humor lacing her tone.

Wes jolted, realizing he'd been staring. "No. Nothing."

She scrunched her brows, looking at him like he was being

weird. Probably because he was. He needed those stupid Tetris pieces inside of him to settle the hell down into nice straight lines.

Dolly got up to grab some more tea, asked if anyone wanted any. Hailey offered to help her.

When they came back, Dolly was telling Hailey about a spice mix she used with chicken.

"I'd love the recipe," Hailey said. "We make a Fiesta Cup that's popular. I'm always looking for new ideas though." She looked at Wes. "Leo is really great with coming up with salad combinations. He was actually talking about going to culinary school."

Wes's heart gave an extra pump. "He's a good kid. I'm glad to hear he's enjoying it. He's in a tricky situation, living at home. He's not sure how much he can get for scholarships but his parents make too much for him to get a lot of financial assistance."

"We should be looking into offering a scholarship of some sort," Chris suggested.

"Maybe something that isn't just for teens heading to college," Wes said, an idea humming in his brain. "I was chatting with a guy who came to pick his kid up from the coding class a few weeks ago. He was asking about adult training. Turns out, he'd been laid off after ten years with his company and wasn't sure how relevant his current skills were. He needs to keep paying his bills while getting retrained. That's tough in any economy."

"I think that's a lovely idea," Dolly said. "There are lots of adults who need help but it's not always easy to ask for it. I've only just squared away the medical bills from my husband's passing. Even with my pension, I'm still tight every month. But who's going to hire an old woman like me?"

Hailey set her cup of tea on the table. "I would." Everyone looked her way. "If you're serious. Things are busier than I could have hoped at the shop. If you can make salads, work a cash machine, do prep work, I'd be happy to give you some hours."

"Don't mess with me, honey. My heart isn't as young as it used to be," Dolly said, giving her a sassy smile.

Hailey laughed. "I'm not messing with you. Bryce and Leo are great but I'd love to designate one of them to deliveries, which means I need more counter help."

"How about the catering? How's that going?" Everly asked.

He saw her mouth tighten but no one else seemed to notice. "It's getting harder to split my time. I've got a couple more scheduled that I need to do. The side work helps with the rent increase but I don't enjoy it. The shop is everything I wanted." She gave a "what can you do" shrug.

Wes glanced at his brothers. He wanted that property more than he'd wanted any acquisition in a while. He couldn't help wondering if that was because he saw its potential or because of the woman sitting next to him. *It's okay if it's both.*

"Well, I would be happy to accept a job at your shop," Dolly said.

"Excellent. We'll exchange information and get you set up for training."

They chatted back and forth a bit more before Grace clapped her hands together. "Present time."

Noah laughed, kissed the side of her neck, agreeing with her.

It wasn't until later that evening, when he was dropping her back at her place, that he and Hailey exchanged gifts. He hadn't wanted to do it in front of everyone else. He'd spent the last three weeks working all the kinks out of the app he'd created for her store.

On her couch, in the dim glow of her Christmas tree lights, she stared at it, pressing the options, squealing with excitement every time something popped up. "I cannot believe you made this. How will I know when someone orders something?"

Her legs were crossed but she was bouncing on the couch, making his weight shift. He laughed, explaining how he'd connect it to her server and computer at the store.

"It'll print out the orders. You'll designate a pickup spot, just like other restaurants. You have the extended options of having them pay in advance. It'll take some time to get used to it but it's got a lot of capability."

Without warning, she threw her arms around him, her phone still in hand. She smelled like Christmas cookies and Hailey. He hugged her back, his chest tightening as his heart beat harder.

He'd already accepted the fact that she was an important part of his life, that he was more attached to her, even as a friend, than he'd planned. But when she was close like this, he wanted more. He wanted to keep holding her and forget all his worries. He wanted to fully immerse himself in her and forget it was in his genetics to fail in this particular area of life. *Your brothers didn't.* They hadn't seen the full depths of what he had.

It was more difficult than he imagined to pretend they hadn't kissed. To not relive it constantly. They'd made the right decision. They were friends. No matter how she looked at him sometimes.

"I'm glad you like it," he said, stroking a hand down her hair. It was so soft, smelled so good.

Hailey leaned back, her hands resting on his shoulders. Their faces were close enough that they shared the same air. Their eyes locked. He had a flash of watching the first of a series of rom-coms together—*When Harry Met Sally.* What had Harry said about being with the person you wanted around for good? Sure, he meant it in a romantic sense and that wasn't them but he wanted Hailey with him. By his side. He wanted to see her succeed, share that success with her. She was the only person he'd let see into his soul with his art.

Though, he hadn't known she looked so deep. The framed print of a colored version of one of his sketches was still sitting on her coffee table.

"What are you thinking about?" she whispered, brushing his hair to the side.

Wes bit back the groan trying to escape. He liked her fingers in his hair. "I love my Christmas gift, too."

She dropped her hands, sank back into her seat as she looked at it. "I didn't want to cross a line. I know your art is personal but between that and the app, Wes, you're selling yourself short."

He ran a hand through his hair, trying to shake off the tingle of awareness lingering from her touch.

"I'm working on a number of other things right now. I love this picture. I love that you had someone ink it and you framed it. It'll remind me I have an outlet when things are difficult. But that's all it is, Hailey. Just like kickboxing for Chris or surfing for Noah." He thought about his brothers telling him to do what he loved. What was stopping him?

She nodded. He could see in her gaze that she accepted his words, his reasoning. She wouldn't push but that didn't mean she believed in him any less. Yeah. He wanted to start his year with her by his side. Clearing his throat, he tried to think of how to phrase it to make sure there were no mixed signals.

"I was wondering if you wanted to spend New Year's together. We could have dinner, hang out. Maybe watch some movies?"

Hailey unfolded her legs, set her phone down on the table. "That sounds really nice. I wish you'd asked sooner."

"Why? You have a date?" He grinned.

She looked at him, the answer clear in her gaze. His stomach sank at the half smile she offered.

"I do."

Well. How about that. No need to worry about mixed signals. Her going out with another man—and he was pretty sure he knew who—was loud and clear.

Careful what you wish for.

30

February

Hailey didn't like the word "resolution." Instead, when the new year started, she'd written an "aspiration" on a little note card and tucked it into the pocket of her purse.

The difference between the two words, in her mind, was one was inflexible—like a grand declaration with no substance. The other, the word she'd chosen, was a wish. A good intention. She was hopeful that she'd achieve the outcome but wouldn't beat herself up if she didn't.

Do what makes you happy. That was her wish. In light of that, she hit send on the email reply turning down the latest catering job.

Her heart beat heavy, rattling her ribs. She reminded herself that even with a few days of post-Christmas lull, she'd been busier than ever. She couldn't keep splitting her attention. The app Wes had designed for her for Christmas was a major hit and pushed her sales up dramatically.

"Why do you look worried, dear?" Dolly carried a large rectangular bucket of smaller tubs filled with veggies she'd just cut. She put them into their holders in the counter.

Hailey closed her laptop, pushed it to the side of the counter, and washed her hands, donned her apron. "Not worried. Just hoping I made the right choice."

"About anything in particular?" The older woman had dyed a

chunk of her white hair pale purple. It was a striking contrast that few could pull off. Dolly managed with flair. Hiring her had been one of the best things Hailey had done and not just for the business. Being with Dolly was like having a doting grandparent with a bit of a wild side hanging around. She had fun stories and a lot of wisdom that only came with age and experience. As someone who didn't have many adults in her life growing up, Hailey had a soft spot for the woman.

"I turned down a catering job." Saying it out loud made her second-guess herself.

"Good. You're too busy to be running all over the place trying to meet everyone's needs. You keep saying every side job is the last one. It's time for that to be true or you'll wear yourself out. You have a successful shop right here. Focus on that."

Dolly didn't mince words. Hailey patted her shoulder. "That's the idea. I still have the one this Saturday. It'll be the real last." An old "friend" of a "friend" had recommended Hailey to an actress hosting a pre-awards party. Or, as she'd called it, a gala.

"How's it going with that charming young man?" Dolly set the empty tub on the counter, grabbed an apron.

She'd gone on two dates with Seth since Christmas. She hadn't told anyone other than Fiona because Piper was too invested. She liked Seth. He was very nice. He'd kissed her once and all she'd been able to think about after was how Wes may have ruined her for any other man's kisses.

It was no good trying to get Wes's kiss out of her brain either. It was permanently engraved in the memory bank. Every single nanosecond of it. She was probably making too much out of a kiss. They'd gone back to normal, like nothing had happened, the day after the party. Mostly.

"Seth is fine. I think you and Piper are more enamored with him than I am." When he'd shown up for dessert on Christmas evening, it should have been awkward but she'd found herself at ease with him. He was funny, kind, and good-looking. When he'd asked her to dinner, she said she'd think about it. Being with Wes, realizing he didn't have any lingering thoughts about their kiss that she could tell, pushed her to say yes. Because the best way to move forward was to move on.

"Well, he's not interested in either of us so if he doesn't make your blood heat, your heart pound, and your head spin, don't waste your time, my dear. Life is shorter than all you young people think."

Hailey thought about that while she switched the CLOSED sign to OPEN. Wes made her body do those things. Seth didn't. End of story. What she needed to do now was get over these feelings for her best friend and put him back in his clearly labeled box. As he'd done with her.

Wes was a master at compartmentalizing. He'd shoved Hailey back into the friend box with ease, then put that box at the back of all the others, tucked safely out of his way. She knew this because, after their Christmas, he was extra careful not to touch her, not to sit too close. Not to breathe her in. Except for that moment he did when she hugged him and she'd wanted so much more than she'd ever get from him.

"I'm going to focus on my store. My family. My friends. The only blood heating I'm interested in is that spice blend you put on my Fajita Cup. Are you ever going to share the recipe?"

Dolly gave her a fun smile. One that warned Hailey what was coming. "If you use it, do I get a percentage of those sales?"

Hailey laughed. Dolly was so much savvier than she wanted anyone to believe. Confident the recipe would sell, Hailey made a mental note to ask Nick about an accountant.

Because she enjoyed going back and forth with this woman, Hailey lifted her chin playfully. "Sure. Four percent on each cup."

Dolly leaned against the counter, tapping a bright-blue nail to her chin. "Fifteen."

Hailey laughed, crossing her arms over her chest. "Eight."

"Ten."

Exactly what she'd hoped. "Done."

"Really?" Happiness lit up Dolly's face.

"It's going to be worth it. We'll build a salad around the spice. Leo had a few ideas after he tried it." Her brain started spinning with employee incentives and how that would work. She'd ask Wes. He'd know.

Dolly walked over, squeezed Hailey's shoulders. "You're wonderful."

Hailey leaned in, gave her a quick hug. "So are you."

～～～～～～

The day was busy. Leo worked on the orders that came through the app. Much like other companies, people could log on to the app, place an order, and have it waiting for them when they showed up. Bryce was taking care of deliveries, while Dolly and Hailey worked the front counter.

Every time a customer walked through the door, Hailey thought about what Dolly had said. *This* made her heart pound. This needed to be her focus.

Like he'd been sent to pull that focus into a giant knot, Wes came in just as they were slowing down.

"Hey," she said.

"How's it going?" He looked tired. He wore a button-up shirt in light gray that softened the blue of his eyes.

"Good," she said.

"You still up for helping me with the class tonight?" He walked toward the back corner table he preferred as Hailey came out from behind the counter.

"Of course." Though he was teaching coding and programming to a group of teens at the center, he wanted to sneak in a quick résumé-building course. He'd asked Hailey to come talk to the class as a business owner, and a woman, as a way to reach some of the quieter kids, in particular the girls. Hailey had happily agreed since she enjoyed being there. She loved how Wes and his brothers were involved with the rec center. It made her more aware of the impact she wanted to have. If she could help those kids take the steps they needed to have a successful future, she was all in.

He sat, gestured to the seat across from him. "Do you have a minute?"

She sat. "I do. The app is doing great, Wes. I don't know how to thank you."

"You don't have to thank me. It's just an app."

She laughed. "One that has increased my revenue enough to offset the rent in a very short period of time. At least, for this month." She realized that was all she could really do—take it one step at a time. She had big-picture ideas for what she wanted for her store but right now, it was all about building momentum.

"That makes me happy." He said it with a hint of a smile but his eyes told her something else.

"Then what's wrong?"

He tugged at the collar of his shirt. He did that when he was worried about what he had to say. "Do you mind if we shop on Sunday after brunch?"

She winced. Right. She hadn't handled the last schedule change so well. "Of course. That's fine." She bounced her eyebrows. "You have a hot date?"

The corners of his mouth creased.

Hailey swallowed, her heart dipping down into her stomach. "That's great. Why do you look like you've been sentenced to death?"

Wes looked at the table, tapped it with his index finger. "I just don't want things to be awkward between us."

Worry flickered in her chest. "Why would it be?" Her lungs felt smaller, like they couldn't take in enough oxygen.

His gaze locked on hers. Was that pity? Did he think she was pining for him between salads? Setting her hands on the table with more force than she meant to, she leaned in.

"I think it's great. You should be getting out there, Wes. You need to find a woman that actually makes you feel something. Something you can't walk away from." Like us. Like *me*.

His mouth dropped open. "Hailey."

She stood up. "You made your feelings clear, Wes. I'm not lounging around in a corner licking my wounds. I'm dating Seth. I'm happy."

Okay, that was overstating the whole Seth thing since she didn't plan on going out with him again because it just wasn't *there* between them. But Wes didn't need to know that.

"Also, I'm busy this Saturday, so I would have had to bail anyway."

A couple customers came through the door. Dolly greeted them with her enthusiastic hello.

"Hailey."

She turned back to face Wes.

"What?"

"I'll see you tonight?"

What he meant was, "We're okay, right?" She sighed. For all his confidence and compartmentalizing, he was surprisingly in need of reassurances that they were all right. That their friendship would remain intact. Unharmed. Hailey was starting to wonder how much of that was about his feelings for *her* as opposed to his need for consistency and routine.

"We're fine, Wes."

Do what makes you happy. Maybe she needed to take a closer look at her own intentions. Because something had shifted when they kissed. It couldn't be undone. Pretending it hadn't mattered to her was *not* bringing her any happiness.

31

Wes tugged at his tie. When had the damn things become so uncomfortable? Maybe it wasn't the tie. More likely, it was that he'd agreed to escort Ana to this stupid party tonight. He hated this sort of thing: the false smiles, weak handshakes, pretending people mattered who didn't. Everyone here was looking for that one connection that would mean their big break.

"I think I should have offered you more than a drink before we left," Ana said, her hand tightening on his arm. Her pink nails looked brighter against the black of his tux. What the hell was he doing in a tux in the California heat?

Trying to feel a spark for someone who won't pull you into a rabbit hole of emotion. There had to be a happy in-between. Something in the middle of cordial arrangement and all-consuming lust. He hadn't stopped wanting a partner—someone he could talk to, laugh with, rely on. But it needed to be someone who wouldn't make him lose sight of his own goals, his own needs. What he *needed* was to fall for someone who wouldn't rip him to shreds when they walked away. Saying yes to Ana wasn't a reflex after finding out Hailey was still dating Seth. At least, he told himself it wasn't. *Getting pretty good at lying to yourself.*

"Sorry. It's been a while since I wore a tux." He smiled at her. She was beautiful. She could have easily been one of the actresses or models that her company catered to. She fit in easily with them in her silk blue gown, her hair tucked into a clip that sparkled with real diamonds. *She's not Hailey.* The thought sucker punched him.

Laughter floated around them like the candles in the pool. Lights were strung across it, people hovered in small groups. Tall tables with long white linens were artfully placed around the patio. Delicious food in tiny portions sat untouched because most people at these things didn't want to be caught with their mouth full.

Ana turned to him so they were facing each other, very little space between them. In her heels, she was the same height so it was easy to see the heat in her gaze. Heat he didn't feel anywhere other than the back of his neck because of this freaking tux.

"It's been a long time since I helped a man out of one. But I'd be happy to try when we leave."

Well. That was forward. He stared at her, willed himself to feel something for this woman. In his mind, as far as his heart and emotions were concerned, Ana was perfectly safe. He could fall into this relationship and not break when it was over. Not turn into an asshole like his father had after his mother had left. He'd be able to pick up and move on.

Yet, instead of jumping at the offer, which held no appeal for him—*she isn't Hailey*—he stopped her hand from playing with his tie. Gripping it, he removed it from his chest, shaking his head.

"That's not where this is going between us, Ana."

Anger and color rose in her cheeks but he couldn't lead her on. Wouldn't.

"I need the restroom," Wes said, stepping back. Weaving through the crowd, he headed for the house. The sprawling estate belonged to a beloved Hollywood starlet who had a niece trying very hard to follow in her aunt's footsteps. Throwing this awards gala tonight had been a surefire way to gather some of the most well-known and up-and-coming stars in one place. Life was all about connections. In this setting, Wes felt zero. In this crowd, he was completely untethered.

Wes stepped through the oversized open French doors, the tux becoming more uncomfortable with every step.

He pulled his phone out, standing in a stark white hallway with a massive chandelier. He texted his brothers. They needed to find the connection between Vanderben and who he wanted to invest with. If they could find a connection to something that showed his hand, they could persuade Vanderben to sell. Maybe without throwing him a bunch of overpriced offers.

Voices tumbled around him; the scent of spices, herbs, and overwhelming perfumes assaulted him. He wanted to go home. He was tired of playing games and pretending the last six weeks hadn't been a futile exercise in pretending he couldn't still taste the sweetness of Hailey's lips. That he hadn't noticed the change in their rapport. That he didn't hate it and spend his nights wishing things were easy with her again.

He turned back toward the terrace. Wes needed to find Ana and tell her he was leaving. That coming had been a mistake and nothing was going to happen between them. Not tonight, not ever.

Through a sea of well-dressed strangers, he saw her by the pool house. He weaved his way in and out of conversations, losing sight of her by the time he reached the edge of the pool. Irritation mounted as he walked forward, the voices and laughter seeming louder, more grating. He was about to text Ana and get out of there when his heart hitched in a way it only did for one face. One person. Like his wishing had brought her to him.

Before his brain, feet, and mouth could work in tandem, a tux-clad guy standing in front of Hailey gripped her arm, leaning into her, crowding her space.

Hailey.

Wes's feet moved on their own, cutting a path as he watched her eyes widen. She said something Wes couldn't hear, tried, unsuccessfully, to tug her arm free. Wes's heart rate hit new heights.

32

This night could not get any worse. Hailey yanked her arm from Dorian's grasp as Wes surged through the crowd toward them. *What is he doing here?*

"I mean it; this is pathetic, Hailey. What did you think would happen? I'd see you and want you back?"

She looked up into Dorian's dark, angry eyes. Why had she ever thought he loved her? Cared about her? Wanted a future with her? The man she'd fallen for may never have existed.

She rubbed her arm where his fingers had pinched. "I know it's hard to believe, given the size of your ego, but I'm not here for you. I'm working."

Dorian gave an unpleasant laugh as Wes came to her side. There was something in Wes's gaze she'd never seen before. Something possessive and almost . . . untamed. Dorian turned, gave Wes a dismissive look, then leaned into Hailey again, reaching out with his hand.

"Unless you want that hand shoved down your throat, I suggest you don't touch her again," Wes said. His voice was low, steady, and laced with barely leashed anger.

Dorian scoffed at him, eyed Wes up and down. "Who the hell are you?"

It took her a minute to surface from the shock of Wes's reaction. "What are you doing here?" Hailey asked him.

God. That tux was seriously working for him. But she did not need him coming to the rescue with some misplaced best-friend complex. She could take care of herself.

"Is everything all right?" Ana appeared, resting her hand on Wes's arm.

Hailey's heart felt like someone had shoved a nail into it.

"Everything is fantastic. I was just complimenting the waitstaff on the wonderful desserts," Dorian said smoothly. He stepped into Ana. "Lovely to see you again, Ana."

She looked from Hailey to Dorian, gave a tight smile. "You as well, Dorian. Congratulations on your new role. I've heard good things about the show." She looked at Hailey as she stepped closer to Wes. "Hailey. How are you? I had no idea you were working this party."

Hailey swallowed the bitterness rising in her throat, unable to look away from where Ana's hand lay on Wes's arm. *Of course that's why he's here.* "I'm great. Just finishing up actually. Hope you all have a really great night. Dorian, it was unpleasant at best to see you again."

She tried to walk away without rushing as bile rose in her throat. *Ana. His date is with Ana. You knew this would happen. You told him it should happen. You all but pushed them together, saying how great they looked next to each other.* She yanked off her apron, catching her hair and tugging as she pushed her way through the crowd. She'd set out the desserts, she could leave. She'd figure out getting paid later. Tomorrow. Never. Whatever. She just needed to get out of there.

She'd made it to the back door where the "help" parked. Anger and hurt, along with a heaping dose of humiliation, kept her tears at bay. Of all the nights for her past and present to collide. She pulled open the door to her SUV, grateful she'd locked her purse inside. She wasn't going back into that house for her dishes or anything else tonight. She just needed to be anywhere but here. She'd left this fake, fickle town for a reason.

"Hailey." Wes slammed a hand on her door, leaned over a little like he was out of breath. "You should play football with the way you weave in and out of groups." His breathing was choppy.

She glared at him. "Just a little trick the *help* learn. How to move and be invisible." Her voice cracked on the last word. That's how she'd felt standing there with Ana next to him.

Hailey didn't have money and she laughed too loud at jokes. She didn't like four-inch heels, didn't care if her purse was Prada or The Gap. But she thought those things didn't matter to Wes, despite his upbringing. Clearly, they did. It wasn't that he wasn't interested in a relationship. It was that he didn't want one with *her*. Even after the kiss that had chiseled beneath her friendly feelings, leaving nothing but longing, he didn't feel the same. Worse, if he did, he was able to deny it and move on. Clearly, Hailey was no better at reading someone now than she had been with Dorian. When the hell was she going to learn?

"Hailey." He stepped around the door, crowding her so she stepped back, her butt resting on the driver's seat.

"You should go back to your party, Wes. I didn't realize your *date* was this event. With Ana. It shouldn't surprise me though. You fit with these people." She didn't. She'd never been more painfully aware of that than right this minute. *I don't want to fit with them. I want to fit with Wes.* Pain lodged like a sharp wedge in her ribs.

"You and I both know that's an insult." He was staring at her like he hadn't seen her face before.

She gave a harsh, unhappy laugh. "It is. It absolutely is. But that doesn't make it less true."

"That was your ex."

She swallowed. "It was."

Hints of his earlier anger still hovered in his gaze. "I've never felt that kind of anger before. When he grabbed you, an actual haze clouded my vision." Wes reached out, ran a hand over her arm where Dorian had squeezed tightly. There was agony in his tone and expression. "Are you okay?"

Her lip wobbled. Why did he have to sound like he cared so much? *Because he's your friend.* She laughed again, bitterly. The pain in her arm was nothing compared to her heart.

She moved her arm, willed herself to keep it together for just a few more minutes. "I'm fine. I need to go. I'm sure Ana will be wondering where you are."

He ran both of his hands through his hair. "I don't care and it's not a date like you're making it sound."

She crossed her arms over her chest. "None of my business. We're friends. You've made that implicitly clear. *Painfully* clear. There's nothing between us other than that. Who you sleep with is your business."

"I'm not sleeping with Ana." His voice rose. He took a deep breath. "I'm not sleeping with anyone."

Hailey's tears wanted to make an escape and the relief she felt over hearing that didn't help. "Don't care."

He stared at her, moved closer. "Yes, you do." Her butt pushed against the buttons on her seat.

Don't cry. Don't let him see you cry. "No, Wes. I don't. I'm done chasing people who don't want me. That's why I left all of this bullshit behind." She swung her arm out, almost clocking him in the chin as she pointed toward the house where the party could be heard. "I'm done with not being enough. I'm happy with who I am, what I've done with my business and the life I've made for myself. I do not have time for drama or smoke screens. I can't do this." It just didn't make her happy anymore.

"Do what?" His voice cracked, his nostrils flared.

"Pretend I don't feel more for you than I do. I didn't mean to or want to. Trust me on that one. Something changed between us the night we kissed. Probably before that, for me. We can't undo it and we can't go back. Seeing you with her . . . it's a reminder that it isn't about chemistry or wanting with you. It's about that internal checklist of what makes a good match for you. It's knowing that I'm not it. I'm not enough for you. I can't live like that again. Not even as your friend."

Something flashed in his gaze. An intensity she hadn't seen before. "Not enough?" The words were practically growled.

She pushed off the seat, her chest bumping into him. She started to talk but he cut her off.

"You think this is because you're not enough?" The last two words sounded like they were ripped from his lungs.

She couldn't stop the tears that escaped. "I *am* enough." It had taken her too long to realize that to forget it now just because Wes didn't want her the way she wanted him.

He leaned down so their noses were practically touching. "You are the opposite of not enough. You're too fucking much. I can't breathe anymore when I'm with you."

Her jaw tightened even as her heart cracked. "Well, let me fix that for you. I'll get out of your life, you'll be able to breathe, and live happily ever after with Ana."

With her chest heaving, breath sawing in and out, it was hard to say which of them was angrier.

"I don't want happily ever after!" he shouted. "I want you!" He leaned closer and her hands went to his chest. "Dammit. That came out wrong."

He wanted her? This whole fight was about how he didn't want her. Confusion warred with her need to get away from him before he saw her sob. She was close. A few tears wouldn't be enough to relieve this aching pressure. His forehead fell to hers as his hands gripped her hips in a way that ignited her from the inside out. The connection poured salve into the cracks he'd created in her heart.

"It isn't because you weren't enough, Hailey. It's because I'm terrified you could become everything."

She felt like she'd jumped off a high dive board in a blackout. "What?"

"I want to kiss you," he whispered. "I've wanted to since I stopped kissing you that night. It's all I can think about. You're enough. You're so much more than enough. I'm scared I'll mess this up. That I'll destroy what has become the most important relationship in my life. It'll kill me if I do but having you think you're not enough is worse."

Her hands slid up around his neck, his hold on her loosened even as his body moved in, lined up with hers perfectly. "It's okay to be scared. I can handle you scared. I just need to know I'm not the only one feeling whatever this is between us."

His arms tightened around her waist. "You're not."

"Then kiss me. We'll figure out the rest later."

When his lips touched hers, it was like setting a match to straw. Instantaneous heat that couldn't be slowed or contained. A fire that had finally been given the oxygen it needed to truly blaze. She dove into it, into him, willingly and without doubt. She was all in.

33

In hindsight, she probably shouldn't have driven with that much lust surging through her system. Were there laws against that kind of distraction while operating a vehicle? Wes's hand was a welcome weight on her thigh. *Wes's hand is on my thigh.* She couldn't stop thinking about all the other places she wanted it. Her breath shuddered out.

"I'm not going anywhere," he said, leaning over to kiss her shoulder. She tightened her grip on the wheel, cursing traffic in her head. "You can slow down. I'd like to get home alive."

She shot him a glance. "Trust me, we will. I have plans for you."

She looked back toward the road but not before she saw the way his gaze heated. His fingers pressed into the sensitive skin of her leg. "Jesus, Hailey. I don't think anyone has ever looked at me the way you do. It's intoxicating."

Smiling, she put her hand on top of his, linked their fingers. "Get used to it."

Hailey's gaze flitted to Wes, who was staring at her. She had to ask. "You're really not *with* Ana?"

"I'm not," he said, his voice low and genuine. "I haven't been. I agreed to go to the party with her because it seemed like a good business decision. Plus, I was trying to distract myself from wanting you. What about Seth?"

Heat flooded her cheeks. "I haven't gone out with him since early January. I already told him I had no intention of more dates."

"But you said . . ." His voice trailed off.

"I've been going crazy trying not to want you, Wes."

"This changes everything," he said quietly.

Their exit appeared; Hailey switched lanes. "I know." *Please don't change your mind. Please.*

Wes's fingers trailed up along her neck, touching the back of her ear. "You're beautiful."

Doesn't sound like his mind is changing. Nerves made her scoff. "I'm dressed like a maître d'. It's hardly the gown—"

"Don't." His tone was gruff. "You're stunning. Regardless of what you're wearing. You are the only light I see."

She sucked in a sharp breath. "Is that a rented tux?" They were close to his apartment now.

"Of course not. Why?"

She grinned at his tone then focused on the road. "I just wanted to know if I needed to be careful about ripping the buttons off."

His laugh was deep, incredibly sexy. She felt absolutely giddy. The rest of the ride felt like a dream, like it couldn't possibly be true, but as they walked-ran to his apartment from the parking garage, it all became more real.

He emptied his pockets when he got into his place, setting his keys, wallet, and cell phone where he always did before turning to face Hailey, who stood by the door. She slowly removed her purse, hung it on the wall hook.

Wes stepped toward her and as much as she wanted him, she was no longer willing to rush. She wanted to savor. To remember every minute of all of this.

Nerves, excitement, and happiness welled inside her like dozens of lights being flicked on. He stopped in front of her, his gaze on hers, his hand coming to her shoulder. With one finger, he traced her collarbone through her plain, button-up, white dress shirt. Heat streaked under his touch, over her skin. His eyes watched the path of his finger, which he brought down the center of her shirt to the top button. His gaze flickered to hers, making her breath catch.

"This changes everything. Our friendship. We can't go back," he whispered.

"That's okay." She stepped closer. "What I want is in front of me."

Their mouths met, eager but soft, nearly reverent. His touch was electric and Hailey suddenly knew this was different than anything she'd experienced before. Their journey from the entryway to his bedroom was a slow dance of soft touches, deep kisses. The music was their combined breaths, the swish of clothing as it fluttered to the floor. When he came down over her on his bed, he used both hands to brush her hair away from her face. She didn't even remember it coming out from the elastic.

She reached up, stroked her hand across his cheek. There was so much feeling building inside of her—she knew what this was, for her at least. She didn't know if it would ever be love for him, but the way he looked at her, the way she felt in this moment, it redefined everything she'd thought she'd known about the word.

"You're so much more than enough," he whispered. His lips grazed her forehead, her cheekbone, butterflying across the bridge of her nose to the other cheek, down to her chin. Finally, his mouth came back to hers, his lips insistent.

She wasn't sure if she said the words out loud but they flickered in her brain on repeat. *You're everything.*

~~~~~~~~~

Hailey stared at the ceiling of Wes's room, unable to keep the smile off her face. He nestled into her side, his breathing soft against her neck, his hand on her stomach. Life was full of moments that got built up to epic proportions only to fall flat or, at the very least, be nowhere near as great as hoped. This was not one of those moments. This was everything she'd hoped for, and even though she knew she was getting ahead of herself, it felt *right*. The long-term, white-dress kind of right she could see now she hadn't had with Dorian. With anyone, until Wes. They fit. Saturday-night shopping, Sunday brunches, his family and hers. His contented sigh fluttered wisps of her hair. *Here and now. Focus on that.*

Her stomach growled. Loudly. Wes lifted his head, his gaze a sexy kind of sleepy that made her want to stay in his bed for good. His lips tipped up at the corners.

"I should feed you." His voice was husky, his hair a mess.

"I wouldn't say no to food." But first. She leaned over, pressing her hand against his surprisingly defined chest. He didn't love to work out like his brothers but that hadn't stopped him from staying in very good shape. He was lean, sexy muscle beneath that tux. And she could kiss him anytime she wanted to.

His hands went into her hair as he flattened on his back. If her stomach hadn't growled again, they likely would have been there longer. Instead, he grinned, pressed a kiss to the tip of her nose, and nudged her away.

"How about eggs?"

She watched him get out of bed, grab his boxers. When he caught her staring, his eyes darkened—the ocean at night with a hint of stars shining straight into her heart. *Oh man, you're in trouble.* She'd decided to dive but hadn't realized she'd launched herself right into the deep end.

He tossed his shirt at her. "Stop looking at me like that or we won't get food."

"Humans can last a surprisingly long time without food," she told him, pulling the soft T-shirt over her head.

Wes chuckled. "But food gives them energy to do the things they enjoy."

When she stood, he was right there, making their bodies brush. He looked down at her, making her heart clutch. "That means you enjoyed—" Her gaze darted to the bed.

Wes pulled her close, his hands on her hips like that was their spot. "Was that not evident?" His gaze was serious, his tone soft.

"I just want to make sure—no regrets?"

His hands moved up, cupped her jaw. "There's no room for regret, Hailey. I feel too many other things." He kissed her gently. "Only good things."

She went up on her tiptoes, wrapping her arms around his neck. That was a damn good answer. "Same."

Over eggs, they talked about random things—his brothers, their girlfriends, Fiona and Piper. It wasn't until he laughed at something Jason had said to Nick that Hailey realized things had been stilted between them for weeks now. Until tonight. Things felt "normal" with a huge side of freaking awesome.

"This should make brunch interesting tomorrow," she said, taking his plate and hers to put in the dishwasher.

Wes leaned back in his chair, ran a hand through his hair. "I suppose it will. The good news is we can tell everyone in one sitting."

She washed her hands before walking over to him, putting her legs on either side of his as she sat on his lap. His hands came immediately to her hips.

"Most people. I'll tell Piper in the morning."

One hand wandered up her back, under her shirt. "What will you tell her?"

Hailey's fingers played at the base of his neck. She felt the slight tremor of his body. "That you fell for my charms and are hopelessly hooked."

He laughed. "Hmm. Maybe I'll tell my brothers the same about you."

Her brows rose. "They will, for sure, say you are without charm."

Wes frowned, his fingers causing tremors in her own body as they danced over her back. "They absolutely will."

She kissed his neck where it met his jaw. "They'd be wrong."

"It's safe to assume that while we're an us, there's no one else?"

His words were like an unexpected blast of cold water. She

leaned back, her fingers stilling. She didn't want to be upset. He was still Wes. Practicality was his middle name. "I don't want anyone but you."

"Same."

His words toyed with her confidence but she needed to know. "Did you have an end date in mind?"

Wes's forehead creased. "Of course not. That's not what I meant."

"*While* we're an us?" Her jaw tightened.

Wes reached up like he'd noticed the slight movement and stroked his thumb over her jaw. "I don't want or intend to but I'm going to mess up, Hailey. It was part of why I fought this. I'm not romantic like Chris or suave like Noah."

"I'm only interested in you."

He nodded, his thumb easing the tension along her neck. "Which I'm very grateful for. But I've never been particularly good at emotional relationships with anyone outside of my siblings. Even then, it's not always easy. You know my flaws—as much as I tend to voice my concerns even if they aren't what people want to hear, I'm not adept at sharing my emotions. I try to fix things that aren't mine to fix. I'm scared of feeling too much but with you, I can't help myself. That's new for me. I'm not looking at the end. I want this between us. Enough to jeopardize a friendship that means more to me than you know."

"I didn't want to risk our friendship. But I couldn't fight this."

He leaned in, kissed the underside of her jaw. "I'm glad. I don't want you to. I want you, and I think our friendship only makes whatever this is between us that much stronger."

She tilted her head to the side. "I know you're cautious about your feelings but I'm clear on mine. I'm crazy about you, Wes. I'm not saying that to corner you or scare you but as reserved as you can be about your feelings, I need to be able to express mine. I don't want to feel like the one who's in deeper."

He stopped kissing, stopped moving, and met her gaze straight on. "You're right. I'll be careful. I'm here with you, Hailey." His hands gripped her hips again, his fingers pressing in. "*Right* here. With you. There's nowhere else I want to be. Don't doubt that."

His grip tightened, one hand going to her butt as he stood, her legs wrapping around his waist. "I should have said you're mine. And I want to be yours. That you're all I can see. The only one I want."

His kiss consumed her, sweeping away the last ashes of uncertainty. There was no room for it in the way he touched her, the words he whispered against her skin. They were all in. Together.

34

Chris tossed a crumpled straw wrapper at Wes, pulling his attention from where Hailey was laughing with a customer.

"It's about time," he said, looking over at Noah. He and Noah exchanged a look.

"What?" Wes looked between them.

"That you fell flat on your ass in love," Noah said.

Wes frowned, leaned forward. "We've been together for a week."

Noah shrugged. "I knew with Grace the minute I looked at her."

Chris gave a quiet, almost shy smile like he was remembering something. "Same for me."

Wes stiffened. "Well, that isn't this. I'm very happy. I care about her a great deal but as I said, it's been a week." Though, he was quite certain he *could* feel what they did and that thought kept him up at night.

"Just remember that doesn't matter on Valentine's Day. Whether you've been together twenty minutes or twenty years, you know to get her something, right?"

Wes crossed his arms over his chest, looked down his nose at his brother, his lips quirking. "I'm older and smarter than both of you. Of course I'll get her something. I'm not a complete idiot." He was quite proud of the Tiffany's diamond bracelet he'd already bought. Fine, the idea had technically been Ari's. She'd sent him a picture of one she'd recently bought and Wes immediately thought the shimmer of diamonds would look lovely on Hailey's wrist.

Noah held up his hands. "I'll back off." He stared at Wes a moment longer. "It's nice to see you happy."

Wes didn't know what to say to that. In general, he was a happy person and always had been. He enjoyed his job, most of his family; he'd had a predictable but enjoyable social life in New York. But Noah meant something more than that. He was a different kind of happy now, and it must show. Like it did on his brothers.

"Where are we at with Vanderben?" Chris asked, pulling something up on his iPad.

Noah shook his head, his expression darkening. "We're not. I think we need to pull the plug. He's in over his head but still trying to play hardball."

Wes's stomach cramped. "I don't think we should be hasty about walking away."

Chris frowned, set his tablet down. "We're not. But we shouldn't jump into something just because we like the area or the property. I agree with Noah. We should bow out of this one. I have a bad feeling."

Wes nodded. Two against three. It was done. Except it didn't feel like it was when he looked over at Hailey again. He was so proud of her determination and success. He'd seen CEOs with everything at their disposal who didn't put in a tenth of the heart and effort she did. She didn't deserve to have it ripped out from under her before she'd had a chance to soar.

"I actually have something I'd like to talk to you guys about," Noah said.

Wes picked up his coffee, putting a mental pin in his worries. "What is it?"

"The area around the community center needs new businesses. It got me thinking about this place, the high rent, and how it impacts the tenants. What if we purchased the strip of buildings across from the rec center? We redo it, offer cuts on the rent to local business owners based on their willingness to give back to their own community."

Wes turned the idea over in his head. "I've checked those places out. It needs updating. Possibly a lot."

Noah nodded. "I didn't come without information." He flicked his finger across the screen, opening his own tablet.

Wes saw Hailey watching him. When their eyes connected, she winked at him. The muscles around his heart tightened but his smile grew wider.

Noah snapped his fingers, smiling widely. "Hey. Flirt later."

"You'd look good with coffee all over you." Wes arched his brows.

"How about we focus so I can get back to work?" Chris leaned over Noah's shoulder.

"It definitely needs updating. It'll cost us some money but I've made a lot of connections so far. I can get a lot of deals on the supplies and labor. Even giving a reduced rent, we'll earn a profit and be able to return the investment."

Noah showed them the projections. They were good. His smile betrayed his excitement. "Can I start putting the paperwork together?"

Both Chris and Wes were on board. It was a solid plan.

They finished discussing the project, assigned tasks to themselves, and agreed to chat later. Hailey came over with a cup of fruit, layered with whipped cream.

"Thought you might want a to-go cup," she said, sitting across from him.

Dolly was working today. Her bright hair didn't move an inch as she excitedly pointed out options to a customer. She was settling in well. Hailey had a reliable, charmingly eclectic staff.

"Thanks. Looks like it will be a busy day," he said, taking her hand across the table. He loved touching her, the feel of her soft skin.

"Hope so. What are you up to later?" She glanced over when two more customers entered the shop, then zeroed in on him again.

"I was hoping to make dinner for this really beautiful woman," he said.

She arched her brows as she nodded slowly. "Noah teaching you how to be suave?"

Wes laughed. "Noah thinks he could teach me lots of things."

Hailey squeezed his hand. "I don't think you need Noah's help with anything."

He wanted to haul her toward him, kiss her until neither of them could breathe. Which was ridiculous because the middle of the salad shop was hardly the place. Sometimes, it was difficult to get a handle on all the feelings she evoked.

"You know what next week is?" He didn't want her to think he wouldn't remember Valentine's.

"Of course. We don't have to do anything fancy. I was actually hoping I could cook you dinner."

"Will it be salad?"

She laughed, stood. Walking closer, she put a hand on his shoulder, leaned down, and brushed her lips across his. "I promise it won't be. My place?"

He nodded. "Sounds perfect."

~~~~~~~~~

Wes was surprised by the level of excitement he had as he waited outside Hailey's apartment. They'd had a busy week and she'd gone to her cousin's the last couple nights in a row to help with hand-made Valentines all the kids were making for their classmates. It felt strange to miss her but he did. He wasn't sure if he'd ever get used to this restless rush of wanting that came along with Hailey but being with her soothed it to some degree.

She opened the door wearing a soft blue shirt with little silver heart buttons all the way from her cleavage to her waist. His mouth watered. She wore a pair of black pants and her bare feet showed pink toenail polish that he found incredibly sexy.

"Hey there, Valentine."

He laughed, stepped into her, and caught her in a kiss he wanted to take deeper. Given that his hands were full and she hadn't shut the door yet, he kept it brief.

"What did you bring?" She stared at the generic gift bag and the bottle of wine. "I told you I had everything."

He shrugged, slipped off his shoes as she shut the door. "Never hurts to have extra wine and I brought you some treats from Tara's. If you don't want them, though?" He held up the bag.

She laughed, made a grab for it but he held it out of reach. "For after dinner." He followed her into the kitchen, where something smelled amazing. He inhaled deeply. "What are we having?"

She walked to the stove, took the lid of the pot, and stirred. "I felt like Italian. Minestrone soup, lasagna, and homemade rolls."

He tucked himself behind her after he set his things down on her tiny table. Wrapping his arms around her from behind, he pressed a kiss to her neck. How was this so easy? His whole life, he'd assumed this level of intimacy would be hard to achieve or would feel draining. Instead, it lifted him like a double shot of espresso. He felt like she was made for him. The transition from friends to lovers felt like it was a path they'd been meant to take.

She arched her neck, encouraging him to press his lips along the column of skin.

"I can't decide what smells better. You or your cooking."

She laughed, setting the lid back on, then turned in his arms. "You get to have both so you don't have to choose."

When he bent his head, she met him halfway. He loved when she arched up into him, like she couldn't wait to be closer. When he pulled away, he ran a hand over her hair. "You look great."

"So do you. Why don't we have some wine? We can start with soup in about twenty minutes?"

He nodded, grabbed the glasses while she opened the wine.

Following her into the living room, he was brought up short. He'd been so focused on her, he hadn't noticed the setup. In the living area, she'd laid out a checkered blanket, set it with a bouquet of roses, linen napkins, cutlery, and pretty white dishes.

"I should have brought you flowers," he said to her back.

She turned, wine in hand. "Why? I have some."

He laughed but cursed himself in his own head. "I still should have brought you some. Hopefully, my gift will make up for it."

She shook her head like he was talking nonsense. Lowering herself to the blanket, she stared up at him. "There's nothing to make up for. You're here. It's all I wanted."

He nodded, glad she felt that way but grabbed the bag he'd brought before sitting down with her.

"Does that mean you don't want your present or the treats from Tara's?"

They both set their wine on her coffee table. She scooted closer, hands out. "If it's chocolate, you know I want it."

He pulled out the little box of heart-shaped mini brownies Tara had made. Hailey's gaze widened. "Yum. Those look delicious."

He nodded, opened the box, fed one to her. When she moaned with pleasure, his stomach tightened, his skin heating. "I think I'm jealous of a brownie."

She laughed, coming closer so she could cuddle up to him. "You're just as delicious." She pressed her mouth to his, giving him a taste of the chocolate. Her hands went to his chest but he didn't want to rush. She made him so happy. He wanted to show her he could do the same.

"There's more," he said, pulling back.

Her hands moved lower. "I certainly hope so."

Wes laughed. "Stop for a sec. I want to give you your present."

She shifted, frowned at him. "If you insist."

Wes pulled the gift-wrapped box from the bag he'd carried the brownies in, handed it to Hailey, his heart thumping way too fast.

She took the box, looked up at him through lowered lashes. "What is it?"

He laughed. "Why do people always ask that?"

One of her shoulders lifted but she hesitated, her hand on the bow. "I only made you dinner."

Wes cupped her cheek. "It smells incredible. I'm going to want to give you things, Hailey. I wouldn't do anything I didn't want to. Please just enjoy it."

She smiled at him—a full Hailey smile—and there was no better gift she could give. Unwrapping the box, she hesitated again when she came to the blue box, running her fingers over the engraved lettering. Her breath hitched, her gaze darting up to his. She looked almost . . . wary. He frowned as she opened the box with what seemed like trepidation.

Inside the Tiffany box, the diamond bracelet was nestled in a soft silk cloth. She sucked in another sharp breath, her fingers touching it so delicately it was like she thought it would break.

When she looked up, her expression took him by surprise. "What is this?"

He smiled. "It's a bracelet. Let me help you." He reached for it but she shook her head, set the box down. "What's wrong?"

"Wes. It's been two weeks. You got me a diamond bracelet from Tiffany's. I made you dinner and yeah, I bought you something, but it only fits me so really, we both benefit."

Now he was curious but he'd have to wait. He did his best to keep his gaze focused on her face. "It's just a bracelet. I wanted to buy you something pretty. Something that shines the way you do."

"Flowers are pretty."

Dammit. He knew he should have grabbed some. "I'm sorry about not bringing flowers."

She shook her head again, this time getting to her feet. "No. Not flowers in addition. Flowers would have been fine. *Nothing* would have been fine." She was pacing, putting wrinkles in the picnic blanket.

He stood up, stopped her with hands on her shoulders. "Talk to me. What's wrong? If you don't like it, it won't hurt my feelings. We can take it back, exchange it. I have an account with the company. It's Ari's favorite store."

Her shoulders sagged; he felt it under his hands. "I don't need diamond jewelry. Where would I even wear it? Grocery shopping with you on a Saturday night? Jesus, Wes. That probably costs the same as my rent on the shop for a couple months." She waved toward the kitchen. "I made you minestrone! I bought lingerie. That's it."

The word "lingerie" stuck in his head and clearly distracted him because when he moved his gaze back up, she was glaring at him, folding her arms across her chest.

"Sorry," he said. "You can't say 'lingerie' and not expect some distraction."

One side of her mouth tipped up. "You won't be seeing it until you tell me that you get it." She stepped forward, putting her hands on his chest. "I care about you. Not your money. In fact, the money thing is a deterrent, if you want the truth."

"How can money be a deterrent?" He hated that he was messing this up with her.

She ran her hands over his chest. He stopped her hands because he couldn't focus while she did that.

"Did you buy me that bracelet because it made you think of me? Because it suited me? Did it call out my name?"

It was hard not to look away. "Not exactly. My sister sent me a picture of one she'd bought. She really loved it, it was pretty, and I thought of you."

"I don't want to feel like I can't keep up with you but we both know there's a discrepancy in our finances."

He pulled her over to the couch, down onto his lap. "That doesn't matter to me. I don't need anything. I wanted to buy something to make you happy. Because you deserve it."

Her fingers played with his hair. "That part is sweet. I'm not trying to be ungracious. I love that you wanted to give me something to make me happy but you know I'm uncomfortable with expensive gifts. Our relationship has changed but that hasn't. I truly only need and want you, Wes." She leaned closer, brushed her nose against his. "You are so much more than enough."

Wes couldn't help but smile at the way she threw his words back at him. "So I can't buy you something when I want to? That hardly seems right."

"You can buy me something if you want to but not because you think it checks off a box in the 'good boyfriend' column. I would have been happy with just the brownies. Gifts should show your connection with the person. They should *suit* them, show you know them, you *get* them. I won't ever be able to give you diamonds but I'm pretty sure I know how to make you happy."

He pressed his forehead to hers. "You do. I want the same. I want to make you happy."

"You do. I've been happier these last couple weeks than I can ever remember being. That comes from your texts, your voice, you showing up at my house with brownies. Making me pancakes last Sunday even though we were going for brunch. I can't accept the bracelet, Wes. I'm sorry. It's too much and if you ever give me a piece of jewelry, I'd like it to reflect me."

He understood that. She might feel as precious as diamonds to him but if he had to choose something right now based on what she said, he'd choose something with a rainbow of colors. Something that made him smile even when the sun was hiding.

"Can I have a do-over?"

She groaned. "So you can buy me something else?"

He shook his head. He wasn't an idiot. He caught on quick. "I was thinking of making you something."

Her smile was brighter than the bracelet. "Now you're getting it."

She kissed him, her hands running through his hair, and he shifted, intending to lay her down on the couch, but she got up off his lap.

"Where are you going?"

She gave him a sly, sexy grin, her fingers going to the top button of her shirt. "Gifts should be bought with that person in mind." The button released, her fingers going to the second one. Wes shifted on the couch as she continued unbuttoning one by one. When she pulled the two sides apart, let the fabric trail off her shoulders, drop to the ground, he forgot how to breathe. Which was fine. He didn't need air when Hailey stood before him in pink lace.

"I'm starting to see what you mean." He barely recognized his voice.

Her fingers went to the button on her pants. "This was actually on sale. Does that take away from your appreciation?"

He shook his head emphatically but words were beyond him.

"It's not about the money or the name brand. It's the thought."

He nodded as the pants slipped over her hips. Swallowing thickly, he moved to the edge of the couch.

"The thought. Got it." He found his voice.

She laughed, stepping out of the pants and toward him. "You're a quick learner."

He grabbed her hand as he stood, pulling her against him. "Right now, I want to learn how to keep that smile on your face."

"That's easy. Kiss me."

That, he could do.

35

Fiona turned the computer so Hailey could see. It was absolutely impossible not to give a little squeal. She squeezed her friend's shoulders, leaned over.

"This is adorable. I love it."

Fiona grinned up at her, pointing to the screen where she'd created a flow chart graphic that helped the reader choose a salad. It was fun and unique.

Hailey took the chair beside her friend, eager to try it out. The shop had been closed for an hour when Fiona texted, asking to drop by. Hailey had been making a schedule—because she had employees—and cleaning up.

"Let's try it," Fiona said. She pointed at the first question. "Do you like a little spice?"

There was a yes or no option, each with arrows pointing to different choices. "Yes." Her gaze followed the arrows. She laughed, reading the choices aloud. "Jalapeño hot or black pepper hot? Black pepper but only because that's a big gap in preferences."

Fiona laughed, scrolled down a touch. "Wimp. Okay. Meat, yes or no?"

Hailey shrugged. "No."

Another arrow pointed down and Fiona scrolled to the bottom of the graphic, revealing a cute graphic of a salad cup.

"House special," Hailey said, clapping her hands together. Below it were the ingredients in very small font: mix of lettuces, red peppers, cucumbers, shaved almonds, shredded cheese, and homemade croutons with oil and pepper dressing.

She reached around Fiona's shoulders, hugging her from the side. "You are so awesome. I love this. I think I might put it on the take-out menus."

"That would be perfect. I'll share the graphic on social media and you can put it on your website."

Fiona often dropped by the shop since she could write anywhere. It was nice having her there. She closed her laptop, picking up one of the coffees she'd brought from Tara's for each of them.

"Things okay with you and Wes?"

After Valentine's Hailey had phoned both Fiona and Piper to talk about the evening and Wes's gift. She'd been tempted to accept it, fawn over it because he was so happy to give it to her, but he'd have seen right through her façade. What they shared was real, which meant she had to be honest with him.

"Yes. I think he gets it but I still feel bad."

"Money can come between people. You told him how you feel. I don't think you need to feel bad. I do wish you'd snapped a picture of it."

Hailey tried to smile. "I'm falling in love with him." She stared at the patterned tabletop, tracing the barely noticeable circles.

When Fiona didn't respond, Hailey looked up. Fiona set her cup down. "Sorry. Was that supposed to surprise me?"

Huffing out a laugh, she picked up her own coffee but didn't sip. "It's too soon. I mean, I wouldn't let him give me a gift, which in his world was really nothing much, yet I'm thinking about a future and how much I want him in it."

Fiona rubbed her shoulder. "Listen, from what you've said, you already tried to fit into a world where you didn't feel like you belonged. If you can't be straight with him when he goes over the top, then you're not as steady as you think you are. Has he given you any reason to think he's upset or hurt?"

She smiled, thinking of the text he'd sent this afternoon, telling her he couldn't wait to see her tonight. "None."

Dropping her arm, Fiona began packing up her laptop. "Then stop sweating it. Enjoy it. Live in the moment. You two can't be in the same room without drooling over each other so I'm thinking he feels the same way."

Giving her a mock glare, Hailey stood up. "I do not drool."

Fiona laughed, touched the corner of her own mouth. "You've got a little right there just from talking about him."

Hailey's tension eased with the laughter. "Get out."

"On my way. See you Sunday."

"Fi?"

Her friend turned, waited.

"Thank you. For the graphic, for being my friend. You're another reason I'm grateful I moved here."

Fiona rolled her eyes but leaned in for a one-armed hug. "You're a big sap. But I'm glad too."

Locking the door after her friend, she decided to do one more check to make sure she was ready for the next day. The massive whiteboard calendar Wes had bought her months ago hung in the kitchen beside the walk-in fridge. Her phone pinged before she made her way to it. Pulling it out of her pocket, she saw it was an email and swiped it open.

Frowning, she leaned against the fridge and read the email from one of their regular lunch contracts. They were canceling. No explanation. She typed a quick response, thanking them for their business, asking if there was anything she could do to make the service better for them, and offering a discount if they changed their minds.

Tucking her phone away, she told herself it was just one contract. It would be okay. Looking at the board, she erased the company's name. They had thirteen other weekly contracts. That was huge. Super important and one of the reasons she'd been able to stop the catering. It made up a substantial piece of her business.

But it bothered her that the one company that canceled was a referral from Ana.

~~~~~~~~~~

Wes greeted her with a wide boyish smile that immediately brightened her mood.

Going up on tiptoes, she kissed him, loving how he leaned down to meet her halfway. His hand went to her hip.

"I missed you," he said.

The admission smoothed away any lingering tension from the end of her day. She cupped his cheek. "Careful. You might be getting addicted."

She didn't need to show all her cards. He laughed, closed the door behind her.

"I'm surprisingly okay with that. What's in the bag?"

She followed him through the apartment, detouring to the kitchen to put the bag in the fridge. "I brought fruit cup salads with a twist."

When she turned, he was right there. She laughed. "You're awfully cuddly. What's going on?"

He bobbed his eyebrows. "What's the twist?"

She went up on tiptoes, kissed his smooth jaw. "Brownies."

He laughed. "Why did I even ask?" He took her hand, pulled her to the couch. "We'll eat after."

She tucked her hand in the back pocket of his jeans as she followed. He didn't wear them often but damn they looked good. "I like the sound of that."

Wes glanced over his shoulder, shooting her one of those droolworthy smiles. "We'll do that after, too."

She laughed when he turned, pretended to toss her on the couch.

He came down with her, landing beside her. "First, I want you to play a game."

"A game?" She shifted on the couch, getting more comfortable by tucking her legs under her. She'd gotten decent enough at his favorites but she didn't love any of them in particular. They'd spent several evenings with him playing while she came up with new salad recipes or read.

"Yup." He opened the laptop.

"Don't we need your console?" He had several and though she, again, didn't have a favorite, his excitement was contagious. "Is it new?"

He glanced at her from the corner of his eyes as he typed something. "Brand-new."

He put the laptop on her lap, glued himself to her side. The screen was blank.

She looked at Wes, leaning over to kiss his cheek. "You're so excited."

He turned his face, met her gaze. "I just want you to know I heard you. I want you to know you matter to me."

Her heart slid right in his direction. "I do know that."

Wes practically bounced in his seat and gestured to the screen. "Hit the space bar, follow the directions."

She did as he asked, completely unsure what to expect. Following the instructions on the screen, she used a combination of arrows, the mouse, and the keyboard to walk an adorable character, named Wes, through a series of tasks. His goal was to get through the maze to an equally adorable character, Hailey. By making the correct choices—flowers over diamonds, chocolate over chips, dogs over cats, tea instead of coffee—he was able to open new pathways. She purposely chose a couple of wrong answers to see what would happen.

Covering her mouth, she tried to stem her tears, pointing at the screen when on-screen Wes sat down, head in his hands, revealing his disappointment. Then she got another chance to try, making the right choices. When he finally cleared the path to on-screen Hailey, the two characters kissed. Little hearts floated over their heads.

Unable to stop the tears, she set the laptop down on the table. When she turned to fully face Wes, he winced. "You're crying. Do you hate it?"

She sniffled indelicately but was too overwhelmed to care that the ugly tears were trying to show up. She shook her head. "I. Love. It." She had to slow the words, put emphasis on each one so she didn't accidentally swap "it" with "you."

Her breath came out shaky. Wes reached for her, ran his thumb under her eyes. "Hey. Hey. Come here," he whispered.

She curled into him, swallowing down the tears. "You are quite possibly the sweetest man in the universe."

His chest rumbled with laughter under her cheek. "The chances of that are slim but as long as you think so, that's all that matters."

They lay there for a while, her breathing him in, doing her best to get her emotions somewhat contained. Hoping she didn't look like a puffy mess, she leaned back, smiled up at him. Wes stroked her hair away from her face, pressed a kiss to her cheek, trailed along, up, over her temple, across her forehead.

Before his lips touched hers, it occurred to her he'd created a game. An actual on-screen game.

She started to share how happy she was but his lips touched hers, making her forget about anything else. She'd tell him later, how much he meant to her, how proud she was. Right now, she put her effort into showing him.

36

April

Wes didn't keep things from his brothers. Ever. Until now. As they each took their seats around the table to listen to their lawyers, his foot bounced up and down.

"What's wrong with you, man?" Noah leaned in, tapped him with his hand.

"Nothing."

Noah arched a brow, looked to where Wes's leg continued to dance on the spot. He stopped.

"Meeting Hailey's cousin and family later. Guess I'm nervous."

"We met them at the restaurant," Noah said.

Wes frowned. "For five minutes. This is different."

"Equivalent to meeting the parents?" Chris asked, leaning in from the other side.

"Pretty much."

Chris smiled. "You clean up okay. You'll be fine."

"Let's get started," their lead counsel, Leonard Reiner, said. He was an older, distinguished man who had a long, successful career fighting for the underdog against men like their father. He worked for them and with them to do things right once and for all. "Your father has agreed to drop all proceedings if these conditions are met."

The other lawyers and assistants passed papers forward. Wes

scanned the list. Their father wanted rights to intellectual property Wes had created, or would create, in the cybersecurity sphere. He wanted a percentage of their investments in exchange for them breaking contracts with his company.

"This is bullshit," Noah said, tossing the paper back. "We didn't *break* anything. We're his sons."

Chris flipped through the pages.

"He means by leaving before the contracts expired on any of the investments we brought in. He's claiming by not staying, we breached several contracts. Which is ridiculous since he could buy or sell whatever he wanted without giving us notice."

Wes's shoulders tightened like an overwound spring. "What does he want? What's his endgame?"

Leonard sighed, steepled his fingers under his chin. "In some ways, I think this is his attempt to hang on to whatever sort of relationship with the three of you he can. Even if it's volatile." Leonard had taken the time to learn everything he could about their father. Between what the brothers had shared and people he had spoken to, he knew more than enough to want to be in their corner.

"I don't think so." Noah scoffed, pushed back from the table, heading to the side bar where he poured some water.

"You don't want this fight," Leonard said.

Chris looked up. "He has an endgame proposal, doesn't he?"

Wes sat up straighter, knowing the answer from the look on their lawyer's face.

"He's to be married at the end of July. He wants all of you there."

Noah slammed the glass down. "Who does this? Who manipulates their children like this?"

Wes didn't know what to say in response to that. Noah started to speak—if Wes had to guess, he'd say his brother was about to use a lot of unfriendly words. Chris sank back in his chair. Wes hated knowing his father still had the power to hurt them. He felt like he'd worked his whole life to protect them, shield them from this kind of manipulation. This had to end.

"I'll talk to him," Wes said.

"I'd advise against that unless I'm present," Leonard said.

"You're not taking the brunt of his bullshit." Chris's expression was hard. Only their father brought that out in his brothers.

"We can't keep fighting like this. I'll be the go-between. We need to end this. It's pulling us away from the things we really want. Let's focus on that."

Noah walked over, stood by Wes's chair. "You don't agree to anything on our behalf. You don't agree to take one for this team. He doesn't get his way. On anything."

Wes nodded. He'd do whatever was necessary to keep their father from wrecking everything they'd built. "Sit down, Noah. I've got this. Let's talk about the Mayville Street Shops."

The conversation shifted, moved through the tension talk of their father always brought. His brothers told him they'd face their father as a united front but Wes wanted to finish it for them. He owed them. As their older brother and for going around them on his most recent investment. Guilt tugged at his conscience, but he told himself they'd have done the same. Doing the right thing didn't always mean it was right for everyone.

~~~~~~~~~

Hailey greeted him in the back of her shop. She was dressed casually in a pair of cropped pants and a pretty tank top, and her hair was pulled into a ponytail. He didn't love the way his heart actually jumped toward her every time but he was getting used to it. It was easier to acknowledge it, accept it, than worry about it.

"Hey." She wrapped her arms around his neck, kissed him. He had to admit, he wouldn't have thought the chemistry between them would remain so . . . charged.

"Everything good?" He kissed her back then opened the door to his truck for her to slide in.

She nodded, waiting until he joined her in the vehicle. She'd been doing some inventory and ordering. He knew she'd lost a couple lunch contracts, which had upset her, but the rush of spring breakers through March had kept her busy enough to refocus.

When he pulled into the traffic, heading toward her cousin's, he felt her gaze.

"Guess what?"

He smiled over at her. "Like really guess or are you just starting your story that way?"

She laughed. "You're so literal. I'll just tell you. We have a meeting tomorrow morning before any of the shops open. We received an email from a new owner. We've been bought and—" She paused.

When he stopped at a light, he looked over. Her smile was enough to flip everything inside him upside down and shift it back into place. "And?"

"The rent is being dropped. Not only that, the new owner—a Genevieve Montroe—is willing to put a rent freeze on for two years for any shop willing to commit to contributing to a community lunch or breakfast program."

Wes's heart squeezed painfully tight, stealing his breath. "That's amazing. On all accounts."

Staying hyperfocused on the road, he clenched his fingers on the wheel as he listened to her excitedly explain some of the ideas she had for how to help and contribute.

"I know you and your brothers decided not to invest but maybe it's for the best."

He nodded. "Things sometimes work out as they should."

Hailey's hand came to his neck, her fingers playing at the base of his skull. Just like that, with a simple touch, his fingers relaxed.

"Sometimes they absolutely do."

Her cousin lived on the outskirts of San Verde in a beautiful residential neighborhood with wide tree-lined streets. It looked like the kind of place neighbors held block parties, where kids grew up together. The house itself was two stories with a detached garage and a large yard. White with gray trim, it was a quintessential family home.

Growing up, Wes and his brothers used to be able to hide for hours from his parents because their house was obnoxiously large. Despite being full of fine art and Italian furnishings, it felt empty. He'd always preferred his grandparents' brownstone. After the divorce, his mother had bought a similar one. They spent a lot of time there and Wes could remember being . . . happy. Without all the arguing, a weight had lifted from his young shoulders. But as the boys got busier in their teen years, his mother started to travel. He wished they'd held on to that time a little longer.

"This is it. Piper and Nick are awesome. They're really excited to meet you," Hailey said.

"I hope I pass," he said. They got out and he came around to the passenger side to take her hand. In his other, he had the bottle of vintage wine he'd purchased from a local collector.

Hailey gestured to it. "You didn't have to do that."

"You wouldn't show up at my family's place with nothing."

She stepped into him. Just breathing in the scent of her hair and *her* calmed the storm inside of him. He was tying himself up in knots over some of his recent choices but when she was close to him like this, everything quieted. He liked it. He was happy.

"I'm really glad you're here. Have you met a girlfriend's family before?"

He shook his head, laughing. "Not since my prom. Hopefully, Nick won't give me the evil eye and a lecture about his gun collection."

She nudged his hip, letting them into the house. "We're here," she called out. She turned to him, whispered, "Nick doesn't have a gun collection."

Children's voices rang out along with the sound of feet running overhead. When Nick and Piper appeared in the hallway together, Wes did his best to not appear nervous.

"Yay! I'm so glad you're here," Piper said, pulling Hailey into a hug.

Wes shook Nick's hand, passed over the wine. Piper hugged him like they were long-lost friends. The kids, Jason, Alyssa, and Cassie, were bundles of energy that talked from the second they saw Hailey and Wes. Jason took Wes's hand while the girls took Hailey's, leading them through the house to the backyard. Wes missed Nick's comment on the wine as Jason explained how he was learning to dive in the deep end of the pool, but he saw the man's appreciative expression.

Piper laughed at something Nick said. "We should leave them and go drink that wine," Piper said, loudly enough for them to hear.

Wes's gaze zipped to Hailey's. Hers was sparkling with amusement. "She's joking. Mostly."

It was easy to settle into conversation. Nick was an investment banker and Wes was excited to talk to him about the newest project he and his brothers were putting together.

"It makes me happy to see people of your wealth and status give back," Piper said.

Wes did his best not to blush. Their grandparents had instilled the importance of giving back. It had resonated with everyone in the family except their father. "I think a lot of people in my position do the same."

"A lot of them don't," Piper said.

Nick nodded, clearly enjoying the wine. "She's right. A lot of times, people give to get. Even if it looks generous, there's an internal motivation no one else was aware of. You and your brothers should be really proud of the work you're doing."

They had BBQ steaks with prawn skewers, the wine was fantastic, the company entertaining and funny. But Wes couldn't get Nick's comment out of his head. What was Wes's motivation for the choices he'd made? Was it selfish? He didn't think so. When he'd talked to his mother, she'd been completely on board with the investment in the San Verde Square. In fact, she was thrilled to be designing a living space directly above Hailey's store. Once he figured out how to tell his brothers, they'd have the office space they wanted. Hailey's and Tara's rent was safe. It was a win-win all the way around.

So, why did he feel guilty for not telling the people who mattered most to him?

37

May

The buzz of saws and banging of hammers made it hard to hear the customers. Hailey leaned in, asked the woman to repeat herself. According to Tara, the owner of their shops was renovating the upstairs space for a variety of purposes. She never knew how Tara got all the good gossip but figured it might have to do with being around longer. Or more employees with their ears to the ground.

Once things quieted down, she left Bryce and Leo in charge, going next door to meet up with Everly, Grace, and a friend of Grace's. Everly had texted earlier that morning and asked if she could join them for coffee and brownies.

The bakery was still bustling with the end of the afternoon rush and it hit Hailey that she no longer had reason to envy the flow of customers. Tara waved from the counter, then pointed toward the back. Folk music played from the speakers. It would be so lovely if they had outdoor patios. With the summer temperatures starting, she could imagine how nice it would be to have the outdoor element.

Grace, her friend, and Everly were tucked in a back corner near a display of quirky items for sale. There were mini coffee cups, little glam bags with BAKED written in gold across the front.

Grace stood, gave Hailey a hug when she arrived at the table. Everly smiled at her as she sat down.

"This is my best friend, Rosie." Grace pointed to the other woman.

With dark curls surrounding a cherub-like face boasting a bright-red-lipstick-painted smile, she was immediately likable. Hailey shook hands with her across the table.

"Nice to meet you."

"You too. I've heard lots about you," Rosie said.

"Most of it is probably true," Hailey said, wincing.

Grace playfully swatted her. "All good things."

Everly laughed, nodding. "Mostly," she said quietly.

Hailey laughed. She'd noticed that each time she saw the radio show producer, she was a little more open. Wes had explained the story of how she and Chris got together. Having gotten to know Everly a bit now, she couldn't imagine how hard it would have been for this woman to go on a bunch of basically blind dates.

"You own the salad shop next door?" Rosie asked.

Hailey picked up the coffee Grace had already ordered for her, took a sip. A loud clang from upstairs interrupted her answer. They all glanced at the ceiling.

"The new owner is renovating. The salad shop is my business but we don't own the space."

Rosie nodded. "I'd love to get up there and see what they're doing."

Grace grinned, using a fork for her brownie. "Rosie and I are both designers. We've been working together on several projects."

"That's exciting for you guys. By the Cup was a sub shop before I moved in so most of it was ideally set up but I got to pick out my furniture and accents. I enjoyed it but I don't have an eye for those details." She gestured to Grace. "Your house is so beautifully decorated. I can't even imagine pulling that all together."

She took a drink as Grace said, "You won't have to worry about it. When you and Wes buy a place, Rosie and I will take charge. Trust me. We're not subtle. Everly already knows I'm barreling full steam ahead when she and Chris finally choose a place."

Hailey choked on her coffee. She coughed loudly, wishing the renovations upstairs could drown her out now. Grace rubbed her back.

"Are you okay?" Everly asked, a small smirk playing on her lips. "Grace, you nearly killed her with the 'buying a house' comment."

Hailey nodded, set her coffee down. "I'm fine." She tried clearing her throat, doing her best to catch her breath.

Grace smiled. "What? Noah said he's never seen Wes so happy. It's not a stretch at this point in our lives that the people we're with are the ones we're choosing." Grace angled herself on the bench seat to look more fully at Hailey. "You are totally in love with Wes, so don't even deny it."

Hailey couldn't help but laugh. "I haven't actually said a thing."

Rosie's laugh was loud and fun. "Never mind Gracie. She sometimes forgets she's not a wedding planner."

Giddy nerves tickled Hailey's ribs. "Wes and I have only been dating for a few months."

"Not everyone is okay with jumping in headfirst," Everly said to Grace affectionately.

Hailey bit her tongue. Oh, she'd jumped *and* landed. But that didn't mean she and Wes would be advancing their relationship that soon. If she knew him, and she was pretty sure she did, he'd have a carefully designed schedule for where their relationship was headed. And because what Grace said was true—she *did* love him—she wasn't entirely sure she was ready to unearth his plans. Because what if they were entirely different than the dreams she envisioned when she slept beside him at night?

"Trust me, the only thing I did with my head when I met Noah was butt it against his," Grace said with a scoff.

"I can attest to that," Rosie added.

The women entertained her with stories of Noah and Grace

becoming neighbors. By the time she went back to the shop, she felt like she was floating. There was something incredibly empowering about having a group of women in her life who cared about her happiness and success. Women who realized that hers didn't impact theirs. She'd wanted so much to dish about Wes but it didn't feel right. He was private and more reserved than his brothers. What they had was theirs.

Leo was sweeping the floor when she returned. Bryce was wiping down tables. The pounding upstairs continued.

"Hey guys. How'd closing go?" She locked the door behind her.

"Good. It was busy today," Bryce said. "There was a phone call about a possible dinner delivery tonight. You had nothing else on the calendar so I said yes."

Leo looked up. His dark hair had grown long enough to fall over one eye. "We were going to make the salads after we do this then Bryce said he can deliver."

"You guys finish up here. I'll take care of the orders and delivery."

"You sure?" Bryce asked.

She nodded. "Of course. If I haven't told you guys already, you're doing an awesome job and I'm so glad to have you guys working here."

Both of the boys sort of ducked their heads, averted their eyes, and mumbled something appreciative and complimentary in response.

Hailey laughed, washing her hands before pulling on her apron. "Mushy moment over. Finish up and get out of here."

It didn't take long to make the salads despite the order being for twenty. They'd only ordered two types. She wasn't sorry she'd let the catering jobs go but she was surprised by how many companies wanted the convenience of take-out for their employees. Pleasantly surprised. She packed up the orders, loaded them in her SUV, and dialed Wes on the way to the business section of town.

"I was just thinking of you," Wes said into the phone.

Happiness warmed her skin. "That's nice to hear."

"I'm just about to head into a meeting. Did you want to come by later?" She heard muted sounds in the background.

"Absolutely. I just have a delivery then I'm heading home. Maybe call me when you're done?"

"Sounds good."

Hanging up, she was grateful for time to go home, shower, and change. She'd spilled olive oil on her jeans when the container slipped while she was making dressing. Fortunately, they were mostly work jeans so she wasn't too worried that the stain was unlikely to come out. She pulled into the large, nondescript parking lot. It was one of those multibusiness places. Bryce's instructions said second floor, 217. A security guard saw her coming and held the door for her.

"Thank you," she said, giving him an appreciative smile.

"No problem. Where you headed?" He walked toward the elevator, glancing at her.

"217."

He nodded, pressed the up arrow. "CoreTech." He pointed to the ceiling then stretched his arm out. "Get out, turn right, go down to the end of the hall."

Hailey hoped her face gave nothing away but as she stepped onto the elevator, her stomach cramped uncomfortably. It was a coincidence. That's all. Ana may not even have placed the order. If she did, she'd have no way of knowing that Hailey would deliver herself.

The tub of salads felt unsteady in her hands. The elevator doors opened. She took an extra second to take a deep breath, let it out. She turned right and walked down the hall. When she reached the end, the glass door was open. There was no one at the reception but Hailey caught sight of a windowed room with several people around a table. Ana caught her gaze through the glass, smiled, and opened the door.

"Dinner as promised, guys. Come on in, Hailey."

Hailey gritted her teeth, walked past Ana, set the box down on a side table near a mounted whiteboard with information written all over it. She turned, ready to leave, when she saw Wes. He stood from the end of the table and hurried toward her.

Looking at Ana, she wasn't surprised to see a look of satisfaction on the woman's face. She'd seen it many times in her life, particularly when she lived with Dorian.

Wes approached, put a hand on her arm. Ana turned before he could say anything.

"Aidan, can you pay the salad girl, please. Don't forget to add a tip." She turned to Hailey. "Thank you so much for coming all this way. My brother will take care of the bill."

Ana's brother joined them. Hailey could *feel* Wes seething beside her. Tension emanated off him like steam from a boiling pot. Aidan frowned at his sister.

"Hailey. Lovely to see you again," he said, taking in the scene before him. To his credit, he sent his sister an unfriendly look.

Biting her tongue, refusing to let the woman bait her, she simply nodded curtly then gave him an amount.

"Wes, you look upset. I thought you'd be happy to have Hailey get some business," Ana said.

"Hailey's business is none of your concern. This crosses a line, Ana."

Murmurs started behind them as people came to choose salads.

"Jesus, Ana," Aidan said under his breath, pulling several bills out of his wallet before passing them to Hailey. "What did you do?"

"*I* didn't do anything. Other than attend an event with a date," Ana said.

Wes's cheeks went pink and Hailey felt horrible. He hated confrontation, scenes, being the center of attention. Stepping toward the door, knowing the others would move with her, she swallowed down the hurt and anger she felt.

"It wasn't a date," Wes said.

Hailey put a hand on his arm and he stepped closer, wrapping his arm around her shoulder. She looked at Ana, whose gaze was filled with empty satisfaction.

"This isn't the time or place. And really, there's nothing to discuss." She waited until Ana looked *at* her. "I've done nothing to you. I'm sorry you feel slighted but you're a strong, beautiful woman. I'm not sure what your goal tonight was but you're better than this. Wes wasn't with you. I didn't steal him. It doesn't matter if you get more friends to cancel their contracts with me, it won't change anything. Do you even like Wes or is it just that he chose me?"

Shock widened Ana's gaze.

"What contracts?" Wes looked at her.

"Goddamn it, Ana. Wes, Hailey, I'm sorry." Aidan shoved his hands in his pockets.

Ana stiffened her shoulders. "I'm not sure what everyone is upset about. I ordered salads. You guys eat, she gets business. Win-win."

Hailey nodded. "Keep telling yourself that. Thank you for your business. Aidan, nice to see you. Wes." She took a second, not caring that Ana stood before her in a freaking designer pantsuit while she wore oil-stained jeans. Whatever else Hailey might be unsure of, she knew, without a doubt, Wes wanted to be with her. She ran her hand up Wes's chest, into his hair, and kissed him. "I'll see you at home."

With that, she turned and left. Proud of herself, she waited until she was in the elevator to collapse against the wall and let out a string of swear words.

38

Wes's pulse scrambled, like it was short-circuiting. The last time he'd been this mad was because of *her* ex. This time . . . it was Ana. When he saw Hailey walk into that room, his heart had leaped, scaring the hell out of him. He didn't understand emotional games, didn't play them, but he was smart enough to recognize them in the slyness of Ana's smile.

When Hailey left, he'd had to fight the urge to quit on the spot. The guilt he carried over making one huge decision without his brothers was enough to stop him from doing it again. But he did make it clear to Ana that he'd never wanted her that way. It had always been business. Hailey was gone when he got to the parking lot so he'd headed home.

He could still picture her, standing tall, standing up for herself. She was amazing. He'd tried phoning her but got voicemail. Hopefully, she'd be at his home shortly after he arrived.

When he got there and let himself inside his apartment, he had visitors. Just not who he'd hoped.

"The keys were for emergencies," Wes said to his brothers, putting his own key in its spot on the table by the door.

Noah and Chris were sitting on his couch, beer in hand, watching sports.

"Make yourselves at home," he said, tucking his shoes in the closet, shrugging off his jacket. "Maybe it's better you're here. I need to talk to you guys." Time to spill his guts. He'd thought he could help everyone along, smooth out all the red tape, then do a "big reveal," but now it just felt like keeping secrets.

Chris looked at him but Noah practically snarled, "About fucking time. Better late than never, I guess?"

Chris sent Noah a warning look. "Knock it off."

Something was up. He grabbed a beer of his own, started into the living room when the buzzer went for his apartment. "That's Hailey."

Noah started to swear, increasing Wes's own irritation tenfold. "I don't know what your problem is but hang on to it for a minute." He buzzed Hailey in, meeting his brother's gaze, glare for glare.

He opened the door in time to see Hailey step off the elevator. His rib cage shrank, making his breath tight. She looked gorgeous, with that auburn hair still slightly damp around her shoulders, a cute pair of patterned leggings, and a long off-the-shoulder gray shirt.

"Hi." Her smile when she saw him made him feel ten feet tall. What was it about her?

Wes leaned in, overwhelmed with how happy he was to see her. He kissed her, pulled back, then leaned in for more. When he pulled back, she looked up at him with a confused, blinking gaze.

"Are you okay?" Her hand rested on his stomach.

"I should be asking you. I'm so sorry about earlier."

She shook her head, moved around him to go in. "Not your fault. Oh. Hi, guys."

Wes shut the door behind them and followed her into the living area. Both Chris and Noah stood, offered their spots. Hailey laughed, shook her head, and sat cross-legged on his huge ottoman, dropping her bag beside it on the floor.

"I'm good here. How are you guys? I had brownies and coffee with Everly and Grace today. I met Grace's friend Rosie."

Both of his brothers shook off some of their moods and engaged with Hailey. It made him happy they all got along well.

"The patio around the pool is just about finished. We'll have a BBQ when it's all done," Noah said. "You guys can stay over."

Wes nodded. That would be great. Hailey looked at him questioningly. He smiled at her but answered Noah. "That sounds good."

He didn't know where to start. Clearly his brothers were here for a reason but he didn't want to get into his own confessions with Hailey here. Not yet. Plus, he wanted to see if she was really okay about Ana.

Chris and Noah exchanged a glance. Of course, it was Noah who threw the bold statement at them. "I'm guessing you two are serious?"

Hailey's gaze widened.

"Goddamn it, Noah. Have some tact. We're not doing this now."

"What's going on?" Hailey's voice was nearly timid. It didn't suit her.

Noah stood, gesturing back and forth between them. "I'm not waiting. This isn't about tact, it's about honesty. What the hell, Wes?"

To his credit, Chris winced, shrugged an "I'm sorry" at Wes, but he stood, moved next to Noah.

"You guys know." Son of a bitch. He should have just told them.

"Know what?" Hailey asked, looking at him.

"There's construction going on at your place?" Noah asked Hailey.

She nodded uncertainly. "Yes. The new owner is remodeling. I think she's planning on a huge apartment or something. I'm not sure. Tara always knows more than me."

Noah and Chris looked at Wes. He set his beer down on the coffee table, refusing to squirm under their censure. He opened the patio door, stood by it for a minute.

"Wes? What's going on?"

He turned and looked at the three of them.

Noah shook his head. "If you wanted it that bad, fine. Why go behind our backs?"

"That's not what this was, Noah. We decided it wasn't right for SCI. But I felt strongly about it."

"Should I go?" Hailey reached for her bag. His brothers looked at him, brows lifted.

Wes gave a deep sigh. "You should stay but know, you'll likely be mad at me by the time they're done."

Her fingers gripped her bag and she pulled it onto her lap like it was security. "Okay. You're worrying me."

"I know the owner of your building. My brothers decided not to invest."

Her shoulders sagged with what seemed like relief. "Oh. Okay. I'm sorry it didn't work out for you guys. It would have been nice to have your meeting space just upstairs."

Chris's mouth tightened. Noah smiled at her. "We'll probably still do that."

Hailey looked at him. "What am I missing? I don't like games. What's going on?"

One more reason to like her: she didn't like games. She didn't play them and looking at this from behind, he could see he'd made a pretty big mistake.

"The new owner is our mother."

If she hadn't been firmly planted on her butt, she looked like she would fall over. "I don't understand."

Wes shoved both hands in his hair then tugged at his tie, pulled it off, and tossed it on the kitchen table. "It wasn't the right investment for our company but I still felt strongly about the space. So, I spoke to my mother, asked her to weigh in. She's been thinking about moving to California or at least having a place here. I mentioned the area above the shops. Sent her some pictures. She loved it."

"You let Mom invest her money in something we agreed wasn't

a good investment," Chris said. His brother's tone was disappointed. It felt like a kick in the gut.

"Not a good investment for *us*. But for Mom, it *is*. She'll have more space at a better price than if she'd bought a condo. She'll be finishing the two small apartments that have been empty for months because of the cost. We can have the meeting area; she even said she'd charge us for it. Plus she'll have rent from the shops. It works for everyone."

Hailey sucked in a breath. "Wait." She took a deep breath. Like sucked in for a full five seconds, then released it. She met Wes's gaze. "Did you suggest your mother buy the shops to help me with the rent?"

He continued to stare at her, unwilling to regret making her life easier. It was a good move for everyone. "That was a factor in my decision, yes. But that doesn't mean she would have purchased them regardless. She's thrilled. It's a good investment. I wouldn't put my mother in a bad situation."

Hailey stood almost as if in slow motion. "That's good to hear. But, if I'm understanding correctly, what you *would* do is go behind everyone's backs, including mine, to make sure my rent was reasonable."

He shoved a hand in his hair. Everyone always told him he was too black and white, too literal. Now he understood. What he'd done was in the gray area. Technically, what she said was true but it was more complicated than she said. "We would have lowered it if we'd bought it."

She nodded, pursed her lips. "But you didn't buy it. Why would an owner move in and lower the rent?"

"Because she's a *real* businessperson who understands what the previous owner charged was ridiculous. He was operating on fear, trying to undo bad investments. She'll profit on these shops even with lowering the rate. With what that guy was charging, everyone would have had to move. You would have had to look for a different space."

"Was it a favor?" She stepped closer to him. He felt like prey.

"Yes. No. *No*. Not a favor. A smart move for everyone."

She turned to his brothers. "In your honest opinion, was this a smart move for everyone?"

Noah's gaze widened before he looked down to study his feet. "Not for Wes," he muttered.

Chris elbowed him. "Hailey, Wes is smarter than anyone I know. He never would have suggested the investment if my mother wouldn't do well. He only *ever* has people's best interests at heart."

Wes swallowed. "Thanks, man."

Chris shot him a glance. "But it's always in everyone's best interests to be up front. Especially when you have a partnership."

Wes didn't know if his brother meant their partnership or him and Hailey.

"Hailey."

She shook her head, held up a hand. "I tell you a Tiffany bracelet is too much after two weeks, you seem to get it. I didn't think it needed to be said but apparently you need it spelled out pretty clear. Nearly four months is too soon to buy real estate to save your girlfriend's ass. Especially when said girlfriend has told you more than once that I can take care of myself. I don't want anything from you other than *you*, but that's too much for you to wrap your head around, isn't it?"

Noah muttered, "Oh shit."

Walking closer, hoping to get the situation under control, he reached out. "Hailey, I didn't buy the place. I didn't rescue you. But would it be so bad if I did? You matter to me. Do you think I'm just going to let your dreams fall apart when I can stop it?"

She shook her head. "So, you support me, listen to me. You help me brainstorm ideas but you don't reach into your pockets and bail me out." He started to speak but she held up her hand. "Or ask your mom to do it."

He stiffened, dropped his hands. "Speaking of hiding things. Why didn't you tell me you'd lost two contracts because of Ana?"

She stormed toward him, poked his chest. "Because my business is mine to take care of. I'm not going to cry to my boyfriend about a couple of lost lunch contracts through her when I filled those spots in seconds."

"We should go," Chris said, hedging toward the door.

Hailey shook her head. "No. I'm leaving. You stay." She started to go but turned. "I thought when you made me that game that you really did understand me. You spend so much time looking for ways to solve other people's problems, even when they don't want you to, you end up creating more. I don't need saving. I saved myself when I showed up here. I know you have money but that isn't the part of you I see. I see the guy who laughs at corny jokes, always puts his keys exactly where they go, makes lists for fun, and is an incredibly talented artist. But you need to start looking back, Wes. I needed someone to see me, all of me, and believe I could do what I set out to do with or without them."

He shoved his hands in his pockets, his jaw tightening. "I won't apologize for wanting what's best for you."

Noah and Chris groaned in unison.

"That's part of your problem. You think *you* get to decide what that is. But I make my own choices."

"Don't leave like this." The word "stay" sat heavily in his mouth. He didn't want her to go.

"I'm leaving before I say something I'll regret."

She walked by him. He fought the urge to reach out and yank her against his body, hug her until she could feel all his emotions trembling inside of him. But he wouldn't. This was exactly what he'd feared. That he'd want her so badly, he'd let his emotions rule his decisions. He was thrilled his mother owned the shops. Should he have talked to her? Maybe. But he couldn't chase after her only to have her walk away regardless. Space and time would give them both clarity. That was rational. Logical. They'd come to an agreement somewhere in the middle.

"Dude. You're an idiot," Noah said.

"Shut up, Noah." Chris shook his head, sank down to the couch.

He hated fighting. It was part of why he tried to control the narrative. But maybe his need to sort things out in the way he deemed right really was getting in his way. His heart hurt. *See? Emotions muddle everything up.* He'd been so sure he was right, and now? He just didn't know.

"Just out of morbid curiosity, what did you want to talk to *us* about?" Chris let his forearms drop between his legs.

Wes sank down to the spot Hailey had vacated. "This. I didn't mean to keep it from you guys. I'm sorry. I was just trying to get things in place before telling you. But I also wanted to talk about CoreTech. Ana was horrible to Hailey. I'd like to drop them as a client."

Noah hung his head then pinned Wes with an angry glare. "Let's not make any more rash decisions. I'm not saying no but let's let it sit for a while."

God. He was doing it again. Acting on emotion. Of course they needed to let it sit. Discuss it.

Chris looked at Wes, studying him closely. "Why did she call you an artist?"

He ran his hands through his hair, held on to it as he looked at his brothers. He felt like he was treading water. "She's seen my art. I made her a video game. It's nothing."

His brothers both looked at him, their mouths open. Their expressions might have been comical if he didn't feel so heavy.

"Man. You really are clueless," Noah said.

Wes let out something close to a growl, dropped his hands, and stepped up to his brother. Chris came between them immediately, a hand on each chest.

Wes stepped back, an unrecognizable feeling settling heavy inside of him. "What the hell is wrong with you two?" He didn't mean to yell but everything felt hazy, like he was reaching for something just out of his grasp. "I've been here for both of you for everything. Now, when I'm struggling, trying to figure shit out, you give me a hard time?"

Noah's chest deflated. He clapped Wes on the back. "We just want you to be happy, bro. You keep getting in your own way and messing that up."

Wes stared at the space where Hailey had been. "How do you two do this?"

Chris stepped beside him. "Do what?"

His chest was hollow. "Feel so much."

Noah flanked his other side, all three of them staring at the seat. "I'd like to say you get used to it but I don't know if you do. Maybe just lean into it?"

Wes breathed in through his nose, filling his lungs, breathing out slowly. He'd fooled himself all these years that it was an active choice not to fall for a woman. His brothers told him it wasn't something he could control once he met the *right* woman. He hadn't believed them. Now, no matter what choice he made, he could end up alone and heartbroken. Worse, he could hurt Hailey. There wasn't even anything he could have done differently. Once he'd let Hailey into his life, his heart took over. He could deny it, fight it, but really, he had no control over anything.

39

Hailey ignored Wes's texts and calls. She wasn't sure how to make herself calm down. She tried deep breaths, staring at the ceiling, a glass of wine, music. Nothing worked. Her skin didn't feel right. Nothing did. She knew she was proud—knew it was because she was so scared to really rely on someone and trust their feelings. Trust that they wouldn't leave or let her down.

In the end, she went to the beach. It *was* California, after all. Not bothering with anything other than her phone, with her ID tucked in the case, she drove to the nearest one, parked, and settled herself on the sand to stare at the water.

The last several years had been an exercise in figuring out not only *who* she was but also who she *wasn't*. She didn't want to push Wes away simply because he wanted good things for her. She scooped up a handful of sand, let it fall through her fingers, frustrated with herself. Dorian hadn't given enough. Wes was giving too much. Was she just hard to please? No. Because underneath both relationships, what she wanted was the same: She wanted to be *seen*. Accepted. And loved anyway.

The waves rolled in a mesmerizing rhythm. Seagulls dove in the distance. A few people, farther down, were splashing in the surf but this late in the day, it was quiet. God, it'd been a long day. After about an hour, no further into solving her own problems than she'd been earlier, she got up, dusted her clothes off to head for her vehicle.

On the way, she passed a food truck and her stomach growled. Waiting in the line, she chatted with the guy for a couple minutes while he made her two fish tacos.

"By the Cup? I was there a couple weeks ago. That's a great shop you've got," he said. He'd wrapped a green bandana around his head to hold his hair out of his face.

"Thank you," she said. It was the first thing in hours that had made her smile. "It's going really well."

"Rent can be steep. You ever get tired of being locked into one place, I've got a buddy who helped me get my truck up and running." The guy passed her a card.

She stared at it a moment, then looked back up at the guy— Chase. "Thank you. That's really nice of you."

He laughed like her comment was funny. "No problem. I mean it."

She started to walk away but turned back. "Why?"

He'd picked up a cloth but his hand froze in midair. "What?"

Hailey stepped back toward the truck. "Why would you help me? You don't know me."

Chase laughed, the creases around his eyes deepening. He set the cloth down, leaned on his forearms. "Why not? Your salads are good. People like variety. Trucks have a lot of benefits."

"But why help a stranger?"

He stared at her a minute, tilted his head to the side. One of his dark, curly locks tumbled over the bandana. "When we stop looking out for each other, the world gets scary."

She nodded, smiled at him, and thanked him again. She'd told herself that she wouldn't ever rely on anyone again but that wasn't the way life worked. The whole way home, she thought about that, about Wes wanting to help her only to have her push him away. Sure, he'd gone overboard, but it wasn't just for her. It was for his mom, his brothers, himself. She might have been a deciding factor but if they were going to share a life together, they *should* be factors in each other's decisions. But he'd never hid who he was. If she wanted to be accepted, she needed to do the same. The truth was, she'd do anything for him. So why didn't she trust that his interests were for the same reason as hers?

Feeling exhausted, she didn't phone him or text when she went home. She'd talk to him in the morning, say sorry for her part in things. She couldn't have a partner if she was unwilling to lean on him, at least as much as she wanted him to do the same.

~~~~~~~

Hailey wasn't running behind for once. Since she'd hired Dolly, her time had freed up some and she no longer felt like there was no way to accomplish her to-do list. *Another example of how letting someone in, trusting them to help and not let you down, works out in your favor.* Hailey still needed to run a few errands before she went into the shop. Most importantly, she needed to talk to Wes.

She didn't, however, expect him to be on her doorstep when she came out her front door.

In a gray sweater and jeans, his hair mussed, he looked like he hadn't gotten any more sleep than she had.

"Hi," she said, standing on the bottom step, bringing her eyes level with him.

"Hi." He touched her waist, stepped into her, their lips a fraction apart.

"I'm sorry," she whispered.

His gaze widened. "You are?"

She nodded with a smile, put her hands on his shoulders. "I am. I think we need to talk about some boundaries. But I shouldn't raise my hackles quite so high."

His grin was belly warming. "I'm sorry, too. I should have talked to you."

"Do you want to come up for a cup of coffee?" She could do errands later.

"You don't need to get to work?"

She was already unlocking the door. "Dolly is opening."

As if they'd come to an unspoken agreement, they waited to fall together until they were in her apartment. His lips touched hers tentatively at first but she stepped into him, pulled him closer. *You're mine. And I want to be yours.* She needed to trust his words, his actions, *and* his intentions.

When he pulled back, he used both hands to sweep her hair away from her face. "I know I can be difficult."

She laughed. "Well, I think I might have a couple faults of my own."

"I didn't mean to go behind your back. Well, I did, but I won't again. The thing is, I really think this space is great for my family. I didn't do it *just* to help you. I know I have some boundary issues but I promise you, I'll work on it."

Hailey felt like she physically melted into him. "I need to work on a few things of my own. Like trust. And also believing that just because you want to help me doesn't mean you don't think I'm capable."

His eyes widened. "Hailey, you're one of the most capable women I've ever met. You're amazing."

He really believed that. She ran her hands up and down his arms, so happy he was there. "I just don't want you to think your money has anything to do with my feelings for you."

He laughed. "Trust me, I know that. You forgive me?"

"Do you forgive me?"

He nodded. "We've survived our first big fight," he said, kissing her cheek.

Hailey patted him down, earning a sexy arch of his brows. "Making sure you didn't bring any stupidly expensive jewelry."

Wes's deep laugh filled the last dredges of worry. "I know better."

She pulled him over to the couch where they sat side by side, her legs thrown over his lap.

"Is everything okay with Chris and Noah? I didn't think about it until after but they don't usually just show up like that, do they?"

"No. They'd found out from Grace and Everly about the construction. Noah, being Noah, got curious. He looked up the sale. They were there to kick my ass."

She tilted her chin down. "Poor baby."

He laughed. "You don't mean that. They're no longer mad at me either, though Noah doesn't want me to dump CoreTech as a client."

Hailey's back stiffened. "Why would you do that?"

Wes sighed, lowered his hand to her knee. "Because I won't tolerate the way Ana treated you."

"Wes. I don't need you to fight my battles. Ana's issues with me have nothing to do with business."

His fingers squeezed gently. "I know but the behavior is unacceptable. If that's how she does business, I want no part of it." He paused. "Why didn't you tell me about the contracts?"

Hailey fidgeted, avoiding his gaze. "I guess because I thought you'd be protective or mad."

After tilting her chin up with his fingers, he met her gaze. "What's wrong with that?"

Wanting to protect her? Support her? Nothing. *Intentions.* Wouldn't she be upset if someone treated him that way? "I replaced those contracts with others immediately. I didn't want to impact your business."

"You're a big part of my life, Hailey. How other people treat us will impact the other person."

She nodded. "Just tell me you and your brothers are okay."

Wes laughed, tapped her nose. "We'll always be okay."

Hailey kissed him on the cheek. "Look at us, communicating like champs."

He laughed, kissed her, letting his mouth linger. She didn't have that much time before work. She wrapped her arms around his neck, squeezing hard. "I'm so glad you were here this morning. I want things to be okay between us."

He pulled back, stroked her hair. "So do I. It's good that we know we can work through things reasonably. It bodes well for our future."

She nuzzled against him, wondering how long she could put off going into work. "Well, when you put it like that, I'm so very glad we made up." The questions bubbled up inside of her. She tried to shove them down, live in the moment. Instead, she went with a statement. "I'm glad you think about us having a future." It gave her permission to hope.

Pulling her up to sit, he kept his arm around her shoulder. "I'm a little old to be investing time in a relationship otherwise."

Hailey swung her legs to the floor. "Guess I nabbed you at a good time then," she joked.

Wes took her hand, traced his finger along the back of it. "I worried, when we first got together, that it would ruin things between us. The sexual, romantic piece. I didn't want to lose my friend. Instead, it's just enhanced everything that was already great. I'm glad we took the chance."

She turned her head, the declaration stuck in her throat. Her heartbeat danced in the base of her neck. "Me too," she whispered.

Wes leaned toward her, brushing his lips with hers. The kiss was so sweet, so soft. Hailey was pulled into the moment, the man.

"I love you," she whispered, her lips skimming his. Life was too short to keep it to herself.

Wes's body jerked, making Hailey go rigid against him.

"What?" The word was scratchy, like his throat went dry.

She laughed nervously, easing away as she rubbed her hands up and down her legs. *It's okay. You know he's different, it takes him time to wrap his head around his feelings.*

Wes angled himself toward her, waited for her to look at him. When she did, his gaze was wary. Uncertain. "What did you say?"

She cringed. *Too much, too soon.* Pushing up off the sofa, she grabbed her purse. "Never mind, Wes. It was just a slip." It would be fine. She'd got caught up in the moment and thrown it at him without any warning. They'd laugh about it one day.

He stood as well, letting out a sigh of what could clearly be called relief. "Okay. Thank God."

She whirled on him, stared, wondering if he realized what he'd said. How it would make her feel. She *did* love him. She didn't have the best timing but that didn't make it less true. "Thank God?" She shook her head, her lips trying to form words. "What's that supposed to mean?"

Wes shoved his hands in his pockets. "Hailey. It's not like you didn't know this going in."

"Know what?"

"That I'm not . . . that love isn't—" He stopped, shook his head. Pacing away from her, he almost seemed to be mumbling to himself. He stopped in front of her. "I care a great deal about you. You are very important to me. But you've known since the beginning of our acquaintance I'm not the declaration, marrying kind of guy."

Now she huffed, wrapping her arms around her purse like a security blanket. "I didn't ask you to marry me."

"Okay."

They stared at each other. Hailey blinked away the tears that threatened. It was fine if he didn't love her back but did that mean he never would? He was the one who brought up their future.

Swallowing past the lump in her throat, she asked, "Just out of curiosity, where do you see this going?"

Wes pulled his hands out of his pockets, a V forming between his brows. "I don't like that question."

Hailey's laugh felt like acid in her throat. "I'm not particularly enjoying this conversation so I guess we're even."

He let out a frustrated sound. "Things are great between us. Why do we have to do this?"

"Wes, you got your mom to buy my building because you were worried about my rent. But you're mad because I love you?"

Shock registered in his expression. "You said it was a slip!" He pointed at her.

"Yeah, as in, I shouldn't have said it out loud." The buckle of her purse was digging into the spot between her breasts but she only held tighter.

"But you love me?" He sounded . . . heartbroken.

What the actual hell? "I can't help how I feel." At least, not to the extent he clearly could.

"Of course you can. We both can." He closed the distance between them. "We're a great match. We make each other laugh, we're attracted to each other, we enjoy each other's company. Can't that be enough?"

"You'll never love me?"

His gaze answered before his mouth. "I don't want to be in love. I don't want to get married or have children."

Her throat went dry. She wanted all of those things. She nodded her head, up and down, up and down, like the movement could absorb the pain of his words.

Wes gripped her shoulders. "That doesn't mean we can't be together. I *want* to be with you. So much."

"I'm not asking for declarations or promises but I don't know if I can just go forward knowing you never want those things with me."

"It's not *you*. It's those things I don't want. We can be—we *are* happy together."

Pain radiated through her body with the truth of what he was saying. "I can't be in another relationship where I'm the only one who's willing to give. Who's willing to fall all the way. I told you this."

He dropped his hands but Hailey wasn't done. "Wes, you're scared. I think you care about me more than you want to. Isn't it possible that you're just afraid to admit how you really feel? To me and to yourself?" His behavior, his words—not at this particular moment but usually—suggested that he could love her. That he might already.

Wes stared at her like she'd lost her mind. "You don't make any sense. You sell salads but eat sugar, you'd give the shirt off your back to anyone but get mad when I step up to help, you've been on the wrong side of love but still throw the word around like a naïve person who doesn't know any better."

Hailey tossed her purse to the couch and stepped into his space. She wanted to touch him, pull him close, make him *feel* what she felt. Instead, she worked to gentle her tone. "Believing in love doesn't make me naïve. It makes me brave. The fact that I was hurt makes me stronger, more sure of what I want. I'm not afraid to ask for it or want it. You think you can slot everything into its own box but life doesn't work like that. *I* don't work like that."

"You're supposed to learn from your mistakes," he said haughtily.

All gentleness fled. Hailey's heart fell right down to her shoes. She squared her shoulders. "Screw you, Wes. I did learn. I learned that I'd rather get hurt again than be too damn scared to feel anything real. All the money, the investments, the control over your feelings you're so proud of? Those things seem safe but playing it that way makes you a coward. If you can't give yourself completely, let yourself fall even if it means you break, you'll never be truly happy. And if you can't at least try, we aren't going to work out."

His hand clenched and unclenched. She saw the tightness in his stance, the coldness in his gaze. "I hate to be the one to tell you this but love and happiness rarely go hand in hand."

He walked out before she could ask him to go. When the door closed behind him, Hailey stood there, wondering how the hell everything had changed. She didn't realize she was crying until the tears fell to her chest, rolling along her skin. She continued to stand there, frozen. What had she said to him? That she'd rather hurt than not try? *Well, you tried.*

Lowering herself to the corner of the couch, she tucked her knees up so she could wrap her arms around them. She squeezed tighter, trying to lessen the impact, but there was no way. There was no way not to feel every word he'd said, the look in his eyes and the realization that not only could he not love her back, if given the choice, he wouldn't.

Was this better? Feeling this way? Like her heart was paper being torn apart, every shred landing in a discarded pile on the floor? She felt like she was watching herself from outside her body. Through the trembling and the tears, she knew, deep down, on some level, that she'd be okay. But she'd never be the same.

40

Hailey grinned at the customer until her cheeks ached. "Thanks for coming in." She started cleaning the counter as Leo came back from his break.

"Hey. I'm going to head out to do the deliveries," he said.

Turning her head, she nodded. "Great. Can you make sure to drop the envelope I tucked in the box with Rob at the gym? He wants to expand his order."

Leo nodded, hung up his apron. "You bet. You okay, Miss Hailey?"

Pushing her smile back in place, she looked at him. "I'm fine, why?"

"I just . . . I don't know, you seem different." He shrugged.

Different? Like what? Like someone had plucked her heart out of her chest and she was now operating at a deficiency? She pictured one of Wes's games where every time she lost, one little red heart disappeared. She nearly laughed at her own thoughts.

"Nope. I'm good. Thanks for doing the deliveries."

He stared at her a moment longer then left through the kitchen. She was dicing cucumber when Tara walked through the door. She'd purposefully avoided Piper's and Fiona's texts because she was no longer in a place in her life where she was going to let a little thing like having her heart obliterated derail her goals.

She was fine.

"Hey, Tara. How's it going?"

Tara's brown curls framed her round face. Hailey had slight eyelash envy and considered asking where she got them done.

"Hi. I'm good. How are you?" She had a paper in her hand.

Hailey came around the counter, leaving the veggies, wiping her hands on her apron. "I'm good. Things are busy. What's that?" She gestured to the paper.

"Esther had the idea to do a newsletter for the shops. We thought it would be a good way to do specials, share upcoming promotions, and get the word out. I wanted to show you and get some ideas of what you'd like to add."

Taking the paper, she looked over the layout, saw the examples others had put for their shops. Two for One Tuesday was advertised at several of the shops.

"This is really great. It's a wonderful idea. You could put these flyers somewhere like Rob's gym or other high-volume places."

Tara nodded. "That's a great idea. Do you want in on the Tuesday specials?"

Hailey wiped her hands on her apron again. "Actually, do you have a minute? I wanted to ask you about something."

Tara regarded her with an easy smile. "Of course."

They sat at one of the tables, Hailey gripping the apron in her fingers. "I've been thinking about a food truck. I wanted your opinion. I hope it's okay to ask." She took a deep breath. "I admire you and love what you've done with your business. Esther told me when you started, you only had three signature desserts and coffee." Hailey wanted to build and grow. But maybe here wasn't her place.

Tara smiled as if happy memories were filtering through her head. "It's been a few years now. Yeah, those first couple years, when more of the shops were empty, it was tough. But three desserts turned to four, then six. I hired a woman named Maddie who owns her own business now. She knew how to make fancy drinks so that got added to the menu. I think a food truck is an amazing addition but I would caution you against too much too fast. When I started, I wanted to add a full menu but a friend suggested I start small. Make them want more."

Hailey let go of her apron, put her hands on the table. "Oh. No. I meant a food truck instead."

Tara didn't bother trying to hide the surprise. "Oh." She frowned. "Why? Things are going so well." She leaned in, folded her arms.

Hailey did her best to sound like she was reciting the specials, that the words didn't affect her. Didn't drag across the spot where her heart had been with sharp little nails. "They are. I'm not sure if you know but Wes's mother is the new owner. He encouraged her to buy the place. I don't know . . . at first I was mad he wanted to swoop in and save me. It turned out to be more than that. Not all about me." She let out a bitter laugh. "But I don't know if I can stay. Not with." Tears threatened and she looked toward the ceiling. "It's just too close, you know?"

"Wait, I thought you and Wes were doing great. You're so good together." Tara leaned forward, covered Hailey's hand.

Her words felt like a sucker punch. They *were* good together. Tara was in *his* circle, not hers. Asking a business-related question was one thing—that took enough nerve on its own. She was *not* falling apart in front of Tara. "We broke up. Which is fine but, as I'm sure you can guess, makes things more awkward. I'm just looking at other opportunities."

Tara squeezed her hand. "I'm so sorry. I don't know him as well as Chris but he's a good man and I haven't ever seen him smile the way he does with you."

Hailey tried to swallow repeatedly like she would on an airplane. "We want different things." She was so proud that her voice didn't crack. "He's a wonderful man. I hope he finds what he's looking for." There. Take that back to Wes. She was cool, calm, and collected.

Compassion shone in Tara's gaze, making the lump in Hailey's throat grow.

"Sometimes people have what they didn't realize they wanted right in front of them. They just need help opening their eyes."

Hailey pasted on a smile. "I doubt he sees it that way." Or that he ever would. He was too convinced love wasn't for him.

Tara leaned in again. "Sweetie, I was talking about you."

"What?" Her voice cracked, she covered it with a cough.

"You came here so full of dreams about your shop being successful. You started from scratch, you're doing fantastic. Why would you walk away from that? You need to focus on what you can control, Hailey." *Ha. Wes would like that advice. Why can't you control this ache?*

"I don't want to be indebted to anyone." She didn't ever want to feel like she owed anyone anything or that she hadn't earned what she'd gained. She'd basically been on her own since her early teens, learning not to rely even on the people closest because they didn't have the time or inclination. It made her strong. Strong enough to face this. *But are you facing it if you run?*

"What makes you indebted? You haven't even met Wes's mom. Am I indebted to her as well? Is she doing us a favor?" Tara pointed to the roof. "At the moment, that favor is giving me a headache."

Hailey tried to think of how to explain herself. "Of course you don't owe her. Wes didn't feel compelled to make sure your rent wasn't an issue."

Tara shook her head, clearly not understanding. "Listen, if he wanted to, I'd be fine with that. But that's me. There's nothing wrong with wanting to do this on your own. You *are*. But it's human nature to want to help the people you care about. Those Jansen boys walked away from the power money brings to show that they understood their ability to make a difference. To do things, be part of things they care about. Things that matter. I'm guessing that Wes wouldn't put his mother in a situation that didn't benefit her."

"Well, no." He might not love Hailey but she was sure he loved his mother.

"They're estranged from their father. I'm guessing the compassionate, amazing pieces of their personality are in some way directly connected to their mom or just their close relationship with each other."

Hailey realized she'd probably get to meet the woman, but not how she'd hoped.

"I'm sure she's lovely."

Tara nodded. "And smart."

"Of course."

"Smart enough not to do something just because one of her sons likes you."

Something painful stabbed Hailey's chest. She nodded. "Liked. Not loved."

Tara made a nurturing sound that must have been the secret code to all of Hailey's emotions because they unraveled in an instant. She covered her mouth with her hand, trying to contain it, to stop it, but the sob escaped.

"Oh, sweetie." Tara hurried around the table, wrapping her arms around Hailey, murmuring softly, encouraging her to cry if she needed, that everything would be okay.

But she was wrong. Nothing would be okay. She'd lost more than a lover, a confidant, a boyfriend. She'd lost her *friend*. The person who made her laugh, who teased her about forgetting to set alarms and didn't mind being teased about the overabundance of the ones he had set. A person who in so little time had come to know her well enough to complete her sentences, see the best in her, and make her believe anything was possible. Just not love.

41

Wes ran his hand over his face, frowning at the rasping sound that followed. When was the last time he shaved? He pulled open the door to let both of his brothers into his apartment. They said nothing as they shuffled past him in suits.

Instead of joining them in the living room, he went to the coffee maker.

"Wes," Chris said.

Wes turned from making coffee. "What?"

"We had a meeting. You flaked. What the hell?" Noah said.

His brows scrunched closer as he tried to remember his schedule for the week. His brain felt a little fuzzy. Glancing at the counter, he was surprised to see his couple of beers had turned into seven empties. Apparently, he'd had a pity party for one last night.

"Sorry." He went back to making coffee.

"Sorry? That's it?" Chris's voice held no judgment and he appreciated his brother that much more for it.

"Blink twice if your body has been invaded by aliens," Noah said, coming around to get his face in Wes's.

Wes's lips quirked even as a steady, uncomfortable bass began to beat at the base of his neck. "Remind me about the meeting."

"It was a board meeting. For the rec center. When was the last time you forgot anything? What's going on?" Chris flanked the other side of him.

"I guess I had more beer than I thought. I must have slept through my alarm." He glanced around after pressing start on the coffee maker. "I'm not sure where my phone is."

His brothers followed him into the living room. His laptop sat open on the game he'd made for Hailey. He'd worked through every single combination last night. All roads led to her. Jesus. What a fool he was. He started to close the laptop.

"Wait, what is that?" Noah, being Noah, picked it up without permission.

Wes's gut turned in a way that had nothing to do with his hangover.

Chris sat beside Noah, forcing Wes to move down on his own couch. They pressed start and worked through the game. Wes waited, the muscles in his shoulders pulled tight.

"This is awesome," Noah said, laughing with genuine joy. He looked over at Wes. "Pretty basic, but it's fantastic. Did Hailey love it?"

He nodded. And him. She loved him. Or thought she did. That's what happened: people confused affection and their desire to not be alone with a word that had deadly potential to wreck lives.

"Can you expand on this? Could you create something more complex? Different levels? More players? Could you do something like add another character into the mix—almost like a bad guy?"

Wes ran both hands over his face then stared at Noah. "Yes. To all of your questions. But I'm not going to. It was just a stupid gesture that, in the end, wasn't worth my time." It was good that they'd parted ways. Better now than years from now when she was dropping hints with wedding magazines.

Noah pressed some buttons that made a sound Wes didn't recognize.

"We'll come back to that, but first tell me if you've made other games and if these graphics are yours," Chris said, taking the laptop from Noah.

Wes looked over, frowning. Had he added to the code last night? He didn't remember. "Wait, why are there two different paths?"

Chris glanced at him. "You created it, dude."

Wes took the computer. Now, instead of just Hailey being the end goal, there was a miniature Wes character in the right corner. Clicking the keys, Wes unlocked the path that led to him on his own. Shit. He must have included that. See? Even drunk, he knew he was better off taking a road that led to him being alone. When he got through the maze, the little version of himself jumped up and down with a speech bubble over his head reading, "You are alone." His stomach sank. The character's cheesy smile crumpled as he then crumpled onto the ground with another speech bubble popping up. It read, "For the rest of your life."

"Damn. That's dark, man." Chris shook his head.

"What did Hailey say to that part?" Noah's voice was strained, his face scrunched.

Wes swore. "That part wasn't there when she saw it. I must have added it last night."

Getting up, Wes went back to the kitchen. He needed a shower. He definitely needed to shave. It had been a few days; why didn't he feel more like himself? Why the hell had he added that dark option for his game? Not wanting the answers to his own questions, he shook his head, as if that could clear the cobwebs.

Taking a long drink, the bitter liquid burning his tongue and the back of his throat, he hoped the caffeine would kick in quick. He heard his brothers arguing under their breath. Might as well say it out loud. He turned, leaned against the counter, crossing one ankle over the other.

"Hailey dumped me."

If he didn't feel like he was going to throw up, he would have laughed at the way both of their heads swiveled in his direction.

"What?" Chris stared.

"Whoa, dude. Way to bury the lead." Noah shook his head. He got up, went to Wes's fridge, and pulled out a beer.

Wes looked at him, frowning. "It's morning."

Noah twisted off the beer cap, took Wes's coffee, and set the beer in his hand. "No, it isn't. And if you're hungover, which I haven't seen since you were about twenty, you need this first."

Chris joined them, pulling a chair out from the table, swinging it around to straddle it. "What happened?"

The bottle was cool in his hand as he clenched his fingers around it. He didn't want the beer but it felt good to hold on to something.

"We've known each other close to a year; she knows I don't want to get married and have a family. We could have stayed together longer but she insisted that if she loves me and I don't feel the same, it's not worth it. Since when is having someone in your life who complements you, whose company you enjoy, a waste of time? She didn't think it was a waste to be friends even though we weren't throwing meaningless declarations around then." He set the beer down too hard, making it slosh over.

"Chris?" Noah looked at his brother.

Chris nodded. "Right. Okay. Where to start. First, you're an idiot."

Noah pointed at him. "Excellent point. Exactly where I would have started."

"Secondly," Chris said, nodding again, "what do you mean you don't want to get married and have kids? Fine if Hailey isn't the one, but do you mean never?"

"I would have stuck on the idiot thing longer but we can totally swing back around," Noah said, grabbing a kitchen chair so his pose mimicked Chris's.

Wes glared at them. "Since always. Why would I do that to myself? To someone else? To children? Do you not remember how awful it was in the days leading up to the divorce? The yelling and accusations, then the way Dad tried to use us as bargaining chips?

The way he threatened Mom with us if she went after any sort of settlement aside from the one he'd drawn up?"

To their credit, both of his brothers looked a little lost. That's what he'd always wanted for them but suddenly, the burden of being the only one to know felt like it could drag him to the ground. He shoved both hands through his hair.

"It's not like you two are ring shopping. I was self-aware enough to tell her up front that I didn't want all that. Maybe you two got lucky, the conversation hasn't arisen. You won't talk about prenups at all so what do I know. But I don't see you heading down any aisles." He paced to the patio, pulled open the sliding door.

"I want to marry Grace. I hope we have kids." Noah's voice was quiet.

"I love Everly more than anything. All I want is to have her be my wife. I just don't want to rush her." Chris looked uncomfortable before he asked, "Is Hailey just not the one?"

The one. Everything. "No. Trust me, if ever I was going to dive off that plank into shark-infested waters, she'd be the one I'd do it with. But come on, guys, look at the statistics. Doesn't that worry you?"

Chris shrugged. "Not more than losing Everly."

Noah's brows bounced. "When have I ever not beat statistics?"

"It seemed like you two really fit. Do you care about her at all?"

Wes whirled so fast he felt dizzy. "Do I care about her? Of course I do. But when I do things to show that, she gets all mad, tells me she loves me, then dumps me because I don't say it back."

"Can we insert the idiot thing again?"

Chris smacked Noah. "It's okay not to want marriage and kids, Wes. But it surprises me. Is that really how you feel or is it because of how we grew up? What *do* you feel, Wes?"

Wes swallowed. "Right now?"

Chris shook his head. "No. When you're with her."

Walking back and forth across his kitchen, he tried to put the words together to describe what being with Hailey was like.

"I feel like I've found a secret code that unlocks a different world that only I'm allowed to be part of, that only I know how to navigate. Even the hurdles feel more manageable with her there. It feels like everything fits perfectly into place even when it doesn't all make sense." He sucked in a breath. "I feel happy."

"It seems cruel to point out the idiocy now," Noah said in a genuinely perplexed tone.

"I'm not an idiot. I'm protecting her. Protecting both of us. What do I know about love? Nothing. That's what. Absolutely nothing. We don't just jump in and hope for the best with business. How can you do that with love? With emotions, when they can be unstable? When they can change? This isn't a game where I can win more lives or defeat the bad guy. There's no prize. Just a broken heart and an inability to breathe because I've put too much stake in a person who isn't me."

He didn't realize he was shouting until he stopped.

"Can I tell him?" Noah stood up.

"Don't be a jackass, Noah," Chris said.

Approaching Wes, he put both hands on his shoulders, looked him square in the eye. "It's too late."

Wes stared at him, wondering what that meant. His head hurt.

"You already love her."

He shook his head. "No. I've been very careful about my feelings."

"Your heart doesn't give a shit," Noah said, shrugging like what he was saying was of no consequence.

Chris stood up, knocked Noah's arm so he dropped them both. "The thing is, this isn't something you can plan, control, or navigate. You love her. You can tell yourself you don't but the emptiness you're feeling is the truth. That's what you have to look forward to now, so I have a question."

He crossed his arms. "What?"

"The way you're feeling right now? Would you rather feel this for the rest of your life or take a chance, admit what you really feel, and do everything in your power to hang on tight and never let her go?"

The silence felt like a weight on his chest. Breathing through his nose, he thought about what he was feeling right now compared to how he felt in Hailey's presence. He thought about the way she looked at him, the part of him that had felt like dancing when she'd said the three words. The way his heart leaped when he saw her.

"But what if . . ." He trailed off.

"There's no guarantees, man. Not in real estate, investments, or love. But we've done pretty well trusting our instincts," Noah said.

He stared at his brothers, wondering if they could be right. Hailey had called him a coward. Was she right, too? He was definitely scared, but a more terrifying thought jumped around in his brain: What if he had to live the rest of his life without her?

Was it possible that telling her he loved her—admitting that he did—was less scary than walking away? On one hand, the idea of professing his feelings made his skin itch, but the idea of never trying, never seeing her again made his body feel like there was an empty cavern no amount of light could fill.

"I need to get her back," Wes said.

"Man, that took a while," Noah said, grinning.

Chris laughed. "Come on, Noah. We took our time figuring out how to get it right, too."

Noah nodded, clapped Wes on the back. "He's right. We did. Which means, we can help."

42

The next few days were a bit of a blur. Noah and Chris got it in their heads that Wes had been holding out on them as far as his ability to create computer games. Wes didn't see how this could be a surprise to them seeing as he'd created multiple apps and accrued interest on the revenue from those.

He was happy they were pushing him to explore ways to pursue creating a full-version game, if for no other reason than it was keeping him busy. It kept him from standing outside Hailey's door, begging her to talk to him, to forgive him. He'd learned enough about her now to know that a simple "I'm sorry" wasn't going to cut it. He'd hurt her. More than that, he'd diminished her trust in what they shared.

He knocked on the door, his nerves feeling like needles poking into his skin. When Piper answered, she gave him a cool glare but gestured for him to come in.

"I appreciate you seeing me," Wes said. It'd been a week since he last saw Hailey. It had taken all of his willpower to avoid her shop, avoid calling or texting.

"This better be good." She led him into the kitchen, where Fiona was waiting. The other woman didn't smile at him.

"Fiona." He nodded.

"Wes."

Right. At least Hailey had strong, loyal supports in place. "Thank you for letting me come here."

"You hurt her. When Dorian left, she went into planning mode. It was like she'd known it was over even before it was. Sure, her pride took a hard hit but it didn't knock her down. Not completely." Piper held his gaze as she relayed this information. "You did. There's a piece of her that's changed. How are you going to fix it?"

Wes shoved his hands in his pockets, his heart hurting with the realization of the pain he'd inflicted. This was what it was like to love someone? You felt their pain more acutely than your own? The need to fix everything he'd broken was spiraling inside of him. He'd spent considerable time thinking about that very thing. His need for control, his desire to fix and help was his way of making sure he took care of the people he cared for. The people he *loved*. But there was more to loving someone than just "fixing" things.

"I'm not sure I can."

Both of their mouths dropped open so he hurried on. "I hurt her and I can't even begin to tell you how much I hate that I did. I can't undo it or go back in time. Hell, I may mess up in the future and hurt her again. Though, it'll never be my intention to do that. If I could absorb her hurt, I would. Instead, I want to show her how much she means to me. I want to show her that she's part of me and it'll always be my goal to fill her life with happiness, not tears. But I need help." The words were unfamiliar to him.

Maybe he was overly hopeful but he was almost positive he saw a sheen in Piper's gaze and a hint of a smile on Fiona's mouth. In an unintentionally synchronized move, both women crossed their arms over their chests. They didn't tell him to leave so he shook off his nerves, approached the counter, and set his hands on the edge to give himself something to hold on to.

Then, he put everything out there, telling them how he felt and what he was willing to do to prove it.

43

She was not wallowing. She refused. Which was why Hailey said yes when Piper invited her for dinner. Nick and the kids had gone to see a movie. She'd managed to avoid more than talking on the phone with her cousin for the last ten days. She worried that even though she was holding it together, functioning as she should, one look at Piper would be like tugging the bottom block out of the Jenga game.

Taking a deep breath, she shook her arms, hands, and body a little just to reset herself. *You're fine. You're not a blubbering mess. Life happens. Hearts get broken. You are rocking the salad world. You have friends. You are loved. Maybe not by the man . . . nope, veering off track there, Hailey. You are fine.*

She knocked. Piper opened the door, her smile soothing some of the sadness in Hailey. Pulling her into a hard hug, she rocked back and forth.

"I love you. And I truly believe I'm not the only one." Piper pulled back, kissed Hailey on the cheek, then skirted around her, nudging her inside.

"What are you doing?" Hailey stood in Piper's entryway as her cousin descended the couple of steps.

Piper turned, purse slung over her shoulder. "Moving out of the way so you can get what you deserve." Piper pointed. "Shut the door. Go inside."

Hailey did as she was told, leaning her head against the cool wood. When she turned, pressing her back to the door, she wondered why Piper thought she deserved time alone. She'd thought, for sure, Piper was going to go all mama bear on her, pamper her, let her cry it out over wine she'd saved for just such occasions.

She pushed off the door. She'd grab the wine, head out to the pool deck, and enjoy the quiet. She left her shoes and purse by the door, padded down the hallway to the kitchen.

Smiling, she walked to the glass of red that was already sitting there. She picked it up, sipped. Deep breath in, out. She was going to be okay. It might not feel like it in those moments between sleep and waking when it all came rushing back. But she would be.

Heading toward the sliding doors, she smiled wider when she saw Piper had turned on the twinkle lights strung around the edges of the patio.

Sliding the door open, she was surprised to hear music playing. As she closed the door behind her, she wrinkled her nose.

"Really, Piper?" The eighties classic "I Want to Know What Love Is," by Foreigner, played through the outdoor speakers.

There was a small partition that blocked her view of the pool but once she'd rounded it, everything inside of her came to a pause. Set up beside the pool was a table for two with a white linen tablecloth. Candles flickered from the center of the table, adding a subtle glow. The twinkle lights seemed to dance to the tempo of the music.

Wes stood beside the table dressed in a pair of dark jeans and a black T-shirt. Her heart thrashed against her rib cage. She felt her pulse everywhere. The wineglass was heavy in her hand.

He clutched a handful of colorful flowers. She didn't know the name but they were like petaled rainbows.

Wes walked forward, stopped in front of her. "This moment is the first one I've been able to breathe properly since I left your side."

She stared up at him, sure she was seeing things, hearing things. "What are you doing here?"

He took a deep breath, and she felt it fan across her skin when he exhaled. "Anything I have to in order to show you I was wrong. To show you what you mean to me." He extended the flowers. "These were so bright and happy. It made me smile just to look at them. They reminded me of you."

Her breath whooshed out of her lungs as she closed her eyes, then opened them. She took the flowers, hoping he didn't see her hands shake. "I know I matter to you, Wes. And I miss you. I do. But we can't go back to being friends. At least not yet. Maybe one day. But not yet."

He took the flowers and the wine, walked to the table, and set them down before coming back to take her hand. He led her to a chair, held it out. She sat and Wes pulled his chair directly in front of her so their knees were touching.

"This is more than friendship, Hailey. So much more. You were right about me. I was scared. I was a coward."

She shook her head, doing her best to stuff down her emotions. "You were right, too. I knew who you were, what you wanted and didn't want out of life. You can't make someone love you back. Let's just call it even and hope that in the future we can be in the same room without it hurting."

He shook his head. "No."

Hailey's brows moved up. "Excuse me?"

"I never wanted to be in love. From what I'd heard, what I'd seen with my brothers, it was the equivalent of jumping out of an airplane with a chute you're only hopeful will work. There are no guarantees. Those three words seemed more like a watered-down farewell than an expression of how the other person alters someone's life just by being part of it. My father would say it to calm my mother and his subsequent wives and girlfriends, appease them. My mother says it so often at the end of a conversation, I've heard her say it to her hairdresser and masseuse. I'm not even sure if she knows she's saying it or if it's just habit. So how meaningful can they be?"

Hailey's lips twitched so she gave into the small smile. "Maybe they're really good at what they do." What he said made so many things make sense. The emotion in his voice seeped into the cracks of her heart.

He laughed, reached out to take her hands. "You make me laugh. You call me on things when I don't make any sense. You have the most amazing heart and work ethic of anyone I know. You're not afraid to reflect, to dig deep and see what you can do to make the world around you better. You not only started over but you flourished. You've changed me."

Tears pushed. "I wasn't trying to. People shouldn't have to change for love." Though, maybe they changed because of it.

Wes scooted closer, his knees going on the outside of hers. "That's not entirely true. I mean, isn't that what life is? Growing, changing, making the effort to be better? To be more? To realize the ways we're preventing our own happiness?"

She shrugged. "I guess."

"When I hit a wall in my coding, I have to go around, under, over, basically tearing apart every step I made to see which one was wrong. When I did that to myself, when I pulled apart my mistakes, trying to figure out where I went wrong so I could stop feeling so lost, so *empty*, without you, I figured it out. I thought by controlling my feelings, by refusing to say the words, there was no way to fail. I was stupid enough to believe that not saying the words meant I could stop myself from *feeling* them. I was so sure I could chart the course of my future without being hurt. The irony is, I put up a roadblock in my head and around my heart, refusing to admit to being in love because I told myself that way, nothing could hurt me. I thought there was nothing more terrifying than falling in love with you. Than having my heart in your hands."

She pulled her hands back, set them flat on her thighs. "But?"

Wes held her gaze, his confident and sure. "But that's nothing compared to how scared I am that you won't forgive me, that you won't believe I love you enough to fight for you, to change and grow. That I know now why people say those words. I know what they mean, at least to me."

She blinked back the tears. "What do they mean?"

He nodded his head. "They mean I'm vulnerable. I run the risk of you hurting me or worse, me hurting you. But the reward of owning them, of telling you every single day that I love you, that I will always love you, well, that's like nothing I've ever known. I want to weather hard times and argue over which version of *Overboard* is better. I want to spend my life with you, accepting you and loving you for exactly who you are. And nothing could be scarier than the thought that I've missed my chance. That I'm too late."

She felt shaky. She spoke around the lump in her throat, the words wobbling a bit. "The first."

"What?" The word came out gravelly.

"The first version is better. There's no reason to argue about it."

She saw the sheen in his gaze, or maybe it was a reflection of her own eyes. He took her hand again. "Okay. We'll take that off the list. I agree to defer to your judgment on romantic comedies."

She looked around, realized the song he'd chosen was on a loop. "Speaking of."

He smiled like she'd given him a prize. "Every romance we watched had several things in common. Grand gestures in those movies need a soundtrack, a sufficiently changed hero, and proof that he's seen the light. The funny thing is, I spent more time watching you than those movies. I might not have the romantic hero down but I know what makes you smile, I know who you are and who I am when I'm with you."

A half laugh, half sob escaped. "What if you get scared again?"

Wes stood, pulled her against him, swaying softly to the music. "Have you ever noticed there's always a dance scene, too?"

"Wes." She wanted this but she had to be sure.

He pressed his forehead to hers. "Nothing seems as scary when you're with me. I want you to feel the same about me. I want you to rely on me. Trust me. The truth is, I'm still scared. I like being able to predict the outcome, plan for it. But I couldn't plan for you or the way you obliterated the walls around my heart. Go figure, the one thing I don't plan turns out to be the best thing that ever happened to me. I couldn't have planned it but I'm willing to tell you and show you that I love you. If you want that. If you still want me. If you still love me."

His gaze flashed with an uncertainty that squeezed her heart. She cupped his cheeks, surprised to feel a couple days' growth against her palms. "I know you're new to this but it doesn't go away just like that. When you love someone, they're part of you. It's not something you can just turn off like a switch. That's why it's so hard when things are over."

"I don't want to be over."

"Me neither," she whispered.

"Does that mean you still . . ."

One tear slipped through. "Love you? Yes. I do. Of course I do."

He laughed. "Thank God."

Their kiss was soft but full of unspoken promises that Hailey held close to her heart. When she pulled back, she ran her hand over his cheek again.

"I don't think I've ever seen you without smoothly shaved skin."

He pressed his hand against hers, holding it to his face. "I've been a bit preoccupied. I have something for you."

Her body tensed, making him laugh. He kissed the tip of her nose. "Don't worry, it's not from Tiffany's."

"It's not that I'll never want anything from there," she said, dropping the wide-open hint to see his response.

He pulled her against him, kissed her hard enough to make her forget where she was. "The only thing I'm scared of anymore is being without you. I'm not running. One day, I'll give you exactly what you want from there or anywhere else you choose."

Tears burned her eyes. Needing to lighten the mood, she gestured toward the dome-covered dishes. "Well then? What's the surprise?"

He held her chair for her, lifted the dome. A small heart-shaped chocolate cake sat in the center. In cursive, *H.S. + W.J.* was written on its top. She laughed then noticed the laminated page beneath the cake. Lifting it by the base, she set it aside and picked up what looked like a glossy magazine insert.

"What is this?" she mused, looking at it, her smile growing with every second. It was a quiz. Like one of the ones Fiona's magazines published.

Wes sat beside her. "I already took it."

He had—he'd circled his answers for each question. The title was, "Are You in Love?"

There were ten questions, each asking about varying situations that were personal to Wes and Hailey.

She laughed at number three: *Would you give her your last piece of chocolate?* He'd circled *Without a doubt.* Number five asked: *Are you willing to be vulnerable if it means proving how much you care?* Again, he'd answered *Without a doubt.*

When she got to the end, there were three options for answers:

❒ You might as well walk around with a shirt that says, "Yes, I'm in love"

❒ You are so in love you're walking around with cartoon hearts in your eyes

❒ You are utterly, absolutely, fully and completely, irreversibly and forever in love.

She looked at Wes through her tears. "Those are some options."

"Read the one I got," he said, pointing to what he'd circled based on his answers.

Clearing her throat, determined not to cry, she read, "You are utterly, absolutely, fully and completely, irreversibly and forever in love. While this could be scary to someone like you, you are smart enough to know that storms can be weathered together, that everything is better with Hailey at your side, that she's more than a friend, she's the person who sees you, makes you see yourself and pushes you for more. You're in the 'first person I want to talk to every day and last person I want to talk to every night' kind of love. This kind of love is not to be taken lightly. It's real and it's not going anywhere."

The page shook in her hand as a few more tears escaped. "Did Fiona help you with this?"

He nodded. "Yes. She helped me and made it sound a lot better than I could. For future reference, she's a harsh editor. But every bit of it, of all of them actually, is true. I love you, Hailey. I'm sorry it took me so long to say it back."

She threw her arms around him, hugged him tightly as she kissed his neck. "I love you, too. And you know me well enough to know I'm a big fan of the phrase 'better late than never.'"

With his arms wrapped around her, the music still on the same song, and the lights dancing in the early dusk, Hailey no longer wondered what happily ever after looked like. It would look like whatever they made it, together.

Epilogue

Hailey bit the inside of her cheek so she wouldn't cry. Everly looked like a princess in her white gown. With a sweetheart neckline, the elegantly classic shape of the A-line skirt, and the custom-made, silver, sparkly Converse, Everly belonged in a magazine titled *Wedding Day Perfection*. Her hair was pulled back off her face with thin tendrils softly falling.

"Is it weird I'm more nervous about walking down the aisle than I am about getting married?" She stared in the beveled mirror while Stacey, in a gorgeous navy body-hugging dress, double-checked Everly's back snaps.

"No. You hate being on display. Just remember that the only people in the room that matter are you and Chris. Your dad—if he can stop crying—will hold you up if you feel faint. Count the steps like we practiced."

Everly nodded repeatedly. When she turned, spread her arms wide as if to say, "Well?" Hailey and Grace gripped each other's hands.

"You're perfection, Evs." Grace, whose dress was similar but not identical to Stacey's, said, a linen handkerchief clutched in her other hand.

"There are not enough words to adequately describe how incredible you look," Hailey added.

Everly huffed out a breath, put a hand to her stomach. "Okay. I can do this." Then her face broke into a grin that made her eyes shine brighter than the sun or the moon. "I *get* to do this. I get to marry Chris."

Stacey waved a hand in front of her face. "Argh. Stop. No tears. I will not cry."

Everly nudged her friend with her hip. "You'll break by the end."

Stacey handed out champagne flutes so they could toast the bride. When they finished, Hailey gave each of them a quick hug so she could slip out, get to her seat. She was excited to see Wes in his tux. The small wedding was mostly family, with just a few friends.

Hailey had only briefly met Wes's sister that morning when she'd flown in with Wes's mom. A smile stretched her lips. His mom was cool. There were other words to describe her: funny, elegant, genuine, but cool captured it all. Hailey had learned within a half hour of meeting her landlord last year that if she hadn't wanted to buy the shops, she wouldn't have. Not even for one of her sons. She also learned the woman had a keen business sense of her own.

She and Hailey were investing, together, in Leo, who would run By the Cup's food truck. This new venture was one more thrilling piece of her life that, some days, didn't feel real.

Heading down the hall, she heard the murmurs from the beautiful space where the wedding was being held. She stopped short when she turned the corner and nearly ran into Wes.

"Hey," she said, smoothing her hands over his black tux. "You look wonderful. Not as good as the bride but pretty damn good."

He chuckled, pulled her closer. "Back at you. Though, I haven't seen the bride." He leaned back, his gaze moving up and down. The heat in his eyes made her grateful she'd splurged on something new he'd never seen. She'd hidden it at the back of their closet.

"I'll peek at her out of respect but I'm pretty sure my eyes will be glued to this dress all night."

"Shouldn't you be with Chris? Is he nervous?"

Wes kissed her softly. "He's not. He's been ready to marry her since they met. Sometimes you just know."

She laughed as his fingers came to the chain at her neck. He played with it, lifting it in his fingers.

"And sometimes it takes a bit to figure it out," she said, grinning at him.

The antique-style baguette engagement ring he'd given her that morning was on the chain. He ran his finger over it before tucking it back under the high reverse V-neck collar of her gown.

"I may take a while to catch on but I'd say it's worked out okay," he said, kissing her again. "My mother and Ari are only staying through the weekend. I'd like for us to tell them together. We can tell everyone else after Everly and Chris are back from their honeymoon."

She nodded, still exhilarated that he'd asked her to marry him. He was the firstborn but he'd be the last to marry. Noah and Grace had surprised everyone six months earlier with a big party at their house which turned out to be a wedding. Grace's pseudo father, Morty, had officiated, just as she'd done for him the year before.

"Whatever you want," Hailey whispered.

Wes pulled her close, pressed his forehead to hers because he seemed to need the connection. "I have everything I never knew I wanted."

"I knew I wanted these things but I didn't know how much finding the right person, finding *you*, would fill all the spaces in my heart and my life. I guess what I really dreamed about was finding someone to love me every bit as much as I love them."

"Here's to dreams coming true," he said against her lips.

She smiled into the kiss. Life rarely followed a straight path,

324 | Sophie Sullivan

but the curves and unexpected detours had a way of leading to the exact right place. Wes took his place between Chris, who had anticipation written all over his face, and Noah, who had that easygoing grin. Hailey's heart did a happy dance, and she was more grateful than she ever could have imagined being for the bumps and hiccups that had led her here. To him. To all of them.

Acknowledgments

It's hard to believe the Jansen brothers' journeys are done. I have absolutely loved writing this series. I'm so grateful to have been given the opportunity to do so. It is truly a group effort. Thank you, readers, for loving the characters, for wanting more. Thank you to Headline Eternal for the UK versions of my books. I didn't say it in the last two books but it's an honor to work with you guys as well as with St. Martin's Press. It still amazes me that I have multiple covers of my book, different versions. Thank you, Fran, for being my constant champion. Thank you, Alex, for believing in this series, in me, and for making me a better writer. Thank you, Cassidy, Sara, Rivka, and all of the SMP team. There are so many people that helped make this book what it is and I'm grateful to all of you. Thank you to my family: Matt, Kalie, Amy, my mom. For loving my words and loving me and supporting me. To Brenda—you're like an emotions manager—you should ask for a pay raise. To Sarah and Tara, Nicole, Addie, Stacey and Cole: you make me believe in myself and my stories. Thank you. To all the bloggers, readers, and people who've read my books, shared them, enjoyed them: thank you so much. Not only do I get to share my stories, but I've made friends and connections that will last long after the book closes.

I hate when things are over. But because books are amazing things that you can read repeatedly, maybe it's not really the end.

About the Author

Brenda Mallory

SOPHIE SULLIVAN (she/her) is a Canadian author as well as a cookie-eating, Diet Pepsi–drinking Disney enthusiast who loves reading and writing romance in almost equal measure. She writes around her day job as a teacher and spends her spare time with her sweet family watching reruns of *Friends*. She has written *Ten Rules for Faking It* and *How to Love Your Neighbor,* and has had plenty of practice writing happily ever after as her alter ego, Jody Holford.